# REDEMPTION'S SONG

*Second in a series of*
JENNA'S CREEK NOVELS

## Teresa D. Slack

**Tsaba House**
Reedley, California

All scripture quotations, unless otherwise noted, are taken from the King James Version of the Bible.

Cover and text design by Bookwrights Design
Senior Editor, Jodie Nazaroff
Author Photo by Andrea Lundgren


Published by
Tsaba House
2252 12th Street, Reedley, California 93654
Visit our website at: www.TsabaHouse.com

Printed in the United States of America

First Edition: 2006

Library of Congress Cataloging-in-Publication Data

Slack, Teresa D., 1964-
Redemption's song / Teresa D. Slack.— 1st ed.
      p. cm. — (Jenna's Creek series ; 2nd)
ISBN-13: 978-0-9725486-2-5 (pbk. : alk. paper)
ISBN-10: 0-9725486-2-9 (pbk. : alk. paper)
1. Teenage girls—Fiction. 2. Ohio—Fiction. I. Title.
PS3619.L33R43 2006
813'.6—dc22
                                                2005032826

To Robin Sorrells,
My sister and very first "best friend".

# *Acknowledgments*

Before the publication of my first book, I thought all one had to do in order to create a book was write a good story. I didn't realize how much blood, sweat, and tears go into the finished product.

From cover art, to marketing, to guiding me through the maze of publishing, I want to thank everyone at Tsaba House for their hard work in getting my stories into the hands of readers.
Thanks to Senior Editor, Jodie Nazaroff whose wonderful editing skills and infinite patience transforms my rough drafts into readable fiction.

A special "thank you" goes to Pam Schwagerl, President of Tsaba House, who saw a series inside my first Jenna's Creek novel. Thanks for your enthusiasm, vision, and for your willingness to take a chance on an unknown author.

*"For there is nothing covered, that shall not be revealed; neither hid, that shall not be known."*

—Luke 12:2

# Chapter One

*July, 1974*

"Jamie, can I come over tonight?"

Jamie Steele's grip tightened around the telephone, her heart hammering in her chest. Her relationship with her boy friend, Jason Collier had progressed beyond the point of asking permission to see one another long ago. They'd been going out exclusively—of course exclusively; he was the first and only boy she ever really dated—since last summer. They had met at Wyatt's Pharmacy in Jenna's Creek where she got her first job. Jason was assigned to train her to fill the position of the drugstore's newest stock girl. At the time she figured her new boss, Noel Wyatt, didn't like her very much and was trying to force her to quit. Why else would he put someone as interesting as an old shoe in charge of training her? Jason thought of nothing besides work. She doubted he had a life outside the drugstore. But over the course of the summer, she realized underneath his gruff exterior beat the heart of a funny, ambitious, caring individual.

Had it not been for Jason's support and friendship last summer, after her dad was killed in a car accident and her discovery that he had been suspected of a terrible crime twenty-five years earlier, Jamie didn't know how she would have survived. Especially since some people in Jenna's Creek thought it was better to go on thinking her dad had killed his old girlfriend and disposed of her body, rather than discover the truth. But the truth had come out; partly due to Jamie's grim determination to uncover all the facts that had been overlooked in the first investigation, and partly because the missing woman's remains were finally discovered.

The mystery of what really happened to Sally Blake had consumed Jamie from the moment she first heard of the young woman on the day of her father's funeral. James, Jamie's violent tempered father, and Sally had left a party together after a very public fight which included knocking over a refreshment table and exchanging blows. Sally was never seen or heard from again. Since finding out the whole story last summer, Jamie was determined to put the past behind her and move on with her life. That included forgiving her father for the cruel way he had treated her, her younger sister, Cassie, and most of all, their mother who died six years ago from cancer. Forgiving had been difficult. Forgetting, Jamie feared, would be impossible.

Now that classes were over and Jason was no longer living on a college campus two hours away, he came to the house nearly every evening after work to see her. Often the two of them relaxed side by side on the front porch swing, talking or simply gazing at the corn field on the other side of the blacktop road. They went for walks through the woods or played Yahtzee in the kitchen with Cassie. Every now and then, they went into town for something to eat, and occasionally caught a movie. Working his way through college, Jason couldn't afford to take her on actual dates every week. Jamie didn't mind. They were content spending time together, which made his present behavior especially odd.

"Yeah, sure, Jason, you know I'll be here," she said aloud, while telling herself not to get worked up over nothing. The strange ring in his voice didn't mean a thing.

"I have something I really need to talk to you about," he said.

Her insides twisted tighter into a knot. This definitely wasn't good. Either he was dumping her, or about to suggest they move their current relationship to the next level; neither of which she particularly wanted just now.

She managed to keep her voice steady. "Okay, great. Whatever." She winced and cursed her brain for not coming up with a reply that consisted of more than one-word sentences. "You're welcome to join us for supper if you'd like." Now she sounded like she was talking to a long lost relative. She took a deep breath, told herself to calm down, and added, smiling, "You know how Grandma Cory loves feeding you."

Jason didn't seem to notice her discomfort. "I work 'til eight so I'll get something to eat in town, but thanks anyway." There was a moments silence on his end, and then, "And Jamie?"

"Yeah?"

"Um...well...I'll see you after work."

"Okay, Jason. Bye." She held onto the receiver, giving him one last chance to say whatever was on his mind. A click on his end sounded in her ear. Whatever he meant to say would have to wait until after eight.

Jamie replaced the phone on its mount on the wall and left the kitchen. There was no need to mention Jason coming over tonight to Grandma Cory or Cassie. They knew to expect him at any time on any given night. He had become a steady fixture around the old farmhouse in the past month since Jamie graduated from high school and his classes at the university let out for the summer. During the school year while Jamie finished her senior year at South Auburn High School and Jason was earning his Bachelors' Degree at Ohio University in Athens, they saw very little of one another. He came home every other weekend and during his breaks between quarters, but even then he worked as much as possible at Wyatt's Drugstore.

Jamie worked at the drugstore too, on weekends and after school, and had little time left over for socializing. Now that it was summer break, Jason put in even more hours at the drugstore. Though he was the recipient of a few small scholarships and some financial aid, the brunt of his college expenses fell directly on his young shoulders. His father was disabled and his mom had left years ago, so Jason needed to work as much as he could.

Jamie didn't share Jason's financial concerns about starting college. Even before her father's car accident last summer, Jamie and Cassie had lived with their paternal grandparents on the family farm since their mother's death. Grandpa Harlan was disabled and Grandma Cory received Social Security to supplement her small income from running the farm. That meant Jamie qualified for federal grants that would pay whatever fees her various scholarships from high school didn't cover. All she needed to concern herself with was pocket money and a new wardrobe befitting a college freshman.

She couldn't wait to start college. While a little nervous about leaving home for the first time, her excitement over the future outweighed any anxiety about sleeping in a strange bed or sharing her life with an unknown roommate. Best of all, she would be with Jason all the time. Now that he had earned his Bachelor's Degree, he would be working toward his law degree while she acclimated herself to collegiate life. She could handle anything knowing Jason was on the same campus.

She headed upstairs to her bedroom. She had at least an hour to herself before evening chores or dinner preparations required her attention downstairs. She threw herself across the bed, propped herself up on her elbows and rested her chin in her hands, allowing an unobstructed view of the cloudless summer sky outside. From this position, she could see nothing more than treetops and sky. She couldn't see the open pasture to the west that led to their nearest neighbor as the crow flew, or the narrow blacktop road that disappeared around the bend just past their property line. As of this moment, nothing else in the world existed other than the bed beneath her, the patch of vivid blue sky outside the window, and Jason; always Jason.

What could he want to talk to her about? She stared hard out the window and replayed the short phone conversation in her head. It wasn't so much what he had said, but what he hadn't said. He sounded so serious, even more so than usual. Something was up, but what? Surely he didn't plan to change the status of their relationship. Not steady, practical, focused Jason. It wasn't that he didn't love her. She knew he did, even though he hadn't said as much. And she loved him. Neither had been in a hurry to put their feelings into words with so little time spent together over the past nine months, sometimes as much as a month going by with barely a long distance phone call from the campus in Athens to tide her over. For now, each concentrated on their individual goals. Jamie wanted a college education as badly as Jason wanted a law degree.

No, Jason wouldn't be making any announcements tonight. He certainly wouldn't ask her… No, of course not; with four years of law school ahead of him and her just starting college, his practical mind would balk at serious commitment.

That left only one possibility. She groaned and rolled over onto her back to stare at the mildew stained ceiling above her head. Jason was dumping her, pure and simple. She might be a naïve farm girl, but even she could see the writing on the wall.

Jason's compact car pulled into the driveway ten minutes after the hands on the grandfather clock by the front door read eight o'clock. Apparently, he hadn't even gone home first to change out of his work clothes. The supper dishes had barely made it into the cabinets when fourteen-year-old Cassie spotted his car. She turned away from the kitchen window as a sly smile lit up her china doll features.

"Romeo's here. And what's that he's carrying, flowers?"

Jamie straightened the damp dishtowel on the rack inside the cabinet door under the sink and pushed it closed with her knee. Hoping to hide the desperation on her face, she pushed her sister away from the window to look for herself.

"I thought college boys couldn't afford flowers," Cassie observed, her smile widening with every word.

"Oh, hush," Jamie warned. Inside her heart was fluttering. Cassie was right; Jason couldn't afford flowers. She got to the window in time to see him slam the door shut with his free hand and turn toward the house, the modest bouquet of summer flowers swathed in green tissue paper clutched in his other hand. She couldn't see his expression clearly from this distance, but he seemed—nervous or afraid. Neither one sat well on her stomach, along with the cooked cabbage from supper.

"I wonder what he's up to," she said under her breath, more to herself than Cassie.

Cassie nudged Jamie in the ribs with her elbow. "Maybe I know."

"You don't know anything."

At that moment Jason looked up and caught sight of the girls watching him through the kitchen window. He grinned sheepishly and threw up his free hand in greeting. He headed for the back door.

Jamie waved back and stepped away from the window. When Jason disappeared from view around the corner of the house, she ran her hands through her shoulder length, brown hair and tucked an errant corner of her blouse back into her jeans. "I look awful, don't I? I wish I'd done something with my hair."

Cassie gave her a wary glance, taken aback by her sudden un-characteristic concern over her appearance. She lived and worked on a farm. She didn't worry when she perspired or broke her nails. She'd been raised to ignore splinters, calluses and bad hair days. Jason had seen her at her worst—and her best—and liked her anyway.

"What are you getting so worked up about?" Cassie wanted to know. "It's just Jason. You see him every day."

"No, I don't, not everyday."

Jason tapped at the screen door. "Anybody home?" he called out as he let himself in.

"Smooth, Jason," Cassie said, teasingly. "You saw us from the driveway. You're as jumpy as Jamie tonight."

Jason edged into the kitchen, smiling at Cassie's observation, but from his expression, she must have hit the nail on the head.

"Jamie, Jason's car's outside," Grandma Cory said, coming into the kitchen from the front of the house. "Oh. Hi, Jason, I see you're already in here."

Jason's eyes darted from one Steele woman to another. Cassie was right again; Jamie had never seen him so jumpy either. Her heart twisted inside her. Just what did he want? And why did he have those flowers in his hand?

"Evening, Mrs. Steele," Jason said after finding his voice. He looked down at the flowers in his hand and then helplessly at Jamie. "I—um—Jamie, would you like to go somewhere to talk? I mean, if I'm not too early. Are you busy?"

"Looks to me like she's no busier than she ever is," Grandma Cory said gruffly. "There's no need for you to stand there hanging onto the door handle all night, Son. Come on in and me and Cassie will give you two some privacy."

"We will?" Cassie asked, crestfallen.

"Yes, we will."

"No, Mrs. Steele," Jason objected. "You don't have to leave. Jamie and I can—"

"Jason, will you sit down, for lands sake?" Grandma Cory instructed, sounding put out, but there was no mistaking the twinkle in her eye. "You're making me a nervous wreck. Cassie and I'll go watch TV with Grandpa. If you decide to go somewhere to talk, there's no need in letting me know." She took hold of Cassie's hand and led her from the room.

Jamie saw her own surprise reflected in Cassie's face. Grandma Cory wasn't usually so accommodating. Did she know what Jason was up to or had the flowers tipped her off to the apparent importance of the occasion, as they had Jamie? Whether she knew or just assumed, she sure seemed in a hurry to get Cassie out of the room.

"You two behave yourselves now," Cassie called over her shoulder from the doorway. "Nice flowers, Jason."

Jason watched until Grandma Cory and Cassie were safely out of sight and then stepped to Jamie's side. He kissed her cheek and held out the flowers, his smile tight and quavering. Jamie took the mixed bouquet offered her and lowered her nose dutifully into the tissue paper. The flowers didn't smell like much of anything except wet foliage and the inside of Jason's car, but she smiled anyway, intensely aware of the spot where Jason's lips had grazed her cheek. She had only received flowers one other time and those were a dozen red roses on Valentine's Day. This was the first of July, nowhere near Valentine's Day, or her birthday, for that matter. This bouquet meant something—something big. She gulped. Good news or bad? She didn't know which she was more prepared to hear.

Was it customary to bring flowers when you broke up with someone? If so, it seemed like an incredible waste of money and effort. Since Jason was her first boyfriend and she'd never actually been dumped, she wasn't sure of the protocol.

"They're beautiful," she said and lowered herself into a kitchen chair.

He sat down in the chair opposite her and reached across the table to take her hand. "So are you."

Jamie kept her eyes on the flowers, too anxious to risk looking into his eyes. He couldn't be dumping her, unless he planned to make this the gentlest breakup in the history of doomed relationships.

"I guess you're wondering what this is all about," he said.

She nodded and willed herself to look at him. "Well," she croaked, "as a matter of fact…"

"Let's take a walk," he said rising to his feet, the chair scraping noisily across the linoleum.

Jamie jumped up after him. "Um, okay. Let me put these flowers in some water first." She went to the sink and rummaged underneath for a vase or a mason jar. None were to be found. A water glass would have to do for now. She'd look later after he went home and she could breathe again.

Outside in the still evening air, Jason took her hand and started across the yard in apparently no direction at all. When they were a good distance from the house, the lengthening shadows of a summer's evening closing in around them, he stopped walking and turned to face her. Jamie watched his long, slim fingers encase hers. She always liked watching his hands while he worked; efficient, capable, as if working with no conscious thought on his part. In all the time they worked together in the stockroom at the drugstore where he trained her, she never saw him start something he couldn't finish. She'd never seen him make a mistake. He was a man possessed when a job needed to be done. Nothing else mattered until he saw the task completed. Nothing or no one—not even she—could distract him from the job at hand.

"Jamie," he said, his voice firm yet tender just like his hands. "I have something really big to talk to you about, something that's going to affect both of us forever."

Jamie's heart skipped a beat as she brought her eyes up to meet his. She couldn't miss the excitement in his voice. Knowing him, he'd held it in all week, stewing over it, meditating, debating on the best way to put his announcement into words.

"What is it?" she murmured, gazing up into his smoky, blue gray eyes, all the while terrified of what he might say.

Without another word he took off walking again, momentarily pulling her off balance. The sliding barn door stood open. Even though the chores were done for the night, Grandma Cory would come out to check on everything one last time before going to bed. She had gone through the same routine every night for the past forty years.

Jason led Jamie into the barn and pulled her down beside him on a large flat-topped tack box. The Steeles hadn't owned a horse since they had finally been able to afford a tractor. Horses were "expensive and impractical these days" Grandma Cory insisted every time the girls voiced their dream of owning one after seeing a beautiful specimen in someone else's field. No amount of reasoning or vain promises could dissuade her. Nothing ever changed Cory Steele's mind once she settled on something. Nowadays she stored tools and an assortment of farm implements inside the padlocked box once intended for brushes, bits, bridles, and whatever else a horse owner needed.

Jason took her hand in his and brushed a strand of hair away from her face with the other. "Jamie, I don't know how to say this."

His silence lengthened. Jamie, who always considered herself a patient, somewhat passive personality, couldn't take it anymore. "Just say it, Jason," she burst out. "You've been avoiding it for the past twenty minutes." No matter how badly she wanted to hear what he came to say, she found herself holding her breath and dreading his words.

He looked surprised at first and then relieved that she'd forced him into action. "I've never felt about anyone the way I feel for you." He tightened his grip on her hand and she squirmed within his grasp to arrange her fingers into a less painful position. "I haven't really had a family or anything like most people," he went on, unaware of her discomfort. "After Mom took off when I was a kid, Dad totally shut down. Mom was the one that held us all together and without her, we just sort of drifted along like we would get back to living as soon as she came back. Well, that never happened. I don't even know for sure where she's at. Dad doesn't talk about her and I learned a long time ago not to ask questions. He's been sick for as long as I can remember. He's getting worse all the time. Or maybe he just wants it to look that way; like it's his way of holding me here. We've never been close like some fathers and sons. I can't open up and talk to him. You know what I'm saying?"

For the life of her, she wished she did, but he lost her somewhere around the not asking questions part. She nodded anyway, afraid he'd feel the need to expound if she didn't. All she really wanted was for him to get on with it. She would decipher his ramblings later.

"You're the first person who's been really important to me." He scooted a little closer on the tack box and gazed into her eyes. "I love you, Jamie."

Jamie's heart caught in her throat. He loved her; he'd finally said it. She knew it was true but why did he tell her tonight? What else did he have in mind? *Please, don't say another word*, she silently begged. *I don't want anything to change. I'd like things to stay just the way they are—forever.*

"Jason, I—"

He pressed a finger to her lips, silencing her. "I don't know how I'd get along without you. You mean so much to me."

"I—"

"I got a letter last week," he said, shifting gears so quickly she forgot her apprehension. For a second she thought he was still talking about his mother. Then he added, "I've been accepted to law school."

"What? I...I thought you were already registered for law school...in Athens."

His eyes clouded over, and she felt her pulse race. "Well, I was. I mean I *am* registered there, and I *was* planning on going."

Jamie didn't like the conversation's sudden shift in direction.

Jason continued, unaffected by her lack of enthusiasm. "I applied to a few other schools too. I'm sure I told you about it. And, well, I've been accepted. I think Noel may have had something to do with it." Noel Wyatt, the owner of the drugstore where Jamie and Jason worked, had recognized Jason's potential when he hired him a few years ago and had taken him under his wing. He became the father figure Jason lacked at home and had done everything he could to encourage the young man to follow his dreams of becoming an attorney. How much encouragement, Jamie was about to find out.

"He sent out I don't know how many recommendations for me," Jason was saying. "They're offering me a full scholarship and everything. I can't believe its happening. I don't know how Noel even talked me into applying. I figured I'd just embarrass myself. I never dreamed in a million years they'd want me, especially enough to offer me a full ride."

"Jason, wait a minute." Jamie leaned away from him so she could get a better look at his face in the deepening gloom of the barn's interior. With his sandy blond hair slicked back away from his face with whatever it was guys used on their hair, his blue gray eyes seemed larger and more expressive than usual. Or maybe his hair had nothing to do with the glint in his eyes. "What are you saying? Who wants you?"

"Stanford."

Her brow furrowed as her confusion mounted. "Stanford, Connecticut?"

"No, not Stamford, Stanford University—in San Francisco, Stanford Law School," he added proudly, his chest puffing out just a little.

She was beginning to understand. "Stanford," she echoed her voice barely a whisper, "In California?"

His smile widened. "I'm pretty sure that's the only one."

"So you're...the flowers...all this is for..."

"Jamie, this doesn't change anything," he said quickly. "I meant it when I said I love you. That'll never change."

So this was his big announcement; the reason behind the flowers. He hadn't come to dump her. He hadn't come to propose. He came to make a fool of her. "You're wrong, Jason. This changes everything. You're leaving to go to California." Her voice rose in pitch. "What about me? What about Ohio University? They have an excellent law program. You said so yourself a hundred times."

"They didn't offer the package Stanford did. Don't you see? They're offering to pay for everything. I'll really have to keep my grades up, of course, and I'll be on a work study program while I'm there, but no more student loans. No more grant applications. They're even including room and board. Oh, Jamie, you don't know what a load off my mind this is. I haven't had any help getting through school besides a few small alumni scholarships. You know how tough it's been on me. But now...and it's *Stanford*." His eyes lit up. "I can't pass this up."

Jamie wouldn't cry; she refused to give in to the tears pushing their way out of her chest into her voice, her eyes. "So Athens isn't good enough for you anymore. *I'm* not good enough. You want to go to California and become some big city attorney. Just turn your back on everything and everybody you know."

"No, that's not what I want. I never said anything about staying in California, just studying. It's a full scholarship. You're supposed to be happy for me. Can't you see? This is good news." He reached for her hands again, but she jerked them away, out of reach. "You've got to understand," he implored. "With a degree from Stanford, I'll be able to get a job with any firm I want. It's the opportunity of a lifetime."

"What about your dad? Have you told him you're going to run off across the country and leave him here to fend for himself?"

"Yes, I have, and he's thrilled. I think he's just glad he won't have to worry about feeding me for the next four years."

She stood up and turned away from him. "Well, I'm glad everything's working out so well for you." She was about two seconds away from giving into some kind of feminine hysteria, and she couldn't care less. "I don't even know why you bothered to come out here and discuss it with me. You could have just waited until you were some hotshot attorney at some hotshot law firm in San Francisco, and then sent me a postcard."

"Jamie, aren't you listening?" He stood up behind her and put his hands on her shoulders. "Just because I go to school out there doesn't mean I won't come back after graduation. Ohio is my home. This is where my life is."

She spun around to face him, her fists clenched at her sides. "Give me a break, would you? You won't come back to this," she threw her arms into the air, indicating the barn around them, "after spending four years in San Francisco. Why would you?"

Her lack of understanding confounded him. "Why are you acting this way? I thought you of all people would understand the practicality of all this. I'll get an excellent education most people only dream of—totally paid for—and then I'll be able to do what I want for the rest of my life."

"I'm sick of being practical," she shrieked, any semblance of grace and decorum abandoned into the barn's rafters. "I'm sick of being understanding. I thought we were going to school together. Now I find out, you only planned on going with me because you had no other options. Now that Stanford's waving this bone in front of your face, you've forgotten all our plans. Isn't that right?"

Jason's shoulders sagged in defeat. "This is what I've wanted since I was a little kid," he said softly. "Yes, I'm excited about this bone they're waving in my face. I saw it as an answer to prayer, something like divine intervention making it possible for me to get a great education—for free. I kind of thought you'd see it that way too. Now you're accusing me of using it to get away from you. This has nothing to do with you, Jamie." When he saw the hurt those words brought to her face, he hurried on. "I love you." He reached for her hand again. "But it would be stupid to pass up this opportunity."

Jamie jerked away from him. "Well, we can't have anybody

accusing you of doing something stupid now, can we? Being accepted to Stanford means you must be brilliant. Staying in Ohio with the woman you love would be *stupid*."

She watched as his jaw clenched and unclenched. Maybe she was being too hard on him. Maybe she should calm down, take a deep breath, and try to see things from his point of view.

Jason dug his toe into the soft earth of the barn floor. "I guess I'd better go."

She pursed her lips and crossed her arms over her chest. No, she didn't want to try to understand why he couldn't wait to get away from her. She was right, and he was wrong. If he cared anything about her, he wouldn't even consider Stanford's offer. He had some nerve insinuating God was somehow involved in sending him clear across the country to pursue this selfish dream and that if she was a good Christian, she'd see it too. Apparently he didn't see their future the same way she did.

"Yeah, maybe you'd better," she said stiffly.

She followed him out of the barn to the back porch, rigidly silent, hating him and hating Stanford. He looked back one last time before heading to his car, but she turned away and went into the house through the squeaky back screen door, letting it slam behind her. She heard his car start up and the crunch of gravel as he backed out of the driveway onto Betterman Road.

She caught sight of the colorful bouquet of flowers in the water glass on the counter. She closed her fist around the stems, crushing them in her grasp, and gave them a toss out the back door. His attempt at a peace offering—he wouldn't have brought them if he thought for one minute she would support this selfish, cold-hearted decision.

"Was that Jason leaving already?" Cassie asked from the doorway. When she saw the look on Jamie's face and the trail of water droplets leading from the empty glass to the back door, she turned and headed back into the living room. For the first time in her life, she did the wise thing and didn't ask questions.

# Chapter Two

A lternating between self-pitying tears whenever she thought about a future on the college campus without Jason, fury toward him for thinking she would be happy that he was moving across the country, irritation toward Noel Wyatt for interfering in other people's lives, and bitterness at herself for not being happy for him when it was so important to him that she be, Jamie didn't sleep more than a few fitful hours. She awoke the next morning with her brown eyes swollen and puffy, feeling like they were filled with grains of sand. All she could think about was clambering out of bed and down the hallway to the bathroom where she could get a drink to soothe her dry, scratchy throat.

Except for the sounds of Grandma Cory downstairs in the kitchen—probably sitting on a kitchen chair, pulling on her old boots, her hair pinned back in a tight, practical bun, her lips pursed in concentration as she went over everything in her head that needed to be done before breakfast—the house was as still as a tomb. Cassie never got out of bed until Grandma Cory yelled at her from the bottom of the stairs that it was after seven o'clock, the day was already half wasted, and if she didn't get up soon she might as well stay in bed all day. Not that staying in bed all day was ever an option.

That's when Grandpa Harlan would get out of bed too. Now, instead of rising early like he used too and going outside to do some harmless jobs like gathering the eggs or watering the vegetable garden, where he couldn't do any real damage, he would sit at the table and wait silently for his breakfast. Then he'd move to the living room to either play his country music records on the old record player, watch TV game shows, or wander aimlessly around the barn yard as if looking for something he had lost.

Jamie hated to see the changes in him. They had come about so quickly. Only a year ago, he spoke to her every morning on his way out the door to get to his chores, whistling an old Bluegrass tune, a smile on his face, pleased with any simple job he completed—even completely incorrectly. Those days were gone. He didn't whistle, he seldom spoke, and he never looked pleased with himself.

The words had never been uttered aloud, but the family knew it wouldn't be long before Grandpa Harlan was no longer with them. Whether matters beyond their control forced him into a nursing home—something the V.A. doctors had been vehemently suggesting to Grandma Cory for several years—or he mercifully slipped away in his sleep, his time on the farm was waning.

Jamie knew it was the natural order of things. As a born again believer, she knew there was an eternal home waiting for all God's children, a better home than any mortal could imagine; one where Grandpa Harlan wouldn't be old and feeble-minded. He'd experience no more sickness, and he wouldn't be a danger to himself. He would be a young man again, happy and strong, coherent and useful, just as the good Lord designed him.

Heaven would be a better alternative than a nursing home, but either way, she couldn't stand the thought of seeing him go. Their relationship had always been a close one. She remembered him swinging her up on his shoulders for piggy back rides, his strong hands grasping the fodder twine around a hay bale as he hefted it into the loft, his firm, gravelly voice telling her a silly, scary story he made up on the spur of the moment as they walked hand in hand through the woods. Back then she hardly noticed the dementia's gradual progression, and when she did, it seemed only natural for her to assume the role of caregiver and him the role of child. When he became agitated or contrary, only she could soothe him. When he was sick and sleepless from a new medication, he wouldn't stand for anyone else but Jamie to read to him.

Now even those days were gone. Grandma Cory still administered his medication, made his appointments, and bullied him into the car when it was time to go. He no longer needed Jamie, but oh, how she needed him.

She hurried past his closed bedroom door and back through her own, refusing to let her mind dwell on what her life would be like when he was no longer in it. For now, the sun had not yet reached its golden fingers around the house to shine into his bedroom window. He slept as soundly as a baby, apparently in no distress. He would awake soon, dress himself, go downstairs and begin another day just like the one before. She would watch his slow, methodical deterioration and know he was one day closer to meeting his Lord.

Jamie softly closed her bedroom door behind her and sat down on the windowsill. She gazed out at the fog lifting off the distant hills. She turned her eyes to the east and Jenna's Creek, a town of about ten thousand residents, which slowly encroached upon the surrounding farmland more and more every year. She imagined Jason already out of bed, fully dressed, ready for work. She could see him frowning at himself in the mirror as he dragged a razor across his angular jaw, thinking of her, disappointed that she hadn't reacted the way he'd hoped over the biggest news he'd ever received.

She rested her elbow on the wooden pane and sighed. She had to admit the whole idea of Stanford was pretty cool. If any of her friends had been accepted there, let alone awarded a full scholarship, she would have been beside herself with delight. But since it happened to Jason, all she could think of was how it would affect her. She realized she shouldn't be so angry. This was the opportunity of a lifetime; one she shouldn't begrudge him. He had worked too hard not to take advantage of a free ride to a top notch law school.

She shook her head in dismay at her own selfishness and turned toward the bureau for a pair of shorts and a T-shirt to wear outside while she did her chores. After chores and breakfast, she would come back up here to shower and get ready for work. Jason would be at the drugstore by the time she got there for her shift.

She would apologize, congratulate him with a kiss, and try to work up a little enthusiasm.

Like always, business was jumping by the time Jamie arrived at the drugstore for her noon shift. Wyatt's Drugstore was nearly an institution in Jenna's Creek. It carried everything residents could find a use for besides the usual pharmaceuticals of the bigger drugstore chains that were creeping stealthily across the country. Situated on the corner of Main and High Streets, it faced the county courthouse across the street and was adjacent to the two national banks that occupied the remaining corners of the intersection. On any given day, residents from all over Auburn County thought of a reason to stop in the drugstore while they were in town.

Jamie hurried through the crowded store to the short staircase in the back that led to her boss's office. After punching the time clock outside the office door, she raced back downstairs to the stockroom where she knew she'd find Jason. Today was Friday, a big delivery day, and sure enough Jason was positioned in front of a stack of boxes, a clipboard with an attached invoice in hand. A new stock girl—Jamie thought her name was Kim—stood nearby, awaiting instructions. Jamie smiled at the memories the scene evoked. Not long ago, she'd been the stock girl in training, trembling in Jason's capable presence. He was easily the most feared individual at the store, even more so than their mild-mannered boss who had a smile and encouraging word for everyone.

In typical Jason fashion, he didn't look up from the invoice when the heavy stockroom door creaked as Jamie entered. The new girl smiled at her, relieved to see a friendly face.

"Jason," Jamie said from the door.

Jason's head snapped up. The wariness was all too evident on his face.

Jamie gave him an encouraging smile and moved toward him. Jason smiled back—relieved that she hadn't come to pick a fight with him—and handed the invoice to the new girl. She looked down at it as if it might come alive in her hand and then stared questioningly at the back of Jason's head.

"Hi," he said, taking Jamie's hands in his.

"I've only got a minute," she said, peering up at him through dark lashes. "I work till closing tonight. Do you think we could go for a ride afterwards? I really want to talk."

Jason cocked one eyebrow. "I don't know. My ears are still ringing from the last little talk we had."

Jamie blushed and squeezed his hands. "I know. I'm so sorry. I've been unreasonable. That's what I want to talk about. I'm still mad about you going to California. I think it's crummy, but…" She rose up on her tiptoes to draw eye level to his five-foot, ten-inch frame. "…I'm willing to talk about it like a civilized adult. If I think about it long enough, I may even let myself be happy for you."

They left Jamie's car parked in the alley behind the drugstore after closing and drove out of town in Jason's car. She didn't ask where they were going as he turned in the opposite direction from her house. Eventually he pulled the car over on a deserted stretch of Highway 18, a quiet road a few miles out of town. Highway 18 was frequented by young lovers looking for privacy. Jamie and Jason didn't come here. If they wanted to be alone they needed only go as far as the front porch on Betterman Road. Too much unsupervised time together only led to trouble; besides the fact that Grandma Cory would kill her if she knew she was alone in a parked car with a boy.

Jamie knew Jason's desire for privacy was not so he would have an opportunity to take advantage of her. He probably just didn't want Grandma Cory, Cassie, or half of Jenna's Creek to hear her yell at him again.

He killed the ignition and turned a little in the narrow seat to face her. "Jamie." His voice was as soft and soothing in the graying light of a late summer evening as the look he gave her. "I'm so sorry this happened."

His hand slid across the space between them, seeking hers. She grasped it and turned to him in the seat. "No, Jason, I'm sorry. I shouldn't have reacted the way I did. You were right. It was supposed to be good news. I was just so…" She swallowed hard. She wouldn't cry. She was here to celebrate, not make him feel worse about earning the scholarship. "I know I'm being childish, but I don't want anything between us to change."

He squeezed her hand and brought it to his lips, "Neither do I. If I had my way, Harvard or Princeton would've called," he said. "That way, I'd only have to hitchhike halfway across the country a couple times a year to see you. But it didn't happen that way. Stanford wants me bad enough to pay for it. I've gotta go."

She looked up at him through glistening eyelashes. "I know," she admitted, hating herself for siding with reason. She wanted to stay mad. She wanted to give him an ultimatum; if he didn't stay, they were through; he was the most selfish man on the planet; if he left her, he would never forgive himself.

He slid his hand up her arm to her neck. "I don't want to leave with it like this."

"I know," she said with a sniff to hold her unshed tears at bay. She pressed her lips together. She wasn't going to cry. If she started, she might never stop.

He leaned forward and kissed her. "Jamie, I love you," he murmured, resting his forehead against hers.

"I love you too." The admission slipped effortlessly from her lips. How could she let him go? How could he even consider going, knowing how they felt about each other? How did anyone walk away from the one they loved? She couldn't do it; she didn't have the courage. She put her arms around his neck and clung desperately to him. *Don't go; don't go,* she cried inwardly, but too much of a coward to say it aloud.

Jason breathed two words into her ear.

"Marry me."

The tears that were so close to spilling on his shoulder froze just behind her eyelids. Her ears were playing tricks on her. His news last night had put her in such a fragile state, she was hearing things. He had not just proposed. Jason Collier would never suggest marriage after getting a full scholarship to Stanford. How impractical was that!

She leaned away from him to study his face to make sure she heard what she thought she heard. "Jason, what—"

"Marry me," he repeated, louder this time. His lips found her ear, her chin. "Go to California with me. If you don't get accepted to Stanford, there are plenty of other schools in the area. If you can't get the financial aid, we'll work it out when the time comes."

"Jason, I don't want to go to California."

He stopped kissing her and narrowed his eyes as if the thought had never occurred to him. Then his gaze softened. "Then say you'll marry me, and we'll do it when I get back in four years." He leaned in for another kiss.

She pulled completely out of his grasp and moved back to her side of the little car. For a brief instant she let herself imagine accepting his proposal and moving to California with him. It was all so romantic. Like straight out of a movie. Then she realized it wasn't what either of them wanted.

"Jason, you don't want to marry me. I kind of thought that's why you came to the house with flowers last night, but you don't want to get married and neither do I—at least not yet."

Even though she knew him well enough to know she was right, the relief that flashed briefly across his face was a tad insulting.

"We don't have to right away," he said. "We can wait a couple years, take our time. By then we'll both be ready." He put his hand behind her neck to pull her to him.

Jamie stiffened. The romantic notions from a few moments ago were gone. She was beginning to get annoyed. This was not how she imagined her first proposal. "What if we're not ready in a couple of years? What then?"

He shrugged. "We'll worry about that when the time comes."

She took his hand and removed it from behind her neck. He sighed angrily and straightened up, resting both hands on the steering wheel. "Neither of us is ready to even think about getting married," she exclaimed, "you know that as well as I do. If you really wanted to get married, you would've asked me last night before you sprang Stanford on me."

"I had to do something," he snapped. "You were so mad. I expected you to understand and when you didn't, I figured the only way to get you over being mad is to get engaged before I left. Then you'd know I'm serious about coming back."

This evening kept getting worse and worse. "So, this is a sympathy proposal!" she shrieked, her voice echoing off the windshield, "Every girl's dream come true. You think the only way to make me stop pouting is to ask me to marry you? What do you think I am, a five-year-old? I don't want to get married. Not now. And I don't want you to stay here to please me."

"Well, forgive me for not knowing what you want, Jamie. I can't read your mind. I never expected this Stanford scholarship, but since I got it, I'm not turning it down." He brought his hand down hard on the steering wheel, making her jump. "When I got the acceptance letter, I was more excited than I've ever been in my life. It was a dream come true. I thought you'd be excited too."

"Oh, I know how excited you were, Jason," she said sarcastically. "Did you have to be so happy about it? Couldn't you have at least pretended to be a little disappointed that it wasn't OU or Ohio State offering the scholarship? All you can think about is Stanford. 'Ooh, look at me, a big time law degree from a big time California law school! Ain't I special?' Even if we did get engaged, I don't know if I'd want you by the time you got back, you'd be so full of yourself. And you sure wouldn't give me the time of day; not after spending four years surrounded by all those beautiful, tanned California girls. They'd smell you and your law degree a mile away."

"Why do you keep insisting I'm going to change into someone you hate just because I'm going to Stanford? Could you give me a little credit? If you were going away, I'd give you the benefit of the doubt. Don't you think I'm a strong enough man to withstand whatever temptation you see me encountering out there? Don't you have any faith in me at all?"

"I don't want you to go, okay?" The tears let loose, and she was beyond the point of caring what he thought if she broke down in front of him. "I want you here with me. If you leave, you'll never come back. You'll see there's a lot more to the world than what me and Jenna's Creek, Ohio can offer you. You'll realize you can do a lot better than this; better than me, and you'll never come back."

"Jamie." He sighed and pulled her into his arms. This time she didn't resist. She fell against him and gave into her tears, great quaking sobs that wracked her body. Yes, she was feeling sorry for herself. Yes, she was admitting her greatest—and most irrational—fears just to make him feel worse about choosing Stanford over her. But she couldn't help it. She wanted him to be as miserable as she was.

Finally she stopped crying and pulled away. Jason leaned across her and rummaged in the glove box until he found a crumpled tissue to give her. She noticed dampness on his cheeks from his own tears. "I'm sorry for acting like a big jerk," she said, after blowing her nose. "I am happy for you, or at least, I'm trying to be."

Jason smiled and wiped a stray tear from her cheek with his thumb. "I knew you were underneath all that attitude. But you've gotta believe me. I am coming back."

She tried to smile as she wagged her head back and forth. "You may think you will, but you'll start getting offers from firms all over the West Coast when you graduate, and then, what'd be the point?"

"Do you always have to see the negative in every situation?"

"Not always."

"Jamie, I love you. Don't you think you're more important to me than some exciting job in a high rise office building with a starting salary that'll make my eyes bug out, my own secretary, parking space, and company car…?"

"Okay, okay, I get it. You'll hate everything about California and will come running back to me and these cold Ohio winters as fast as your tanned legs can carry you."

Jason put one hand on the steering wheel and the other on the key in the ignition. "Do you feel like getting something to eat before I take you home? It's getting late. Your grandma will think I've got you somewhere taking advantage of you."

"Maybe she'll think I'm the one taking advantage of you."

"I wish." He gave her a wink and turned the key. The four-cylinder engine sputtered to life.

They rode back to town in silence, holding hands across the empty space of vinyl between them. Jamie's anger had been cried out but the sadness remained. What would she do without Jason? He asked her to marry him. If the circumstances had been different, would she have said yes? She allowed herself a moment to imagine what it would be like to be married to Jason, living in a little apartment off campus, both of them attending classes during the day and discussing their dreams every night wrapped in each other's arms.

Was her hasty negative response to his proposal a mistake she would regret the rest of her life? She may never get another chance. She loved him and he loved her. What if he never came back? What if she let the only man she'd ever love get away because of pride or whatever it was that made her answer so quickly? Was there someone else out there for her? Had God removed Jason from her life to enable her to find Mr. Right?

No, God wasn't saving her for someone else. He wasn't behind this move to California; just some benign West Coast alumni board who thought they were doing the right thing by offering a full ride to a disadvantaged Ohio pre-law student.

# Chapter Three

J amie hated to see the summer end, and it sped by at an alarming rate just to spite her. Nearly every night in bed, she stared at the ceiling until she fell asleep, too tired of crying to cry anymore. Her tears were gone, along with her excitement of attending college in the fall. Fall meant Jason was leaving. She would go to Ohio University alone like every other freshman; friendless, scared, with no idea of what to expect.

After church on Labor Day weekend—her last Sunday morning in Jenna's Creek before moving to campus—Noel Wyatt held a party at his house on Bryton Avenue in Jason's honor. All drugstore employees were invited, along with Noel's friends and business associates, Jason's friends—not a large portion of the guest list since Jason wasn't the outgoing type—and Jason's father, someone Jamie had yet to meet.

Cassie couldn't wait to get to Bryton Avenue and spend the afternoon with every influential person in the county. Noel's house alone was enough of an event to get her chomping at the bit about going. Jamie had to admit she wanted to see his house as much as Cassie. She had visited his mother's house several times for dinner or just to talk since going to work at the drugstore, but never Noel's house. The beautiful brick Federalist occupied a large corner lot, its circular driveway entering Bryton to the south, and exiting Marple to the east. The front of the house was barely visible from the street, secluded from view by a mass of impenetrable oak and elm trees. As Jamie maneuvered her car along the tree-lined driveway between shiny Lincolns and wide-bodied Cadillacs, the sisters gaped in awe as more and more of the grand house came into view.

"Oh, Jamie, it's beautiful," Cassie said with a sharp intake of air. "Noel's wife must have been out of her mind to divorce him and leave all this."

"She was rich already," Jamie pointed out. "I'm sure this wasn't such a big deal to her."

Everyone in Jenna's Creek knew the story of how Myra Curtsinger broke Noel Wyatt's heart—at least they thought they knew, including Jamie and Cassie.

Noel had met the young debutante from Lexington, Kentucky while attending college in the 1930's. The marriage ended abruptly after only two years, the young Mrs. Curtsinger-Wyatt unable to adapt to small-town life in southern Ohio, or to her small-town—and in her opinion—small-minded husband. Jenna's Creek was scandalized. Self-respecting folk didn't divorce in those days. Occasionally a husband failed to come home or a young wife disappeared with someone else's husband, but it was never talked about. It was better to assume both had met an untimely end than to imagine they were living in sin somewhere; probably out west where those things weren't frowned upon, but in Jenna's Creek the oath of marriage was a bond not readily broken. If a divorce actually made it to the courts, the guilty parties usually moved away to spare their families the humiliation.

In Noel Wyatt's case, no one in town was sorry to see the ex-debutante go. She wasn't one of them. She never would have fit in anyway. But it was inconceivable that she would leave Noel. He represented the best Auburn County could produce. He was the last male heir of the founding family of Jenna's Creek. He had money, power, status, yet remained a man's man. Everyone loved him, and consequently blamed Myra Curtsinger for everything that could possibly go wrong in a marriage. Surely Noel had done nothing wrong, except try to love a woman who possessed absolutely no redeeming qualities.

The town's only regret over Miss Curtsinger's departure, was how she had broken poor Noel's heart. Even forty years later, no one considered her worthy of the name Wyatt. If not for that, why else would he never have remarried? They had finally resigned themselves to the fact that Noel would never find love again, making one of their daughters the happiest and most indulged woman in Auburn County.

No one except two people in the entire county knew the real reason behind Noel's bachelorhood.

"Well, I'm sorry," Cassie contended. "No matter how rich you were, this would be hard to walk away from."

Jamie's car reached the side of the house where she wriggled it into position between a Town Car and a Chrysler New Yorker. If possible, the back of Noel's property was even more spectacular than the front. The grounds were immaculately landscaped—probably professionally—another thing unheard of in Jenna's Creek. A white board privacy fence running along the perimeter blocked from view the alley that came out on Marple Street.

"Oh, Jamie, this place is incredible," Cassie gushed, her voice lowered so the other guests, who were now within a stone's throw of the car, wouldn't hear.

Jamie didn't comment. She was as impressed with her surroundings as Cassie, and thought it a little sad that Noel never had anyone to share his blessings with, but all she could think of was how this party today meant Jason was leaving and probably never coming back. Cassie didn't seem to notice Jamie's grave mood. She exited the car as soon as Jamie shut off the engine and was headed across the lawn in the direction of a huge white tent set up in the center of the back yard.

Jamie got out and gave the car door a good hard slam to insure it stayed closed. Uncle Justin and Grandma Cory had given her the car for Christmas. It was a good enough running used car, but it had its little quirks that sometimes made her fantasize about a new one. Fantasizing was all she'd ever do, at least until she was out of school and working somewhere making real money.

Cassie blended effortlessly into the crowd. There were lots

of kids she knew from school, the privileged offspring of Noel's friends and associates. Station in life meant nothing to her. She believed all men were created equal in God's eyes, and if it was good enough for the Almighty who was she to dispute it?

For the thousandth time in her life Jamie wished she possessed a hint of her sister's self-confidence. But Cassie was prettier, more interesting, charming, and definitely more outspoken—period, end of story. While she plowed headfirst into a situation, totally unconcerned about whether she would make a fool of herself or not —which of course, she never did—Jamie hung back, reserved and timid. Working for the last year at the town's pharmacy, first in the stockroom learning the ropes from Jason, and then out front behind the register for the whole town to see her mistakes, had helped bring her out of her shell. But still she lacked Cassie's natural-born charisma. She figured some things couldn't be taught; you either had it or you didn't. Cassie had it. Jamie...well, she didn't.

She looked up to see Jason coming toward her. "Jamie." He gave her a quick kiss.

"Some turn out," she said, eyeing the crowd. "Noel went all out, didn't he?"

"I've never been so uncomfortable in my life," Jason said, tugging on his shirt collar, buttoned up to his throat and topped off with a handsome tie. "I don't know who half these people are, but they keep slapping me on the back, calling me 'old man', and stuffing twenty-dollar bills in my shirt pocket."

"Oh, you poor thing," Jamie said, rolling her eyes. "It's a hard life."

Jason grinned. "Well, I guess the twenties in my pocket aren't so bad, but I do feel like a fish out of water. You know how I hate these kinds of situations."

"Don't worry about it. They all know you're Noel's protégé. That makes you equal to them. Besides, they want to make sure they've minded their P's and Q's in case they ever need your help once you're defending corporate America."

"I wish you wouldn't say things like that every time it comes up about my going to law school. Not all lawyers are leeches, you know, stepping on whoever they have to, to get what they want."

Jamie swallowed hard, wishing she hadn't opened her mouth. "You're right. I'm sorry. I didn't mean it that way. I guess it was my attempt at a pretty bad joke. I didn't come here to ruin your party."

He looked at her face, his expression drawn and guarded. Jamie clasped his hand. "Jason, I really am sorry. I'll be good. No more *attorney* digs."

He looked into her eyes, searching for sincerity. Apparently satisfied, he pulled her into his arms and kissed her.

"Hey, hey, none of that." Noel Wyatt was working his way through the crowd toward them. "This is a respectable neighborhood." Jamie and Jason's boss was tall and broad shouldered. His once dark hair was now streaked with gray, but he still had a flat stomach and firm jaw line. Jamie knew he had to be about Grandma Cory's age, probably around sixty, but she never would have guessed by looking at him. He had the vigor and vitality of a man much younger.

She drew back from Jason, her cheeks hot. Of all people to catch her and Jason kissing, she wished it hadn't been him. Noel grinned impishly, clasped a hand on each of their shoulders, and steered them toward the white tent. "Now that you're here," he said to Jamie, "we can get started." He ushered them into the tent to a long table in the center, calling for attention from his guests as he went. A large ice sculpture in the shape of a mortarboard tilted up on one end sat in the middle of the table. The sculpture was surrounded by red and white rose petals—the colors of the Stanford Cardinals Jamie had learned over the course of the summer—floating in a recessed pool of crystal clear water. He pushed Jason to the place of honor behind the ice sculpture overlooking the guests and drew Jamie up beside him, crushing her shoulder into his rib cage. A flashbulb popped in her face. She prayed it wasn't someone's intention to have the picture printed in the paper along with a long-winded story on the society page. People did things like that in small town newspapers much to the younger generation's chagrin.

"Okay, everyone, everyone, if you could all gather in." Noel's big voice boomed across the yard. "Yes, let's all crowd in. Okay. That's it. We all know why we're here. My friend, Jason here," he thumped Jason on the back, nearly sending him into the mortarboard sculpture. "In, what is it now, five days...yes, five days he'll be going off to earn his law degree at Stanford University in California."

Everyone in the tent and yard erupted into applause. Jamie leaned forward so she could see past Noel. Jason's face turned red against his starched collar. He caught her eye and she smiled encouragingly. If Noel realized how difficult this public display was for Jason, he didn't let on. Like Cassie, Noel didn't have a shy bone in his body and couldn't understand anyone who did.

"Jason's been a great employee," Noel continued, "and someone I'm proud to call a friend. He's more deserving of that scholarship than anyone I know. But we all remember what it's like to be a poor college student far from home. Well, those of us who can remember back that far." He cocked his head in the direction of a cluster of well-dressed gentlemen and winked. The comment was met with good-natured laughter and elbow ribbing. "So, if any of you windbags can see fit, I'm sure it wouldn't hurt ole Jason here," another sound thump on Jason's narrow shoulders, "one bit to take some of your moldy money off your hands."

More laughter and applause flowed from the crowd of aging bankers, judges, and businessmen as they remembered their own first trip into the world. Jamie doubted there was one among them who had ever been a poor anything, but they seemed to enjoy remembering themselves that way.

Jamie saw Jason cringe again at Noel's plea for his friends to hand over more money. He would rather be anywhere but here in front of all these people. He was probably plotting his escape as soon as good manners permitted. Noel lowered the hand that had been resting on Jamie's shoulder and put both arms around Jason, pulling him into a massive bear hug. He whispered something into Jason's ear and laughed and Jason laughed too, his discomfort alleviated if only by a degree.

Noel turned back to the crowd and called for attention again. "I knew when I invited you all here today I was going to have to feed you." More goodhearted affirmation came from the crowd. "Pastor Rice," he said to a man in the crowd, the pastor of the church he attended along with Jamie's family, "could I ask you to bless the food for us, and of course, Jason here."

Finally Noel was quiet and Pastor Rice eagerly lapsed into a two-minute blessing of food, company, fellowship, Jason, and almost anything else he could think of. Jamie bowed her head along with everyone else under the tent, listened to the breeze flapping the sides of the tents, the birds in the trees, and a mother shushing a small child. She smiled to herself as Pastor Rice droned on. She thought of the menagerie of people gathered here in a big back yard on Bryton Avenue—somewhere she'd probably never be again—and her heart wrenched inside her. Next week she'd leave for Ohio University in Athens, Ohio and college life. Jason would be in San Francisco by then. No matter how good his intentions or the promises he made, she doubted she would see him again for at least four years and maybe never. Welling tears tickled Jamie's nose and she pinched it to hold them back. When Pastor Rice finally finished his blessing and amen's sounded throughout the crowd she raised her eyes and saw Jason watching her. Her lips twitched in an effort to smile. He opened his mouth to say something, but was swept away as Noel pushed him in the direction of the buffet line. He threw another glance at her over his shoulder as he disappeared into the crowd. Jamie looked away. She sniffed and wrinkled her nose, determined not to cry in front of everyone. She wouldn't ruin Jason's big day by feeling sorry for herself. As she took her place in the buffet line she wondered just how much her life was about to change.

When Jamie turned away from the buffet table with her plate filled with potato salad, shrimp, and chicken, even though she had no appetite, Jason was right beside her. He took her elbow and turned her around. "Come sit with us," he said. "There's someone I

want you to meet." He set her plate down in front of an empty folding chair at a large round table. Everyone at the table had stopped
eating and was watching her. Noel and his mother, Lucinda Wyatt,
sat across from them. Several others, whom Jamie recognized from
town but didn't know by name, were seated around the table.

Jason looked down at the man to his right. "Dad, this is Jamie
Steele. Jamie, this is my dad, Burton Collier."

Mr. Collier wiped his hands with his napkin and then raised his
right one to shake Jamie's. Despite the warm afternoon, his hand
was cool in hers. He was a little man, as if he'd shrunk during his
adulthood instead of growing. He seemed smaller, more withered,
and older than his true age. Jamie knew he was of poor health, but
had never heard Jason expound on his condition. Why didn't she
know more about him? What kind of girlfriend had she been to
Jason in the past year that she knew so little about his home life?
She wasn't sure if Jason was embarrassed for her to meet his dad or
if he was uncomfortable showing her off to his father.

Jamie smiled warmly, "Nice to meet you, Mr. Collier."

"You too, Jamie, I've heard a lot about you." He pulled the
empty chair next to him away from the table and motioned for
her to sit down. Jamie sat down with Jason taking the chair beside
her.

"Jamie," Mrs. Wyatt greeted her warmly from the other side of
the table. "How are you, dear? I hear you're headed off to college
next week, too."

"Yes, Mrs. Wyatt." She usually loved talking to Noel's mother,
but today her heart wasn't into polite conversation.

"I imagine you're looking forward to it."

"Mmm," she nodded her accent and picked at a section of
hard-boiled egg in the potato salad.

"How I envy you young people," the woman to the right of
Mrs. Wyatt spoke up, "starting out fresh without a mark against
you. You don't realize how fortunate you are."

"They won't realize it either," said the loan officer, "until they're
too old to appreciate it, that is."

The woman nodded in agreement. "When we're young, all we
can do is look forward and wish we were older. Then when we're

old, we spend our time looking back wishing we could recapture the carefree days of youth."

Jamie smiled politely and nibbled at her salad. Ordinarily it annoyed her when adults talked about young people as if they couldn't hear conversation going on less than two feet from them. At this moment she didn't care what anyone said. She concentrated on swallowing her potato salad and tuned them out.

"You're going to love San Francisco," the man on Jason's left told him, "there's a lot of history and culture in that town. Not to mention the miles of beaches and all those tanned, blonde coeds to go along with it."

"Jason's going there to study, Howard," another woman—apparently Howard's wife—admonished. "He won't have time for a beach full of coeds."

"There's always time for coeds," Howard said with a laugh. The men at the table joined in. Jason blushed and chewed frantically on a piece of shrimp. Jamie wished she hadn't sat down at this table. The last image she wanted on her mind before Jason got on that plane headed west was him frolicking on the beach. She didn't want to imagine him having any kind of fun whatsoever.

Much to Jamie's relief, Mrs. Wyatt turned to Jason's father and changed the subject. "Burton, how are you going to do with Jason so far away? It'll be awfully quiet around the place without him."

Mr. Collier set his fork down and looked at her. "I always knew this day was coming. I'm just glad the boy's getting what he's worked so hard for."

Jamie washed down a mouthful of chicken with a long drink of her iced tea. She didn't hear the rest of the conversation. She hadn't even considered how this move would affect Mr. Collier who had come to depend greatly on Jason. All she had thought of was her own needs and pain in seeing him go. But if Mr. Collier could put his own needs aside in support of Jason's best interests, who was she to think only of herself?

She reached for Jason's hand under the table. She twined her fingers through his and smiled. He squeezed back and smiled, relieved. Today wasn't about her. She needed to stop thinking of her own self and consider what was best for Jason. He deserved the scholarship. It hadn't been awarded out of pity, but of worthiness.

After nibbling at her food and pretending to follow the conversation, Jamie left the table and tossed her paper plate in a strategically placed garbage can. Cassie moved up beside her, smiling from ear to ear. She didn't notice Jamie's long face. "Isn't this wonderful, Jamie? I'm having so much fun. Have you noticed all the gorgeous boys here?"

Jamie tried to focus on what she was saying, "Uh huh, gorgeous."

"Oh, Jamie, stop your moping. You're bringing me down. Have you seen Uncle Justin and Aunt Marty? They're here somewhere." Cassie cast her eyes around the crowd. "They were asking about you earlier. I think they figure you'd be upset."

Jamie sighed. "And I suppose you told them how miserable I am. I wish you'd mind your own business and stop worrying about me."

Cassie held her hands up in front of her. "Oh, believe me, you're the last person I'm worrying about today. Life's too short and I am having too much fun. If you'd just look around and see Jason isn't the only fish in the sea you'd have some fun too." She leaned closer and whispered conspiratorially. "In fact, there's some pretty rich fish swimming around in this fish bowl. You might be better off than you ever would've been with sweet little Jason."

"Just remember, little sister, you're not even allowed to date yet," Jamie pointed out. "It'll be some time before Grandma Cory gives you permission to go fishing."

Cassie squealed with laughter. "I'm just looking, Jamie. For future reference, you know." She arched her eyebrows and wagged her head in the direction of a handsome young man by the punch bowl as a case in point. She nudged Jamie with her shoulder and moved off into the crowd.

Jamie watched her go and smiled to herself, her depression momentarily lifted. How did Cassie get to be so flippant? Nothing ever seemed to bother her, like making lemonade with life's lemons. She doubted Cassie would ever suffer from a broken heart, but then again, would she ever allow a man to mean enough to her that she grieved when he was gone?

Maybe she could learn something from her little sister. All Cassie was interested in was having fun. She didn't take life seriously. When a boy proved silly or not worthy of her time, she knew there were plenty more out there to take his place. Of course, in her case, that was always true. Cassie got attention wherever she went. Even though nature hadn't been as kind to Jamie, she didn't have to hang her hopes on one man. Jason was leaving whether she was ready or not. That didn't mean her life had to end. She wasn't interested in finding someone to take his place but she didn't have to wallow in pain the rest of her life either. Like it or not, she had to accept that she and Jason were about to part, probably for good.

Five days remained before Jason would get on that plane to San Francisco. She didn't want to spend those last five days being angry at him. He felt guilty enough about leaving without her making everything worse. Besides, these were her last five days too. She didn't want to spend the next four years looking back on the five days she made his life miserable.

Cassie was right, life was too short.

She stayed on the fringe of the crowd the rest of the afternoon. Jason gave her as much attention as he was able. He would put his hand on her shoulder or around her waist for a quick hug when they had a moment. He'd place his hand on her neck under her hair and pull her close for a kiss now and then. She concentrated on being happy for him and forced her mind off her own misery. It was all a part of growing up, this terrible pain; what didn't kill you, made you stronger. Didn't someone say that once? It was probably some masochist who enjoyed pain. But she would learn from this. She'd grow into a more caring, understanding individual—wouldn't she?

She knew now what else she had to do. It was also a part of growing up.

It was getting close to church time when Jamie pulled Jason behind a hydrangea bush for a good-bye kiss. "Cassie and I are leaving," she said after he released her. "We've got to go by the house to pick Grandma Cory up for church."

He squeezed her hand and kissed her forehead. "Thanks for today, Jamie. You've been great."

"Not so great," she admitted. "But I'm trying."

"Can I come by tonight after church? I know you've been here all day, but it seems like we haven't seen each other at all."

"Sure, that'd be fine. We need to talk anyway."

"Sounds serious."

"We'll be home from church around eight-thirty," she said, forcing a smile. "I'll see you then." She didn't have the heart to say anything more.

A cool breeze rustled the dried cornstalks standing in the darkened field across the road. Jamie and Cassie used to scare each other with stories of a scarecrow coming to life and walking the fields in the late summer dusk. The night noises were such a part of her world. She seldom heard them anymore, especially on nights like this when her heart lay heavy in her chest.

She led Jason out to the front porch and sat beside him on the old porch swing. She rested her head on his shoulder and he set the swing in motion with a push of his long legs. The silence lengthened. Jamie tried to think of nothing more than the breeze on her face and sound of the cows lowing from the direction of the barn. She wished the next few moments could last forever.

Finally she lifted her head from his shoulder and began what had been on her mind all evening. "Jason, I'm sorry I've been so awful all summer. I know I shouldn't have made you feel bad about taking that scholarship at Stanford."

"It's all right, Jamie. You've already apologized. Just forget about it."

"I know, but when I apologized before, I didn't mean it."

Jason laughed. "You didn't, huh?"

"No, I didn't. I was sorry for treating you so rotten, but I pretty much knew I couldn't stop myself. I was still mad at you for leaving me. Now when I say I'm sorry, I really mean it because I'm not mad anymore."

"You're not?" He studied her under the amber porch light. "I'm not sure if that's a good thing or not."

"It's just that I know you have to go," she explained. "It's all part of growing up; leaving childhood behind and all that song and dance. We're not children anymore."

The swing came to an abrupt stop. "Why do I get the impression this conversation's leading up to something?"

"Your attorney's intuition, I guess."

"Well, go ahead and say what you've got to say then."

Jamie put one hand on his jaw, he needed a shave. Further proof he was a man. She had to let him do what he was going to do. "Kiss me first. You may not want to in a few minutes."

"There's no chance of that ever happening." He lowered his face to hers and kissed her deeply.

When she opened her eyes, she said, "I love you, Jason. I always will."

"I love you too."

"You know what I'm going to say, don't you?"

"I wish I didn't."

"This has to be our last night together," she said simply.

His eyes widened. "Why? We still have five days. I want you to ride along when Noel takes me to the airport."

She shook her head. "I can't. It hurts too much already. I could never watch you get on that plane and then ride all the way back here from the airport in Noel's car, crying my eyes out."

"Don't I have any say in this? I want you there with me. I want to say good-bye."

She shook her head, more determined than ever. "No, we have to say good-bye right now, tonight. And..." her voice cracked as she struggled to go on. "We won't be seeing each other anymore, not summers or holidays. I don't even want you writing to me while you're at Stanford."

"Jamie, that's—"

"No, Jason. I'm trying to be fair to you and you need to be fair to me. My heart can't take anymore of this." A tear welled up in her eye and splashed on her cheek. She brushed it aside and went on. "I'm already going to miss you more than I can bear. I want a clean break, not so I can get on with my life and see other people, and definitely not so you can do the same thing. I want you out there in San Francisco just falling apart from missing me. But seriously, I have to start moving past this hurt. I can't do that if I keep finding letters from you in my mailbox or if I'm counting the days till you graduate in four years. What if in four years something happens and you don't come back?"

"I told you that won't happen."

"Jason, things change. You could get the offer of a lifetime by some firm out there that you just can't pass up. Or...or you could meet someone. Then we'd be going through this all over again." Her voice broke. "I can't keep going through this every four years."

"Why are you the one deciding this for both of us?"

"I'm not deciding anything, Jason. Circumstances have made all the decisions for us. Remember that first night when you said you thought the scholarship was an answer to prayer. I was so mad at you for seeing it that way, but maybe you're right. Maybe God has a divine purpose in sending you to San Francisco like this out of the blue. I can't be the one holding you back. But I also know I can't sit by the phone for four years not knowing if you'll ever come back."

Jason wrapped his arms around her and pulled her close. His voice was a hoarse whisper in her ear. "I want my five days, Jamie. You can't do me this way. I'm not ready to say good-bye tonight."

She stiffened and pulled away from him. "Don't ask me for that."

Maybe it wasn't fair for her to make all the decisions, but she couldn't worry about being fair right now. None of this was fair. It wasn't fair that he was going to California without her after the two of them had planned for a year to go to Ohio University together.

He rocked her back and forth in his arms and their tears mixed together. No words would bring her comfort at this point, so he didn't even try. They cried and held onto each other, knowing everything was changing and nothing they did would stop it.
Growing pains, first love for both of them, no hard feelings—just heartache; they would mend and eventually contemplate opening their hearts to another. But tonight as the cool night air brought the first warning of the approaching autumn, frogs gurgled on the pond, and Grandma Cory and Cassie tried to pretend they didn't know what was happening on the front porch. Neither Jamie nor Jason could imagine a future without the other.

# Chapter Four

The Saturday after Jason's party at Noel Wyatt's house Uncle Justin drove Jamie to the campus in his most recently acquired blue Ford sedan. Uncle Justin had driven new blue Fords for as long as Jamie could remember. Every other October he drove to the dealer's in Blanton to trade in his barely two-year-old vehicle for a showroom-new model. Aunt Marty would grumble and try to coax him into getting a white or a gray one, or even a Chevy, but he would smile and come home with nearly an exact replica of the car in which he left the house that morning.

Jamie sat in the back seat with Cassie and gazed out the window at the bumper to bumper traffic. It seemed like every one of the ten thousand or so students who would reside in the dorms had arrived on the same day with their parents and every last relative they had in tow. A lanky young man with a mop of shaggy sun-bleached hair streaming down his back dashed out in front of them to cross the street. Uncle Justin mashed the brakes to avoid hitting him and the car behind them honked in protest. The young man didn't break stride.

Jamie thanked God for the twentieth time since arriving on campus that she wasn't behind the wheel. Freshmen weren't allowed to have vehicles on campus so any time she wanted to go home, she'd have to call ahead or bum a ride from one of the other ex-South Auburn High School students who had chosen to attend Ohio University.

Uncle Justin smiled and reminisced about his own school days, trying to convince Jamie of what a wonderful time she'd have. She barely heard a word. She looked again at the tiny clock on the car's console; ten-fifteen. If everything was on schedule, Jason's plane had taken off from the Columbus Airport five minutes ago. He had a two-hour layover in Chicago before heading on to San Francisco. He had never flown before. Neither had she. She imagined him leaning back into the seat—a nervous wreck—and gripping the armrests as the jumbo jet gained altitude. A stewardess would come by and ask if he was all right and offer to do anything she could do to make his flight more enjoyable.

Cassie decided the best way to alleviate Jamie's depression was by pointing out every decent looking male they passed. Nearly anyone in pants qualified. "Jamie, you've got to meet him," she said, pointing to a tall, dark-haired fellow hurrying across the brick-lined street in front of them.

"Oh, okay. Pull over, Uncle Justin, and I'll tackle him."

"Ask him if he has a cute friend," Cassie shot back, as if Jamie was actually considering leaping out of the car.

"I didn't come here to meet guys," Jamie reminded her.

"Then why, for crying out loud, are you here? You'll never get another opportunity to see so many gorgeous guys in one place the rest of your life"

Aunt Marty laughed and turned around in the front seat to face the girls. "Give her a chance to get her bearings first, Cassie. But don't worry, as soon as she figures out where everything's at and what's what, she'll find time to meet a few young men."

Jamie stared out the window at the line of cars inching their way forward. She didn't care what Cassie thought. Meeting men was the farthest thing from her mind. She had spent the last five days getting ready for this moment, packing the last of her clothes she'd be bringing with her and saying good-bye to the farm. Jason had called twice. Both times she refused to come to the phone. She wasn't behaving out of spite, she told herself. It was all she could do to keep from bursting into tears at the mere thought of him. They had said their good-byes that night on the porch. She couldn't do it again. If she heard his voice she would want to see him and then she'd be right back at square one. He was gone and not coming back. The sooner she got that through her head and into her heart, the better off she'd be.

Last spring when she toured the campus with Grandma Cory, Cassie, and Jason everything had looked exciting and promising. Now with the confusion of the traffic, a bout of carsickness brought on by all the starting and stopping, horns blaring in every direction, and people shouting and running into the path of Uncle Justin's Ford every two seconds, she wanted nothing more than to turn around and go home; home to the farm and peace and quiet, back to familiarity and serenity. This was insanity. She didn't belong here, especially with all these men. Worthless creatures that make you fall in love with them then up and leave you to fly clear across the country. Who needed it?

"Begley," Uncle Justin announced when he spotted the street where they would find Jamie's dormitory building. "I think this is you, honey."

Jamie looked out the window at the tall imposing red stone building in front of her. It would be her home for the next four years. Funny, it hadn't looked so threatening last spring. While Uncle Justin waited for a parking space, ten minutes elapsed before they were finally able to exit the car. Uncle Justin moved to the rear of the car and popped the trunk lid. Back at the farm as Jamie stuffed what seemed like everything she owned into the trunk, she thought she was bringing too much. Looking around at the other cars parked next to the building, with mattresses strapped to the roof racks and boxes spilling out of every window, she hoped she had brought enough. Surely she wasn't responsible for her own mattress. She hadn't read that in the brochure.

Uncle Justin sighed and grabbed a box from the trunk, "Looks like we'd better get started. I'm only allowed to park here for unloading."

Jamie grabbed the largest suitcase, the one Grandma Cory wanted returned to her this afternoon when she was through unpacking it, and followed Uncle Justin toward the building. He was walking like he knew exactly where he was going, weaving his way through the throng of excited students and anxious-looking parents. Jamie sidestepped somebody's little brother who nearly crashed into her and hurried to catch up.

The hallway to her second floor room was even more congested and treacherous than the roadways leading to the dorm and the parking lot out front. Girls and parents spilled out of doorways. Duffel bags, suitcases, and legs of students lounging on the floor and leaning against doorframes, had to be stepped over. Some would smile upward at whoever stepped over them but most seemed totally oblivious to anyone else being in the building.

Jamie hated it already.

The door to her room was still locked when Uncle Justin turned the knob. Good, maybe her roommate—whoever she was—had decided not to come.

With so many helping hands, her side of the tiny room was soon transformed to resemble a miniature version of her bedroom at home. The rose and green quilt Grandma Cory made for her graduation covered the narrow bed. Uncle Justin hung the framed print he and Aunt Marty bought her last week. Cassie helped her set up her typewriter and office supplies neatly on the desk at the foot of her bed.

Before Jamie knew where the time had gone, Uncle Justin looked at his watch and announced somewhat regretfully it was time to go. Fear reared up in Jamie's head, but at the same time she looked forward to having the room to herself, if only for a few minutes, before her roommate arrived.

"Oh, Jamie, this is so exciting," Cassie said, throwing her arms around her neck. "I wish it was time for me to go to college too. The only place I get to go is dumb old South Auburn. What a waste of time."

Aunt Marty snapped another picture with her new Polaroid and handed the picture to Cassie. Cassie immediately began shaking the picture, even though Uncle Justin had assured all of them when he gave Marty the new camera for her birthday that shaking did not speed the developing process. Aunt Marty stepped forward and put her hands on Jamie's shoulders. "Have fun, Jamie. It's not as scary a place as it seems right now. You'll get used to it."

Jamie sank against Aunt Marty and wished for a moment she was going home with them. "I hope so."

As soon as Aunt Marty stepped aside, Uncle Justin pulled Jamie into a rough hug and kissed the top of her head. "You behave yourself now, and don't worry about anything. We love you and we're here for you. All you have to do is pick up the phone and call us."

"Anytime, honey, day or night," Aunt Marty put in, after snapping another picture. "In fact, I want you to call me Monday night after your first day of classes. I want to hear everything. I'll be waiting by the phone."

"Okay, Aunt Marty."

Cassie looked up from the pictures she held in each hand between her fingers and thumbs, careful not to bump them together. "Me too; call me as soon as you've talked to Aunt Marty."

"I'll fill you in, Cassie," Aunt Marty told her. "Your grandma might not appreciate all these long distance calls."

"She won't care. I want Jamie to call me Monday night."

"Come on, ladies," Uncle Justin said pointing them toward the door. "We can discuss this on the way home. Bye, Jamie. We love you."

Another flurry of kisses and professions of love followed before Jamie was finally alone in the room. The hallway began to clear out and the noise level—though still mind-numbing—had lessened. She wanted to sink onto her bed and cry but decided if she did, she might cry all night.

A knock sounded at the door, and Jamie looked up to see a chestnut-haired girl with baby blue eyes stick her head into the room. "Hey. I'm Valerie Howell, your neighbor on the right," she said, exposing a row of white, even teeth. "Those your parents leaving?"

Jamie was relieved she hadn't given in to the urge to cry. "No, my aunt and uncle," she replied, "and my kid sister. I'm Jamie Steele."

"My folks just left—finally," Valerie said as she entered the room. "I think Mom was hoping I would invite her to stay overnight. Fortunately they've got a long ride home. They won't be dropping in for unexpected visits. Where're you from?"

"Jenna's Creek; about two hours south of here in Auburn County," Jamie replied.

"I'm from Shaker Heights, near Cleveland."

Jamie nodded back as if she was familiar with northern Ohio. "That is a long drive."

"Where's your roommate? Mine's off checking out the campus or something."

"I haven't seen anything of her yet. I'm sure she'll turn up."

"No doubt about that. Well, hey, Jamie, it was nice meeting you. I'm sure we'll be seeing plenty of each other."

❀

In that fuzzy region between sleep and wakefulness, Jamie became aware of someone standing over her. She gasped and sat up in bed fully awake, her heart beating a rapid tattoo in her chest. For the briefest instant she couldn't remember where she was.

"Easy there," a deep voice said from the darkness, "I didn't mean to scare you."

Jamie fumbled in the dark for the lamp.

The overhead light came on first. She threw her hands up over her eyes, unable to make out details of the figure standing over her.

The figure barked out a one-syllable throaty laugh. "Sorry about that. I was hoping to get settled in without waking you. It's late, and we all got classes in the morning."

Jamie blinked and lowered her arms as she grew accustomed to the harsh florescent light. Blurry details of the tall blonde before her quickly assembled themselves together and registered in her brain. "I presume you're my roommate."

An easy, infectious smile settled over the girl's attractive features. "You presume correctly. I'm Robin Lamphear. I really didn't mean to wake you, but since you're up now, do you mind if I put my stuff away with the light on? It'll go much quicker that way."

Jamie motioned with her hand. "Sure, go ahead. I'm Jamie Steele. Do you mind if I ask why you didn't get here till now?" It was Sunday night. She'd been on campus over twenty-four hours and had given up on her roommate showing up before classes started Monday morning.

Robin laughed in the now-silent dorm and tossed her long, blonde hair away from her face. "No, I don't mind. You wouldn't believe the night I've had. I was supposed to be here yesterday like everybody else, but nothing worked out like it was supposed to. For one, something came up with my folks and they couldn't bring me down. I'm from Saginaw, Michigan by the way. Where're you from?"

"Jenna's Creek, Ohio," Jamie mumbled through a yawn. She couldn't help but wonder what could've come up to justify not getting your daughter to campus on the proper day, but she was afraid if she asked, her roommate would launch into an awfully long explanation.

"Well, like I said," Robin continued in a loud nasal accent Jamie had never heard spoken in southern Ohio, "my folks were at it again this morning. Mom hasn't spoken to Dad since he moved out last year with Becky. Becky's his girlfriend. Mom just hates her. She's only twenty-eight—Becky, not Mom." Robin laughed at her own joke and threw open the closet door. It reverberated against the concrete wall with a solid bang.

"You've got to be kidding," her voice rang out. "Is your closet this small? Where in the world do they expect us to keep our stuff? You'd think with all the money our folks are shelling out, they'd be a little more charitable with the closet space. Am I right, Julie?"

"Jamie," Jamie corrected and covered her mouth with her hand to stifle another yawn. She sighed and sank into her pillows. "Listen, Robin, I'm beat. I had a really long weekend. Everybody was so keyed up last night I didn't get much sleep, and like you said, we've gotta get up early."

"Oh, hey, I get where you're coming from, man," the tall blonde assured her. "We can talk tomorrow. When's your first class?"

"Nine."

"Bummer, I can't believe I'm rooming with an early riser. Personally, I prefer sleeping in. My first class isn't till noon. I guess we know who got the better schedule, huh? You don't make a lot of noise in the mornings, do ya? I am not a morning person, I'm warning you now." Her loud braying laugh filled the room. It reminded Jamie of the sound Grandma Cory's Farmall tractor made when started on cold winter mornings. Robin rummaged in her bag for hangers, making more noise than Jamie thought coat hangers could make. "I'll be done here in two shakes, 'kay? Don't pay any attention to me. Maybe we can get together for dinner at the cafeteria tomorrow night. You know, compare battle scars; night, night, sleeping beauty."

"Um, okay, night," Jamie said as she rolled over to face the wall and covered her head with her pillow. What she wouldn't give to be at home in her own bed staring at her own uneven, water-stained wall. She was beginning to wonder if this whole college experience might not be over-rated.

# Chapter Five

For the first week Jamie cried herself to sleep every night. She had been advised against going home too soon. "Stay on campus and get used to college life," everyone told her. It seemed like good advice, and she doggedly adhered to it, even though there was nothing she wanted more than the familiarity of the farm. Everything here was different and she hated all of it. Even the water tasted different. She grimaced every time she swallowed a mouthful. The sad part was she knew when she did go home for her first long weekend it would be the water out of *her* tap that would taste peculiar.

The din outside her room made it almost impossible to fall asleep before two a.m., but at least it muffled her despairing sobs. If Robin noticed her adjustment problems, she never let on. The sanguine blonde could sleep through anything it seemed, not that it mattered. She preferred the mod to their room where she always found a like-minded individual in search of mischief long after Jamie turned in for the night.

Jamie tortured herself with thoughts of Jason: where was he, what was he doing, had he found someone to replace her, did he miss her as much as she missed him? Knowing him like she did, it was safe to assume he was immersed in his studies, not giving her or finding her replacement a second thought. Jason could survive without any outside stimulus. She probably never crossed his mind; that knowledge alone made her toss on the bed even more and caused the tears to flow that much harder.

She reminded herself time and again that she had been the one to break things off. He had promised to come back after law school and take up where they left off. She was the one who wanted no part of a tenuous, long distance relationship. Such an arrangement could never work. Too much could change between them. No matter what he promised, he would realize sometime over the next four years he had nothing in Ohio to come back to, including her. Her heart couldn't take the risk of facing such a painful rejection.

How dare he get over her so quickly! While she writhed in her bed in abject misery, he slept like an angel with no thought of her whatsoever. Oh, she hated him! She hated Noel Wyatt for his role in getting Jason that scholarship. She hated California and all the phony coeds vying for his attention. She would show him. She would succeed in her studies, make the dean's list, graduate early with honors, and forget he ever existed. She'd find a handsome engineering student with brains that made Jason's look like sweet potatoes and make him fall in love with her. Then she'd dump him, breaking his heart just like Jason had done her. That would show him.

It was more than alternately hating, loving, and missing Jason that kept tears streaming down her cheeks after the books closed and lights went out for the night. She had never been out of Jenna's Creek for more than a night or two in her life. She missed Grandma Cory's grouchy reminders for her and Cassie to stop gossiping and get their chores done. She missed Cassie's endless debates over who was better looking, Mick Jaggar or Paul McCartney, even though Robin did much of the same thing about the boys on campus. She missed the symphony of cicadas and crickets lulling her to sleep, and the smell of rich, green meadow grasses wafting through her bedroom window. She missed the sounds of Grandpa Harlan's nightly TV programs coming from the living room while she and Cassie washed the supper dishes. She missed his awful country music emanating from the old record player and Grandma Cory's complaints about "that sinful, honky-tonk music."

On the up side, there was always something going on and something new to look forward to every minute on campus; depression, yes, boredom, no. Still, she missed her family and dreamed of home. Apparently, she was the only one who did.

Robin invited her everywhere she went; she couldn't understand Jamie's preference to stay in the dorm and study. The lack of sleep did nothing to slow her down. But Jamie declined most offers. Her work demanded her full attention. She couldn't risk slipping in her grade point average and losing her scholarships. While she wasn't the only student on campus relying on scholarship money, she was apparently the only one worrying over it.

She caught a glimpse of him out of the corner of her eye. She turned quickly imagining something familiar in his features, but the young man had already turned away and disappeared into the crowd. It wasn't the first time she thought she recognized someone from back home, only to realize she was mistaken. More often than not the familiar face she imagined seeing belonged to Jason, standing on the other side of the cafeteria or just at the edge of her peripheral vision. Even though her brain knew he was in San Francisco having the time of his life, her imagination couldn't help running away with her, forcing her to double check in case it wasn't merely her eyes playing tricks.

But this guy didn't remind her of Jason. He was taller, over six feet, and broader through the shoulders. His hair was darker, almost black, and cut short around the ears while long and thick on top. She knew him from somewhere or he reminded her of someone she knew. Seeing the occasional familiar face from Auburn County happened all the time. Every year several students from the tiny area where Jamie spent her entire life made Ohio University their school of choice. The campus wasn't that big; she couldn't expect to never run into someone from back home.

She went into the classroom and found a seat.

"Jamie Steele? Is that you?" said a voice from over her shoulder.

Jamie looked up into the eyes of the dark-haired young man from the hallway.

He smiled and pushed an unruly lock of hair out of his eye. "I thought that was you," he said, lowering himself into the empty seat beside her.

That strangely familiar face, those intense dark eyes— "Eric?" she asked hesitantly; carefully putting a name with the face. "Eric Blackwood! I didn't know you went to school here."

"I thought I saw you in this class the other day," he said. "But I couldn't get close enough to say anything before old man Brushart started in. How's it going?"

"Great. I'm getting used to being away from home and enjoying myself. Unfortunately, this class is tougher than I thought it would be. Math has always been one of my easier subjects, but I think I bit off more than I could chew when I signed up for Calculus my first quarter."

He nodded and smiled knowingly. "Yeah, I started out with Math 113 last year so hopefully I can handle this."

"I just hope I survive."

"Don't worry, you will. I seem to remember you were a brain in high school." His smile widened, and again she thought he reminded her of someone with his square jaw and straight, aristocratic nose. "I really miss Jenna's Creek," he said. "It's cool to see someone from home."

"I think so too. I've already been so homesick I just lie in bed and cry." She blushed and lowered her eyes to her notebook. She couldn't believe she'd opened her big mouth. She had been careful to keep her homesickness to herself, and then to go and blurt it out in front of someone like Eric Blackwood.

Eric grew up in Jenna's Creek, just as she had, and graduated from South Auburn High a year ahead of her. They attended the same high school, shared a few classes, ran into each other at ball games and pep rallies, and occasionally exchanged greetings in the hallways. That had been the extent of their relationship. A typical high school loner, Jamie kept her head too deep in books or the clouds to really get to know anyone—except Jason. Eric Blackwood, on the other hand, knew everybody and everybody knew him. He was naturally bright and popular. He participated in various extra-curricular activities and blended smoothly into nearly every peer group, whether acting as head of the debate team, first trombone in the marching band, or star pitcher on the softball field. Besides his dark good looks and humble charm that garnered attention from the female population, he was amicable and friendly with a ready smile and upbeat attitude that endeared him to the rest of the male student body and faculty alike. It was impossible to dis-like him. No wonder he and Jamie moved in different circles.

Still, he was from back home. That made them instant friends on campus.

For the next hour Jamie focused her attention on Professor Brushart and his notes on the blackboard and tried to ignore the handsome gentleman to her left. After class was dismissed in the professor's typical melodramatic manner, she sighed and closed the textbook; another complex assignment to be finished by the next session. She knew where she'd be tonight while her uncon-cerned friends littered the hallways of the dorm and the surround-ing green. How they could relax and have fun with an impending assignment hanging over their head was beyond her.

"I'm starved," Eric said as he unfolded his legs from under the seat. "D' you feel like getting something to eat?"

Was Eric Blackwood actually asking her to join him for lunch? The discouragement over the assignment vanished. "I was think-ing about getting a sandwich and going to the park. After this class, I usually need a break. It's a gorgeous day outside."

"Mind if I tag along?"

"Um, sure."

"Great. We can reminisce about home." He leaned over and took her books out of her hands. "Lead the way. I'm right behind you."

The snack bar two buildings down was always crowded, re-gardless of what time of day Jamie stopped in. It was conveniently located and accepted campus meal cards so Jamie often grabbed a snack there between classes, along with most of the rest of the student body. Today the line moved quickly and in minutes she and Eric were back out in the glorious September sunshine, their sandwiches and drinks in hand.

Eric juggled the waxed paper bag containing his lunch with the books still in his hands. "Here, I'll take yours." Jamie reached for the bag.

"No, I'm fine. You take the drinks and I'll handle the sandwiches." They rearranged their packages as they made their way through the moving sea of students to a small park on the north green.

"What are you majoring in?" Eric asked after he located an empty bench under a canopy of red maple leaves and settled onto it. This was always a first question on campus.

"Health Services Administration; I'd like to be a hospital or nursing home administrator. Next year, I'm going to apply for a job at the health care clinic on campus. I'm really looking forward to that."

Eric nodded. "Sounds like you and I will be taking a lot of the same courses. I switched from Chemistry to Microbiology this quarter. I'm planning on going into pharmaceuticals or clinical research, something like that."

"Great. Now I know who to come to when the Calculus gets to be too much."

"I don't know about that, but I'll do what I can."

Jamie snapped her fingers. "I remember now. You won the Benjamin Wyatt Memorial Scholarship when you graduated, didn't you? Impressive; I imagine you'll be a lot more help than you're letting on."

He shrugged. "Maybe I just got lucky."

"Oh, I'm sure. That's the best scholarship awarded in Auburn County; a full ride toward a Bachelor of Science degree. Noel Wyatt, your benefactor, is my boss, or I guess he's still my boss, anyway. I'm hoping he'll still need me to work during winter break. I could use the money."

"You work at Wyatt's Drugstore?" Eric asked while removing the paper wrapper from his straw. "Maybe you can put in a good word for me. I could use a part-time job myself."

"Sure, but I doubt it'd be necessary. Noel's always helping out starving students. Besides, you're family."

Eric gave her a sideways glance, his sandwich halfway to his mouth. "Family, how do you figure?"

"You're related to the Wyatts, aren't you?"

"Not that I'm aware of."

"Oh. I'm sorry. I thought when your mom came to the drug-store last year to talk to Noel… from the way she was acting that night, I just assumed—"

From the look of confusion on Eric's face, Jamie could see he had no idea what she was babbling on about. She stopped talking. She bit her tongue and inwardly kicked herself. Noel had asked her not to mention that visit to anyone. Now she could see why.

"What night?" he asked.

Jamie didn't want to be the one to explain the whole scene to him, when he apparently knew nothing about it. It had happened during her first summer working at the drugstore, and she'd only heard enough of the conversation to get the general idea of what was going on. Abigail Blackwood had come to the store one evening after closing when Jamie was alone in the store with Noel. Eric's mother had taken him to see a neurologist in Columbus that day where the doctor diagnosed him with epilepsy. She was understandably upset; she had cried on Noel's shoulder and expressed her fears and concerns for Eric's future. Noel consoled her, explaining that his sister suffered the same malady and lived a perfectly normal life with the aid of medication. After Mrs. Blackwood left, he asked Jamie not to mention the visit for the family's privacy, he had explained. Jamie had drawn the conclusion that he meant his family as well as the Blackwoods.

Until this moment she hadn't mentioned the after hours visit, except for the phone call she made to Noel's mother a few days later to express her sympathy. She wished Lucinda had told her then the two families weren't related; that there must have been another reason why Abigail Blackwood came to see Noel that night. Then she wouldn't be sitting here right now in front of Eric with her foot in her mouth.

What was she worried about? More than likely the secret wasn't even a secret anymore. Surely Eric's friends, relatives, and even some of his teachers and casual acquaintances knew of his medical condition. There was still a social stigma attached to epilepsy, but he must have gotten used to it after all this time.

"It was on the evening you got home from seeing your neurologist in Columbus," she explained, "the one who diagnosed your...condition. Your mom was really upset. She was confused, but I think relieved that they had finally found out what was wrong with you. I happened to be at the store that night when she came in. I was waiting for Noel. He was going to give me a ride home. Anyway, I didn't mean to be eavesdropping or anything. It was pretty quiet in the store and I overheard her crying. She told Noel what the doctors said about the epilepsy. He explained what he knew about it, and that was it."

Eric was quiet for several minutes, staring into space, Jamie and their lunch forgotten.

Jamie couldn't tell if he was upset because she knew about the epilepsy or because his mother had taken the news so hard? "I'm sorry, Eric," she said finally. "I shouldn't have brought it up. But don't worry about your mom. After she cried on Noel's shoulder a little bit and got it all out of her system, she was fine."

He turned to look at her, his gaze accusing. "That doesn't make any sense. Why would she go to Noel Wyatt and cry on his shoulder? She doesn't even know him. Are you sure it was my mother?"

It was Jamie's turn to stare. "Um, I guess so; Abby Blackwood, right? And Noel told me later you were the same Eric who graduated from South Auburn that year. That's how I knew who your mom was."

His shoulders sagged and his gaze softened. "Yeah, I guess it couldn't be anyone else. I'm sorry. I just can't figure out why Mom went to see Noel Wyatt about me. She's not the type to cry on anyone's shoulder, especially someone she barely knows."

"Maybe she figured he'd know something about it. He *is* a pharmacist and he said his sister has epilepsy." Jamie didn't figure her theory held much water, since Abby didn't know Noel's sister was epileptic until he told her that night, but she wouldn't point that out to Eric just now.

"Yeah, maybe."

"Eric, I'm sorry," she said, feeling inadequate. "I must've misunderstood the whole thing. I mean, no one actually said you were related to Noel or anything. I just assumed…"

"No, don't worry about it," he said, giving his head a shake and causing that same stubborn shock of dark hair to fall over his left eye. "You didn't do anything wrong. I just overreacted."

"I didn't mean to intrude in your private life," Jamie said. "About you being sick, I mean. It's none of my business."

"No, no, it's all right," he said again. "I'm not embarrassed about being epileptic, if that's what you mean. I don't even think about it anymore. I'm just thankful the doctors finally figured out what the problem was. I was tired of being sick all the time. Now as long as I take my meds, I seldom think about it."

Jamie relaxed. "Good. I mean, it's good you're getting along so well."

"Well, hey," Eric said, making a visible attempt to lighten the mood, "maybe you could put a good word in for me at the drugstore when we get back home. Even with the scholarship, I always find myself short on pocket money. Dad's pretty cool about giving me a few bucks now and then, but I hate to ask every time I want to spend a dollar."

"That's kind of the situation I'm in," Jamie said, glad the tension was past. "I've got scholarships and financial aid for tuition and fees, but there's always little stuff you don't think about needing money for, like hairspray and make-up."

"Yeah, I hate it when I run out of that stuff." Eric grinned, and she wrinkled her nose at him to cover up her embarrassment. She didn't know what made her say that in front of him. She didn't normally talk so freely in front of people she barely knew but something about Eric put her at ease.

The two settled back on the bench and finished their meal in silence, looking out over the small manmade pond, the leaves' vibrant colors reflected in the shallow water. Two squirrels chattered at each other and disappeared under a holly bush. Growing up in the country, Jamie had never encountered as many squirrels as crossed her path on campus every day. Hunters, fear of civilization, and the neighbors' cats kept the ones at home safely out of reach. Here, there were no natural predators, and the squirrels knew it.

Eric carried Jamie's books as far as the lobby of her building. "It was great seeing you," he said as if they had been close friends in Jenna's Creek. "Let's get together again."

Jamie hoped he wasn't saying it to be polite. This had been the nicest afternoon she'd spent since coming to campus. "That'd be great, I mean, if I ever get my head wrapped around this Calculus."

"Since we're going to be working on the same assignments, we may as well do them together. I can meet you back here in a couple hours and we can see if we can knock the lid off this thing. We can work in the mod if you want or go to the library."

"Sure," she exclaimed, and then hoped she didn't sound too eager. "Here would be fine. I haven't found any fantastic study partners yet. My roommate is great, but she thinks I'm a little too much into this studying thing. Her words, not mine."

Eric chuckled. "It seems I do remember you were a little bookworm. But, hey, I mean that in the nicest way."

"Good. That's how I took it."

Eric grinned and handed over her books. "Well, then, I'll see you around seven if that's okay. I'll come by after I get cleaned up from my daily run."

"Okay." She discreetly gave him an admiring glance from head to toe. That explained the physique. "I'll meet you down here at seven. Don't be late."

"Don't worry. I never am."

"So, you have a study date?"

"It's not a study date. Eric's from back home. There's nothing to it."

Robin rolled her eyes toward the ceiling. "Sure there isn't. There never is. So what's this guy from back home look like?"

"He just looks like a guy." At Robin's arched eyebrows, Jamie added. "Okay, a really cute guy with great runner's legs."

Robin slapped her hand on the desk. "I knew it. I could tell by the way you came floating in here."

"I wasn't floating."

"Believe me, girl, you were floating. And I must say it's about time. The rest of us were starting to worry about you. Spending all your time down in the dumps, that my-world-is-coming-to-an-end look on your face, pining away over somebody you won't even talk about."

"Was it that obvious?"

Robin grimaced. "We knew it had to be a guy, or else you were just plain weird. I was kinda leaning toward weird myself."

"Funny."

"He must have been something," Robin went on, "this guy you haven't been able to get over. Let me guess, the conversation went something like this." She lowered her voice and knit her eyebrows together. "'Now Jamie, you know you mean the world to me, but I've been seeing someone else. She has everything you don't; money, personality, a good body.'"

"Robin!" A pillow went sailing from Jamie's side of the room, narrowly missing her head.

Robin threw the pillow back at Jamie and fell back on her bed laughing.

"For your information," Jamie said through her own laughter, "it was my idea to stop seeing him." She stopped laughing and caught her breath. Talking, or even thinking, about Jason had a way of sobering her. "He got a full scholarship to law school at Stanford. I didn't want a relationship with two thousand miles and four years between us."

Robin sat up on the bed, her mouth agape. "Sometimes you're too practical for your own good, Jamie. A law student at Stanford—wow! I bet he was gorgeous too. You could have just strung him along while you had your fun here, like with your new study partner. I'm sure that's what he's doing at Stanford. Then when he came back, if he was still interested in starting something with you, you could decide if you still wanted him or not."

Jamie shook her head. "No way, I can't live like that. For one thing, I don't know how to string people along. What you see is what you get. And even if I could, I have too much respect for him to treat him that way."

"Well, suit yourself," Robin said with an indifferent lift of her shoulders. "Personally your way doesn't sound like much fun. If he comes back and the two of you are still crazy about each other, it may be too late because you broke it off."

"I'll just have to take that chance. If our relationship was meant to be we'll end up together anyway, even if I did make a mistake by breaking it off. I try to put those kinds of things in God's hands and let Him work out the details. He knows what's down the road, so I'll have to trust Him."

"I think if there is a God, He's too busy keeping us from doing something stupid like blowing each other up to worry about you and your ex-boyfriend's little problems."

Jamie's eyes widened. "What do you mean, if there's a God? You believe in God, don't you?"

Robin shrugged. "I don't know. I guess. I've never really thought about it that much."

"And I never thought there wasn't a God."

Robin cocked her head. "So you believed what everybody told you, without asking questions?"

Jamie thought about it for a minute. Robin was right; it had never crossed her mind to doubt what her mother, grandmother, and Sunday school teacher told her. She trusted them. She went to church every Sunday, earned star stickers for memorizing Bible verses like all the other kids in her Sunday School class, respected her elders, handed over her offerings with no clue of where the money went, and never—not once in all her life—questioned the existence of God. She liked the thought of a sovereign God reigning in Heaven with only her best interests at heart. And she couldn't see any reason to doubt her beliefs now. "I guess so," she admitted. "I never thought to ask questions. I've had God's presence pointed out to me for as long as I can remember, so I see Him everywhere I look. It takes more faith to believe we're here as some cosmic accident, than to believe a divine Creator put us all here for a purpose."

She felt satisfied. She had just convinced herself, if not Robin, that her faith was based on her own beliefs and not something someone told her to believe.

Robin cocked her head. "I see your point there. But with all the wars, crime, and people running over each other to get ahead, I really can't see God. I think most people are like me and would rather handle their problems their own way than do what you said and put their trust in a God who may or may not exist."

Jamie had never encountered an actual person with Robin's views. She knew they existed because she heard their crazy ideas every day on television and in magazines, but until this moment, she had never met someone with the idea that the world no longer had a use for God. She had convinced herself only the godless heathens of Hollywood and New York City believed that way. Not anyone in Ohio, the heart of the conservative Midwest. The possibility hadn't even occurred to her that Robin might not be a believer. Of course, she was from Michigan. Who knew what they taught people up there!

Robin got up from her bed and plopped down on Jamie's bed beside her. She rested her hand on her shoulder. "Hey, I'm sorry for teasing you about your boyfriend. I know how hard it must have been to break it off with him. I can't imagine loving somebody who's suddenly two thousand miles away."

"No, it's not that. You didn't upset me."

"Good." Robin slapped her hands against her thighs and stood up. "I want us to be friends. We've got a whole lot of living together to do in the next year. Now, what are we going to do about this study date of yours? We can't have you going out of here looking like that." She cast a dubious glance at the smock shirt and slacks Jamie had worn to class. "You'd embarrass me to death." She flung open the door to Jamie's side of the closet. "Hmm, what have we got in here? We need something that'll maximize your long legs and minimize that big behind."

Jamie jumped up and craned her neck to look over her own shoulder. "Hey. What's wrong with my—"

"And something that doesn't look like my mother would be caught dead in it," Robin continued.

"Robin, I told you this isn't a date. My heart's in California."

Robin rummaged through coat hangers and didn't bother turning around. "Your heart may be in California, but I'm going to find a man for the rest of you if it kills me."

Jamie chewed at a rough spot on her thumbnail as Robin tore several selections from their hangers and tossed them over her shoulder onto the bed. Robin's mind was on clothes and dates and not on the existence of God. Anything Jamie said at this point would be inappropriate and ill received. Still, she had to say something, didn't she? She couldn't let Robin go on doubting God's existence and believing her attitude was all right with Jamie. It wasn't all right. The Bible said all men would stand before God one day and answer for their deeds, whether they believed in Him or not. But how could she tell Robin that without sounding like she was preaching at her?

"Oh, this is hopeless," Robin said suddenly. She hurried to the door of their room and stuck her head into the hallway. "Valerie. Gina," she called out. "Get in here. It's an emergency."

Within thirty seconds Jamie was surrounded by half the girls on the second floor, each of them thrusting tops under her chin—most of which were borrowed from closets up and down the hall—to see what went with what and arguing about which cosmetic products would make the most of her regrettably ordinary features. It was nearly seven o'clock before they were satisfied that she was properly attired for her study date with Eric.

Jamie never did come up with a way to broach the subject of God's existence with Robin.

# Chapter Six

"Hello, Noel? It's Jamie Steele."

"Oh, hi, Jamie," Noel said. "How's our college girl getting along?"

"Great, thanks. I'm home for the weekend, and I thought it'd be a good time to call you. I wanted to remind you I'll be home for winter break the day before Thanksgiving. I don't go back till after the first of the year, so if you need me to work at the drugstore..."

"Sure, Jamie, I'm looking forward to having you back. I always need extra help around the holidays. Many of the full-timers want time off."

"Well, since you brought it up," she began hesitantly, "you wouldn't need an extra set of hands by any chance, would you?"

"Maybe. Why?"

"I ran into Eric Blackwood here on campus and he's looking for a job."

An uncharacteristic silence lengthened on Noel's end.

"Eric Blackwood," she repeated, to jog his memory. "He's the one who won your memorial scholarship two years ago. He and I got to talking about part-time jobs—"

"Oh, yes. Eric." His voice sounded hollow to her ears. "I'll have to think about it."

"Oh, hey, I didn't mean to put you on the spot or anything. If you don't need him, he'll understand. We were just making poor student comparisons and it came up that I worked for you." She didn't mention the part of the conversation about Eric's mother crying on Noel's shoulder or Eric's reaction to it.

"Well, like I said, I'll think about it and see what I can do."

"Thanks, Noel. I know he'll appreciate it."

"What? Oh, sure."

Jamie got the impression she no longer had his attention. She couldn't blame him; he had plenty on his mind these days, especially now that Noreen Trimble was gone. Noreen Trimble had worked her entire adult life as Noel's pharmacy assistant in the drugstore. Without her, Noel was lost. He was working on another assistant, who made it clear she was just filling in until a permanent solution could be made.

Last winter Noreen had confessed to the murder of Sally Blake. She had refused a jury trial and made her plea to the judge instead. According to her, Sally had been killed accidentally when Noreen pushed her over a couch, causing her to hit her head on a heavy metal boot scraper. Instead of notifying the authorities, Noreen had hidden Sally's body. For twenty-five years no one knew what had happened to Sally until her body was recovered on the property of Noreen's uncle.

Many of Jenna's Creek's residents felt that Noreen had been improperly imprisoned. She had suffered enough by keeping the secret to herself for twenty-five agonizing years. Others believed if Noreen had actually killed Sally accidentally during an encounter she never would have disposed of the body.

Jamie tried not to think of it at all. For twenty-five years the good people of Jenna's Creek had held her father to blame in Sally's disappearance because of their relationship and the fact that he was the last person seen with her. In the year that had passed since the truth had been discovered, not one person had apologized to her or the Steele family for believing James Steele had killed Sally. She was of the mindset that Noreen probably had not intended to harm Sally, and shouldn't have to spend the rest of her life in prison. But she didn't know the whole story. She was in no position to cast judgment, nor did she want to. The whole ordeal brought to mind too many painful memories of her father; memories she would rather not dwell on.

"Stop in and see me when you get home, Jamie, and I'll give you a schedule," Noel said, breaking into her disturbing train of thought. "Don't worry, I'll let you enjoy Thanksgiving dinner with your family before I put you to work."

She started to thank him again but he had already hung up. She set the phone back in its cradle and stared at it a moment. Maybe she shouldn't have bothered him about hiring Eric. He obviously wasn't thrilled about it. Did he know something about Eric that she didn't? Was he concerned that Eric's medical condition might interfere with his job performance? Next time she'd mind her own business and let prospective employees apply at the drugstore in person. Still, this wasn't the first time Noel hired someone on the basis of a reference from a current employee, and he already knew something about Eric. After all, he'd won the Benjamin F. Wyatt memorial scholarship.

She turned away from the phone and headed down the hallway to her room. She'd caught Noel at a bad time—that was all. Eric would go to the store and talk to Noel himself and Noel would remember who he was. Eric would get the job, he'd turn out to be a great employee, and she'd have no need to feel guilty for recommending him.

Noel replaced the phone in the cradle and sat back in his chair. This was a fine kettle of fish. How was he going to get out of this one? There was no way he could allow Eric Blackwood to work in his store. It would be too uncomfortable. He would never know a moment's peace from wondering when someone would notice the incredible likeness between himself and his new employee.

The whole idea of assigning the boy tasks, signing his paycheck, and treating him like any other employee was another thing Noel didn't think he could do. He pictured himself hiding inside his crow's nest office, the bustle of the store below him, his eyes fastened on Eric pushing a broom or helping a customer find something, and knowing the boy could never be anything more to him than a minimum wage employee.

Noel wiped his hand across his face. He had fallen in love with Abigail Frasier when she stopped in the drugstore every morning on her way to the factory where she and so many women worked during the war years. Though he didn't suspect it at the time, Abby loved him back. He didn't speak up when she announced her beau was returning from the battlefields of Italy and wanted to marry her. It was a regret he would live with the rest of his days. Just like the regret of what happened ten years later.

Noel remembered it like it was yesterday; sometimes he wished it was. It was the autumn he had his heart attack. He'd been ignoring his health for years, just as his father had done before him. In those days, before the insurance companies balked at paying a patient's bills, Noel was prescribed a month's bed rest upon release from the hospital; no work, no stressful situations. It may as well have been a prison sentence.

Abigail Frasier, who was now Mrs. Jack Blackwood, came to see him. It was then that she told him she loved him and always had. Their affair lasted three months. When Abby discovered she was carrying Noel's baby, she broke off the relationship and told him the child would be raised as her husband's.

For years afterward, Noel held it against God that his punishment was so severe. He deserved the happiness other men took for granted, he reasoned. Finally he realized he had forced this punishment upon himself through his own actions. He had sinned against God, Jack Blackwood, Abby, their son, who could never know his real father, and against his own flesh. Noel now realized the ramifications of that sin more than any man, for he paid dearly for it every day of his life.

It was safe to assume nothing had changed. Jack still did not know Eric's true paternity since Noel had not received any beatings, threats, or demands for cash in the past twenty years. Regrets, mistakes, recompense; that was the story of his life.

Eric wouldn't be applying for work at the drugstore if he knew who Noel Wyatt really was. The only time he had spoken to Abby since learning she was having his child was the night she came to the drugstore to tell him Eric had been diagnosed with epilepsy.

Noel stood up and shoved the chair back from the desk with the backs of his legs. He strode around the desk and threw open the office door. His work was waiting for him downstairs. He needed to get out of the cramped space. He needed noise, confusion, impatient doctors, and disgruntled patients screaming in his ear; anything to push back the loneliness that always overcame him when he thought too much on the woman he loved who would never be his, and their son who could never know his real father.

The morning after Thanksgiving, Jamie rose early and rushed through her chores. She'd been home since Tuesday afternoon when Grandma Cory and Cassie picked her up from college after her last exam. Finals were over, winter quarter wasn't scheduled to begin for six weeks, and the turkey and dressing she gorged herself on yesterday had digested. She was ready to get back into a normal work routine.

Like always, heading down the same roads into town on her way to Wyatt's Drugstore to pick up her schedule, Jamie thought of Jason. Today marked twelve weeks to the day since she'd last seen him. She was finally able to go a few hours without thinking of him, so long as she stayed busy and refused to give into the temptation to just fall down and cry. When he did flit across her mind with his sandy blond hair, smattering of pale freckles, and quirky smile, a familiar ache lodged in her chest. She missed him so much.

She waved hello to the ladies behind the cash registers as she made her way to the pharmacy counter where she knew she'd find Noel.

"Jamie? I thought that was you."

Jamie stopped mid-stride and turned to see Barb Beekman moving quickly down the Housewares aisle toward her. She stepped into the woman's outstretched arms. "Hi, Barb. How was your holiday?"

"The usual; the kids were all in, I cooked too much and ate too much." Barb patted her stomach. She had worked the drugstore's lunch counter for almost as long as Noel had run the place. Jamie and the many customers that passed through the store on any given day could always count on Barb for a smile and friendly word.

Jamie answered the standard questions about her first quarter at college and then asked where she could find Noel. "I'm here to see about my schedule for the next six weeks."

"Good. I'm glad to hear you're coming back, if just for a little while. Noel's in his office. You be sure to stop and talk to me before you leave. I want to hear everything that's been going on at college."

"I will," Jamie promised on her way to the back of the store. She climbed the short flight of stairs to the suspended cubicle office, a sort of crow's nest perched above the stockroom where Noel could easily observe all of the goings on below him through a large tinted window.

Noel's booming voice ushered her inside on the first knock. "Good, you're here. How's it feel to be home?" Before she could answer, he rushed on, too busy or impatient for small talk. The store had been closed Thursday and he planned to catch up on the lost day of business. "Got your schedule right here," he said, waving a slip of paper in the air with his nearly illegible handwriting scrawled across it. "Kind of jotted it down in a hurry this morning, so if you have any problems, let me know."

"I'm sure it'll be fine," she said, taking the slip of paper out of his hand without sitting down. She folded the paper and stuffed it into her pocket with hardly a glance. "Noel," she began, "have you had a chance to decide if you could use Eric here at the store?"

He didn't look up from the ledger in front of him, "Hmm?"

"Eric Blackwood. Remember, I mentioned him to you when I called from school." Noel still didn't look up so Jamie plunged ahead. "I haven't talked to him in a few days, but I think he's still planning on coming in to talk to you about a job."

"Um hmm," Noel's head wagged up and down slowly, distracted again, apparently rapt in his paperwork. "I've been thinking about that situation," he mumbled, penciling in figures in a column.

Jamie waited for him to finish his thought, but he didn't speak. Seconds passed. Finally she spoke; "Should I tell Eric a good time to stop in and talk to you?"

He looked up, pinning her in place with a faraway expression in his dark blue eyes. He almost looked like he'd forgotten she was in the room. "I'll be here all weekend," he said after an incredibly long pause. Without waiting for a response, he plunged back into the ledger.

Jamie backed toward the door and felt for the knob behind her in case he had anything to add—he didn't. What was going on with him? He usually talked a mile a minute about everything, even when he was behind schedule. He hadn't even asked about school. He was usually interested in that kind of stuff.

After spending a few moments with Barb and a few other employees, Jamie left the store. She didn't have Eric's phone number but he had told her where he lived in Jenna's Creek. The town was too small for someone who'd lived there as long as she had to get lost. She would drop in and tell him that Noel would be expecting him anytime over the weekend to discuss a job. She wouldn't mention that Noel wasn't exactly on pins and needles in anticipation. Halfway down Mulberry Street on the north edge of town, she found the large, white two-story house Eric described with the wrap-around porch and yard surrounded by a low wrought-iron fence. She pulled into the driveway and parked behind a dark sedan. Before her knuckles made contact with the glass pane, the front door swung open. "Jamie. Good to see you. How's your holiday going?"

She smiled in response to Eric's enthusiastic welcome, equally happy to see him; almost too happy. What about Jason? Was he out of her system already? Just because their relationship was as finished as yesterday's turkey, didn't mean she wanted to go down that road again. Eric was just someone to talk to, her faithful study partner, she told herself; smart, funny, nice to look at…and here.

"I thought I'd see if you were up to studying some Calculus."

His eyes darkened a moment before he realized she was kidding. "No way—I'm through with Mathematics for a while, got to give my brain a chance for the swelling to go down." He backed into the interior of the house. "Come on in. What are you doing out and about besides recruiting study partners?"

She stepped into the dark paneled hallway and explained her visit to the drugstore, minus the account of Noel's apparent disinterest. "He said he'll be in all weekend," she finished. "I'd stop in today if I were you. He likes to know people are anxious to get to work."

"I plan on it. I need the cash. You want to sit down. I'll get us something to drink. If you're hungry, the kitchen's full of leftovers. I can put together some turkey sandwiches."

Jamie had eaten enough turkey yesterday that she feared she might sprout wings, but her stomach reminded her it was getting close to lunchtime. There would only be leftover turkey at home anyway. "Sure, sounds good." She followed him through a combination dining room/family room and into a large kitchen. The walls were painted a cheerful yellow. Blue and yellow plaid curtains covered the window and back door glass. Eric indicated a chair at the kitchen table and opened the refrigerator door.

Instead of sitting down she moved to the wall-to-wall wood cabinets. "I can help." So much space, she marveled upon opening a door over the sink. Not like the tiny metal cabinet at home and the outdated pie safe and Hoosier cupboard. She bet the Blackwoods didn't even have to store their pots and pans in the broiler drawer under the stove.

"Where do you keep the plates?" she asked over her shoulder, opening another door.

"Next one over," he answered as he pulled an assortment of Tupperware containers from the refrigerator and set them on the counter.

"Are you hungry, Eric?" a voice asked from the doorway. "Oh, I see you have company. That's good. I thought you might be in here talking to yourself again."

Eric pushed the door shut with his elbow and set a bowl of some type of pasta salad and a jar of mayonnaise on the table. "Hey, Mom, I told you I only talk to myself because I'm the most interesting person in this house. This is Jamie Steele." He wagged his head in Jamie's direction. "We're in school together. Isn't that cool? We both went to South Auburn and hardly knew each other then we go to OU and become friends."

Friends—Jamie hadn't really thought about it, but she realized she had come to appreciate Eric. Everything about him was easy; no complications, no attachments, just what she needed now, an uncomplicated friend.

"Nice to meet you, Jamie," Abby responded.

If Mrs. Blackwood recognized her from that night at the store a year ago when she told Noel about Eric's epilepsy, it didn't show on her face. Of course, they'd only seen each other a few minutes in the darkened store. If Jamie didn't already know who she was, she might not recognize her either.

"I'm glad to know there's someone from Jenna's Creek at the college to keep an eye on Eric," Mrs. Blackwood was saying. "You'll let me know if he gets into any trouble, won't you?"

Jamie looked from one to the other and noted the merriment in their eyes. Both wore the same expression; teasing and open, but that's where the resemblance ended. Eric's eyes were a deep, almost bottomless blue while Mrs. Blackwood's were a pale gray. At over six feet, broad shouldered, and powerfully built, Eric dwarfed his delicate and petite mother. He must take after his dad, she figured, most boys did. Still there was something about him that reminded her of someone. She'd seen that expression, that face, before even though she was pretty sure she'd never met Mr. Blackwood.

"Don't worry, Mrs. Blackwood," she said, joining in the teasing. "The first time Eric steps out of line, I'll let you know."

"Hey, that's not fair," Eric blustered. "The only reason I went to OU was so I'd be far enough away from Jenna's Creek to have a little fun without getting caught."

"I guess you didn't go far enough, did ya?" Jamie quipped at which time Mrs. Blackwood smiled and patted Jamie on the back.

"Perfect, an ally, now I can sleep at night," she said as she pulled open a drawer and began setting utensils on the table. "Jamie, make yourself at home. There's plenty of food. Eric's sisters were in yesterday with the grandkids and I made way too much food. Help Eric clean up these leftovers, or we'll be eating them through Christmas."

"I'll do what I can but I'm afraid we've got the same situation at our house."

"I'm sure you do."

"Guess what, Mom?" Eric broke in. "Jamie found me a job."

"A job? It's about time."

"Yeah, at Wyatt's Drugstore. I'm supposed to go in this weekend and talk to Mr. Wyatt. I'll probably go today. You know, make a good impression."

Eric didn't notice the blood drain from his mother's face as she asked, "Wyatt's Drugstore?" She shook her head. "I don't think so."

Eric's jaw went slack and his eyes widened. "What? Why? You just said it was about time I got a job. I haven't had any luck looking anywhere else, and I need the money."

Mrs. Blackwood peeled the plastic wrap off a plate of sliced turkey, avoiding eye contact with anyone else in the room. "It…it's just not a good idea."

Eric would not be dissuaded. "Mom, there's no reason why I shouldn't apply for a job there. I'm going."

Jamie lowered herself into a kitchen chair and stared at the turkey on the plate Mrs. Blackwood set in front of her. She hoped she wouldn't have to witness a fight in the Blackwood's lovely modern kitchen.

"Not if your father and I decide against it."

"But why would you decide that? I know Dad won't have anything against me getting a job. I'll ask him about it when he gets home."

"You'll not bother your dad about it. If I say you're not working for Noel Wyatt, then you won't; case closed."

"But Mom, you just said—"

Mrs. Blackwood cut off any further protest from Eric with a we'll-talk-about-it-later flick of her eyes in Jamie's direction. Jamie saw Eric's struggle. He wanted to finish this discussion that was making no sense to him, but didn't want to start something in front of company.

Mrs. Blackwood rinsed her hands in the sink and dried them thoroughly with a paper towel. "You two enjoy your lunch. It was nice meeting you, Jamie." With no further reference to the job she adamantly opposed, she left the kitchen.

Eric sat down opposite Jamie and began to fill his plate from the various dishes in front of them. "Sorry about that. I have no idea what's wrong with Mom. She knows I need a job."

Jamie didn't answer. For all she knew, Mrs. Blackwood had a perfectly good reason for reacting to Eric's news the way she did. Just like Noel probably did for his strange reactions every time Eric's name came up. Maybe something happened between the two of them years ago, and they hated each other. That seemed unlikely since Noel was the one Mrs. Blackwood turned to in her distress over Eric's health problems.

Jamie thought back to Noel's reaction that night in the store. He had been genuinely shocked at her arrival but also pleased, as if seeing an old friend. She suddenly remembered a comment Mrs. Blackwood made that night. "I waited to come when I thought you'd be alone." Why would she want to see Noel alone? And, where was her husband? Wasn't he as torn up over Eric's condition as she was?

Nothing about the situation made sense to Jamie, especially Mrs. Blackwood's insistence that Eric not work at the drugstore and Noel's apparent reluctance to hire him. But, it wasn't the first time she didn't understand why adults behaved the way they did.

Eric plied her with as much food as she could possibly hold before turning the topic of conversation to school. He didn't mention his mother's odd behavior again. Jamie decided she didn't need to worry about it either. It was none of her concern. After a piece of pecan pie she couldn't resist, she made her getaway.

"My first day back at the drugstore is Monday," she told him as he walked her to the door. "If everything works out, maybe I'll see you there."

"I'm sure it will. With Dad and me working on her, Mom will come around. Thanks a million for everything."

"No problem. I'll see you later."

She hurried home, knowing everyone at the farm would be wondering where she'd been all morning.

# Chapter Seven

During her first quarter on campus, Jamie thought a six-week break between the fall and winter quarters would be long enough to get bored with the ho-hum routine of the farm. Instead, between her chores and her job at the drugstore, the time flew by. Before she knew it, it was Christmas. Working all the time had its advantages; she was too busy to think so much about Jason, and she had plenty of money to buy Christmas gifts for her family. She exaggerated her poor student status to Cassie while hiding a beautiful crimson sweater in her closet. Cassie would go crazy over it Christmas morning. She had a pair of driving gloves stowed away for Uncle Justin and a Conway Twitty album for Grandpa Harlan, although she didn't think he remembered that Conway Twitty used to be one of his favorite country music singers.

For Grandma Cory, she and Cassie had pooled their money and bought the most boring gift in the world but something they knew she'd like—a cast iron skillet; not an easy thing to find since all the modern kitchens were switching to Teflon. But Grandma Cory wasn't interested in progress. The old ways were good enough for her. The girls scoffed at her old-fashioned notions behind her back, but they had to admit her cornbread and blackberry cobbler tasted like heaven on earth baked in the fifty-year-old skillet she used since marrying Grandpa Harlan.

Jamie found a faux pearl and diamond lapel pin for Aunt Marty at the jewelry store. She hadn't meant to spend so much money on one gift, but as soon as she saw it in the glass case she knew nothing else would do. She could imagine Aunt Marty's expression when she opened the velvet box. It would be worth every penny. She wanted to show how much she appreciated everything she and Uncle Justin had done for her since she started making plans for college.

Packages, empty store bags, scotch tape, ribbon, and rolls of wrapping paper littered her bed. Christmas was in three days. She wanted to get everything wrapped and under the tree today. While concentrating on making every package worthy of its contents, she didn't hear the phone ringing downstairs until Grandma Cory called up to her.

The phone lay abandoned on the kitchen counter by the time she got downstairs. Grandma Cory had moved on to some chore she was in the middle of. Grandpa Harlan was in his usual seat in the living room, staring at a big wheel whirling around and around on the television screen while an unseen studio audience cheered for the grinning contestant.

Jamie picked up the phone, turning her back to the TV in the next room. "Hello?"

"Jamie?" a familiar voice said. "It's so good to hear your voice."

She nearly dropped the phone. "Jason?" She stretched the telephone's cord to reach into the living room and sat down hard on the arm of an occasional chair. She took a deep breath. "I wasn't expecting to hear from you."

"I know you told me not to call," he explained, "but I couldn't help myself. I think about you everyday. I miss you like crazy. I'm so lonesome out here."

She wanted to remind him he was getting exactly what he wanted, that he had no one to thank but himself if he was lonely, but the words couldn't find their way to her lips. His voice was music to her ears. Tears pooled in the corners of her eyes. Thankfully he wasn't here to see them.

"I miss you too," *you big jerk.* "How's Stanford?"

"It's still here." She could tell he was smiling into the phone. Had he expected her to hang up on him? He needn't have worried. "How about you?"

"OU's fine, well, you know, it would be a lot better if you were here." She bit her tongue; she hadn't wanted to admit that.

A silence hung in the air. She wanted to hear him say he'd made a big mistake; he couldn't go on living without her; he was coming home on the first thing smoking. What was he hoping to hear from her—encouragement, understanding? She didn't know how much of either she could offer.

"How are you enjoying California?" she asked casually.

"It's all right. I haven't had much time for sight seeing yet, but the campus is beautiful."

Jamie laughed. "Leave it to you to go all the way to California and never leave campus."

Jason joined in the laughter. "I didn't say I never leave campus. It's just…oh, you could always see right through me. I'm usually here, studying or working. And to be honest, I hate it, its eighty-two degrees this very minute. Don't they know it's Christmas? It should be illegal to wear just shirtsleeves in December. I'm telling you, Jamie, it's insane out here. Everybody's crazy. School is keeping me busy, but now that everyone's gone for the holidays, I've got a lot of time to think."

"Is that why you called? You don't have anything better to do?"

"I didn't say that," he said with an edge in his voice. "I called because I miss you. I miss you so much I can't see straight. I can't think half the time. All I think about is you. If I don't get my head on straight, I'm afraid I'll flunk out."

"Oh, for crying out loud, you'd never let yourself flunk out of anything. You're just bored and calling me 'cause you miss home."

"Is that what you think?" The hurt and anger in his voice stabbed at her heart.

She no longer knew what she thought. "Maybe, a little," she said, losing steam. "You wouldn't have waited this long to call me if you missed me as badly as you say you do."

"You told me not to call," he cried out. "You said you wanted a clean break. I was just giving you what you wanted."

"Yeah, well, you could've put up a little bit of a fight. You could've refused. You just rolled over and played dead, as usual. You never fight for anything that's important."

"I'm fighting for this, my future, or don't I have a right to one? I guess you would rather I just stayed home and married you and ended up a nothing like my old man?"

"Who said I wanted you to marry me?" she shrieked. "Why, I wouldn't do such a thing to you, Jason. I mean, I would hate to think I was the reason you ended up a nothing. I know the law schools in Ohio aren't good enough for you. You're a big shot Stanford Cardinal now. I wouldn't want you to have to hang around here with us nothings."

"I can't believe you're acting like such a child. All I wanted to do was hear your voice. I wanted to wish you a Merry Christmas. I love you, Jamie. I think about you everyday. I've been here for the past three and a half months thinking I've made the biggest mistake of my life, but after talking to you, maybe it's a good thing we got away from each other when we did. I guess these things never would've been said if I'd stayed home like you wanted me to."

"Well, I'm sorry I wanted you here with me," she choked out. She cast an anxious glance in Grandpa Harlan's direction, but he was completely absorbed in his TV program. She gripped the phone and made a conscious effort to lower her voice. "I guess I'm selfish. But I can't help it. I love you too, or at least I thought I did."

"So, you're not sure anymore because you aren't getting your way?" He took a deep shuddering breath. "You're right, you are selfish. You can't see any other side of a situation but your own. It's a shame it took me so long to figure that out."

She wished she could start this conversation over again. It wasn't going like she'd imagined when she picked up the phone five minutes ago. She was saying more than she meant to out of anger and loneliness, and she knew he was too, but it was too late to take it all back. Maybe it was better their feelings were out in the open. "You're right, I am mad because I'm not getting my way. But I'm not pouting because I don't have shoes to match a new dress. This is a big deal, and sometimes I think I'm the only one who realizes it."

Another shuddering sigh came from Jason's end. When he spoke, his voice was under control. "Jamie, I know this is a big deal. I don't think you realize how hard it was for me to accept this scholarship. It crossed my mind a thousand times to turn it down before I ever told you about it, but I just couldn't. I had to come to California. It had nothing to do with us it was just the way things worked out."

"I know," she conceded, her voice barely above a whisper. She went back into the kitchen and started pulling open drawers in search of a tissue, paper towel, or something else on which to blow her nose.

"I still don't intend to stay out here after I graduate. I want to come home to you, if you'll have me."

"Jason, I know you have the best intentions. But I can't expect you to feel the same way in four years as you do now. And you can't expect me to sit here and wait just in case you do." She located a crumpled Dairy Queen napkin in a drawer and blotted the end of her wet nose. "I love you, but I still think a clean break is the best thing."

The silence lengthened again. "If that's what you want…"

*No, I wanted you here with me in the first place*, she wanted to scream. "The drugstore's not the same without you," she said aloud, hoping to ease the tension, "very boring."

"So Noel's got you back for winter break, huh? I should've known."

"I couldn't stay away."

"Yeah, it gets in your blood." He sniffed and she imagined him wiping his nose, too, two thousand miles away. "Well, hey, tell everyone there 'hi' for me, will you?"

He sounded so lonely. She wished she could take back every mean thing she'd said. Why did she have to fight with him at

Christmas as if he wasn't feeling rotten enough on a strange campus in a strange city without a friendly face in the whole time zone? "Yeah, sure, I'll tell them."

"Okay, well, thanks Jamie. Bye."

"Bye, Jason." They both hung up quietly, not wanting a loud click to offend the other. What Jason did after hanging up, Jamie would never know. She, on the other hand, ran out to the barn, climbed the ladder to the loft and threw herself into a pile of hay where she cried until the damp weather whistling through the cracks in the wood siding drove her back inside the warm house.

Jamie's heart wasn't into celebrating the holiday. The elation she'd experienced over the anticipation of seeing her family's faces on Christmas morning when they opened the gifts she'd so thoughtfully purchased, could not be recaptured after Jason's phone call. She missed him so much. She wanted everything to go back like it was before last summer. Back when they both thought they were going to OU together; Jason pursuing his law degree and she, working on her Bachelor's in Health Sciences. If he hadn't left she wouldn't be so lonely at school, unable to relax and make friends like all the other girls in her dorm. She wouldn't be so lonely right now, missing him, wanting him beside her for the holidays, hating it that he was all alone and miserable in California.

*He's not alone. He is never alone who calls himself a child of God.*

But he's miserable, I heard it in his voice. And so much of it is my fault. I am acting like a child, just like he said.

*All things work together for the good of them that love the Lord, for those who are called according to his purpose.*

Is this his purpose, Lord? Is it mine? Were You behind this opportunity to study at Stanford like Jason said? Was I standing in his way of fulfilling the purpose You have for his life, or was he standing in mine?

Either God wasn't answering her questions, or she wasn't hearing the answers.

# Chapter Eight

J
amie worked until the store closed on Christmas Eve. Business
was brisk and her shift passed quickly. It seemed all of Jenna's
Creek had last minute shopping to do. She stayed at the cash
register, her fingers flying over the keys and bagging customers'
purchases until six o'clock when Noel closed the store; two hours
earlier than the usual time, in honor of the holiday.

It took another twenty minutes to close out her register and
take the moneybag to Noel's office. At the foot of the stairs she ran
into Eric. She had seen him working out on the floor all day, but
never had a chance to say hi.

"What a day," he said breathlessly. "Are all holidays like this?"

"Pretty much, but Christmas is the worst."

"You got all your shopping done?"

"I finished up the other day. I'm as ready as I'll ever be."

"You don't seem very full of Christmas cheer. Is everything all
right?"

"Just a long day," she replied in way of explanation. She
hadn't told anyone about her conversation with Jason—not even
Cassie—although some of their exchange had been overheard, and
her mood afterwards helped fill in the blanks.

Eric ran a hand through his dark hair. "I've been meaning to
ask," he began, "if you have any plans for New Year's Eve. Some
friends from my church are having a party. We all grew up together
more or less, and we try to do something on New Year's Eve while

the rest of the world is out partying. It's always a lot of fun. I was thinking you might go with me, how about it?"

Jamie gulped. The last thing she wanted to do on New Year's Eve was go to a party with a bunch of strangers and pretend like she was having a good time. She was kind of looking forward to spending the night in bed feeling sorry for herself, with a half gallon of Rocky Road ice cream to keep her company. "I don't know if I'd be much company at a party," she admitted haltingly.

"Sure you would, it's no big deal. We just play games and laugh a lot and there's tons of junk food to eat. I promise to have you home by daybreak."

"I don't know—I really shouldn't."

Disappointment played across his rugged features. "I guess our group does sounds pretty dull to some people, but we like it. I just thought since you went to church and everything, it'd be something you'd enjoy."

"Oh, it's not that," she said quickly. "It does sound like fun. It's just that…the thing is, Eric, I broke up with my boyfriend a couple of months ago, and with it being Christmas and all…well, I don't know about a party. You'd probably regret inviting me."

"I'm sorry, I didn't know. But maybe it'd do you good to get out of the house just for the evening. I promise I won't regret inviting you." He smiled down at her and arched an eyebrow. It disappeared beneath the lock of thick hair that was always falling across his forehead no matter how many times he pushed it back into place.

She hesitated. It did sound like fun, but how much fun would she add to the mix? Even if Eric didn't regret inviting her, she was sure his friends would wish he hadn't. "I'd better not. I'm sorry, but thanks for asking."

"Sure. Okay, maybe some other time."

"Yeah, some other time," Jamie turned and headed into the stockroom. For the first time, the thought of sitting on her bed in her bathrobe, reading a cheesy romance novel and devouring a half gallon of ice cream didn't seem so appealing. She had always heard whatever you did on New Year's Eve, you were destined to do all year long. What a depressing superstition. Maybe she should reconsider Eric's invitation. What's the worst that could happen? She'd spend the whole night with Eric and his friends, wishing she was with Jason.

Maybe not, maybe she'd have a great time. She liked Eric; he was smart and easy to talk to. Definitely better looking than anything she'd come across on the farm if she stayed home. She did love the idea of spending the holiday with Christian young people who shared her idea of fun. If his friends were half as much fun as he claimed...

It would do her good to get out of the house.

She hurried from the stockroom before she could lose her nerve. She would tell him she changed her mind. She'd thought about it, and the party sounded like just what she needed. If his invitation still stood, she'd be more than happy...

She stopped dead in her tracks. Eric was standing next to the lunch counter talking to Mary Caudill. Mary had been working at the drugstore longer than Jamie. They never got to know each other, mostly because they had nothing in common. Mary dated a lot of different boys and liked to party on weekends while Jamie seldom left the farm unless it was with Jason.

Mary graduated from South Auburn the same year as Eric. She attended a local business college in the next county. She and Eric were probably catching up on what had been going on with each other, Jamie reasoned, although she wasn't sure what a Christian guy like Eric would have to talk about with a girl like Mary. She reminded herself Eric got along with everybody; it didn't matter to him what circles a person moved in.

Jamie scowled and crossed her arms over her chest. Eric sure wasn't wasting any time in finding a replacement to attend his party. He'd have no trouble convincing Mary to accept the invitation. She'd been panting over him ever since he had come to work here and had been doing everything she could to get his attention. Well, if that was the type of girl he was interested in, she was glad she found out now. He obviously wasn't who she thought he was. She just hoped Mary's questionable morals and familiarity with the courser side of the English language didn't embarrass Eric in front of his church friends.

It looked as if she'd be spending New Year's Eve alone after all. Maybe she'd stop by the convenience store on her way home tonight for some ice cream so she could start her celebration a little early. She turned and stomped back into the stockroom before either of them had a chance to look up and see her. She wondered why she even cared.

🌺

"So, how much longer you gonna sit here and feel sorry for yourself?" Cassie finally asked on the twenty-seventh of December.

"I'm not feeling sorry for myself." Jamie had her chin cupped in the palm of her hand while she idly flipped through an old issue of Good Housekeeping at the kitchen table. Man, was she bored. Christmas day had been a dismal affair. She pigged out on ham and Mississippi Mud Cake and spent the day in front of the TV staring at holiday reruns of Andy Griffith and The Munsters. Cassie tried to get her involved in a game of Scrabble—a game she usually avoided since Jamie always beat the socks off her—but she wasn't interested.

By the time the leftovers were put away and the living room restored to some kind of order, Jamie was ready for a peaceful night in her room sulking. She wondered about Jason all alone in California. Did he have anywhere to go for a traditional Christmas dinner? Did he get any presents? She should have sent something, at least a card. She'd wanted to call him. She kept her ear tuned for the sound of the telephone, but it didn't ring all night.

Cassie snatched the magazine away from Jamie and slid it across the table out of reach. "You are too feeling sorry for yourself, and I'm sick of it. I thought college life would be exciting. If you're any indication, it must be the pits."

"This isn't college life," Jamie pointed out, "this is farm life remember? The life you're so anxious to get away from."

"Yeah, but you're in college. Grandma Cory would let you do anything you wanted while you're home if you'd just ask, but all you've done is go to work at that stupid drugstore every day. I thought you'd at least want to go out with your friends once in a while. I thought maybe you learned how to have a good time while you were at college, but no, you haven't changed a bit. You go back to school in a week and you haven't done a single interesting thing during your whole break."

"So what?" Jamie eyed the magazine on the other side of the table. She was about to begin an article on how to restore your figure after childbirth before she'd been rudely interrupted. The sooner she got rid of Cassie, the sooner she could get to it. "How is what I do with my free time any concern of yours?" she asked.

"Because you're ruining it for me!"

Jamie studied her younger sister. Her full lips were pulled into a pout, and her hazel eyes snapped with indignation. She looked so much like the framed high school picture of the girls' mother that Grandma Cory kept on the mantle over the fireplace—their mother's looks and father's charisma; a dangerous combination. "What am I ruining for you?"

"Grandma Cory is never going to let me do anything when I get older because you're not breaking her in. You're supposed to be the one to push curfew limits and get her used to boys coming by the house at all hours. That way, by the time I'm ready to start doing stuff, she'll be used to it. But you're not doing your part. When I'm finally allowed to date, she'll still have all her strength left to fight me on every little point. I won't have any fun. All I'll hear is, 'Jamie never wanted to do that when she was your age. Jamie never talked to me that way. Jamie never went out on a school night.'"

Jamie shook her head. "Cassie, Grandma Cory isn't going to punish you because I don't go out that often. Besides, she knows you're the one the boys are gonna go crazy over. She's already bracing herself."

Cassie didn't argue the validity of Jamie's statement, but she wasn't through arguing her point. "It doesn't matter. She's going to have all these arguments to use against me. And having an older sister like you isn't going to help my chances any. You haven't gone out at all since Jason left. You've spent your whole winter break here at the house or the drugstore. You probably don't do anything at school either, except study."

"That's what I'm there for."

"If you really believe that, you're wasting your time at college. In fact, people with your attitude shouldn't even be allowed to go."

Jamie smiled at the seriousness in Cassie's voice. "I can't help it, Cass. I miss Jason. I don't feel like doing anything. I don't want to go anywhere without him."

"That's the problem. You're too dependent on Jason. I know you were crazy about him and everything, but being with him has kept you from trying anything else. All you did your entire senior year was wait for him to get off work so you two could sit out on the porch and watch the cars go by. I think you really missed out on some good times. You'll be nineteen in a month. He's the first real boyfriend you ever had. Just because it didn't work out between the two of you, does that mean he's going to be the last?"

"You don't understand. I loved Jason. I still do."

"You think I don't understand love?" Cassie voice was filled with hurt. "I understand enough to know you can't curl up and die because he moved to California. Face it, Jason's gone. Get on with your life. The way you're acting isn't healthy. Before long you'll be in your twenties, and all your best years will be behind you."

Jamie laughed. "You're right. I'll be an old maid of twenty with nothing good to look back on."

Cassie nodded her head vigorously. "That's what I'm trying to tell you."

"I wish you wouldn't worry, Cass. I know what I'm doing. One of these days, I'll be ready to get back in that saddle and give love another chance."

Her melodrama went over Cassie's head. "And what am I supposed to do in the meantime?"

"You know, I get the impression there's a more pressing issue at stake here than my impending spinsterhood. What's really going on?"

"Well, if you must know…" Cassie cast a nervous glance around the kitchen and dropped into the chair next to Jamie. She leaned in confidentially, "Amy Bishop is having a party at her house on New Year's Eve."

"Ah hah," Jamie raised her eyebrows with a knowing tone in her voice.

Cassie gave Jamie's hand a smart slap. "Would you let me finish? Her parents are going to be there the whole time, so there's nothing fishy going on. I haven't mentioned it to Grandma Cory yet because, see, the thing is, it's a sleepover. Amy's invited just about everybody from school, girls and boys. Sometime after midnight, all the boys are going home, and the girls are staying to spend the night in their rec room in the basement. Well, if I tell Grandma it's a sleep-over with boys anywhere in the vicinity, you know she'll freak out."

Jamie nodded in agreement.

"Here's where you come in. If you had plans for that night too, she'd be loosened up by the time I told her about the party, and she may let me go. But if she thinks you're going to stay here and bury yourself in front of the TV, she'll say, 'Why don't you stay home and keep your sister company. It won't be long before she goes back to college and then you won't see her at all.' Jamie, if you're not doing anything that night, she won't understand why it's so all-fired important for me to have something to do."

Jamie sighed. "Listen, I'd really like to help you out, but—"

"But nothing, come on, Jamie. Please. It's not healthy for you to be sitting in this house your whole vacation anyway; it's unnatural."

"Well, I was sort of invited to a party."

"Really—where—by who?"

"By Eric Blackwood," Jamie said, resisting the urge to correct Cassie's grammar.

"Who's Eric Blackwood?"

"A boy I go to school with at OU. He works at the drugstore too."

"And you haven't mentioned him?"

"There's nothing to mention. We just study together sometimes."

"Is he cute?"

"Yeah, I guess he's cute, but that's not important."

"On what planet?"

Jamie tapped her index finger against her chin, and studied Cassie thoughtfully. "So, if I do you this favor, what can I count on you doing for me?"

"Anything, you name it."

"Okay. How about getting off my back the rest of winter break? If I want to lie around here till I'm covered in bedsores, it's my business. Got it?"

"Yeah, yeah, got it, you can turn into a turnip for all I care, just soften Grandma Cory up so she'll let me go to Amy's party."

"There's only one problem, Eric asked me to the party a few days ago and since I said no, there's a chance he already asked someone else to go in my place."

"Oh, that's just great," Cassie exclaimed. Then she snapped her fingers. "No, wait a minute. This may not be a problem. All you have to do is tell Grandma Cory you've been invited to this party by this Eric person and let her think you're going. Then I'll tell her about Amy's party, and she'll give me the go-ahead. Then, if Eric has already asked someone else—which would serve you right for giving him the brush off in the first place—you can just tell Grandma that things didn't work out between the two of you. It'll be too late for her to tell me I can't go to Amy's party."

Jamie smiled at her sister's resourcefulness. "Sounds like a plan. Go upstairs and give me a chance to tell her about Eric. I'll just have to figure out a way to finagle another invitation out of him without sounding like a dope. You can ask her about Amy's party sometime after supper. We don't want her to think we've been in cahoots about the whole thing."

"Right—thanks, Jamie, you think of everything."

Yeah, sure, Jamie thought as Cassie hurried out of the kitchen, the usual spring back in her step. She wasn't the one who had to call Eric. If he already invited Mary to the party, it would put him in an uncomfortable position. Even if he hadn't invited someone else yet, she was going to look like a pathetic loser for crawling back to him and begging for somewhere to go on New Year's Eve.

"You thought I invited Mary Caudill to the party?" Eric threw back his head and laughed in disbelief.

Jamie smiled sheepishly at his reaction. "Well..."

Eric's invitation had still been open when Jamie called him after talking to Cassie on the twenty-seventh. After telling her how glad he was that she called back, he had spent the next twenty minutes telling her stories about his friends and parties they'd had in the past.

While getting ready for the party, Jamie had reminded herself she was only going as a favor to Cassie. Now, sitting in the front seat of Eric's car, she was glad she wasn't sitting at home watching Guy Lombardo with Grandma Cory and Grandpa Harlan.

"When I saw you and Mary talking that day after you'd invited me," she admitted in a small voice, "I knew you didn't want to go alone. She is pretty and popular with the guys..."

"There's a reason she's popular. Oh, I'm sorry, what I should've said is Mary and I know each other from school, that's why we were talking. But I know how she is, and I don't think she'd have much fun at a party with my friends."

"Are they that bad?" Jamie asked with a playful groan.

"No, no, you'll blend right in."

"I'm not sure if I should be flattered by that remark or not."

Eric chuckled, "Believe me, I'd choose your company over Mary's any day. Seriously, I'm glad you called. I'm not into the whole boyfriend/girlfriend scene. To tell you the truth, I haven't dated since my junior year in high school and these parties always turn into a couples' thing leaving me the odd man out. Last year, I ended up being the scorekeeper for charades; talk about a lame way to spend New Year's."

Jamie turned sideways in the front seat of Eric's car, a teasing smile on her face. "You're kidding? You were always Mr. Popular in high school. I'd have thought you had girls beating your door down." She lowered her voice and added conspiratorially, "You should hear the way they talk about you in the dorm." She grinned at the blush creeping up his cheeks. Eric Blackwood, embarrassed? If that didn't beat all!

"It's just a personal decision I made a few years ago."

She waited for him to elaborate, but he didn't. She figured his heart had been broken by a failed relationship like hers and he didn't want to take another chance. "I'm sorry, Eric. I shouldn't have teased you. You just surprised me that's all; I kind of thought you were pulling my leg there for a minute about not dating."

Eric gave her a smile in the dim interior of the car. "That's all right. I've been teased by the best for my convictions, I'm used to it."

"Your convictions?" Jamie questioned.

He nodded and looked back at the road. "Yeah, even some of the kids in my church don't understand my decision. As long as a girl's a Christian, they don't see anything wrong with dating her."

Jamie felt like a heathen for asking, but she had to know. "What exactly is wrong with dating a Christian? I thought as long as you're not unequally yoked or anything, it's cool."

"Oh, nothing's wrong with it," he answered quickly. "I'm not saying my decision is right for everybody. I'm just not ready for a serious commitment at this point in my life, there's too much else I've got on my mind right now, so why complicate things with a girlfriend?" He gave her a nervous glance out of the corner of his eye. "Hey listen, I'm sorry if I misled you by the invitation to the party. I just wanted to spend a little time with someone whose company I enjoy. I don't really consider this a date. I should've made it clear when I asked you in the first place. I thought since we were friends and all, we could go together as friends. There'd be an even number for the games, and I wouldn't get stuck playing score keeper all night again."

"So in other words, you used me." She crossed her arms over her chest and gave him a playful scowl.

"Yeah, well, I guess you could say that."

"No problem," she said with a wave of her arm. "As a matter of fact, I'm relieved. Like I said the other day, I broke up with someone this past summer, and I don't want to even think about dating again. If it hadn't been for my sister bugging me about never going out, I probably wouldn't have called you back."

"Is that right? So I guess we used each other."

"It sure looks that way." Jamie relaxed against the back of the seat. This was turning out to be fun already. It was easy to be herself in Eric's presence, just like on campus. "I do appreciate the invitation tonight," she said. "Without it, I would've spent the night in front of the tube watching Guy Lombardo with my grandparents. Can anything be more pathetic than that?"

The party was held at the home of a young married couple from Eric's church. Jamie recognized several of the party guests from South Auburn, many of whom had graduated long before her, other faces she had never seen before. There were young married couples in the group along with other college students, home from their respective schools for winter break. Like Eric said, everyone was paired off in one form or another, and she was glad she had Eric to hang around with. She wouldn't have wanted to serve as score keeper for all the fun games they had planned either.

The conversation was mature and enlightening, not at all what she expected. She had often wondered if she was the only young person in Auburn County who believed in a Savior who died on a cross, that one must live a holy life in order to see God, and life in this day of free love was virtually impossible without God's direction and wisdom. Eric's friends were intelligent, eager to make her part of the group, and appeared to share her beliefs of self-purity. No one sneaked away from the group to be alone with their date. She didn't hear any of the foul language or crude jokes she had grown accustomed to on the college campus.

Friendly hugs between the girls and backslapping and hand shaking from the guys rang in the New Year. A few ardent embraces were exchanged between some of the serious couples, including the married ones among them. But they kept their behavior chaste and appropriate for the sake of the group.

Eric made his way through the crowd, glued to the television set as the ball dropped in Times Square, and approached Jamie. "Happy New Year!" he called out merrily. For a brief second they stood inches apart. Jamie wasn't sure what to expect or what she should do. Then he pulled her into his arms for a brief hug and slapped her on the back like he'd done his male friends a moment before.

Jamie gave him a hammer or two as well before they separated. After his announcement in the car about not dating, she didn't want him to think she was making more out of the evening than he intended. "Happy 1975, Eric, thanks for inviting me."

After midnight, the group split up into smaller groups to play euchre and gin rummy. Jamie and Eric were partners against two other teams, and the game soon became spirited. In what seemed like no time, she realized it was after two a. m.

"Oh, my," she exclaimed, "this'll have to be the last hand. I've gotta get home."

Several others chimed in that they, too, would have to be leaving soon. More hugs were exchanged as the party broke up. Everyone assured Jamie of how much they enjoyed her company and how they were looking forward to seeing her again. Eric helped her into her coat and held the door open for her.

"I hope you weren't disappointed with the party," he said when they were alone in his car headed toward Betterman Road and the Steele farm.

"Oh, no, I loved it. It's exactly the type of evening I enjoy. I always thought I was the only person on the planet under the age of twenty who thought playing cards and drinking Pepsi was fun."

"Great—I knew you'd enjoy it if you came one time." He gave her playful wink. "A lot of people expect a different scene for New Year's Eve. That's why we started having these parties; to give people an alternative to going out and drinking and carrying on. I'm glad you had a good time."

Jamie went to the party as a favor to Cassie and ended up enjoying herself more than she thought she would. Cassie would say it was because of Eric. Who could *not* have a good time while looking into those dark eyes? It wasn't simply Eric's company, Jamie told herself. The group was fun and lively; the games they played energetic, but not so competitive anyone suffered hard feelings. She enjoyed everything about the evening, not just Eric. He didn't date anyway; he'd made that clear. And she wasn't ready to get emotional over anyone yet either.

Eric was a nice guy, nothing more. He didn't want to complicate his life, and neither did she. Besides, with his looks and confident personality, when he did get ready to complicate things, he surely wouldn't settle for a door mouse like her.

"I was thinking," Eric said, breaking the silence inside the car, "if you want, I could drive you back to school Sunday afternoon. I remember what a bummer it was to be a freshman with no wheels and always have to beg a ride off somebody. Besides, it's a lonely trip for me riding up there by myself. I wouldn't mind the company."

Jamie could think of no reason to refuse. The four-hour round trip from Jenna's Creek to Athens was taxing on Grandma Cory. She would much rather sit at home on a Sunday afternoon with her feet propped up than endure the long drive. Aunt Marty and Uncle Justin wouldn't mind missing out on it either. Only Cassie would begrudge the missed opportunity to visit the campus again. She would understand completely though why Jamie chose Eric's company over her family's.

"Sure, that'd be great," she spoke up without hesitation. She really meant it.

# Chapter Nine

"There's a basketball game tomorrow night at the Convocation Center," Eric said as he pulled the car up to the front of Jamie's building on January fourth. "Want to go?"

Jamie wrinkled her nose. "I don't know. I really don't know much about basketball."

"What's there to know? If our guys get the ball through the hoop, we score two points. Everything else, I'll explain as we go along."

Jamie chuckled appreciatively. "Yeah, that much I get. It's just that I grew up in a houseful of women. I don't really see a point in organized sports. I'd hate for you to have an awful time if I don't get into it."

"Isn't that what you said about the New Year's Eve party? Don't worry, there's no way I'll have an awful time. These games are a blast even if you're not a sports fan, you'll see. We'll have fun."

"Okay, sure, tomorrow night, right?"

"Yeah, I'll pick you up about five-thirty. The student section fills up early." A basketball game—what was she thinking? She'd almost prefer having a tooth pulled, but it appeared Eric Blackwood had the ability to talk her into anything.

The winter quarter flew by. After Jamie sailed through pre-Calculus with a B average, her study dates with Eric came to an end. Now, instead of studying, they got together for basketball games. Jamie became quite a fan in spite of herself. He even talked her into attending an away game in West Virginia. She loved everything about it; the smelly bus ride, the enthusiasm of the crowd, the greasy food, and especially Eric's company.

Before she knew it, basketball season was over. Her disappointment, however, was short lived. Longer daylight hours and milder temperatures meant one thing to Eric, baseball.

"I know even less about baseball than I did basketball," Jamie admitted after an invitation to watch his first intramural competition against a team of upper classmen.

"Don't worry. All you need to know is we hit the ball with these long stick things and then run around the bases."

She laughed. He did have a way of simplifying things. Still it was baseball, her least favorite of all sports. Ugh!

"I get the premise, thank you very much. I took P.E. in high school, you know, and baseball was the worst. I never could hit the ball, even when the pitcher walked halfway to home plate and lobbed it to me. Then Coach Courtwright would make me run laps; as if I intentionally have no hand-eye coordination."

Eric seemed amused by everything that came out of her mouth. "You just never had the right coach," he said after he stopped laughing. "After the game, we'll have a little batting practice. As a pitcher, I'm not half bad even when I'm throwing grapefruits."

When Eric took his position on the pitcher's mound and fired strike after strike over home plate, Jamie knew there was no way she could hit a ball he threw to her, regardless of his stellar coaching abilities.

He had been a huge baseball star back at South Auburn according to the weekly write-ups she sometimes read in the local newspaper. But she had never actually seen him pitch. Sitting in the stands with the players' girlfriends and wannabe major leaguers, she listened with half amusement/half pride to their comments. "Who is that guy?" "Why doesn't he play for the school?"

Her favorite one by far was; "He's gorgeous." She had to admit he didn't look half bad standing out there in his pitcher's stance with his unruly dark hair sticking out from under his South Auburn team cap.

"Do you need a ride home this weekend?" Eric asked Jamie when he caught up with her in the dining hall the last week before spring break.

"I don't know. I feel guilty asking you to chauffer me back and forth all the time."

"Hey, don't worry about it. With the gas shortage, we're supposed to be doubling up. Don't you pay attention to the President's fireside chats? Besides, I enjoy the company."

Jamie smiled, warmed to her toes by the compliment, but deciding it best not to read anything into it. "I guess I do too. I hate to admit it, but the trip can be pretty dull with Grandma Cory or Aunt Marty behind the wheel."

Eric selected a fat, juicy apple from the rack and set it on his tray. "It hasn't been that long since I was a freshman and had to depend on Mom and Dad or one of my sisters to drive me home. I bummed rides off friends as often as I could."

Jamie passed on the fruit and followed him to the unoccupied end of a long table. The din of noise made it difficult to hear one's own conversation, and she inclined her head toward his on the other side of the table as they talked. "You've never really talked much about your family. It had to be rough growing up with three older sisters bossing you around. But I never hear you complain."

"I've never seen where complaining does much good, especially in a house full of women where a run in somebody's pantyhose can usher in the end of civilization. Dad and I learned not to make a lot of noise or draw attention to ourselves."

She laughed and nearly choked on a mouthful of soda, "Oh, Eric."

He smiled at her over the top of his water glass. "It wasn't really that bad," he conceded, "Not all the time anyway. The part about Dad and me sticking together was pretty much the truth. We always did all that father-son stuff. He coached my little league team, and we went on Boy Scout camping trips together. You could count on him to tell the scariest stories around the campfire. All the other kids thought he was great."

"That must have been nice." A lump rose in her throat, making her wish she hadn't brought up the subject. "Most men don't have a relationship with their kids at all. They leave everything up to the mom."

"I don't think that's necessarily true. If the dad isn't involved with his kids, it's usually because he's making sure their physical needs are being met and leaving the nurturing up to the mom. At least that's how it was in my house."

Jamie felt like she had been chastised. She didn't want him to think she had anything against men in general, but it was obvious their upbringings were worlds apart. "I suppose it can be that way in a perfect world," she said defensively, "but I know for a fact that most fathers leave the childrearing to the mother, not because they are busy busting their humps to make a living, but because they're lazy and selfish with their time."

Eric sat back in his chair and stared at her, his jaw slack. Jamie lowered her eyes to her plate and wondered whatever possessed her to be so rude. He didn't deserve that, neither did his dad.

When he spoke, his voice was quiet and gentle, not at all angry like she expected. "Where's all this coming from, Jamie?"

She shrugged and blinked away tears, too mortified to speak.

He reached across the table and touched her hand. She raised her eyes to look at him. "I know your Mom died when you were young and your grandparents practically raised you, so I assume your relationship with your dad wasn't all that great."

She shook her head, affirming his assumption.

"I'm sorry if I was insensitive talking about how great my old man was," he continued. "I guess a lot of men are lazy and selfish with their time. Maybe I'm looking at the situation through rose-colored glasses because that attitude wasn't prevalent in my house, but I like to think I'm at least partly right and the majority of men want to be involved in their kids' upbringing."

Jamie still doubted he knew what he was talking about, but she didn't want to offend him or his father any further. "I guess where your background made you see the best in people mine made me a little jaded. I'm sorry about my 'perfect world' comment. I wasn't trying to insinuate your family thinks they're perfect."

"That's good, because we're far from it. Most of the time growing up, I thought my family was as lame as everybody else's. It's just now that I can see how things really were. Mom wasn't too bad either, kind of smothering at times, but whose Mom isn't? She was the June Cleaver type. You know, always baking cookies for school parties and sitting up with me all night when I was sick. She still does it if I let her know I'm not feeling well. If you ever repeat that, I'll tell everyone you're crazy." He pointed a threatening finger at her, and they both laughed.

"Dad and I still have these great talks about whatever's going on in my life. It's been that way as far back as I can remember. He always has time to listen. A lot of adults only know how to talk at you, not to you. They're always trying to get you to admit they're right and you're just a dumb kid. Not Dad, he doesn't push his philosophies off on me. He taught me about God and stuff like that, but in the end, it's always been my decision to make. He never tried to turn me into a mirror image of himself like a lot of fathers do."

"Sounds like the perfect dad. Oops, I used the 'P' word again."

"No offense," he assured her. "Dad is pretty close. We still get under each other's skin, usually when he doesn't know as much about something as I do," he added with a smile. "I just hope I can show my own kids the same kind of respect he's always shown me."

She took a bite of her sandwich and forced it down with a gulp of soda. "It's very noble of you to want to be just like your dad. Most kids want to be the exact opposite of their folks. You know, not make the same mistakes." She took another bite of her sandwich. It was dry and tasteless in her mouth, but she didn't want to look him in the eye.

"What about you? Are you afraid of making the same mistakes?"

"My mother was wonderful, pretty close to the June Cleaver type." *Except Ward never slapped June around*, she thought. "She died when I was twelve..." Jamie's voice cracked, but she felt compelled to continue. "So I guess I never really knew who she was. To me, she was just mine and Cassie's mother. She was funny, honest, and always knew the right things to say if one of us was upset about something. But as far as what kind of person she was, I don't really know."

"If she was funny and honest and caring like you say, she had to be a wonderful person. She sounds a lot like you."

Jamie took the top off her sandwich and began removing the wilted lettuce. No one had ever compared her to Nancy before. Everybody said she was quiet and practical, introverted and hardworking, like Uncle Justin. Cassie was like Mom; beautiful and spirited. No one ever used those words to describe Jamie.

But there had been more to Nancy Steele than her beauty and grace. Jamie's memories were right. She was honest, patient, and long-suffering; a good mother. Jamie could never hope to be as good.

She replaced the top on her sandwich, but didn't move it toward her mouth. "Mom took a lot of guff off my dad, and I never really understood why," she said in a small voice. She looked up from her plate and saw Eric's deep blue eyes were filled with concern. "I guess she thought she was doing it for Cassie and me; probably hoping things would get better, and we could be like a normal family, whatever that is. She had a strong faith in God. When she knew she was dying, she told me and Cassie about how she was going to her mansion in heaven. If she was afraid of dying, it was only because she was worried about us. To her, nothing was more important than family. She believed in marriage. I used to think she was weak for staying with Dad. For letting him run all over her the way he did. But now...well, maybe it took more strength to stay and try to make it work than it would have to walk away."

After a moment of silence, she continued. "I never understood

Dad either. I couldn't figure out if he was just a mean, selfish jerk, or if he treated everybody the way he did her. He must've had some good qualities because he always had friends. Everybody said he was the life of the party. He loved making people laugh. I'll always wonder if that's what made Mom fall in love with him. Was she hoping his negative qualities would mellow with age, or that she could learn to live with them?"

Eric squeezed her hand in reply, sensing no words were necessary.

"If I ever have kids, I don't want them growing up like I did," she stated. "Kids should have good memories to look back on after they're grown, not questions and doubts." She took another drink of her soda. "I'm sorry. I don't mean to sit here feeling sorry for myself about something that can't be changed. You said yourself complaining doesn't help anything. I didn't mean to spend our whole lunch bellyaching. I have plenty to be thankful for. I have a family who loves me and a benevolent government giving me a practically free education. What more could I ask for?"

He reached across the table to give her hand a final squeeze. "I'm glad you're smiling again. But I don't think it hurts to complain once in a while, as long as we don't start enjoying the sound of our own voice."

She leaned across the table toward him. "You are so wise, Eric Blackwood."

He smiled back. "I know. What can I say?"

"If your offer still stands, if you're not sick of listening to me, that is, I'd love a ride home this weekend. I'll call Grandma Cory tonight and let her know everything's under control."

"Mom, I've been looking for five minutes, and I still don't see the casserole dish you're talking about."

Abigail Blackwood turned from the sink in time to see her oldest daughter straighten up from the cabinets lining the floor, place her hand on her hip, and level an exasperated look at her. "Why are you looking down there?" Abby asked, bewildered. "You know that's where I keep the pots and pans. The casserole dishes are up there." She pointed to the cabinet door behind Karen's head.

"Because you told me it was down here," Karen exclaimed, pushing the door closed and reaching for the one above it. "I asked you twice to make sure I heard you right. I know where the pots and pans have been for the last twenty years. I thought maybe you'd done some rearranging now that it's just you and Dad."

"Sorry, I must've thought you meant something else. And it's not just me and Dad, Eric still lives here." Abby turned back to the sink. In all honesty, she had no recollection of Karen asking her any such thing. That didn't mean she hadn't, just that Abby hadn't been paying attention again.

Her mind hadn't worked properly ever since Eric announced he was going to work at Wyatt's Drugstore last Thanksgiving. Of all the places in the county to find a job, why did it have to be there? And what in the world was Noel thinking offering the boy a job? Certainly he could've come up with some excuse why he didn't need him. He could've said he already had plenty of help or Eric didn't have enough work experience. Anything would've satisfied the boy; he wouldn't know any better.

"Mom?"

She became aware of Karen standing at her elbow, "Yes, dear?"

Karen's face was a mask of concern. "Are you all right?"

Karen had always taken her duties as the oldest child to heart. She was the one to make sure the younger children finished their homework, didn't talk back to their elders, and did the chores assigned to them. Growing up, the other children called her 'bossy' and 'little mother', but Karen couldn't quell her naturally occurring maternal instincts. It wasn't just her brother and sisters who benefited from her compassionate heart; anyone, whether friend, stranger, or stray cat could count on her. Her maternal nature had matured along with her. Married six years to Roger Swayne, a delightful man Jack and Abby adored, she had two little ones with another due next month. Abby always figured she must have done something right in raising her own kids to have created such a loving and godly mother as Karen.

Abby wiped her hands on her apron and pulled her daughter into her arms. "I'm fine, sweetheart, just a little distracted."

Karen's face softened a fraction. "You haven't seemed yourself lately. You're not worried about all the time Eric's spending with Jamie Steele, are you?"

A shadow passed over Abby's face for a moment, but she smiled brightly for Karen's sake. It was just like her to worry. "What? Of course not, Eric and Jamie are just friends. I don't know why you brought that up."

Karen's eyebrows lifted a fraction of an inch, reminding Abby of Jack. "I don't know, Mom. The two of them are getting pretty chummy, if you ask me. She's all Eric talks about."

"Oh, Karen, that's silly. They go to school together. They share the same interests and keep each other company at ball games, that's all. You know your brother. He's too serious about his studies to get involved with someone right now. He doesn't even date."

Karen raised her hands in defeat. "Okay, okay. You spend a lot more time with him than I do. I'm sure you know what you're talking about. But personally, I won't be surprised if the two of them end up falling for each other, if it hasn't happened already."

"Falling for each other," Abby said with an indignant huff. "You're right about one thing, I do know my son. He's much too practical to let something like romance sneak up on him. And according to Eric, Jamie's heart still belongs to a boy who's gone off to college in California or somewhere. Now get that casserole dish out of the cabinet where it's been for years and pour those noodles into it."

Abby didn't miss the slight shake of Karen's head before she turned and did as she was told. Abby turned back to the sink. So what if Karen thought she had her head buried in the sand. She knew her son. She knew what was important to him. Nothing would come between him and a college degree; not even a pretty little girl to whom he was dedicating all his free time.

His nonexistent love life wasn't what had Abby out of sorts lately, but rather the truth of where he came from. Especially if he—or anyone else—found out his college tuition was the direct result of the benevolence of his natural father. It was not simply good grades and a winning essay on his application that insured Eric was the recipient of the Benjamin F. Wyatt scholarship. No one in the world knew that besides her and Noel Wyatt and she was determined that no one would ever know. She'd have to be more diligent about focusing on what was going on around her and keeping her emotions concealed if Karen had noticed she was acting out of sorts. She had no intention of letting her twenty-year-old secret become known now. No one must suspect her life was anything more than she'd ever let on.

For as far back as she could remember she had loved Noel Wyatt passionately, madly. It was an irrefutable fact, no matter how difficult it had been to behave otherwise. Over the years she had learned to play the part of the chaste, loving wife of Jack Blackwood. Staying away from the drugstore, turning the other way when she passed Noel on the street, and avoiding conversations where his name was mentioned had been easy. Keeping him out of her thoughts was another matter entirely.

She remembered the first time Jack questioned her. Eric was ten-years-old. Karen had already graduated from high school, and the other girls were right on her heels. It was their twentieth wedding anniversary, and his words had devastated her. She had thought she was doing so well at keeping her true heart hidden from the world.

Jack took her to the nicest restaurant in Jenna's Creek for dinner. Both of them had dressed up for the occasion. She sat across from him at the tiny table, two candles glowing between them, illuminating his face. She knew there was something on his mind, something he wanted to say. She had known Jack her whole life. He could never keep secrets from her. If he only knew what secrets she kept from him...

He reached across the table and covered her hands with his, the fettuccini Alfredo growing cold on his plate. Usually if something bothered him, he totally ignored it. He wasn't the confrontational type, preferring instead to let problems take care of themselves. That night he made no pretense.

His green eyes bore deep into her eyes. "Abby, do you love me?"

She resisted the urge to draw her hands back. They weren't the type of couple who discussed their feelings for each other. Jack loved her; she was fond of him. She did love him, not in the romantic, mushy sense they wrote songs about, but she cared deeply for him. He was the father of her children, most of them anyway.

She loosened one hand from his grip and laid it aside his cheek. "Jack, you know how I feel about you."

He gave her a grateful smile, but she didn't miss the disappointment his eyes. "I know how you feel. What I want to know is if you love me."

Abby felt tears well up in her eyes. How did her life get to this point? Jack was in pain because of her. If only things could've been different way back when, before the lies and mistakes piled up so high. Now it was too late to fix anything.

She had learned to live without passion; had buried her true heart so deep within herself she couldn't have recognized it if she tried. She put her mistakes behind her and never looked back. Still, it wasn't enough. Her own husband was sitting here in this romantic atmosphere on their twentieth anniversary asking if she loved him. What woman wouldn't love such a sweet and gentle man? He was a good provider, always putting the needs of his family before his own. He was good to the children, more than most men could claim. He never put unreasonable demands on them to be someone else as a way to appease his own male pride. Abby cared for him. She appreciated him. She respected and honored him. But did she love him the way she knew he was asking?

"Jack, you're a better husband than I ever hoped for," she answered honestly. "I think the world of you."

His face fell, and a tear slid unchecked down his cheek. "That's what I thought."

Her own face crumpled at the sight of his pain. Why couldn't she just say it? Tell him what he so desperately wanted to hear, whether it was true or not? Would it be so bad to add one more lie to the stack that already threatened to topple over on her? "Jack…"

"It's all right, Abby." He took a quick sip of his iced tea in an effort to compose himself. "I've always known you married me because you didn't want to hurt me."

The table tilted in front of Abby, and she feared she would fall out of her chair. How many years had he known? She had tried to make him think she said yes to his marriage proposal out of consent rather than obligation.

"Jack, no," she exclaimed, leaning toward him and clutching at his hands. "That's not true. You know it isn't true." God, forgive her.

He shook his head dismally. "When I got home from the service, our mothers pushed us together. You know they did. Yes, I loved you more than anything back then. I still do." He smiled at a distant memory. "You should've seen how jealous my Army buddies were when I'd take out your picture and tell them you were my girl. You were so beautiful, too beautiful for an old country boy like me. I knew you could have any man you wanted. I really believed by the time I got home you'd be long gone, fallen in love with somebody worthy of you, probably married with a couple kids. That didn't stop me from telling those guys how you were mine; you were crazy about me; we were going to get married as soon as I got home. Then when I did get home, my wildest dreams came true. My mom was so excited about the whole thing. Your mom was calling the house all the time, the two of them making plans. I kept expecting you to hold up your hands and say, 'Wait a minute, I'm not marrying that jerk.'"

Jack chuckled and gazed deep into her eyes. "Every day I'd pinch myself, thinking this can't be happening. Abigail Frasier can't really want to marry me. I knew your heart wasn't it in. I knew there was something missing, but I didn't want to know what. I thought over time, I'd earn your love. I promised myself that if you actually went through with it, I'd be the best husband this side of heaven. Then you'd love me; really love me with all your heart, that your eyes would light up when I came into a room, and that you'd want to sit on my lap—not because I pulled you down on top of me—but because you couldn't get close enough."

His voice cracked and he glanced away. "I guess you can't make a person love you, no matter how hard you try. I'm living proof of that. I've tried for twenty years and still—nothing."

By this time Abby was crying openly. She couldn't stop the flood of tears streaming down her cheeks or the hiccupping sobs she tried in vain to silence. She wanted to tell him he was wrong; that she did love him she just wasn't any good at showing it. But the words wouldn't come. She stared into her fettuccini Alfredo and cried.

"Shh, it's all right, baby," he said, stroking her hands, his insufferable kindness only making her cry harder. Why didn't he get angry, shout at her that she was a miserable disappointment of a wife, why did he have to be so understanding? "I didn't mean to upset you. I guess I was feeling a little sorry for myself and said more than I meant to."

She shook her head and struggled to speak. "No, no, it's not your fault. I—I'm a horrible p—person, treating you th—this way." She set aside the linen napkin on her lap and fumbled in her purse for a tissue. She couldn't blow her nose on that beautiful napkin.

"I'm sorry, sweetheart," Jack apologized from his side of the table. "I shouldn't have brought it up tonight."

"I shouldn't have made you feel like this all these years. You're a wonderful husband. You deserve better than a cold shrew like me." She found a tissue and blew her nose, aware she'd broken every unwritten rule of manners and decorum.

"There's nothing cold about you, Abby. I've had a wonderful life with you. I just wish you were having as much fun as I am."

For the first time she could be honest. "I am having fun, Jack. I've tried to give you what I knew you wanted and deserved, I really did. It's just that…I guess we were so young when we married, I really didn't know what I wanted. You're right, our mothers did push us into marriage, but I think it all worked out okay." She reached for his hand again. "Don't you?"

His smile was genuine this time. "Yes, it's all worked out. I love you, Abby. I just want to see you happier than you are now. You've been holding back part of yourself our whole marriage, and I wish I could be the one to reach that part."

"It's not your fault," she repeated. "It's never been your fault, it's me. I'll try to do better. Make you happy."

"That's not what I want, Abby. I don't want you to try to love me. You either do or you don't." The sorrow was gone from his eyes, replaced with matter-of-factness. "I don't mean to be making demands on you that you can't deliver. I don't want you to regret marrying me anymore than you already do."

The tears were back in her eyes. "I don't regret marrying you. I've never regretted it." She saw on his face that he recognized the lie as soon as it was out of her mouth.

"It's all right, sweetheart. I know I wasn't your first choice, but for whatever reason, I'm the one who's got you. I love you and I'll do whatever I can to make you happy as long as I'm on this earth."

Jack never mentioned their conversation again after that night, and she never asked what tipped him off in the first place. Just how much he knew, she was uncertain, and she was terrified to find out. One thing was sure, Jack Blackwood was too much of a gentleman to put her in an uncomfortable position again. If nothing else, she loved him for that.

That was ten years ago. Abby had renewed her determination to be a good wife. She did everything she could to provide him a warm, inviting atmosphere to come home to at the end of the day. She prepared his favorite foods, got along with his mother, sat through Monday night football, and listened while he explained stats, plays, and Howard Cosell's dry sense of humor. She knew he appreciated her efforts. For the most part, their marriage was a good one. No one else knew—not even their four children—that her love for him was nothing more than one human being caring deeply for another. No matter how hard she tried, she couldn't make her eyes light up when he came into the room.

Now only Eric remained in the house, and he was off at school most of the time. Elaine, two years younger than Karen, had married a career Air Force man and was living on post in Germany. The family was fortunate to see her once a year, but she was happy with her life and nothing else mattered. Christy, twenty-five and still single, had earned a degree at Ohio University and was working as a paralegal at a law firm in Columbus. She was the only female paralegal in her firm, practically the only one in the whole city. Abby was pleased with the job she had done with her children, but now that they were gone and Eric had gone to work at Wyatt's, she began to wonder what she was going to do with the remaining years of her life.

"You remind me of somebody," Barb said to Eric as he crumpled his napkin and stuffed it into his paper cup.

Eric smiled at her and slid off the stool at the lunch counter. It was the first week of summer break, his first day back to work at Wyatt's Drugstore, and his lunch break was over. "Let me guess, Sean Connery."

"You wish." She stuck out her tongue and pressed it to her top lip as she stared at him. "Seriously, every time I look at you I think I should know who it is. It's been driving me crazy all morning."

"Well, when you figure it out, let me know." He turned toward the stockroom.

"I know who he looks like—too much like."

He turned back and saw Paige Trotter leaning against the outer edge of the counter, her arms folded over her chest.

"Okay, wise guy, who?" Barb demanded.

"Oh, no, you can figure it out for yourself. But it's more than just a resemblance. He looks exactly like someone in this town." The measuring gaze she directed at him made the hair rise up on the back of Eric's neck.

"You don't know what you're talking about," Barb countered. "If you did, you'd let us know so we could make our own judgment."

Paige turned her attention to Barb. "You mark my words the truth'll come out one of these days and set this town on its ear." She turned and stalked back to her customary position behind the register.

Barb watched her walk away and then huffed in annoyance, "Don't let her bother you, Eric. She likes getting under everybody's skin."

Eric nodded and started for the stockroom. The rest of the

afternoon he couldn't get Paige's words or knowing look out of his head. What did she mean by 'the truth will set the town on its ear'? What truth was she talking about? He wanted to think Barb was right, and Paige was just being her usual vindictive self, but something about her expression told him there was more to her words than her usual spitefulness.

# Chapter Ten

Jamie eased into her second year at school much smoother than the first. Now that she was an upperclassman, she was permitted a car on campus. It would make life so much easier. No more hassling Grandma Cory or Uncle Justin and Aunt Marty whenever she wanted a ride home. Of course, with access to her own car, she no longer had an excuse to see Eric as often. They had no classes together, and she didn't need him to drive her around. She couldn't help worrying about being replaced as his study partner by someone smarter and prettier than her.

Why did she even care? Her happiness didn't hinge on Eric Blackwood, the only man on campus who'd sworn off dating and relationships.

At the beginning of last year, she had expected Jason to help ease her into collegiate life. Much of her anger at him for going to Stanford had been fueled by the fact that he wouldn't be here to depend on. Now that she'd survived her first year of college on her own, she wondered if he had been nothing more than a security blanket. She hadn't spoken to him in nine months. She still thought about him, but not in the way she once did. When did she stop thinking of him as her boyfriend on the other side of the continent? When had her heart stopped aching with the need to hear his voice? Was she finally over him? Had the change been so subtle, she hadn't seen it happening?

Where did that leave her and Eric? Had he taken Jason's place as her security blanket? She had to admit, her first year of college had been a lot more fun having spent so much time with him. What did that say about her? Was she one of those women who wouldn't be fulfilled without a man by her side? She hoped not.

Just like last year, her roommate, Robin Lamphear, wasn't in the room when she arrived. She questioned the wisdom long and hard of sharing a room with Robin again. At times, Robin got on her nerves, and she thought their personalities clashed more than meshed. But they had learned to work through most of their differences or live with them. That was the whole point of dorm life.

They even attended a chapel service together last spring, but Robin still wouldn't commit to a belief or disbelief in God. She listened as Jamie talked occasionally about her faith, but expressed no interest in changing her own life. Jamie figured if nothing else, her life might influence the girl, however subtly.

Jamie stayed busy in her room, unpacking and rearranging to make maximum use of the limited space. By six p.m. she finished doing everything she could without Robin there to help. She'd been working for four hours. Just like last year, Robin probably wouldn't show up until Sunday evening, knowing the hardest part of the work would be completed. Jamie checked her irritation. That's how Robin was, and she really didn't mind the extra work. This way, she got things arranged her way, and Robin would have to deal with it.

A tapping sounded at the open door. She looked up to see Eric sticking his head inside the room. Her heart did a weird little flip flop in her chest. Good grief! She'd just seen him the other day at work.

"Looks like you've been busy," he said, looking around.

"Yeah, I'm just finishing up. How long have you been here?"

He stepped the rest of the way into the room, "Since early this morning. I've got my own room this year, and it took me about fifteen minutes to unpack."

"Men," Jamie said with an exaggerated lift of her brow.

"What can I say, we're uncomplicated. I'm on my way to the park for the big welcoming barbecue. Want to come?"

As if on cue, Jamie's stomach roared to life. She winced and put her hand over her stomach. "I'd love to. I'm hungrier than I realized."

Around ten-thirty, Eric walked Jamie back upstairs to her room. As expected, Robin's side of the room was still untouched. Jamie was tired and happy from the evening of activities. She and Eric had pitched horseshoes against some other teams and participated in a three-legged race and egg toss. Eric's athleticism made up for her stumbling attempts and they made it to the final eliminations of most of the games in which they competed. She didn't notice the September evening getting steadily cooler until Eric took hold of her arm to steer her in the direction of the barbecue pit.

"You're freezing," he'd said, surprised. "Let's get warmed up and eat another hot dog, then I'll walk you back."

She enjoyed the touch of his hand on her arm and wished the evening didn't have to end. But this was Eric; to him she was a friend, another sister he needed to take care of and keep in out of the cold. She nodded up at him in agreement. If only she didn't find him so attractive. They stood near the barbecue pit where it was warm and ate their juicy hot dogs before finally heading back to Jamie's dorm. The walk was only five minutes, and they spoke little.

"Thanks for coming up here to get me," Jamie said as she fumbled with the lock in her door. "I never would have found you in the crowd if I'd gone by myself. I can't believe so many people are on campus already."

"Too bad your roommate hasn't shown up yet. She missed all the fun." He took the key out of her hand and slid it into the lock. Jamie stared at the back of his head as he jiggled it back and forth. So, he wished Robin was here. Is that why he came up here in the first place, hoping he could take Robin to the barbecue instead of her?

The key turned in the lock, and the door swung open. "There you go; your home for the next nine months." He smiled down at her, his hand extended. It took a moment for her to realize he was waiting for her to take the key.

"Oh, thanks." She slipped the key into her jeans pocket and stepped inside the room. "Don't know what I'd do without you."

"I'm sure you'd manage." Eric leaned his shoulder against the doorjamb.

What was he waiting for? Was he hoping Robin would magically appear? Had he been thinking of her all summer while he worked with Jamie at the drugstore? He'd never mentioned her, but why would he? He was too polite to risk hurting Jamie's feelings by asking about her roommate. Of course, he didn't owe her anything. They were just friends; if he wanted to pursue a relationship with someone he didn't need to clear it with her first—but Robin of all people?

*Easy, Jamie,* she scolded herself. *You have no right to be jealous.*

Eric straightened up and blew out a puff of air. "Well, I guess I'll see you around, Jamie. I had fun tonight." He looked over her shoulder and then down at his shoes. Why was he stalling? Robin wasn't coming.

"So did I Eric," she responded. "Would you like to get together for lunch or something tomorrow? Robin will probably be here by then."

"Oh, yeah, sure, that'd be great, whatever you want."

"Okay. See you tomorrow around twelve-thirty." She slowly pushed the door shut, and he stepped back out of the way. The door closed and Jamie leaned her shoulder against it. What a rotten end to a perfect evening.

Eric stared at the closed door and pushed a shock of dark hair away from his forehead. *Smooth move, pal, you're a real lady killer. You couldn't even manage a good night kiss,* he thought as he thrust his hands deep into his pockets and moved off toward the stairwell.

Jamie didn't see a lot of Eric—or anyone else for that matter—for the next few weeks. One of her classes had been cancelled before it even began and another wasn't what she'd hoped. She tried to secure a position at the campus health clinic, but couldn't get in touch with the proper supervisors. Robin was in and out of their room with barely a word. She seemed more focused on her classes this year, more determined to prove what she could do to her parents and herself. Jamie often wondered when she disappeared for hours at a time, claiming she had to study, if there wasn't a love interest in her life—a real one this time, not like the loud, beer swilling boys she hung around last year.

Jamie couldn't help feeling a little anxious every time the door slammed shut behind Robin. If there was indeed a mystery man in her life, why didn't she discuss him? Was it someone she knew Jamie wouldn't approve of or would the discovery of his identity hurt her?

While Jamie had always insisted she and Eric were nothing more than friends, Robin suspected it went deeper than that. Was he the reason Robin wasn't keeping her up to date on her personal life?

Jamie told herself she didn't care if Eric liked Robin or anyone else for that matter. She'd made her own decision to steer clear of every young man who looked her way since coming to campus last fall. She wasn't interested in a relationship. She'd had enough of that with Jason. Jason—had he finally moved on, completely over her by now accepting the fact that their long distance relationship would never work?

Eric, on the other hand, would never be anything more than a friend, an old study partner who helped her survive Calculus. He had done nothing to make her think he wanted more, even if she did. He was free to do what he wanted. She should be happy for him if he'd found a soul mate in Robin. He turned his love life over to God years ago, and if God decided Robin was suited for him, who was she to disagree?

Robin entered their dorm room the evening before their first three-day weekend, her usually animated features, drawn and sullen.

Jamie looked up from her desk and frowned. "Robin, what's the matter?"

Robin tried to pull the corners of her mouth into a smile, but gave up almost instantly. "Only everything that could be the matter," she sounded dangerously close to tears for the first time since Jamie had known her. "I just called home."

Jamie dropped her pencil onto her open book and stood up. She leaned her hips against the edge of the desk. "Is everything all right?"

Robin shook her head without speaking, and her long blonde hair fell across her face. She moved to her own bed and sat down. She removed the pillow from under the comforter and hugged it to her chest. Jamie left the desk and sat down next to her.

"My parents are getting a divorce."

"Oh, Robin, no," even as she expressed her sympathy, Jamie reviewed the scant information she had about Robin's family. She thought the Lamphears were already divorced. Back when they first met, Robin had mentioned her dad's girlfriend, Becky or somebody.

Robin launched into an explanation before Jamie could ask for clarification. "Mom and Dad got back together over the summer. Dad moved back into the house with us, and they're trying to work things out. That's why I've been studying so much. I wanted to give them one less thing to worry about. But I guess it didn't matter.

"Apparently—I just found out anyway—Dad moved back home because Becky had kicked him out, and he didn't have anywhere else to go. Then she decides she wants him back. She even wants to get married this time. For the last month or so, Dad's been seeing Becky behind Mom's back—*again*. He's a prince, my old man."

"Robin, I'm so sorry." Jamie wished she could think of something more helpful to say.

"I guess he's tired of going back and forth between Mom and Becky. He's made his decision." Robin sniffed and wiped her nose on the corner of the pillow. "And it's not us."

"Oh, Robin," Jamie sympathized.

"Becky has ruined our family. I hate her. If I could get my hands on her right now, I'd hit her in the mouth."

Jamie sat quietly as the other girl took out her anger on her pillow. She was ashamed of herself. All this time, she'd been secretly accusing Robin of seeing Eric, when all she wanted to do was get good grades to please her parents. Now their marriage was falling apart because two people couldn't respect a man's wedding vows.

"I'm moving back home after this quarter," Robin announced.

"You are?"

"Yeah, Mom wants me to stay here, but she's no good alone. My sister's up there, but she's got her own family and her own problems. If everything settles down, I can always take classes at a city college."

Jamie put her arm around Robin's shoulders and squeezed. "This is really rotten. I feel so bad for you."

Robin turned imploring eyes on her. "Could you do me a favor, Jamie?"

"Sure, anything," Jamie said around the lump in her throat.

"Will you pray? Not necessarily for Mom and Dad, I don't think even God could put the two of them back together, but for me. I'm so mad at Dad right now I think I hate him more than I hate Becky. I mean, how could he do something so rotten to Mom, me, and my sister?"

Jamie understood Robin's feelings completely, having gone through the same thing herself. She put her other arm around Robin and pulled her against her. "Sure I will."

Now that Jamie had her own car on campus and didn't need to depend on him for rides home, Eric was out of excuses to see her. He hadn't realized how much he looked forward to her company until the ball games, car rides, and study dates came to an end. He couldn't do anything about it now. He was the one who had opened his mouth and made a big deal about not dating. He didn't have time for a relationship, he told her. He couldn't change everything mid-stream without looking like a jerk.

From the looks of things, Jamie had no problem with the situation the way it was. A part time job at an electrical supply company that helped pay his share of the rent on his apartment, forced him to miss every football game but two. Both times he invited her, she had readily accepted. Afterwards, she made no demands. She expected nothing more than friendship, and someone to sit next to in the student section at the stadium.

She was apparently happy with their relationship. He didn't know how much longer he could maintain an aloof exterior.

Jamie leaned as far as she could into the wire cage, scooped up the fat, golden-haired puppy, and clutched it to her chest. "Eric, look!" she squealed. "Isn't he adorable?"

"I think he's a she, and *she* costs a hundred dollars."

She raised the puppy to her face. "She's still adorable, no matter what she costs." The yellow puppy let out a plaintive whimper and wiggled in Jamie's hands, trying to get closer to her face. A tiny, rough pink tongue flicked out of its mouth and lapped against her nose. "Oh, Cassie would love her, don't you think? I wonder how mad Grandma Cory would be if I took her home for Christmas."

"She'd be furious, and you know it."

A smiling clerk appeared at Jamie's side. "Haven't you totally fallen in love?"

"No," Eric answered before Jamie could say a word. "We're just looking."

Jamie cuddled the puppy closer for a final hug. A puppy was not a spur of the moment gift even if the recipient would love it. Cassie did not currently have the time or inclination to go through the hassle of properly caring for a puppy. And more importantly, Grandma Cory would kill her if she brought home a puppy without asking, especially one she had to pay for when there were dogs listed in the newspaper every week people were giving away.

The store clerk wasn't dissuaded by Eric's negative reaction. She could see the enthusiasm in Jamie's face. "She's a Labrador Retriever," she said, taking the puppy out of Jamie's arms. "They make excellent pets—and such fun Christmas presents. They love everybody and are so intelligent. They do have lots of energy though, and require lots of space to run around. Do you live here in the city?"

"No," Jamie offered, ignoring the look of warning Eric directed at her. "I live on a farm."

The saleswoman squealed with delight. "Oh, that's perfect. These little sweeties are designed for the country. She'll end up weighing about fifty pounds. She's eight weeks old and the last of her litter. She'll be gone by the end of the day."

"Oh, no," Jamie put her hands on either side of the puppy's face. "What a cutie you are."

"Yeah, cute," Eric said as he took hold of her elbow. "Come on, Jamie, time to go. You heard the lady, she'll find a perfect home by the end of the day and they'll all live happily ever after."

Jamie dropped her hands to her side. "Yeah, I guess."

The salesclerk wasn't ready to say good-bye to a sale. She pushed the puppy toward Eric. "Are you sure you want to pass this one up, sir? Your girlfriend is already in love. Wouldn't she be darling under the Christmas tree with a big red bow around her neck?"

Eric smiled disarmingly and pulled Jamie against him, "Which one, my girlfriend or the puppy?"

"Oh, um, well…either one, I guess," the salesclerk tittered nervously.

Eric turned Jamie away from the pen and pushed her toward the door.

"Bye, sweetie," she said, waving to the puppy over her shoulder as Eric ushered her out of the pet store.

"You shouldn't have teased that woman," she chastened. "She probably thought you were too cheap to buy that puppy."

"Well, she could have asked me. She shouldn't be playing on people's emotions just to move dogs. That's how they end up in homes that aren't suited for them."

"I know, but you should have set her straight that we weren't a couple."

"It was none of her business. Besides, maybe I liked her thinking it." He winked and held her close for another fraction of a second before releasing her.

Jamie looked into his eyes before he looked away, trying to decipher what he was doing. Was he serious or just teasing her the way he had teased the clerk? She hadn't really minded the feel of his muscular arm around her shoulders or the smell of his cologne lingering on her sweater.

He caught her looking at him and gave her a warm smile. She returned the smile and turned her gaze back to the interior of the mall, sighing contentedly. She was glad she came; glad he invited her on this shopping trip with his parents. This was the last weekend before Christmas, and it seemed like all of southern Ohio was at the malls taking advantage of last minute bargains. It wasn't a date; Eric didn't date, she reminded herself. And they weren't a couple. She remembered the feel of his arm around her and shivered. She wondered what it would be like to be his girlfriend, his strong arms around her as he waltzed her around a dance floor. No, he didn't dance either. He didn't do anything that might lead him into temptation.

She respected him, but at the same time, almost wished he didn't have such strong moral fiber.

She felt his hand on the small of her back. She looked up to see him motioning to another store across the mall's main thoroughfare. It took a moment to focus on what he was pointing at and not his hand resting on the small of her back.

Her eyes followed the direction of his pointing finger, and she saw a huge train display set up outside a cigar and tobacco store. "How beautiful!" she gasped. Immediately they started toward the exhibit, Eric's hand still fastened to her back.

The train was moving through a mountain range that reached above Jamie's head. There was a stream, a working waterfall, snow-capped pine trees, plastic wildlife situated randomly throughout the scene, and real nature sounds that could be heard over the train's whistle. They craned their necks for a better view from the back of the crowd as they inched their way forward.

Although fascinated by the train and its mountain ascent, Jamie was too aware of the seemingly scorching heat radiating from Eric's hand. It was the first time he had maintained any kind of physical contact with her. Was he just being friendly or did he enjoy the contact as much as she? *Please move your hand,* she silently begged. *I can't think straight with you touching me like that.* But at the same time, she prayed he would keep it where it was.

Eric leaned in close and said into her ear over the noise of the train's whistle and other shoppers. "Wouldn't it be cool to be on that train right now riding through the mountains?"

She nodded, "Um."

"I've always wanted to take a train ride through Canada. We'll have to do that someday."

She turned away from the exhibit to study his face, but he wasn't looking at her anymore. He was craning his neck to watch as the train disappeared around a huge, plastic mountain. Evidently his casual comment was just that and not some kind of invitation. They slowly moved to the edge of the crowd to make room for other shoppers waiting to enjoy the exhibit.

"Would the two lovebirds care to sign up for a free giveaway?" A small portly man sat behind a card table at the edge of the display, a large cardboard box with a hole cut in the top in front of him.

Lovebirds? Jamie glanced over her shoulder to see who he was talking about.

"The store is having a drawing for a Christmas gift basket of sausages and cheeses," the man explained, looking directly at her and Eric. "No purchase necessary."

"Sure." Eric's hand dropped from its position on Jamie's back, and he took the pencil offered to him. He filled in the blanks with his nearly illegible script, folded the paper in half and dropped it into the box. "Thanks," he said to the man as he took Jamie's hand and led her away from the table.

As they walked, he looked down at her, smiling his gorgeous smile, his thick dark hair standing unruly all over his head, giving him a deliciously disheveled look. She longed to reach up and push it back into place.

"We'd better get out of this place," he said, his dark blue eyes twinkling.

"Why?" she asked absently, still imagining her fingers in his hair.

"Everybody here seems to think we're in love."

Jamie felt a blush creep into her cheeks. She opened her mouth to respond, but couldn't think of the first thing to say.

The teasing grin on his face faded as his gaze intensified. Without a word of warning he leaned forward and kissed her. Jamie hoped the sound of the gasp that escaped her lips couldn't be heard over the hustle and bustle around them. Just as quickly, he drew back and stared down at her. She didn't know what to think.

She froze, one hand resting lightly on his arm. The winter sun shone down through the glass ceiling and dazzled her eyes, making it hard to see his face. She felt more than saw him take her free hand and bring it to his mouth. She focused on his lips against her hand, and the sunspots dancing in her eyes disappeared. When he lowered her hand and moved in to kiss her again, she was ready. She tilted her head, closed her eyes against the bright sun and the crowd bustling around them, and felt his soft lips against hers.

When he pulled away, there was no mistaking the flush on his cheeks. He looked as surprised as she was. A silence lengthened between them. He looked past her into the crowd.

Jamie waited for him to say something. She didn't want to be the first to speak. She wouldn't know what to say anyway.

When he looked back, the seriousness in his deep blue eyes unnerved her. Still holding onto her hand, he led her to a recessed area in the middle of the floor, lined with benches and dominated by a large artificial Christmas tree. She was barely aware of her feet touching the floor. His kiss had left her delirious and breathless. Eric sat down on the bench, angled so he was facing her.

"Jamie," His voice cracked, and he cleared his throat and began again. "I'm sorry. I shouldn't have kissed you."

"Oh, I…" her voice trailed off. Of course, she knew it was too good to be true. It had been a mistake on his part, an impulse he regretted, a friendly gesture she misinterpreted; but what about the kiss of her hand? It was the most magical, romantic thing that had ever happened to her. She could still feel the warmth of his mouth on her fingers. Had it meant nothing to him? Maybe something he'd seen in a movie and thought would be a cool gesture, only to be disappointed?

"I didn't mean to give you the wrong idea."

She wondered if the sound of her heart crashing to her feet was as audible to him as it was to her. She forced a trembling smile.

"Oh, no, Eric, it's all right—no big deal," she added flippantly.

"It was to me," he said, sounding hurt. "That's why I shouldn't have acted so impulsively right here in front of everyone."

She wished he would stop talking. An explanation would only add insult to injury. The day had been perfect up to this point. The hour-long ride through the snow covered countryside from Jenna's Creek to the city, talking quietly in the back seat of his parents' car. The shops lit up for the holidays; children laughing and pushing in excitement to get into a shop before their friends; the excitement of simply being here with Eric; lunch on the pavilion overlooking the streaming crowds below them. Now instead of going home to relive every wonderful moment in the privacy of her own bedroom, she would be tortured with the memory of a kiss he regretted having given her.

"I wanted our first kiss to be special," he went on, oblivious to her misery. "I've been thinking about it for a long time; too long really. I'm sorry."

What was he talking about? Was he sorry about the kiss, or sorry he had taken so long to get around to it?

"I didn't mean for it to be like that," he continued. "But you were standing there, those brown eyes of yours staring right through me. Your hair all messed up from nuzzling that puppy."

Jamie instinctively reached up to smooth it into place.

Eric caught her hand. "And that mouth," he said in a throaty whisper. "I haven't been able to take my eyes off it all day, just watching you talk, watching you laugh. I couldn't wait one more minute. I had to kiss you. I know I should have—"

"Eric?"

"What?"

"Shut up and kiss me again."

All the way home in the car, Jamie and Eric rode in the back seat with their hands clasped across the space between them. Little was said. Jamie was so happy, she could barely think clearly, let alone speak. Anything she said would come out sounding stupid especially since the only thing on her mind was the kisses they shared in the middle of the shopping mall. She certainly couldn't talk about that, not with his parents sitting in the front seat, blissfully unaware of the fire their son had ignited inside her. She doubted even Eric knew what effect his kisses had had. He was so strong in his convictions; he would be shocked and disappointed to know how weak she was at this very minute, sitting only twelve inches away from him, the memory of his lips still burning on hers.

When they pulled into the Blackwood's driveway, Eric told his mom and dad he was driving Jamie home and then escorted her from their car to his. Neither of them spoke until they were nearly out of town.

Eric began the conversation hesitantly; both hands on the steering wheel, staring straight ahead. "Jamie, I've never felt this way about any other girl."

"I know," she whispered, still reliving the kiss and wishing her thoughts were as pure as his.

"I never went looking for a relationship. I figured I'd leave all that up to God." He paused and glanced over at her before going on. "I knew He would send someone to me when the time was right."

"I know." She needed to repent immediately. If Eric didn't know the effect his kisses had, the good Lord did.

He glanced from the road to her. He took his right hand off the steering wheel and reached for hers. "Do you realize our relationship has changed forever?"

"I think so."

"You're not the first girl I've ever kissed." He smiled at her in the dash light. "But you're the first one I *really* wanted to kiss—and I mean *really*. I guess what I'm trying to say is…"

His voice trailed off, and Jamie found she was holding her breath in anticipation. Just what was he saying? Even she knew, in all her naïveté that a kiss to most guys was simply a prelude to something more intimate. If you let them steal a kiss, their brains automatically began calculating how much farther you were willing to go. But with Eric, everything was different; he didn't throw his kisses around. She had wanted him to kiss her for the longest time and didn't even realize it until it happened.

"Jamie, you're the most special person I've ever met. I feel so comfortable with you." He let go of her hand and gripped the steering wheel again. He let out an anguished sigh and stared blindly out the windshield.

She had no idea what he was trying to say. If she could only make it easier for him, "Eric, I had a wonderful time today. I was so excited when you invited me to go. Even though I knew it wasn't a date, I couldn't help kind of wishing it was."

His head snapped around to look at her, "Really?"

She gulped, hoping she wasn't saying too much. "Yes. Our friendship means everything to me. If that's all you ever wanted, it would be all right with me."

The sign to Betterman Road materialized in the headlights and he turned on the signal for a right turn. "I'm so glad to hear you say that."

Jamie tried to quell the disappointment rising up inside her. So he was perfectly happy with the way things were. Would there never be anything more between them? But she couldn't blame him. She said a permanent friendship was fine with her. She was such a hypocrite.

The inside of the car was quiet as Eric pulled into the driveway and killed the engine. Jamie looked at the slightly lopsided farmhouse, several windows illuminated as her family went about their usual Saturday evening routine. She could picture Grandpa Harlan seated in his sagging recliner watching Barnaby Jones. Grandma Cory was probably in the kitchen, rooting around in the deep freeze for a cut of meat to lie out to thaw for tomorrow's Sunday dinner. She imagined Cassie in her room listening to records and looking through a fashion magazine, wishing Grandma Cory considered her mature enough to wear what everybody else on the planet her age was wearing.

Eric turned his body toward hers under the steering wheel. Jamie erased any signs of discontent from her face and faced him. Once more he reached for her hand, and she wondered how long it would take for him to say goodnight so she could climb out of the car and get away from him. She smiled into his expressive eyes and shuddered inwardly. She *was* a hypocrite, a liar. She didn't want to be his friend. She wanted to be…. She hoped the tears would wait until she was alone.

*Oh, God, he said I'm special. He's never felt this way about anyone before. What does that mean? What does he want? Lord, I can't take this. I don't want to be his friend. If he doesn't feel the same way I do, make him go away. Give him a scholarship to Stanford, too, so I'll never have to see his face again.*

"Jamie, you're going to think I'm the biggest idiot," he said, the sound of his voice reminding her she wasn't paying attention, "after all my talk about not dating and finishing my education before I get into a relationship; then I go and do something without thinking it through." He reached out and touched her cheek.

She nearly cringed. *No, don't break it to me gently. You're only making it worse. Just spill it. Let's get this over with.*

"I love you."

Jamie's jaw dropped. Her ears were playing tricks on her. She wanted to hear those three words so desperately, she was hallucinating. She'd read how the human psyche could convince a person of something, simply because of an intense desire for it to be true. She read a story once of a woman whose stomach swelled, and she suffered actual contractions simply because she couldn't accept the doctor's diagnosis that she would never have a baby.

"Jamie?"

Then again, it did look like his lips said what her ears heard. "Oh, Eric," she croaked out, tears dangerously close to the surface.

He traced her jaw line with his index finger. "I didn't plan on this happening," he hurried on. "I didn't think about falling in love at all. Like I said, I left all this romance stuff up to the Lord." His gaze drifted to the darkened shape of the barn out the passenger window. He removed his hand from her face and ran it through his tousled hair. He drew a ragged breath and forced his gaze back to her. "All I know is I've been trying to talk myself out of the way I feel about you for a long time. I can't do it anymore. I want to start spending time together as a couple, pursuing this change in our relationship. But if all you want is to stay friends, I'm willing to do that too."

"Eric, I—"

"I know the way I feel about you," he continued. "I'm hoping you feel the same about me, but even if you don't, that doesn't change my feelings. I'm ready for a change. If you're not, I'm sorry. In fact, I'll be totally torn up, but that's up to you. Either way, I—"

She put her finger on his mouth. "Eric, I understand." The curve of his mouth, the unruly shock of dark hair hanging loosely across his forehead, the fragile intensity in his deep blue eyes, all worked together like a magnet to draw her to him. She leaned forward and kissed him tenderly. He put his arms around her and pulled her close.

Finally they drew apart and she put her hand on the door handle, not taking her eyes off his. "I love you, too." She climbed out of the car and gave him a little wave of her hand. He was still watching her, speechless, as she hurried around the house to the back door. The sooner she was safely out of his sight, the better off her heart would be. She entered the kitchen, her tread light on the worn linoleum, her heart dancing in her chest. Eric Blackwood loved her. How had it happened? How could she be so blessed?

# Chapter Eleven

"Dad, I wanted to talk to you about something before I mention it to Mom."

Jack Blackwood glanced away from the thin ribbon of highway, barely visible between two dingy snow banks, to look at his son. Nearly every day during the month of February, snow had fallen on the southern Ohio countryside. Visibility was rotten, even when the snow wasn't falling. Traffic snarled along even the best maintained highways. Local schools had cancelled classes eight times this month alone. One in need of a tow truck could anticipate a long, frustrating wait. Yet out here in the country, it was easy to forget the inconveniences of driving under a Level II snow emergency. Beyond the edge of the roadways where county crews plowed the grimy, salt-covered snow nearly as high as the hood of Jack's slow-moving pickup truck, the fields were white, pristine, and unmarred by tracks and diesel fumes. The trees stood against the sparkling whiteness like shimmering confections on a cake, glazed with spun sugar by an omniscient baker.

Jack let off the gas and steadied the wheel as the truck approached a potentially dangerous spot where snow had drifted across the highway. He suspected Eric had intentionally chosen this particular moment to speak. Jack would be too focused on the driving hazards to yell at him about whatever he may have done wrong.

This wasn't the first time Eric used a moment in the car when it was just the two of them to spring some big announcement or broach an uncomfortable subject. Years before, the concerns troubling the boy were related to not getting enough playing time on the little league ball field; how his pitching arm wasn't delivering what the coach expected; how he and Tommy Wilson were slacking off in English class—a class they both hated—and now he feared he would be bringing home a C on his report card. Eric was self-conscious about his voice changing later than the other boys; a group of girls giggling and whispering when he walked past; taking showers in gym class; or what the other fellows might say about his naked body.

As time went by, his problems became increasingly uncomfortable for Jack. The interior of the family car was privy to father-son discussions about girls and the derogatory manner in which most of the other boys regarded them. They discussed hormones, sex, and the importance of waiting until marriage.

"The Bible hasn't laid out these rules to deprive you of having fun," Jack had explained when Eric was about fifteen. "They're common sense, practical guidelines to protect you from yourself. When you let your flesh tell you what to do, not only are you falling into sin, but you are also opening yourself up to hurt and anger later. You are sinning against your own body because sexual sin will haunt you the rest of your life. In health class they've warned you all about sexually transmitted diseases and how an unplanned pregnancy can ruin your plans for your future. What they don't bother telling you is the ramifications of acting on your hormones, and the guilt and feelings of worthlessness that go along with it. You're worth more than throwing yourself away on a girl you may not be able to stand the sight of tomorrow.

"The Bible says the two will become one flesh. You will be forever linked with this person, whether you see her again or not. I know your buddies are telling you that in order to prove yourself as a man you need to score with as many girls as possible. Let me tell you, Son, it takes more of a man to exercise self-control and wait until the right girl comes along and marries you. Then you will have a relationship with one person that can never be sullied by the world's ideas of fun."

Eric had seemed to understand that day. He didn't ask many more questions on abstinence, and Jack could see the young man endeavored to live by Biblical principals. He didn't date and when he did go out with friends, he seldom strayed from a select group from their church. Usually they went to ball games, dances, and other public places for entertainment, avoiding intimate locations that perpetuated the problem.

Yes, many of Jack's most fulfilling moments as a parent had taken place in this battered pick-up. He supposed the truck's interior provided a non-threatening atmosphere for Eric. He didn't have to look directly into his father's eyes during an uncomfortable revelation. Jack couldn't respond as he might at home since his main focus was keeping the car on the road. And there was no risk of the exchange being overheard by any of the women in their house.

Now as always, Jack didn't speak; Eric would talk when he was ready.

And, like always, Eric was anxious to have everything out in the open. "I'm going to ask Jamie to marry me," he blurted out.

Jack felt like he'd been punched in the gut. He had learned over the years that these father-son chats could reveal anything, but he wasn't prepared for this, even though in retrospect he should have seen it coming. His first instinct was to say; "This is going to kill your mother." But he didn't. He wanted to point out all the reasons why it was a crazy idea. Eric was too young for such serious contemplations; he and Jamie needed to finish school; there was plenty of time for marriage later, much later; they had no money and no place to live.

He decided to leave those arguments for Abby. "You are?" he said casually.

Eric exhaled, visibly relieved he wouldn't get a lecture; at least not now. A huge, first-time-in-love grin spread across his face. "Yes, I've been thinking about it for a long time. It's all I think about. Now, I know what you're thinking, Dad. You're thinking I don't know her well enough, that we're too young to get married."

"I didn't say that," Jack reminded him.

Eric continued without missing a beat. This talk was obviously well rehearsed. "Well, I do know her, Dad. I know her better than anyone I ever met, and she knows me. I don't have to play mind games with her. For the first time in my life, I can be myself. I can say what I want to say, and she really understands."

"That's a wonderful thing to have with someone," Jack said. "Some people go their whole lives and never find it."

"So you understand?" Eric asked hopefully. At his earnest plea, Jack's heart swelled with such love he wanted to pull the car over and pull the boy into his arms. "You're not going to give me any grief? You're not going to try and talk me out of it?"

"Would it do any good?"

The grin was back on Eric's face. "Nah, it's too late for that."

Jack chuckled and wagged his head from side to side. "I kind of figured as much. Anyway, you'll get enough of a lecture from your mother."

The excitement in Eric's eyes dimmed. "You'll help me explain it to her, won't you, Dad? You guys were young when you got married, not any older than I am now, and you did fine. We will too. I promise you that. I want to make her happy..."

Jack only half listened as his son talked on about how he planned to save enough money for a wedding with still another year left of school. All he could think about was Abby, and how he had wanted to make her happy too. Eric did have an advantage over his old man. At least Jamie loved him in return, not out of duty or obligation, but just because she did. That's all they needed for the foundation of a successful marriage, of course, he couldn't tell him that. He couldn't tell Eric his mother had never loved him like he hoped Jamie would love her future husband. He couldn't tell Eric he was pretty sure he wasn't even his real father.

Abby took Eric's news just as they feared she would.

"You're too young," she roared, her face red and eyes flashing.

"I'm twenty-one years old."

"Don't tell me how old you are, young man. I think I know how old my own son is. Whatever happened to that responsible young man who said he wasn't having anything to do with women until he finished school?"

"Mom, I didn't exactly say that. When I told you I wasn't pursuing a romantic relationship, it was because I had turned the whole situation over to God. If you remember, I asked you to pray about it like I was. I prayed that God would send me the right woman when the time was right."

"And I suppose you think the right time is now."

Eric straightened his shoulders and lifted his chin. "Yes, I do. This isn't a whim, Mom. I've been thinking about it for a long time, and praying. I'm not acting on my own. I truly believe God brought the two of us together. When I first realized I was in love with Jamie, it scared me half to death. Believe me, I wasn't expecting it." The dreamy, head-over-heels look was back on his face. "Don't you think it's cool that she and I went to school together for twelve years and never even looked at each other twice; now all of a sudden, I'm crazy over her—it has to be God working."

"Oh, Eric, that's ridiculous. You don't know God's plans. You're too young, anything could change."

"Abby!" Jack broke in, shooting her a warning look.

Abby didn't bother turning around to acknowledge Jack's voice. Eric's jaw was set in a hard line. His steely blue eyes pierced hers, and she knew he was about to lash out in anger at her. Something he'd never done before. She didn't care. She wouldn't back down. She was right, and he was acting irrationally.

Jack hurried on before Eric had the chance to speak. "If Eric says he's been praying and seeking God in this matter, then we have to trust him. He has never acted impulsively, and we have to trust that it isn't what he's doing now."

Abby whirled around to face Jack. "I don't want to see him get hurt." She took a deep breath in an effort to bring her emotions under control and turned slowly back to Eric. "When are you planning this marriage? Even after you graduate, Jamie still has another year to go. Who do you think will be responsible for paying her tuition? Her husband, that's who, you can't afford that and an apartment. You don't even have a real job. What do you plan on doing about that? It seems to me like you haven't thought this through."

"She's on a scholarship," Eric explained. "And if things get tough, we'll move in here."

Abby's eyes widened even further. "Oh, no, you won't. You can get that idea out of your head right now. If you want a wife so bad, you can support her yourself without any help from your father and me."

Jack reached out and touched her shoulder, but Abby shrugged him off. "I'm against this marriage from the get-go, and I refuse to be the one to pay because you can't keep your hormones in check."

Eric's nostrils flared and his face turned red. "That has nothing to do with it. I can't believe you think that's what I'm doing."

"And I can't believe you think you're old enough to be making these kinds of decisions," Abby went on, undeterred. "Use your head for a change, why don't you? There's no way you can possibly know what you want to do with the rest of your life…" She railed and hollered a little longer before throwing her hands in the air and stomping upstairs to her bedroom.

Jack put a reassuring hand on Eric's trembling shoulder, gave him a don't-worry-I'll-talk-to-her look, and followed Abby upstairs.

"Don't threaten him, honey. You're just going to drive him away," he said upon entering the bedroom.

"I'm not threatening," she hissed. "I mean every word I say."

Jack sat down on the edge of the bed and took her hand. "No, you don't. You know as well as I do, you'll do anything you can to help him out, whether it's before or after he gets married."

She rose up on the bed to defend herself. "If he insists on going against our wishes—"

"Our wishes don't matter," Jack interjected. "He is twenty-one years old. If he was lucky enough to find the girl of his dreams already, I think we should be happy for him, and let him know we're here for him."

"I agree with that, Jack. But why can't he wait until they're both out of school and working somewhere so they have a little stability? That's all I'm asking. They can still get engaged, but they don't need to be in a big hurry to get married."

"Abby, wait a minute, they're in love and obviously desperate to be together. You've seen the way they look at each other. You can't expect them to put their emotions, or their hormones, on hold indefinitely. He's only acting on the natural desires God put in his heart. Remember what it was like to be young and in love..." His voice trailed off. No, of course she couldn't remember. She had never been in love, at least not with him.

Abby looked away too, probably having the same thoughts. Finally she spoke, "Why does he have to be in such an all-fired hurry? He hasn't had any experience with women. What could he possibly know about being a husband?"

"As much as the rest of us know when we become one."

"Jack, whose side are you on? You sound like you're actually pleased about this."

"Honey, this has nothing to do with choosing sides. I want Eric to be happy. And I think, as far as choices go, he couldn't have done better than Jamie."

Abby sighed. "I want him to be happy too, Jack, and I have nothing against Jamie. I'm just saying I don't want to see him make a mistake. What if he's acting in haste, doing something he'll regret later?"

*Like you did,* Jack wanted to ask.

"He'll be fine, honey," he said instead. "Trust your son. Trust the job you did raising him. You had the same fears with Karen and Elaine, and they turned out fine. Stop worrying."

"Fine," she grumbled, "but they are not moving in here."

Jack raised his eyebrows, wordlessly warning her against making statements that could come back to haunt her. Abby sank back against the pillows and threw one arm over her face. "Why me, Lord?" she moaned, but Jack heard the teasing in her voice.

# Chapter Twelve

Jamie pulled her hair away from her face and stared at her reflection in the dresser mirror. Spring break; while a few kids from school—very few since money, or the lack thereof was always a major consideration—were spending the next ten days on a beach somewhere in Florida, the possibility had never crossed her mind. She was where she wanted to be. In her room preparing to go to a softball game—a softball game of all things—to play on Eric's church team against some Methodists from the other side of town. And she couldn't wait to get there.

She stood up and studied her reflection in the mirror on her closet door. She smoothed her hands over the wrinkles of her red team shirt and smiled. She couldn't believe she was a member of a real softball team. She even enjoyed it, although she rode the pine seven innings out of nine. Two weekends ago she stopped a pop fly that had lost its momentum from getting past her in far, far, far right field, and managed to throw it to the shortstop just as the batter rounded second. Ignoring the loud pop in her shoulder and the pain that plagued her for the next two days, she had waved and talked trash like a real ball player. It was the highlight of her sports career.

Later at Gino's Pizzeria, Eric toasted her with his soda glass in front of everybody, giving her full credit for the win. Someone pointed out it was a 10-6 victory, but he insisted without her quick thinking and athletic prowess, they would have been defeated for sure.

Eric loved her. It had been four months since he first said the words, and she still couldn't believe it. But hadn't Jason said the same thing? And she had loved him in return, or she thought she had. *Oh, Lord, what's the difference in how I felt about Jason and the way I feel about Eric?* She prayed. *If I really loved Jason like I thought I did, why did I stop? How do I know I won't stop loving Eric or he won't stop loving me?*

She heard no audible answer. She'd been asking the same questions for four months, and still heard nothing. While she had no idea how Eric would feel about her five minutes from now, she didn't doubt she would always love him.

The weight of the tiny velvet box in the pocket of his jeans strained against his leg with each step he took toward the car. Eric reached into his pocket and pulled out the box before sliding into the car. He opened the tiny box with big, clumsy fingers and took one last look at the sparkling diamond before closing the box with an audible snap and slipping it under the seat. Jamie was going to go crazy. He couldn't wait to see her face.

His plan wasn't set in stone. He was going to give it to her tonight; he just wasn't sure when or how. The ring had been in his possession for a week now. He had gone over different scenarios in his head. He considered the bended knee route—it always worked in the movies—but that seemed overdone. He thought about dinner and candlelight at an expensive restaurant. The only problem with that idea was he had spent all his money on the ring. Somehow a proposal over a foot-long hot dog and a strawberry milkshake didn't scream romance and happily ever after.

He was sure he would know when the moment was right. Maybe after tonight's game. He imagined her running across the field to him, her face shining with victory and exertion and him thrusting the box out to her as she reached his side. She would look down, confused for a moment and then her eyes would light up when she realized…or he would wait until everyone had celebrated and high-fived one another and driven off in their own directions. Then when they were the last car in the parking lot overlooking the deserted field, he would take her right hand—or was it her left—look deep into her eyes, and tell her he loved her more than life itself…

Was he being stupid and immature like his mother implied? What if she said no? He had put so much into this; so much of himself; not just the enormous amount of money that might not seem like much to any other fellow, but in his heart it represented all the feelings he had for her. What if instead of the stunned elation he envisioned on her face, he saw terror, dismay, and a desperate desire to spare his feelings as she struggled for a gentle way to turn him down?

Eric felt a cold sweat break out on his forehead. He was going to be sick. Maybe he should wait a little longer; make sure she felt about him the same way he did about her. She loved him; he didn't doubt that, but maybe she wasn't ready to get married. She was near the top of her class in college. She had more plans for her future than just taking care of a husband and a house full of kids. What if he didn't fit into those plans? What if she saw him as a hindrance to the exciting career she had planned for herself?

His mother was right; he hadn't thought this through. He was rushing into something, letting his hormones and youthful enthusiasm propel him along.

He gave the steering wheel an angry slap and turned the key in the ignition. No, she wasn't right. He *had* thought this through. He loved Jamie and she loved him. He was young, but not so young he didn't know that. She was the one he wanted to spend the rest of his life waking up next to. If he couldn't have her beside him every day for as long as he had breath in his body, he didn't even want to think about the future. There was no way he could know if Jamie's feelings for him were as intense, but he had to take the chance and ask. If he didn't and she somehow got away from him, well, then he didn't know what he'd do.

He tried to forget the engagement ring under the seat and the fear of rejection sitting in his belly like a lead weight, and concentrate instead on the softball game ahead of him. They were playing the Methodist church from East Main Street. The congregation was a lot bigger and they had several older, more experienced players on the team. He and Ray Hallon had gone last week to watch them play against a church in Blanton. He shuddered as he recalled their big power hitter third baseman. He was a brute of a man, pushing forty Eric figured, a little big around the middle, but with a huge chest and arms that made up for any middle age spread. He could slam a ball across the fence without even leaning into the swing and then amble around the bases like he had all day—which of course he did. Against the Lutherans from Blanton, he batted in five guys during his three at bats, not including himself. If they didn't shut him down tonight and keep him from coming up to bat with the bases loaded, they'd suffer the same humiliating loss as the Lutherans.

Eric reminded himself this was just a game between brothers and sisters in Christ; that their power hitter was a pot-bellied deacon with five kids and a reputation for grilling the sweetest ribs at church picnics. They were all out here for a little fun, fellowship, and exercise. But Eric Blackwood liked to win. He was the starting pitcher, and it was his responsibility to keep the deacon from landing a swing, because if he did…well, it was as good as over.

Eric smiled. He loved competition. He knew Jamie only played deep, deep, deep right field to please him and spend time with him, doing something he loved. She did not share his enthusiasm for the game. She would rather sit on the bench and wave to him on the pitcher's mound whenever she caught his eye and cheer the loudest when he struck someone out. That proved she loved him. She wouldn't be here in the hot sun for some other Joe Schmo. He was doing the right thing. He smiled to himself. He would give her the ring when she ran in from outfield to the pitcher's mound to congratulate him. He would turn the team's victory into her moment in the spotlight. She could squeal and show all the other ladies and they would kiss her, and the guys would thump him on the back and call him "Old Man", and even the Methodists would be thrilled. It would be the most incredible moment in both their lives—unless she said no.

Ed, the Methodists' hulking power hitter, crushed Eric's hand in an earnest, vise-like handshake. "I was warned about you, young fella," he said with a grin. "I hear tell you're the hottest pitcher in the county."

Eric's eyes widened in surprise; this man had been warned about *him*. "Well, I've seen you swing," Eric said. "I doubt I've got anything that'll get past you."

"Don't be so sure." Ed loosened his grip on Eric's fingers and landed a playful punch on his shoulder that nearly drove him to his knees. "There's no way us old-timers can keep up with you young fellas. You'll take it easy on an old man, won't you, son?"

"Don't give me any of that old-timer stuff," Eric shot back. "I'm not letting my guard down on any of you for a minute."

Ed laughed and turned to another man in a blue Methodist team shirt. He put his hand on the man's arm, and together they eyed Eric. Ed opened his mouth to say something to his friend, probably a dig about the young, hotheaded pitcher. Before he could get any words out, a tiny girl ran out onto the field. "Daddy, Daddy." Ed looked down, surprised at the interruption. The game was due to start as soon as the umpire blew his whistle. Eric looked at the little girl and then at Ed. He'd seen men, even in the church league that put nothing in front of a game. It was hard to tell by looking at the big guy if he was simply startled by the interruption or about to blow his top over a game delay.

After his initial shock at her appearance on the diamond, Ed leaned over and opened his arms, "Hey, Chipmunk." The little girl leaped into his arms and threw her arms around his neck.

At that moment the umpire's whistle split the air. "Play ball."

Eric took his position on the pitcher's mound as Ed and his teammate headed for the dugout. "I wanted to give you a kiss for luck, Daddy," Eric heard the little girl say.

"You did? Well, thank you, Chipmunk, that's just what I needed." By this time they were too far away for Eric to hear the rest of the exchange. Both were still smiling and talking, the little girl perched on one thick forearm, her cherubic face suspended inches from Big Ed's. Eric watched them, a knot in his throat, until Ed handed the little girl to her mother in the stands.

Time to focus on the game, he told himself. Eric looked over at Vic taking his position on first base and nodded. He turned to make eye contact with Rudy and Bill on second and shortstop respectively. Sandy, Bill's wife was on third base, but she was busy adjusting the bill of her cap against the late afternoon sun's rays and didn't see Eric checking her position. Ray squatted behind home plate and gave Eric his first signal of the day. "I'm here and ready to go," the signal conveyed.

Eric stepped back into his pitching stance and waited for the Methodists' first batter to complete his practice swings. He was ready to play but more than anything he was ready to ask Jamie to be his wife. He wanted what Big Ed had; a smiling wife, a passel of kids, including a bright eyed little girl who ran out onto the field to give Daddy a good luck kiss.

It was well past time for Jack to be home from work. Abby covered his plate with aluminum foil and placed it in the oven. He was rarely late these days; they didn't need the overtime money like they had when the kids were little. The house was paid off after fifteen long years of keeping just ahead of the payments. The vehicles had no liens against either of them. Eric's tuition and everything associated with it had been paid for long before the need arose. Things had settled down in the Blackwood home. Jack talked of traveling in a few years after Eric moved out. Abby agreed, she always agreed. It was the least she could do after a lifetime of being a horrible wife.

She went to the window and looked out at the sedan sitting alone in the driveway. Jack's pick-up truck should pull into its usual spot behind it any minute. It should have been there two hours ago. Jack didn't drink—he never had—so she knew he hadn't stopped off somewhere to enjoy a cold one with his buddies as some husbands did. He always came straight home. She never had to remind him to mow the lawn or change the oil in her car. He rotated tires, changed furnace filters, and cleaned out eave spouts without her ever knowing the jobs needed to be done. Jack was stable, responsible, a good provider; so much more than she deserved.

Eight-thirty; Eric's ball game should be wrapping up soon. She had thought about going; she went to a lot of the games and always had a good time sitting with her church friends, cheering for the handsome, dark-haired young man on the pitcher's mound.

She wondered for a moment what had become of his intentions of proposing to Jamie Steele. He hadn't said anything more to her or Jack about it since his announcement in February. It was now April—was he still making plans? Had he decided it was easier to keep his nosy, big-mouthed mother out of the loop and let her find out the same time as everyone else?

She shouldn't have yelled at him that day. She shouldn't have insinuated that he was only getting married because he could no longer control his animal instincts. It hadn't been fair, but she was angry and scared.

*Please don't let him make a mistake, Lord. Let him know what he's doing, because after he puts the ring on her finger, it's too late for second guessing.*

Eric, her son, the product of her iniquity; she'd do anything to protect him—even from himself.

Her three daughters were like Jack in every way, from their varying shades of curly red hair and green agate eyes down to their knock-knees that rendered them unable to walk and chew gum at the same time. As babies, the trademark Blackwood hair started out as strawberry blonde wisps on bald round heads, growing more vibrant as the years passed. In elementary and middle school, all three girls hated their hair, cursing the unruly copper curls so different from their dark or blonde-haired comrades. As they grew, the brash tones evened out, and they grew to love the way their hair lit up when the sun hit it, making them stand out in a crowd.

Then came Eric; born with a head full of dark hair, deep blue eyes, and a perfectly formed nose, minus the freckles his three sisters despised. A husky, nine-pound, seven-ounce bruiser with a wail that shattered the nerves of every nurse in the maternity ward, he was a sharp contrast to his pale, fragile older sisters. Handsome and rugged from the beginning; people stopped to look at him wherever she went. Abby had been stunned at his resemblance to his father. She held her breath every time anyone looked down into the bassinette; waiting for them to give her a bewildered look and say something like; "Why, he doesn't look anything like a Blackwood." Fortunately for her, the moment never came.

Everyone was too excited over the first male child born into the Blackwood clan in fifteen years to notice the family had never produced such a fine specimen.

Where was Jack? Abby's impatience gave way to fear. Maybe she should call the plant and see if he was working a double shift. If they were working overtime or someone had called in sick at the last minute for the next shift Jack would've stayed and probably not had time to call her; that was all there was to it, she told herself. Still she would feel better if she called. Of course in another hour he would be home anyway, the extended twelve-hour shift behind him. She would wait. She hated to bother them at the plant. They always acted so put out when she called. She didn't want to irritate them and have them take it out on Jack even though he had been there longer than most of them.

She'd wait until ten, if he wasn't home soon after…

For the lack of anything more constructive to do, she went to the phone and dialed the familiar number. "Hello, Mom?" she said when Jack's mother picked up on the other end. This was silly, checking up on her fifty-two year old husband. "Has Jack stopped in there tonight? Oh. No, I'm not worried. Well, I guess I am a little. I was expecting him home a little after six. It is getting late. Yes, I thought he might've stopped in to see you. No, that's all right. I'm sure he'll be in any minute. I didn't mean to worry you. I'm sure he's fine. Yes, okay, I'll have him call you when he gets in. I'll talk to you later. Love you, bye."

Abby hung up the phone and went to the front door again. The sedan still sat alone in the darkened driveway. The streetlight at the end of their driveway had come on. Eric would be home soon. She hoped Jack got here first. She didn't want Eric to see her worried.

Tires crunched in the driveway, and Abby rushed to the front door. She threw it open, relief flooding through her and filling her eyes with grateful tears. A police cruiser occupied the spot where the pick-up truck should be. Two deputies climbed out of the car. Two—when did you ever see two deputies in one car in Jenna's Creek? On wobbly legs Abby stepped out onto the porch.

It was the bottom of the eighth inning. The ball field was not equipped with lights, and the game would be called after this inning. Eric had remained at the mound throughout the game. His right arm felt like a ball of hot lead was coursing through his veins every time he threw one in. He would be sore tomorrow, but he never considered going out. This was the kind of game he loved. Everyone was getting tired. The players were hollering friendly jibes from one side of the field to the other, the younger guys telling the older guys they probably couldn't see in the dark, and the older players calling back that it was getting past their bedtime. It was the third inning before anyone scored. There had been four lead changes since then.

Ed's precocious daughter was asleep on a blanket on the ground, surrounded by other little ones who gave out before their stubborn parents. Wives and husbands called good-naturedly from the stands to get on with it, tomorrow was a workday. Jamie spent much of the game on the bench, having played outfield two innings and struck out both times she went to bat. She took it well, claiming the pitcher was a Philistine. The poor thing had no hand-eye coordination. Eric vowed to make a ball player out of her if it took the rest of his life.

Now that the sun had set, there was a chill in the air. Eric figured this would be his last pitch. The runner on third was a pretty coed with a bouncy pony-tail and a pair of long legs that fit nicely into her blue, team shorts. She was most assuredly the reason the

Methodist team had a full roster of young men. He had struck out the batter after her, a saucy-tongued mother of two with a mean swing that seldom missed. She had been a hard-won out. After her, he and his tired pitching arm walked a thirty-something song leader to first. Big Ed was approaching the plate. He pointed at Eric with his bat and then motioned to the backfield fence.

Everyone in the stands cheered or booed accordingly. "You gotta get a piece of it first." Eric recognized Jamie's voice from their side of the park.

"Strike him out, Eric," someone else called out.

It now stood at a full count; three balls and two strikes. Ed must be tired too, to miss the strikes Eric threw him. One was fast and low, but the other could've been hit by someone with Ed's swing. Eric eyed the song leader on first who was leading off the base. Let him get to second; he couldn't go any farther. The coed on third didn't look like she was interested in stealing home. She had kept those blue shorts clean for eight innings, and he doubted she felt like sliding now.

Eric leaned forward and took the signal from Ray; low and inside as fast as you can make it. No problem. Eric straightened up and reared back to throw. A flash of black metal moving into the parking lot caught his eye, but he didn't miss a beat. This was the last one of the game. As soon as the ball left his fingertips, he knew it was a perfect pitch. Everything was riding on that ball as it streaked toward home. If Ed could hit this one, he deserved the win. The bat moved off Ed's shoulder smooth and easy like he was swinging at a beach ball. The pitch was everything Eric had hoped it would be; inside, low, and as fast as a softball could move. Unfortunately Big Ed was just as fast, low, and inside. With a satisfying crack of metal on rawhide piercing the night air, the ball flew up, up, up, and out over the right field fence.

Big Ed beamed. The crowd came to its feet, even those on the opposing team's side of the bleachers. After all, it was a fine hit. The coed's ponytail bounced victoriously as she danced across home plate and high-fived her teammates lining the third base line in honor of Ed's home run. The song leader jogged in behind her, cheering and waving his arms. Ed's wife rushed out onto the field and met him at third base. The two of them clasped hands and waltzed across home plate together.

The umpire, a stocky farm boy who played left field on the high school team and umpired for the youth league, called the game, and Eric's team hurried off the field to congratulate the winners and assure them they just got lucky. Eric slapped Big Ed on the back and tipped his hat to his wife. It was then he noticed the deputy making his way toward the field.

"Sorry, folks," the deputy said as he cut through the crowd. He looked straight at Eric. "You Eric Blackwood?"

Eric nodded, his tongue glued to the roof of his mouth.

The deputy took his elbow and steered him away from the suddenly subdued crowd. "I'm afraid there's been an accident."

Someone gasped, and Eric was vaguely aware of Jamie materializing at his side. He didn't remember anything else except following the deputy to his cruiser, Jamie following behind, and the once-jubilant softball players dropping to their knees simultaneously in the dirt while the song leader led them in prayer.

# Chapter Thirteen

Someone not paying attention had pulled off a side road into the path of Jack's pick-up. Jack had been unable to react in time and hit them broadside. The car slammed into the ditch by the force of the impact, and Jack catapulted out of the truck through the windshield. The old truck had never been equipped with seatbelts. Abby, Karen, and Karen's husband, Roger, were at the hospital when Eric and Jamie got there. Abby's eyes were bloodshot from crying. Karen stood up first and met Eric at the door. She pulled him into her arms and explained as much as she knew about the accident. It didn't look good. There were extensive head and chest injuries the doctor told them, and that they were doing everything they could.

Eric hurried to his mother's side. She leaned gratefully against his sweat-stained team shirt and sighed wearily. "This shouldn't have happened," she said dully. "It shouldn't have happened."

He encircled her in his arms. Over her trembling shoulder he saw the fear in Roger's face. His heart sank. Roger wouldn't look so worried if he thought Jack was out of danger. In a flurry of shouted demands directed at the nurses' station, Mother Blackwood arrived, her calm sedate husband in tow. She was not satisfied to sit and wait for news, she wanted it now. Jack's father, Pat, tried to settle her down, but she was listening to no one. She wanted to know what was happening to her son.

At midnight a nurse came out and told them to go home. She said that when they finished with Jack, he would be so heavily medicated no one would be able to see him tonight anyway. None of the family budged. Roger offered Jamie a ride home, but she also refused. She sat in the corner watching the scene, wishing she could comfort Eric, but realizing he needed to be close to his mother. Christy arrived around two in the morning, and Karen finally succeeded in reaching Elaine at the Army base in Germany. She wanted a phone call as soon as they knew anything more. In the meantime, she was working on locating the quickest flight back to the States.

At four a.m. a weary doctor with a long face stepped through the swinging doors. "Mrs. Blackwood," he said, going straight to Abby's side, avoiding eye contact with the rest of the family. "Your husband is conscious. You can see him, but just for a moment. It's not good."

A choked sob came from Christy's side of the room. Karen buried her face in Roger's chest. Mother Blackwood glared at the doctor as if he were personally responsible.

Eric helped Abby to her feet where she straightened her back, smoothed the hair away from her face, and resolutely followed the doctor through the swinging doors. Five minutes later, she reappeared. "Eric, he wants to see you."

"How is he?" Mother Blackwood burst out, jumping to her feet. "I want to see my boy. How's my boy?"

Abby took her hand and looked into her eyes. "He wants to see Eric, Mom." Her firm tone spoke volumes to everyone assembled.

Eric glanced in Jamie's direction, barely able to meet her gaze, and then headed down the hallway from which his mother had returned. A solemn looking nurse ushered him into a large room and then behind a curtain. A sinking feeling overcame him as he stepped inside the curtained partition. It was bad; worse than he'd let himself believe out in the waiting room. He wasn't prepared for this. Why hadn't his mother come with him? He could be stronger then; he'd have to be for her benefit. Alone, he felt like a little boy again, surrounded by a group of bullies on the school playground.

His father looked small and fragile in the narrow bed, wires and tubes sticking out of him from every direction. His eyes opened slowly when Eric approached the bed. The corners of his mouth twitched in an effort to smile.

"Eric," he said in a voice weak and barely audible, "my boy."

Eric resisted the urge to lower his head onto his dad's chest and bawl like a baby. "Hey, Dad," he croaked in a failed attempt to sound upbeat. "You'd better get out of that bed, Grandma's pitching a fit."

Jack chuckled appreciatively, and then closed his eyes as pain seized him. He took a deep breath and exhaled laboriously. Eric cringed inwardly. He clasped his father's hand and squeezed gently. There was no squeeze in return.

Jack forced his eyes open. "You take care of that girl of yours for me."

Eric didn't like the direction this conversation was taking. He pasted another grin on his face and answered him as if he was getting ready for a date and Jack was giving his usual words of advice. "Sure Dad, you know I will."

"No, I mean it. Make her happy, no matter what. She…deserves it."

Panic clutched Eric's heart. "I will, Dad. You can kick my rear end if I don't."

Jack ignored his reference to the future. "I love you, boy."

At his words and earnest expression, Eric could no longer hold back the tears. "I love you too, Dad." He hiccupped and choked down a sob.

"I've always loved you like a son."

The combination of pain and medication was making Jack incognizant. Eric couldn't understand what he was saying. "I know, Dad, but you need to rest." He patted his arm. "You shouldn't be talking. You'll wear yourself out."

Jack closed his eyes again to gather his strength and shook his head slowly. "I've got to tell you. Don't…don't be mad at your mother. Promise me, Eric—promise you won't be mad at her."

Eric leaned closer, his face only inches from his father's, to catch the fading words. "I'm not mad at Mom," he assured him. "She thinks I'm too young to get married. That's all. We're not mad at each other."

Jack shook his head. "No."

Eric stared into his father's glazed eyes, wishing he could understand what he was trying to say.

"She didn't mean to hurt anybody," he whispered. "She's a good woman."

Alarm rose up in Eric at the sight of Jack's struggling. "Please, Dad, don't talk. Just go to sleep. We can talk about it later."

"Don't be mad at her. She always did her best. She loved you more than anything."

"Dad, I—"

The nurse stepped around the curtain, looking stern. "You need to leave now. Your father needs his rest."

Jack reached out and grabbed hold of Eric's red team shirt with his free hand. He gazed up into Eric's eyes. A tear slid down his cheek. "I couldn't have loved you anymore if you'd been my own son."

The nurse put her hand on Eric's arm and pushed him away from the bed. "Okay, Mr. Blackwood, I'm going to give you something to help you sleep." She stepped between Eric and the bed, forcing him against a cart of medical supplies. He looked over her head and saw his father's eyes still locked with his. He opened his mouth to speak, but the nurse spun around and gave him a final push toward the curtain. "You've got to leave now. We'll let you know if there's a change."

He could see in her face she wasn't anticipating a change, and if there was, he would not be the one summoned. He stumbled through the opening of the curtain into the emergency room, reeling from the message the nurse's abrupt manner sent. It was bad. Jack Blackwood would probably never leave the narrow bed. They weren't even giving him his own room. His condition was too critical, too uncertain to bother admitting him into the hospital.

Eric stared at the pulled curtain separating him from his dad and wished he knew what to do.

*Pray, Eric.*

He closed his eyes and tried to form a plea in his head, something profound to utter toward heaven that would change the outcome of the situation.

All he could hear were his father's last words. *"I couldn't have loved you anymore if you'd been my own son."* What in the world did it mean?

Jack never regained consciousness. He slipped away peacefully as the sun came up Wednesday morning over the life flight's landing pad in the parking lot. Karen and Christy wanted to know what Jack had said to Eric when he summoned him back to the E.R. Eric could see the hurt in their faces that they missed their opportunity for a final word from their father. By the time the nurses let them into the little cubicle in the emergency room, Jack was beyond speaking. There would be no meaningful exchange between him and his daughters. Eric made something up he thought would satisfy them, unable to tell them the garbled murmurings of a dying man; words that made no sense no matter how many times he went over them in his head. The only one who may understand what Jack had meant was Abby, and he certainly couldn't bother her with it right now.

They scheduled the funeral for Sunday. The delay would give Elaine and her husband time to fly in from Germany.

Eric didn't remember the engagement ring still hidden under the front seat of his car until thirty-six hours later while he lay in bed staring at the ceiling, trying to fall asleep for the first time since Jack's death. He squeezed his eyes shut to keep the tears from spilling onto the pillow. How tragic that his biggest ally in his quest to marry Jamie would not witness their wedding. Without Jack there to see it happen, he couldn't think about marrying anyone. He didn't think of Jamie again in the next three days as he drove his mother to the places she needed to go and stood by her side while she made arrangements to bury his father.

Noel Wyatt heard about Jack Blackwood's death on the radio Wednesday morning like everyone else in Jenna's Creek. He wished he could do something to offer his support for the family, namely Abby. He could only imagine how she must be suffering, but anything he did would look like it was for his own benefit. So he did nothing. He didn't send flowers as he often did when a loyal customer passed away. He didn't send food or call. He stayed back and out of sight while the rest of the town mourned Jack's passing. There was nothing he could do. He wanted to help Abby, to be there for her, but that was impossible.

Jamie called twice that week to see if there was anything she could do. Each time Eric had been distracted or too busy to come to the phone, so she didn't press. She knew better than anyone what it was like to lose a parent. She remembered the unreasonable way she had bristled with contempt whenever someone approached her with condolences or a kind word. Another person's bumbling attempts to understand what you were going through did nothing to soothe the hurt or fill the void.

For her own sake, she wished Eric would call to say he needed her beside him in this darkest hour. No call came. She told herself not to take it personally; each person coped differently. Still her feelings were hurt and she hated herself for it. They had grown so close the past year. She couldn't imagine going through something so traumatic without his support. She wondered if she was as important to him as he had become to her.

She stayed busy on the farm, prayed for the Blackwood family, and told herself to get over her self-pitying attitude. This wasn't about her. Under Grandma Cory's supervision, she baked a meatloaf, a casserole, and a couple of pies to take to the family. All the kitchen work helped to keep her mind off what was happening at the Blackwood home. She wondered if that was how the tradition actually came about in the first place.

Saturday afternoon, Grandma Cory and Cassie went with Jamie to the funeral home for the viewing. While Cassie signed the guest book for all of them, Jamie stood in the doorway between the foyer and the largest viewing room and scanned the crowd for Eric. She hadn't seen or spoken to him since Wednesday morning at the hospital. Through the sea of darkly clad somber friends and relatives she saw him at the front of the room near his mother.

Before she could make a decision about how to proceed, Cassie whispered in her ear. "Let him know you're here. He's probably waiting for you."

"I don't want to push myself onto him," she said. "He knows I'm coming. If he needs me, he'll let me know."

"He hasn't so far," Cassie pointed out. She looked in Eric's direction and then at Jamie. "Besides, it's what you do at these things." She took Jamie's elbow. "Come on."

Karen intercepted them before they progressed more than a few feet into the room.

"Jamie, we're so glad you're here."

After a brief embrace, they separated. "I'm so sorry, Karen. If there's anything we can do…" she finished lamely. Of course, there was nothing she could ever do to ease the family's pain.

Karen waved aside the offer with a shake of her head. "No, no…"

"You remember my sister, Cassie."

"It's good to see you, Cassie. Thanks for coming."

"Grandma Cory's around here somewhere," Jamie said, casting her eyes around the room. "Yes, there she is, talking to those ladies from church."

"Let's go say hi to Mom and Eric." Karen took Jamie's arm and steered her toward the front of the room where Eric and Abby stood amid a cluster of relatives. "I'm sure Eric's anxious to see you."

Cassie gave her an I-told-you-so look out of the corner of her eye as the three of them moved through the throng. When they reached the front of the room, Karen put her hand on Abby's shoulder. "Mom, Jamie and Cassie are here."

Abby turned slowly away from an elderly lady she'd been speaking to and focused on her daughter. Jamie couldn't believe how much Mrs. Blackwood had aged since the night of the accident. Her eyes were dull and glazed. Her hair had been pulled carelessly back into a straggly chignon. She wore no make-up. Jamie leaned in and kissed her papery cheek. "I'm so sorry," she murmured, feeling like a hypocrite when she remembered how such hollow comments had angered her at her own parents' funerals. But what else could she say? What could anyone say?

Abby nodded graciously and smiled through her tears. She pressed a handkerchief to her nose. "Eric," she said, turning to where he hovered just past her shoulder, "why don't you take Jamie and Cassie to get something to drink."

His spine stiffened. He kept his gaze fixed on Abby. "No, I'm fine."

"It's all right, dear, go ahead. You don't have to stand watch over me all day."

"No," he said more firmly, "I'll stay here."

Karen shot Eric a look of dismay and smiled apologetically at Jamie. Jamie moved away, wounded. When they were out of earshot, Cassie said, "Don't let it bother you. He's hurting, that's all."

Jamie nodded numbly, knowing her sister was right. But it didn't make his brusque treatment hurt any less.

Jamie hadn't been here since Memorial Day, and she only came then because Grandma Cory—a staunch believer in honoring the dead—insisted. Several times a year, she made the trip to prune bushes and clip back the weeds and insure the township trustees were doing what her tax dollars paid for. She only made Jamie and Cassie accompany her the last weekend in May—Decoration Day, as she called it.

At this very minute in another cemetery in another part of the county, the Blackwoods gathered around a recently dug gravesite, honoring Jack. Instead of joining the procession of cars that would follow the black limousines to the cemetery after his funeral, Jamie had come here.

At the funeral home, Eric had treated her in much the same way as the visitation yesterday. He was obviously doing fine without her, so she gave into the strong urge to be with her own mother.

She shut off the ignition and climbed out of the car onto the narrow gravel road, just wide enough for one car at a time. The April grass was soft and spongy beneath her feet. The heavy spring rains had turned the cemetery and surrounding pastureland a vibrant green. She inhaled sharply and drew in the smell of fresh mowed grass, rain, and open countryside. She stepped gingerly and cautiously, aware of the decades-old graves under her feet. Her brain reminded her that she couldn't disturb someone's eternal rest by walking across a grave even if she tried, but it seemed inconsiderate nonetheless.

In moments, she reached her destination, stepping carefully over the many Steeles who had gone on before she was born. She paused at her Uncle Jesse's marker, the saddest and most forlorn in the cemetery according to Cassie. *Jesse Ray Steele-Beloved son of Harlan and Cory Steele 1936-1944*, it read.

Jamie knew the story well even though Grandma Cory didn't talk about it. Jesse had drowned in the creek behind the farm one spring. He wasn't supposed to play there, especially by himself, but everyone knew he did it anyway. Uncle Justin, only eleven-years-old himself at the time, found Jesse's body and what remained of the homemade raft he had fashioned from old boards, tobacco sticks, and fodder twine.

Jamie shivered in the warm spring sunshine. She couldn't imagine what it must have been like for a boy to find his own brother's body and pull him from the rain-swollen creek. She tried to imagine young Jesse's final moments, and wondered if he realized what was happening to him as his lungs were deprived of oxygen. Then she realized Grandma Cory must have been haunted for years by those same thoughts. She shook her head and forced herself to look away from the faded gravestone. A person could drive herself crazy with thoughts like that.

From looking around the farmhouse on Betterman Road these days, one would never know Jesse Steele ever existed. The only reminder of him was this small stone bearing his name and a few photographs buried within the pages of the family photo albums. Only Grandma Cory's long face and careful consideration of his gravesite on Memorial Day weekends let her granddaughters know how she still cherished the memories of her youngest son in her heart.

An empty space next to Jesse's grave indicated the spot Grandma Cory and Grandpa Harlan would someday occupy. Next to it, a granite headstone marked James and Nancy Steele's graves. Seven years had passed since Jamie's mother was laid to rest here, and two since her father.

That's why she hated coming here every Memorial Day. Only a cold, impersonal slab of rock represented the two people she loved most in the world. Jamie knelt in front of her mother's name. She brushed aside a few stray cobwebs and grime that had accumulated against the stone over the winter, and bowed her head and cried.

She missed her mom. She missed Eric. She wished she could talk to someone about the conflicting emotions whirling around inside her. She shouldn't expect Eric to make her a part of his suffering if he didn't want to but why was he shutting her out so completely? Had she offended him somehow or was he simply grieving over his father? If it was the latter, she should give him all the time he needed. Her head understood—it made perfect sense; only her heart couldn't see things clearly.

# Chapter Fourteen

Jamie sat on the front porch of the Blackwood home and stared down the street. Eric occupied the seat beside her, but he may as well have been a thousand miles away. They'd been sitting here in silence since coming outside after dinner. Two weeks had passed since the funeral. It had also been two weeks since they last saw each other or even spoke on the phone. Spring break was over and both had dutifully gone back to the university and their studies. Not surprisingly, each felt like coming home at the first opportunity.

She reached out and found his hand on the porch swing between them and entwined her fingers in his. His hand was cool and unresponsive.

She turned toward him and watched him for a moment, wishing she knew what to say. "Eric," she began finally. "Is there anything I can do? I feel so inadequate. I remember what it was like with both of my parents..."

"No," he said, the one syllable cutting her off.

She looked back down the street. After another moment of silence, she loosened her fingers from around his. He closed his fingers into a fist and set it in his lap. "Have I done something to upset you?" she asked.

"No." His voice had a rough edge around it she'd never heard before. "You haven't done anything."

A sick feeling settled in the pit of her stomach and she had to fight to keep from crying. Why was he alienating her? She couldn't sit still any longer.

"I'll go in and see if your mom needs any help with the dishes."

"No." His voice was a bark this time. "She doesn't need any help from you." He stood up quickly, setting the porch swing in motion. "I'll do it." The slamming of the screen door behind him seemed to mock her.

Tears stung Jamie's eyes. She tried to remember why she even came. Karen had called last night inviting her to dinner after church. She accepted the invitation, the whole time wishing it had come from Eric. Now she wished she'd stayed home. If Eric had wanted her here, he would have called himself.

It was no longer just her imagination that he was shutting her out. Everyone noticed. Jamie saw their looks of sympathy around the dinner table as Eric ignored her whenever someone tried to include her in the conversation. Anyone could see he was angry about something, but no one had the nerve to ask what, least of all Jamie.

A moment or two after the door slammed behind Eric, it opened again and Karen appeared on the front porch. She sat down on the porch swing and put a hand on Jamie's shoulders.

"Oh, Karen, I wish I understood why he's so angry with me."

"He isn't mad at you, honey," Karen soothed, wrapping her arms around her and pulling her close. "He's mad at the world. He was closer to Dad than any of us. He doesn't know what to do with himself."

"I wish he would talk to me," Jamie sputtered. "If he's blaming me for something, I wish he'd tell me what it is."

"I think he's blaming himself," Karen said. "Maybe you're just the easiest one for him to take his frustrations out on."

Jamie sighed and stared across the yard. Knowing Karen had a point didn't make Eric's treatment of her any easier to accept. Nevertheless, this was the time for patience and understanding. She needed to concentrate on his needs and disregard her own.

"I think it would be better if I kept at a distance for awhile," she said. "At least until he has time to work through his feelings."

She hoped Karen would tell her that wasn't necessary. Instead she nodded. "That may be a good idea."

The two stood up and hugged one last time. "Tell your mom thanks for the dinner. If any of you need anything," she paused, hoping it would be Eric to need her, "give me a call."

"We will, honey. You know we think of you as one of the family."

Jamie looked back at the Blackwood house in her car's rear view mirror one last time before she turned the corner and it disappeared from view. She wondered if she would ever be like one of the family again.

Eric was putting the last of the dishes in the cabinet when Karen entered the kitchen. "You think you were rude enough to Jamie while she was here? Maybe this time you've chased her off for good."

Eric glanced at her over his shoulder and then moved to the refrigerator. He opened the door and pulled himself out a soft drink. "I wasn't rude."

"Yes, you were, Eric. You didn't have two words to say to her all afternoon, and you went out of your way to avoid even looking at her."

Eric popped the tab on the can and shook his head. "You're seeing things, Karen." He took a long drink.

"What is it, Eric? Are you afraid if you're nice to anyone, we'll all think you're not missing Dad enough or something?"

"I don't know what you're talking about."

"I'm sure Mom appreciates all the help you've been this past two weeks but she doesn't expect you to jump in and take Dad's place. None of us do."

"That's not what I'm doing."

"Then explain it to me, will you? Except for school, you haven't left this house since the funeral. It's not only Jamie you're ignoring. You haven't said two words to any of your friends either. You can't be doing well in your classes with you calling home every night. I know you were close to Dad but—"

"Get off my back, Karen." He slammed the soda down on the counter, sloshing brown foam over the edge of the can. "I don't need you telling me how close I was to Dad. I don't want to talk to you, Jamie, or anybody else. I'm trying to be here for Mom for as long as she needs me, and I shouldn't have to explain myself to anybody."

Abby hurried into the kitchen, Roger two steps behind her. "What's going on in here? I just got the baby down for his nap." Her eyes flitted anxiously from Karen, who was leaning against the counter with her arms crossed defiantly over her chest, to Eric, his eyes glaring with unspoken anger. "Eric, are you all right?"

He finally tore his eyes away from Karen. "Yeah, Mom, I'm fine. Sorry about the noise." He snatched up the soda can and stormed out of the room.

Abby and Roger turned questioningly to Karen.

"Mom, he doesn't need to be coming home from school every weekend," she said, her frustration at Eric now turned on her mother. "He needs to focus on his school work. It'll be time for finals in a couple of weeks. This is too much for him."

"I didn't ask him to come home, Karen," Abby exclaimed. "He did it on his own. He doesn't like me being here by myself."

"None of us do but it isn't Eric's job to baby-sit you." As soon as the words were out of her mouth, she wished she could get them back. "Mom, listen, I'm sorry. I'm just worried about him. He's totally shutting Jamie out of his life, along with everybody else. It isn't good for him to act like he's stopped living. He's still got a job to do and that's getting an education. You need to make sure he does it."

"He lost his father, Karen. In case you forgot, I lost my husband. It's all I can do to drag myself out of bed every morning. I don't have the strength to force Eric to do something he no longer cares about. It's his life; I'll not tell him how to live it." Abby turned and stomped out of the room.

Roger approached his wife and put his hand on her shoulder. "Are you all right, honey?"

Her shoulders slumped, and she leaned against him. "Oh, Roger, I shouldn't have opened my mouth but I don't think I was wrong." She tilted her head back and looked up at him. "Do you think I'm wrong?"

He pushed her head back against his chest and smoothed his hand across her hair. "No, I don't think you're wrong. But arguing with them right now isn't going to help your case."

Karen buried her face in his shirt. She hated it when he was right.

Eric hurried upstairs to his room and shut the door behind him. He sat on the edge of the bed and stared at the dripping soda can in his trembling hand. Why couldn't Karen leave him alone? If he wanted to talk to her, he would. She was as bad as Jamie. Neither of them understood. Mom was all alone now; she needed to be taken care of. Every night he spent at the house he heard her crying in her room, she wasn't eating, her clothes hung off her frame, and the dark circles under her eyes became more noticeable every day. Much of the time, she lay on her bed with a warm cloth over her eyes to ease yet another headache. She wouldn't talk to him when he asked what he could do. She put on a brave front and swore she'd be fine. Eric doubted she ever would.

If it wouldn't upset her so much, he would stop going to school and stay home all the time. Who cared about the tuition money? His mother needed him here. He only had two months left on campus. He prayed she could hold on until then.

His father's last words had kept his mind whirling since the night of the accident. What had he meant; *"I couldn't have loved you anymore if you'd been my own son?"* Of course he was Jack's son, Eric Blackwood. The words made no more sense than they had before.

He suddenly remembered Barb at the drugstore, telling him he reminded her of someone. He joked with her about it and told her she was showing her age and that one of these days the men in white coats would come and take her away.

He remembered the day Paige joined in the conversation. She said it was more than him looking like someone. Someday the whole town would find out. At the time, he never gave her a second thought. Paige was always saying something snotty to someone. She was one of those people who looked for reasons to be in a bad mood. But maybe her prophetic words held some truth.

He didn't resemble the Blackwood side of the family very much. It suddenly occurred to him that he might have been adopted. What if it wasn't mere coincidence that he looked nothing like his three sisters? What if Abigail and Jack Blackwood weren't his real parents? It would explain his health problems. He had filled out form after form about family history during those years of diagnosing his epilepsy. Every one had a list of questions asking if this condition or that disease ran in the family. He always answered as honestly as he could. His parents never spoke up and said, "We don't know anything about Eric's medical history. You see, he's not our biological son. We adopted him when he was a baby..."

It couldn't be true. He was a Blackwood. His parents would never have kept such a thing from him, they would have told him the truth.

He wished he could tell Mom what Dad said that night in the emergency room. For the life of him, he couldn't figure out why Jack warned him against being angry with his mother. What could she possibly have done to anger him? He was sure if he could talk to her about it, she would straighten the whole thing out. She could explain why he didn't look like his sisters; why Dad was afraid he would be mad about something; what he meant by, "I couldn't have loved you anymore if you'd been my own son."

It didn't help him think when Jamie kept calling or coming around to visit, looking at him with those big, brown doe eyes of hers; the ones that could see right through him. What did she want from him, certainly not a wedding ring? He couldn't think past the next minute, let alone far enough down the road to propose marriage. Not when his mother needed him so badly.

He had already decided he wouldn't be going back to school

for the fall quarter. Karen would have a cow when she found out, but he couldn't worry about her reaction. He would get a full-time job and stay in the house with Mom. Maybe when she was on her feet again, he could resume his college career and someday—far, far in the future—he'd be ready to think about marriage again. If not with Jamie, then with someone who could understand why he was making all these sacrifices for his mother.

A week went by without a word from Eric; then another. A mutual friend from his church told her during one of her weekend home trips, that Eric hadn't been to church since the funeral and hadn't returned any calls from the congregation. Everyone was worried about him. The friend asked if there was anything any of them could do. Jamie didn't have the heart to admit she hadn't seen him in weeks either.

They no longer ran into each other at the university, Eric made sure of that. Jamie ate in the dining hall with friends from class and studied alone in her room. Robin had gone back to Michigan, so she didn't have to talk to anyone if she didn't want to.

When classes ended for the summer, Jamie couldn't stand it any longer. She had to talk to someone who could tell her how Eric was doing. She called Karen's house. She received an immediate invitation.

Christopher, Karen's six-year-old met her at the door with his typical wide-eyed enthusiasm, "Hi, Jamie," he grinned up at her through a patch of wild red freckles strewn across his nose. "What'cha doin' here? Uncle Eric ain't here."

Jamie smiled down at him. "I'm here to see your Mommy. Can I come in?"

"Sure. I think she's in the kitchen." Christopher took her hand and pulled her across the threshold. "Mommy, Jamie's here," he called toward the back of the house.

"Stop yelling, Christopher," Karen yelled from the kitchen. "I told you, that's rude."

Thundering feet were heard above them and then down the

staircase on their left. Jamie turned to see a flash of red hair and a green dress catapulting toward them. Rebecca, less than two years her brother's junior, came to an abrupt halt at Jamie's feet. She clasped Jamie's free hand. "Hi, Jamie, what'cha doin' here?"

"She's here to see Mom," Christopher said authoritatively. With his free hand he gave his sister a shove in the chest. "I'm taking her to Mommy. She don't need your help."

"Ow!" Rebecca covered the injury with her hand as any discomfort quickly gave way to indignation. "You're not the boss of me, Christopher. I'm telling Mommy. Mommy!"

Jamie flinched against the piercing wail. Kids! How did people stand them? Relief flooded through her when Karen appeared in the doorway.

"Stop that hollering, the both of you," she said through clenched teeth. "Your brother is trying to take a nap. If you wake him up, I'll wear you out." She turned to Jamie. Her teeth unclenched and her entire demeanor softened in the blink on an eye. "Hi, Jamie. Good to see you. Come into the kitchen."

With her hands still bound by her miniature captors, the three of them trooped into the kitchen after Karen. Karen headed to the refrigerator and opened the door. "Jamie," she said, turning to face her, "would you like something to…" Her smile faded when she noticed her offspring still latched onto Jamie. "You two go outside for a little bit. Me and Jamie are going to visit."

"Aw, Mom," Christopher started.

"We haven't seen Jamie in days and days," Rebecca finished.

Karen jerked a thumb toward the back door, "Out."

"We're thirsty," Christopher said, eyeing the open refrigerator door. "We want a snack."

"Later," Karen said, her tone and posture threatening, "now, git."

Simultaneously they dropped Jamie's hands, lowered their eyes to the floor, and dragged their feet to the back door. With a groan of abject misery, Christopher pushed open the screen door. The sight of the sun shining, the expanse of back yard before them, the swing set and sandbox beckoning, their wounded pride healed instantaneously and they dove off the back porch with all the enthusiasm of an attacking Indian tribe on intrusive settlers.

Karen exhaled. "Sorry about that. I'm not nearly as mean as I look. But in this business, they can smell weakness. Now, can I get you anything to drink?"

"No, thanks, I'm fine." Jamie lowered herself into a chair at the table. "How is your mom doing?"

Karen lifted her shoulders slightly and pursed her lips. "Okay, I guess." She sat down across the table from Jamie. "She doesn't talk to me a whole lot about anything."

"Have you seen her lately?"

"I try. I call every day, but half the time Eric tells me she's sleeping or something and he'll let her know I called."

The two women sat in silence and stared at their hands for a few moments. "Elaine went back to Germany a couple weeks ago," Karen said. "She had planned to stay into the summer, but she said she felt like she was just in the way. Eric and Mom seem to have this little bond between the two of them, and no one else is allowed in."

"I guess it helps Eric to feel like he's taking care of someone," Jamie offered diplomatically.

"Maybe, but it's not healthy. I know Mom is devastated, but she may be taking advantage of Eric. He's too young to be cooped up in that house watching her fall to pieces." Karen stood up and went to the back door to watch the kids playing in the yard.

"I wish there was something I could do," Jamie admitted. "I haven't seen Eric since the dinner you invited me to at your mom's house. He's totally shut me out. I know he's grieving and needs some time to himself, but I can't help missing him." She sniffed and straightened her spine, determined not to cry. "I know I shouldn't be thinking about myself after what he's—what you've all been through. I keep telling myself to be patient, but I want to help him through this. I'm sorry. I shouldn't be bothering you with this."

Karen turned from the door to face her. "You're not bothering me, Jamie, and you're not being selfish. We all know you love him and want what's best for him. We all do. He definitely isn't himself but there's really no correct way to grieve, you know that. Maybe for him, this is totally normal."

"I guess." Jamie didn't say anymore until Karen re-seated herself at the table. "If you talk to him again, maybe you could let him know I'm thinking about him and praying for him."

"I think that's the key, prayer and lots of it."

Jamie went outside and played with the children on the swing set awhile before she left. She felt more dejected than ever.

Karen didn't call her mother's house that evening after feeding her family and giving the kids their bathes like she usually did. She set Christopher and Rebecca in front of the television, baby Alex in the playpen, kissed Roger good-bye, and headed to the house on East Mulberry where she'd been raised. She let herself in the front door like always and called her mother's name. Eric appeared instantly in the doorway.

"Mom's resting," he hissed. "You should've called."

Karen pushed past him and headed for the stairway. "Every time I call you won't let me talk to her. Where is she, in her room?" She reached for the banister.

Eric put a restraining hand on her arm. "Don't bother her right now," he whispered, his eyes pleading. "She's had a hard day."

"Oh, for heaven's sake, Eric, I'm not going to slap her around." She shook off his hand and started up the stairs. "Why don't you turn some lights on in this place? It's like a tomb. No wonder she's depressed."

Eric gave her a withering look and disappeared into the darkened den.

Karen went straight to her mother's bedroom and tapped gently on the cracked, panel door. "Mom?" she called out softly, but cheerily. Without waiting for a reply, she turned the knob. The first thing she noticed upon entering the gloomy interior was her father's smell. Her heart constricted inside her chest, but she forced herself forward. No wonder Mom kept this room closed up—to preserve his presence.

"Karen?" Abby's voice came from the direction of the bed. It was hard to tell in the gloom. "What are you doing here?"

"I came to see how you're doing," she explained. "Eric said you were resting."

"Yes."

Karen's eyes adjusted to the dim light coming in around the pulled blinds, and she could make out her mother's shape on the bed facing the wall. "The kids are wondering where their grandma's been," she said, advancing to the bed. "They miss you."

"I know."

Karen sat on the edge of the bed next to her mother's form under the blanket. "Well, why don't you get your shoes on and I'll drive you over to see them? Alex is saying 'Grandma' now. At least that's what it sounds like. He's talking much sooner than the other two. I guess that comes from having two older ones talking to him all the time." She put her hand on Abby's hip. "Roger misses you too."

"I don't feel like going out tonight, Karen. It's late. I'm all ready for bed."

Karen's patience snapped. She jumped to her feet and strode around the bed to the window. "Good grief, Mom. It's barely seven o'clock." She gave one of the blinds a jerk and it snapped to the top of the window frame, flooding the room with light. Without a word, Abby rolled over to her other side. Unperturbed, Karen gave the other blind a jerk. "Isn't that better?" she sang out. "Now get dressed and come with me to visit your grandchildren."

When Abby spoke her voice was muffled and directed away from Karen. "If they really wanted to see me, you'd have brought them here. I'm not a four-year-old you can bully into doing what you want. Now pull those blinds back down. This is still my house."

Defeated, Karen obliged, but only returned the shades halfway to their original position. Abby was partly right. She was accustomed to having things her way and didn't like it when her orders were ignored. "I'm sorry Mom—I didn't come here to boss you around. I just wanted you to get up and out of this house. I know it's only been a couple of months, but Dad wouldn't want to see you living like a prisoner, ignoring his grandkids. And he'd hate what's going on with Eric. Now that classes are over, he needs to get back to work. He'll be needing money for when he goes back in the fall."

"We've talked about that," Abby informed her. "He may not go back for a while."

Karen couldn't believe her ears. "What?"

"Eric is in no hurry to resume classes, and I think it's a good idea."

"Mom, you can't be serious."

Abby rolled over to face her and sat up on her elbows, "Why not? Am I wrong to want my son here with me?"

Karen didn't try to disguise the bitterness in her voice. "That's the most selfish thing I've ever heard. You cannot expect him to forego his future in order to sit in this house and hold your hand."

She heard the tears in her mother's voice before she saw them spilling down her cheeks. "I'm not being selfish, Karen. I'm lonely. I miss my husband. Eric is the only one of you kids who seems to understand that."

Tears of regret sprang to Karen's eyes. She hurried to the bedside and sat down beside Abby. "Mom, that's not true. None of us want you to feel alone." She wrapped her arms around her, and they cried together. After some time, Karen fumbled on the night stand for tissues.

She apologized again. "All of us want to help you through this, Mom. Elaine stayed for as long as she could to help out. If there's anything more we can do…"

"I know, dear." Abby reached out and patted her hand.

"I'm here for you, Mom. We all are. We love you."

Abby nodded again and continued to stroke her hand.

"But please, don't let Eric give up college," she put in gently, "And what about Jamie? Roger and I kinda figured they'd get married eventually. Aren't they seeing each other anymore?" Karen didn't miss her mother stiffen under the sheet.

"Eric's decided that might not be such a good idea either."

Karen rolled her eyes and stood up. She suddenly needed some air, even if her mother didn't. "Mom, let him have his life back. He'll resent you if you don't."

Abby lifted her chin and turned toward the window. "Everything's changed, Karen. Can't you see that?"

Karen bent over and kissed her cheek. "Bye, Mom. I love you. The kids want to see you. I'll bring them by in the morning."

"That isn't necessary," Abby said as she turned to go.

Karen didn't answer, but on her way down the darkened stairway, she decided she would be bringing the kids by tomorrow for a visit whether Abby wanted to see them or not.

Eric waited until he heard Karen's car start up and back out of the driveway before he climbed the stairs to his mother's room. "Mom is everything all right?" he called through the closed door.

"Yes, dear—you can come in."

He opened the door and stuck his head inside. "Do you need anything before I leave?"

"Oh, are you going out?"

A pang of guilt assailed him at the desperation in her voice. "I—I thought I might go by Jamie's tonight. I haven't seen her since…"

"Oh." Her voice was small and helpless. Eric felt his resolve slipping away. "Have a good time, dear."

"If you need me to stay…" he said, his voice trailing off, silently begging her to insist that he go.

"I just thought maybe I would come downstairs, and we could watch something on television tonight but if you want to leave, that's fine. I don't mind."

Eric exhaled, disappointed, but feeling guilty for even thinking of leaving her alone. He eased the rest of the way into the room. "No, that's all right. I'll bring up the TV guide, and we can see what's on."

Even in the darkened room, he saw her countenance brighten. She sat up and swung her legs off the side of the bed. "Thank you, dear. Check and see if there's any ice cream in the freezer while you're down there. Wouldn't that be nice?"

Eric slipped out of the room, leaving her alone. Abby flipped on the lamp beside the bed so she could read the TV guide when he got back with it. For a moment, she thought of Karen's warning that he would someday resent her for taking his life from him. How ridiculous. She hadn't asked for any of this. She didn't plan on Jack dying at fifty-two. She didn't tell Eric he couldn't go to Jamie's tonight. She had simply pointed out that she would enjoy his company here with her. She let him make his own decision. He chose her over Jamie. How could he resent her when he decided of his own free will?

On his way downstairs, Eric wondered what Jamie was doing tonight. Was she thinking of him? Was she secretly wishing he'd drop by or at least call? It had been so long since he last saw her, since he last heard her voice. He imagined the look on her face if he showed up out of the blue, her surprise turning instantly to delight. He imagined those deep brown eyes with the green and gold flecks lighting up when she realized it was him standing outside under the amber porch light. He imagined the smell of her hair and the weight of her hand in his.

He felt lousy about the way he treated her the last time she was at the house. He had been angry at her—at the whole world—and he couldn't even explain it to himself. He wanted to make it up to her. He wanted to pull her against him, breathe in her scent, whisper her name into her ear, and shed tears of regret and loss on her shoulder.

He thought of the velvet box buried in the sock drawer in his room and wondered if it would ever see the light of day. He couldn't go on with his life as if nothing had happened while his mother slowly fell apart. He had to be here for her and put his own selfish desires—like school and marriage—aside. She came first. She was the most important person in his life.

He had promised his father he wouldn't be mad at her. Now that his classes were over and he was home all the time, it became clear what his father meant when he made his request. The times she needed him—like tonight—and wanted him with her, he mustn't get angry and push her aside. He had to support her, even if it meant ignoring what he wanted and needed; too bad if Karen or Jamie couldn't understand that.

# Chapter Fifteen

Jamie brought her car to a stop near Eric's and climbed out. "Hi, Eric. I'm glad you called." Glad didn't describe it; she was ecstatic. "How've you been?"

"Okay, I guess. I don't get out much with Mom and everything. You know how it is."

At one time she thought she did, but after three months she was beginning to wonder how a twenty-one-year old man could spend every waking moment in his house with his mother.

Summer break was now three weeks old. She was working nearly forty hours a week at the drugstore; Eric hadn't come back at all. As far as she knew, he hadn't even called to see if he still had a job.

"I'd be lying if I said I haven't missed you," she said rather than pointing all that out.

He nodded but didn't answer.

Jamie let her eyes wander around the parking lot, unsure of what else to say. He should be the one to speak first. He'd arranged this little tête-à-tête. He called this morning and asked if he could talk to her sometime today. When she reminded him it was Thursday, July 1ˢᵗ, the day before the launch of Jenna's Creek huge Bicentennial celebration, and she had to work, he was genuinely surprised. With all the TV specials and Bicentennial moments she'd wondered how it could slip a person's mind. She had spent all last week helping to hang patriotic bunting and flags around the store. Across the street on the courthouse lawn were reenactments of the signing of documents by men in colonial garb, women dressed appropriately for pioneer life, and soldiers with muskets patrolling the grounds. Jenna's Creek was abuzz with activity. If Eric would simply look out his front door, he would know that.

He had brushed off her explanation as something that didn't interest him, and suggested they meet at his church after her shift at the drugstore was over. It seemed odd to be meeting here instead of his house or the drugstore, but she wouldn't make demands of him.

After the silence lengthened and he showed no signs of speaking, she finally said; "Do you know when you're coming back to work? Noel's got a new boy working, and he doesn't show up half the time. I think he's about to get fired."

Eric nodded again but remained mute.

Jamie went on aimlessly, wishing he would say something and rescue her from herself. "I'm training a girl on the register. You remember Kim, don't you? I think she started a little while before you did. She's picking up on it pretty well—"

"I might not come back to the store this summer," he interrupted. "Mom likes having me around the house. She needs me right now."

"Oh, I see," she lied. She didn't see at all. "What about earning money for school? Classes'll be starting back before you know it. I'm sure Karen and Christy will step in and take over for you at the house."

"I'm not going back to college in the fall."

Jamie's mouth dropped open, and it took a moment to turn her disbelief into words. "What? You're not serious."

"Yes, I am," Eric said simply. "Mom needs me at home. She isn't ready to be alone."

Jamie fought back tears that threatened to erupt. She hadn't seen Eric since the dinner at his house last April. Just being close to him made her heart break, and now he was dropping this bombshell on her. "Well, of course she's not ready," she said, struggling to keep the tremor out of her voice. "She may never be but I'm certain she doesn't expect you to take your Dad's place. You couldn't if you wanted to. You've got to think about your future. It would be stupid to drop out of college at this point."

"So now I'm stupid."

"I didn't say that." She took a deep breath to bring herself under control. He wasn't thinking clearly. If only she could put her arms around him, force him to look her in the face; then maybe she could talk some sense into him. "All I'm saying is this is your last year. You've come too far to just drop out. By the time classes start I'm sure your mother will be ready for you to go back. She'll be fine."

"She will not be fine, Jamie," he spat forcefully. "She lost her husband of more than thirty years. With your parents' lousy marriage I don't expect you to understand what it's like to lose someone you loved for that long, but it's destroying her. I'm not going to shove her aside and pretend she isn't hurting so I can get on with my life."

Jamie felt her bottom lip quivering, but she was too angry to cry. "I'm not saying this isn't hard. All I'm saying is, maybe you should back off, and let her stand on her own two feet. She's stronger than you think, Eric. Maybe she doesn't need you as badly as you want to be needed."

"You don't know the first thing about what she's going through." His voice rose to a pitch she'd never heard from him before. "You don't lie in your room and listen to her cry herself to sleep every night. I'm the one who's there when she needs someone to talk to. I'm the one keeping her company; not you, and certainly not Karen. She needs me, and I'm not leaving her."

How dare he insinuate she didn't understand pain; that because her parents' marriage hadn't been a happy one she couldn't comprehend his mother's suffering! "If you don't go back to school in the fall, you *are* stupid. You're not doing your mother any favors, you know? You're being an idiot."

In retrospect she knew she shouldn't have called him stupid or an idiot, regardless of how he was acting at the moment.

Eric clenched and unclenched his fists several times. "Well, this idiot probably saved himself from making the biggest mistake of his life. He almost asked you to marry him. Now that would have been stupid."

"No!" Jamie practically screamed in his face, all restraint and concern for his fragile feelings gone. "I would've been the stupid one. I probably would've said yes."

"Aren't we both glad it didn't come to that?"

"Yeah!"

"Yeah, fine! I'm glad I saw through you before it was too late. Now I won't ever have to see you again." He glared at her.

She glared back, seething with rage. He turned to his car and flung open the door. She spun on her heel to cross the ten or fifteen yards of asphalt to hers. She heard his car door slam shut and the tires squealing against the pavement for traction as he sped off. She walked faster, her arms pumping, her breath coming in short gasps, her throat raw from screaming.

He was ruining his life and now he was ruining hers too, the big jerk! A proposal, ha! What a joke that would've been. She was the one relieved that she found out what he was truly like; a mama's boy in the worst possible way. At least she found out before it was too late; before she got stuck with a husband willing to jeopardize his entire future on the word of his mother.

She got in the car and slammed the door behind her. She reached for her purse in the seat beside her and rummaged inside for the keys. They weren't there. She dug deeper, her patience growing thinner by the minute. In a fit of barely suppressed rage, she turned the purse upside down and dumped the contents onto the passenger's seat, half of which tumbled onto the floor and between the bucket seats. She ground her teeth together, losing the battle of controlling her anger. If ever she thought about swearing...

She leaned to her right to slide her hand between the console and the seat...and saw her keys dangling from the ignition. "Ooooh, Eric!" The words came out in a rush, and she laid her forehead on the steering wheel, finally giving in to the tears.

She *was* sorry he wasn't going back to school. She *was* sorry he hadn't proposed to her. She would've said yes and not regretted it for an instant. He was the best thing that had ever happened to her. She loved him and couldn't envision a future without him. Last April, after Jack's accident, she thought if she gave him enough time, enough space, and exercised a little patience and understanding, their relationship would someday resume. Now that day was never going to come. She had called him stupid, an idiot, and had lied and said she was glad he hadn't proposed.

She wasn't glad, she was miserable. She wanted him back. She wanted more than anything to hear his car pull back into the parking lot next to hers, hear him get out and open her car door, pull her into his arms, tell her he was sorry; that he hadn't meant what he said, he loved her, and that she was the most important thing in his life. She wanted to hear him say that he couldn't go on living without her. She would throw her arms around his neck and tell him she hadn't meant any of the horrible things she had said either.

She stole a glance through her tears in the rearview mirror, looking at the place where he had pulled out onto the highway. She drew a ragged, choking breath of air. Not a car in sight—he wasn't coming back.

Eric went straight home and stormed upstairs to his room. It took a few seconds of rummaging through his sock drawer to find the velvet box. As soon as his hands touched it, he yanked it from its hiding place and slung it across the room, not bothering to look where it landed or caring that the box popped open and the ring, freed from the velvet clutches, was sent rolling under the dresser along the baseboard where it finally came to rest against the heating vent.

Throwing the tiny velvet box did little to quell his raging anger. He yanked the drawer open as far as it would go, tore it from the metal drawer guide, and hurled it after the ring. The sound of crashing furniture and the accompanying guttural yell that escaped his throat brought his mother racing into the room.

"Eric? What in the world's going on in here?"

He stood in the center of the room, his arms hanging loosely at his sides, his chin on his chest, his shoulders heaving with sobs.

She crossed the room, stepping carefully over the balled up pairs of socks, underwear, and splintered wood strewn all over the floor, and pulled him into her arms.

"Baby, hush, it's all right."

"No, it's not," he sobbed, clinging to her. "I've been so stupid. I've ruined everything."

"Hush, now. What are you talking about? I'm sure whatever it is, it's not as bad as it seems."

"Yes, it is. It's over." He sniffed loudly, his dripping nose brushing against her shoulder.

"What's over, baby?"

"Jamie," he choked out. "It's over with Jamie."

He didn't notice the tiny catch in her breath or see the relief that flitted across her features. "Oh, sweetheart, tell me what happened?"

"Nothing, nothing happened except we had a horrible fight. It's over," he sniffed again, struggled to compose himself, and pulled away from her. "I don't want to talk about it."

Abby scooped a clean sock off the floor and wiped the tears from his face. She held it in front of his nose and waited while he obediently blew into it. She smoothed his contrary dark locks away from his face. "You can be so hard-headed," she said absently, patting at the stubborn cowlick that never lay in place no matter how often she spit on her fingers and smoothed it back when he was little. "Just like your father."

"Really, Mom," he asked looking directly into her eyes, his gaze intense behind the tears. "Am I just like Dad?"

Her hand froze momentarily in his hair. Then she busied herself folding the soiled sock into a neat ball and stuffing it into the pocket of her slacks. "Sure you are," she said with a light chuckle. "Jamie probably said something you didn't like, and you went off half-cocked and said more than you intended to. All you Blackwood men are the same." She smiled up at him and patted him on the chest before turning away.

His hand reached out and caught her wrist. His dark lashes glistened with tears. "Tell me how, Mom. How are we all alike? I've never seen Dad lose his temper and go off half-cocked. I don't look anything like him. I don't look like Grandpa Blackwood. I don't even look like you."

"Oh, Eric, what's brought this on all of a sudden?" Her attempt at a laugh sounded hollow to his ears. "No, I guess you don't look like the Blackwoods. You take after my side of the family. You're built like my brothers; tall and broad-shouldered. And that chin, you've got the Frasier jaw line; strong and rugged."

"No, I don't," he challenged. He watched her closely for a reaction, but she wouldn't meet his gaze. "Who do I look like, Mom, do you know?"

Her eyes darkened as she brought them up to meet his. "What are you getting at, Eric? I'm afraid I don't appreciate your tone."

"And I don't appreciate secrets. I'm too old to be kept in the dark if there's something you should tell me."

Abby squared her shoulders and set her hands on her hips. "I don't appreciate you throwing furniture around the room." She flung one hand in the direction of where the drawer had hit the wall. A triangle-shaped gouge in the plaster about an inch deep glared back at him. "Look at what you've done to that wall with your little temper tantrum. That'll have to be fixed. I suggest you call Roger and see if he'll come over this weekend and show you how to do it." She spun on her heel and headed for the door, still grumbling. "This whole room will have to be re-painted. I'll never find the right color match."

"Mom, don't leave," he called after her. "I want to talk about Dad."

She paused at the door but didn't face him. "There's nothing to talk about. I have a headache. I'll be in my room."

As soon as the door closed behind her, Eric sank to the floor on his knees and pummeled his thighs with his fists. He couldn't even remember why he'd gotten in a fight with Jamie in the first place. He called her this morning, intending to meet her at a neutral place and tell her about his decision not to go back to school.

He didn't want to talk to her here at the house, and it wasn't a conversation to be had over the phone. She'd be upset, but he hoped to make her understand it was only for a while. Eventually his mother would be stronger—maybe in a year or two—and then he could start thinking about a career again. But she hadn't even given him a chance to explain. She'd said he was stupid. Stupid—how could helping his mother be construed as a sign of stupidity?

He should get up off the floor and call her. He'd ask her if she meant what she said because he sure didn't. He'd apologize for going off half-cocked like his mother said and not taking the time to explain himself better. He would tell her about his conversation with his mother and her reaction over his questions. He would confide in her about what he thought—that he might be adopted. Getting all his questions and doubts out in the open would make it so much easier to think. Jamie would smile that patient, understanding smile of hers, run her fingers through his hair, and tell him his mother loved him, his father loved him, and that even if they weren't his biological parents, it didn't mean a thing. His mom would tell him the truth when she was ready.

*Oh, Jamie, if I could see your face. I'm sorry I blew up today. You're right I have been acting like an idiot, pushing you away when I need you so much.*

But if Mom heard him on the telephone, she'd be the one upset with him instead of Jamie; even more so than she was over his questions. She didn't like it when he called out. She never said anything, but he could tell it bothered her. She didn't want to be alone. Besides, hadn't Jamie said she never wanted to see him again, or had he been the one to say it? Either way, she didn't understand what he and his mother were going through. She wasn't even willing to try to understand. At this point, he didn't need any added aggravation in his life. If she couldn't see his side any better than her actions indicated, he had no use for her.

Abby filled the teakettle with water and set it on the stove to boil. Her hands shook so badly she rattled her cup against several others as she pulled it from the cabinet. What was wrong with her? What was wrong with Eric? She couldn't help but be relieved when he said it was over between him and Jamie. The last obstacle keeping him from staying here at home with her where he belonged was apparently gone. Good.

Why suddenly all the questions about Jack? He never noticed before that they shared no physical characteristics. If he had, it never bothered him enough to ask. What had brought on all these suspicions? Why now? It couldn't have anything to do with his argument with Jamie, she didn't know anything. There had to be something else that got him going.

Abby fished in the drawer for a tea bag. She couldn't very well ask him what put all these ideas in his head. She would have to hope and pray he didn't ask again. She'd keep him busy re-plastering the drywall in his room and re-painting. If he didn't have time to think about anything, he wouldn't ask questions. Eventually whatever it was that got him started would be forgotten. That's all she could hope for anyway.

The sun hung low in the horizon by the time Jamie turned her car into the driveway alongside the little farmhouse. She sat in the car with her hands on the steering wheel and took a few deep, steadying breaths to make sure she wouldn't start bawling again. She shouldn't be so mad at Eric. She remembered her own confusion and fear when she lost her mother at the age of twelve. Her life had been turned upside-down, much like Eric's was now. She, more than anyone, should understand he couldn't be held accountable for what he said or did out of hurt and frustration. She understood that frustration. She would back off, give him a few days or a few weeks, however long he needed. Maybe he was as sorry as she was for everything that had been said at the church. If not, well then, she'd cross that bridge when she came to it.

Maybe their relationship was over. Maybe it had never been strong enough in the first place to handle such a traumatic event. Wasn't it better that she found out now rather than after they were married with a houseful of kids?

Her breath caught in her throat, and she choked back another sob. Kids, she'd never have kids—if she ever decided she wanted any; she was alone. She'd die a shriveled up, bitter, old hag like Great Aunt Lucy who went through men like the rest of the family went through socks. Eric wasn't coming back in a few days or a few weeks to apologize for what he said and give her a chance to apologize back. He was gone; out of her life. Somehow she managed to chase off every man who ever loved her. Just like Great Aunt Lucy.

She didn't want to think about that right now. She opened the car door and got out.

If only her mother were here, she would have someone to talk to; a shoulder to cry on, even if crying didn't change one thing. She had thought Eric understood the way things were between her parents. She remembered the conversation they shared in the dining hall that first year on campus. He was sympathetic when she told him what it had been like between James and Nancy, and how she wanted to give her kids a different life. But at the first opportunity, he had thrown her tumultuous childhood back in her face. He hadn't really understood. How could he, coming from a perfect home with two loving, perfect parents?

The tears welled up again, but she fought them back. Her swollen sinuses were already causing her entire face to ache. Breathing was a chore and turning her head, agony. She wouldn't cry again. Eric Blackwood wasn't worth it.

She threw her purse strap over her shoulder and trudged around the side of the house to the back door. Grandpa Harlan sat at the kitchen table lacing up his boots, apparently on his way out the door to do some real or imagined chore. He never went outside without first putting on his water-resistant boots, regardless of the weather. He looked up and smiled when she came in.

"Hi."

She returned his smile and kissed the top of his head. He was having a good day. Most days he didn't acknowledge her presence. This was a good sign, even if he hadn't called her by name. It wasn't likely he was capable of placing a name with any of the faces that crossed his path these days. That's what the doctors said anyway. For the most part he was happy. They couldn't hope for much else.

"You're late, aren't you?" Grandma Cory announced from the sink in more condemnation than inquiry. "There's still plenty of chores to do around here whether you're working at that store or not." When she looked up and saw Jamie's tear-stained face, her irritation evaporated. "What's the matter?"

Grandpa Harlan glanced over at his wife, but his blank eyes didn't acknowledge the concern in her voice. He stood up and disappeared through the back door.

"Eric and I had a fight," Jamie replied. "More like a shouting match."

"I'm sorry. He's going through a lot right now."

"I wouldn't know," Jamie said haughtily. "I've been excommunicated from his life."

"I'm sure it's not that bad."

"Yes, it is. He never wants to see me again." She crossed her arms over her chest and leaned against the countertop.

"What did you say to upset him?"

"Why do you assume I'm the one who said something out of the way? Did you ever think maybe he's acting like a big jerk?"

"Jamie, I didn't say it wasn't partly his fault, but he's earned the right to act like a jerk. People in his position don't always say the most tactful things, especially if you made him mad in the first place. He's probably feeling as bad as you are right now."

"Then why doesn't he call and apologize? Believe me he said plenty to apologize for."

"Probably because he's hurt and he's proud. You have to be the patient and understanding one, not him."

"I have been patient and understanding. He hasn't said two civil words to me in almost three months, and I've put up with it, waiting for him to come around. But I can take a hint. I can be pretty dense about some things, but when someone says they never want to see my face again, I usually get the message."

Grandma Cory shook her head. "It's your decision to make, Jamie, but the boy needs more time."

"He's not going back to school in the fall. He needs to stay home with his mother. Does that sound like he's thinking clearly? He's given up and I don't want to waste my life with a man who gives up that easily."

Grandma Cory shook her head again. "Go change out of those good clothes and get to your chores. It'll be too dark to see soon. And keep an eye on your grandpa; I don't want him hurting himself."

Jamie's mind kept replaying the hateful scene in the church parking lot as she hurried to finish her chores. More time, how much more time did Eric need? How long should she be expected to wait? No, it was over between them. She couldn't wait indefinitely just to have him decide to spend the rest of his life holed up in that house with his mother. Her heart had been battered enough. First, she loved Jason, but he needed four years to pursue his law degree on the other side of the country. Then she loved Eric, and he needed an indeterminate amount of time to heal from his father's death. She wasn't cold or unfeeling; she just couldn't take anymore waiting around for the men in her life to decide what they needed. She was tired. Couldn't they ever be men, and make a decision without some dopey woman waiting in the wings for them to get to it?

She didn't hear the car pull into the driveway or Cassie's excited calling of her name until she saw her standing halfway between the house and the chicken coop, waving her arms like a madwoman. "Jamie, hurry up. He came all this way to see you."

Her heart leaped into her throat.

*He's here. He has been hurting as much as me. Oh, Eric, I don't know how much of this emotional seesawing back and forth I can take. But I love you. I forgive you. Can you ever forgive me?*

"What's he want?" she called back over the sound of the garden hose running water into the chickens' narrow trough, but Cassie had already turned and disappeared into the house. Jamie shut off the water and left the hose lying across the dirt between the spigot and the trough. She'd roll it up later. What could have changed since she last saw him, his tires squalling on the pavement on his way out of the church parking lot? Oh, who cared! He was here, that's all that mattered.

She ambled leisurely across the backyard toward the house. She didn't want to appear too anxious about seeing him again. She combed her fingers through her shoulder length hair and pushed it behind her ears. She rubbed her hands over her face to erase any lasting evidence of the tears she'd shed. She couldn't have him knowing she'd been boohooing over him all evening.

The security light between the house and the barn came on the instant she passed under it. An omen, she thought with a smile, a good omen; not that she believed in that sort of nonsense.

Voices and laughter from the living room reached her ears as she stepped inside the back door. She heard her grandmother's and Cassie's voices blending with a masculine one. It didn't sound like Eric. Her heart sank for the hundredth time that day. Why had Cassie come tearing out to the chicken coop to tell her Uncle Justin dropped by? Later, she would wring her neck for getting her all excited for nothing. As she moved through the kitchen to the living room door, she realized the visitor was neither Uncle Justin nor Eric.

The man in the living room with his back to her, laughing over something Grandma Cory had said, was Jason.

# Chapter Sixteen

"Jamie, look who's here," Cassie squealed unnecessarily when she spotted her in the doorway.

Jason turned slowly, and Jamie's breath caught in her throat. It took only a fraction of a second to recover from the initial shock and find her voice. "Jason!" She practically leaped across the faded hand-stitched rug and threw herself into his arms.

"Jamie," he wrapped his arms around her in a tight squeeze. "Man, it's good to see you."

"You too, I can't believe you're here," she squeaked out, unable to adequately fill her lungs with air. Reluctantly he released his grip on her, and she moved back enough for a sliver of daylight to pass between them. She kept her hands on his shoulders. His hands remained at her waist.

"What are you doing here?"

"I was in the neighborhood."

"Not quite. You look great.

"So do you."

"What's this?" She raked her fingernails through a short growth of reddish, brown hair on his chin.

"Ah, you know, it drives the ladies wild."

"I'll bet it does." She hugged him again. "I can't get over it. I'm so happy to see you."

"How about staying for supper, Jason?" Grandma Cory broke in reminding them they weren't the only ones in the room. "We were just getting ready to eat."

"I was hoping you'd say that." He kept his eyes on Jamie while he talked. He finally tore his eyes away from her and turned to Grandma Cory. "You can't begin to know how long it's been since I had a good home-cooked dinner."

"You poor thing," Grandma Cory headed to the kitchen.

"Yeah, you poor thing," Cassie repeated with a grin. She grabbed his hand and led him away from Jamie and to the couch. "Tell us everything you've been up to. I want to hear all about San Francisco. Are the guys all as tanned and gorgeous as you?"

"Cassie," Grandma Cory said from the doorway. "I need your help in the kitchen."

"Aw, Grandma, I want to talk to Jason."

"You can talk to him later. I need your help right now."

Cassie shot Jamie a warning look. "Don't talk about anything good till I get back."

Jason waited until Cassie was out of the room before turning back to Jamie. "I can't believe how beautiful you are."

Jamie sat down on the opposite end of the sofa. "Oh? And that comes as a big shock to you?"

Jason scooted across the upholstery, closing the distance between them and took her hands. "You've always been beautiful but now you're a woman. I can't get over it."

"Jason," she said, blushing at the awe on his face, "what did you think would happen; I'd turn into a porcupine?"

"I don't know what I thought. I just didn't expect this."

The blush on her cheeks deepened. She wished he'd stop looking at her that way. "So, what are you doing home?" she asked to get the subject off herself. "Did you go and graduate two years early?"

"Not hardly, everything's right on schedule."

"I am so happy to see you. When Cassie yelled for me to come up to the house, I thought you were…" She stopped herself just in time. "I never expected to see you."

"Especially since a beautiful brown-eyed young lady I know told me to stay out of her life."

Jamie looked down at her hands and blushed again. "Pray tell,

I don't know to whom you are referring, kind sir," she said in a mock southern drawl.

"I guess you wouldn't." She looked up to see him smiling at her. "I'm glad I didn't listen to her," he added softly.

"So am I."

"The table's set. You two can wash up for dinner," Cassie said from the doorway.

"Company first," Jamie said with a motion of her hand.

"I got an internship with a law firm in Cleveland this summer. I've been there since June tenth. They work me thirteen or fourteen hours a day and most Saturdays, but I'm learning a lot. They paid my expenses from California and even set me up in a little studio apartment in a really cheesy neighborhood. Their offices are shut down for the Bicentennial; that's how I got away for the long weekend. The experience is great, and it's much better than last summer when I bused tables at a restaurant in Palo Alto for slave wages."

"Oh, how exciting," Cassie gushed, "busing tables in Palo Alto!"

"Cassie," Jamie said with a chuckle, "He sits here and tells you about working for a real law firm, and you get excited over busing tables."

Cassie was nonplussed. She turned her wide hazel eyes back to Jason. "Was your restaurant right on the ocean?"

"Actually, on the bay, but I'm afraid it wasn't my restaurant."

Cassie looked at Grandma Cory. "I think I'm going to Stanford, too."

"I think you're not," was the immediate reply.

"Why didn't you call and let us know you've been in Cleveland all summer?" Jamie asked Jason before Cassie could protest the injustice.

"Oh, no," Jason said, chuckling. "I seem to remember one Christmas I called here and got my ear chewed off."

"Oops, would that have been me?"

Jason smiled and changed the subject. "So, what have you been up to all summer?"

A brief image of her encounter with Eric less than two hours ago twisted her insides into a knot, but she resolutely pushed it out of her mind. "I'm still at the drugstore working behind the register like always. Have you stopped in to see Noel yet? He'll flip out."

"No, this was my first stop, after the house of course."

"How's your dad getting along?" Grandma Cory asked.

Jason tilted his head. "He has his better days." He looked over at Grandpa Harlan who had shown no sign of recognizing him. "You know, we take it day by day."

"I bet he misses you when you're so far away," Cassie put in.

"Oh, sure, he's glad to have me home this weekend."

The family caught up with Jason throughout the meal. It felt free and easy to Jamie, just like old times. She forgot her swollen sinuses and broken heart as she listened to a very animated Jason woo Cassie with stories of endless beaches, bronzed weight-lifters, and coffee kiosks on the boardwalk where one could sip iced coffee under a candy-striped umbrella.

After dinner, the conversation moved out onto the front porch while Grandma Cory stayed inside to clean up and Grandpa Harlan plunked himself down in front of the television in the living room. Finally, reluctantly, Cassie went inside to allow them some time to catch up in private.

Jason turned toward Jamie on the porch swing and put his hand under her chin. "I never realized how much I've missed you."

This would be a good time to tell him about Eric, but she didn't. The thought of Eric depressed her, and she was having too much fun reminiscing. "I've missed you too. You seem all grown up," she said and then blushed at the sound of it.

"I didn't leave you here, Jamie," he said, his blue eyes intense. "I told you I was coming back. I already have two years behind me. Sometimes it seems like they've flown by; only two more to go."

This was definitely the time to tell him about Eric but what was there to tell? Eric didn't want to see her again. If he did, he'd be sitting here beside her instead of Jason. "I haven't changed my mind, Jason," she said instead. "I don't want to spend the next two years waiting for something that may never happen."

"That's why I'm here." The intensity in his tone surprised her. "I don't want to wait either. I came to take you back to California with me."

At her sharp intake of air, he hurried on. "I'm making good money in Cleveland. I want you to transfer to Stanford and finish your studies there. There are so many opportunities, Jamie, you wouldn't believe it. With your brains, you could get on at any hospital or nursing facility you choose, even without a degree. With one, you could earn as much money as you wanted. It would be great. I'll be graduating in two years and I'm already sending out feelers for firms. They're everywhere. The potential for money is incredible."

"I thought you were coming back here after you graduate? That's what you said all along."

"And I will if that's what you really want. But I think if you went out there, even for a quarter, you wouldn't want to come back either. Think about it, Jamie. You'll love it. I guarantee it."

"Wait a minute, Jason. I can't pick up and move across the country with you. We're not even dating anymore. I don't know anybody out there. I don't know how I'd go about transferring schools. I couldn't take the risk of being alone in a strange place—"

"I'm not asking you to risk anything. I'm sorry. I'm getting ahead of myself. I want us to go out there together, as a couple. I want to get married here before the summer is over and go back together in the fall."

Jamie's mouth dropped open. He rushed on. "I already signed a lease on an apartment in Menlo Park for September. It's kind of small, but it would be all right to start out in. It's better than dorm living, I'll tell you that. We could always look for something bigger once you got out there if you wanted, but I thought for right now while we're still in school, we could stay there to save money. Two years isn't so awfully long. At least we'd be together."

She definitely had to tell him about Eric. She couldn't let him say one more word until he heard all the gory details. Oh, why did he have to show up tonight of all nights? Was God trying to tell her something; sending her a sign that her relationship with Eric was history, and she needed to move on with a man who obviously still loved her? She had been praying and waiting for an answer since April; was this it?

But did she still love Jason? It had been so long since she'd seen him. Too much had happened in the past two years—too much with Eric...

Did she want to live and work in California? Jason made it sound so exciting, but she was a small-town girl. She didn't belong in San Francisco. The thought of it made her a little sick to her stomach, still, it was exciting; California—a whole world away from Jenna's Creek—a one-horse town where everyone with any sense moved away at the first chance.

She wasn't sure she wanted to spend the rest of her life here either, in the shadow of this little farm where she'd been raised. There was so much more of the world she hadn't seen yet. Eric obviously intended to spend the rest of his life hovering over his mother, trying to take his father's place. What kind of life did that offer her? She couldn't sit on her hands waiting for him.

She had entered a career field that offered her work anywhere in the world. She could make a living wherever she chose to go and definitely more of one in California than the tiny hospitals around here would offer.

What would Grandma Cory say? What about Cassie, Uncle Justin, Aunt Marty, and Grandpa Harlan? She'd never see them again; at best, only once every couple of years. Cassie would be all for it. She would want to move out there with them even if she had to sleep on the floor of their tiny apartment in Menlo Park. Grandpa Harlan would forget all about her. He was her main inspiration for entering the Health Care field in the first place. But there were people who needed good long term care in California too. Still, she belonged in Jenna's Creek—didn't she?

What about Eric? If she moved to California, she would never see him again. No, she wouldn't think of him. He no longer fit into the equation.

"Jason, this is huge; too huge for me to give you an answer right now. I mean, I can't even think straight. I don't know what to say."

"Oh, I knew you wouldn't jump on board right away. You've got till Labor Day to think about it. That's when my internship is over. We'll need to have all your transcripts ready by then. But Jamie," he leaned close to her, "more than anything, I want to marry you. I love you. I know you might not believe it, but I haven't looked at another girl out there. I've had my chances, but they meant nothing to me. As long as I had memories of you, I couldn't bring myself to consider anyone else."

He leaned closer, and their lips met. Jamie's heart hammered inside her chest so loud she was sure he would hear it. After the kiss, she sank against him and her arms encircled his neck as if they had a mind of their own. "Oh, Jason, I'm so glad you're here. I've needed you so much." Tears entered her voice, and he pulled her tighter, misinterpreting their meaning.

She couldn't wait another minute to explain about Eric. Jason needed to know. He hadn't looked at another woman while in San Francisco, waiting instead for this moment. She felt almost like she had cheated on him, even though she knew she hadn't done anything wrong. They broke up before he ever left. She told him plain as day she wasn't waiting for him. If he chose to wait for her that was his prerogative, but she loved Eric, not Jason. Eric was the one she saved herself for. Eric was the one she envisioned spending the rest of her life with.

*Oh, Lord, what am I supposed to do; are either of these men the one You have planned for me? Tell me what You want me to do.*

She wished she could go back to bed and start this day over again repeating all her movements, only much slower and with more thought. She wouldn't have gotten into the argument with Eric if she'd taken into account his fragile state of mind? She wouldn't attack him about postponing school to take care of his mother. Grandma Cory was probably right, and he regretted everything he'd said. Yet here she sat in Jason's arms soaking up his strength and warmth. She was so fickle; leaving one man and finding herself in the arms of another within the hour. How did this happen? What kind of woman had she become, a fair weather friend? One who would stand by Eric until things got bad and then jump at the first offer that presented itself?

How could she mislead Jason? He took a job in Cleveland so he could arrange this visit with her. He had obviously spent some time on this plan to get her out to San Francisco into the apartment he leased with her in mind. All the while he was making plans for their future she was falling in love with Eric.

She needed to be alone. She needed to seek her heavenly Father's face. She needed to come clean with Jason before he left this porch tonight and tell him she was in love with another man, even if that man was a louse. She needed to think. Her brain was mixed up sixty ways from Sunday. She didn't trust herself to open her mouth. This was Thursday, the night before the start of a long holiday weekend. He'd go back to Cleveland on Monday. She had till then to explain about Eric. After that, he would probably never want to see her again. There seemed to be a lot of that going around.

Jason drew back and smiled. "Don't try to think it all through tonight. I know it's a lot to swallow. Just give it some thought. Remember, if the only thing you don't like about the whole proposition is living in California, that's easily taken care of. I realize how hard it would be for you to live so far away from your family. I don't care about any place enough to risk losing you. I'd live on the moon if it meant you'd be there beside me. I want you to be happy, and I want to be the one to make you that way."

He took her hands and stood up, pulling her up beside him. She tilted her head back to look at him and realized he wasn't as tall as Eric or his shoulders as broad. His eyes were a bright blue against his bronzed skin, while Eric's were dark blue and bottomless. His sandy blond hair had been streaked by the sun. With his red shadow of a beard, he reminded her of a beach bum she saw the other night on the Rockford Files.

Stop it, Jamie, focus! Stop comparing him to Eric.

She became aware of his lips coming toward hers. She turned her face to avoid the kiss and sank against his chest instead. No

matter what a terrible person she was, Jason was warm, compassionate, thoughtful, and familiar. Did she love him enough to forget
Eric and move to San Francisco? Did she love him at all? Could
she live without Eric? Two years ago she thought she couldn't live
without Jason but she had lived; she'd gotten along pretty well in
fact. Now Eric was the one she faced never seeing again. Her heart
didn't know what to think. Her head wasn't much better off. She
just wanted to lean against Jason's chest and drink in those familiar
blue eyes. She'd worry about all that other stuff tomorrow—she
was a terrible person.

# Chapter Seventeen

"*Lust not after her beauty in thine heart; neither let her take thee with thy eyelids. For by means of a whorish woman a man is brought to a piece of bread…Can a man take fire in his bosom and not be burned? Can one go upon hot coals, and his feet not be burned? So he that goeth in to his neighbor's wife; whosoever toucheth her shall not be innocent.*"

Abigail Blackwood set the Bible down in her lap and stared at the wall. The book of Proverbs might as well have been written about her. She was the evil adulteress King Solomon warned about. She had reduced Jack to a piece of bread. All he had wanted was to love her. For thirty years he did his best to make her happy and in return, he received nothing.

Her cheeks burned with shame every time she recalled the night at the hospital when the nurse summoned her through the double doors. When she reached Jack's bed, he had reached out to take her hand. "Abby," was all he had the strength to say.

She had grasped his pale hand between hers and pulled it to her face. "Oh, Jack," she cried. "I'm so sorry. I'm so sorry."

He tried to comfort her as best he could, and she struggled to pull herself together for his sake. She knew he wouldn't be with her much longer, and she didn't want him to spend his last few moments soothing her.

"Abby," he said after she stopped crying. "I love you. I always have. I want you to love yourself. God has forgiven you and so have I."

At first, she thought he meant for never loving him. She opened her mouth to lie to him one last time; to tell him he was wrong, that she did love him, she had always loved him—but the look in his eyes had stopped her.

"I know, Abby," he said breathlessly, "I've always known. But I don't care. I love you and I love Eric. It doesn't matter that he's not my son."

A sob wrenched itself from her throat, and all the strength drained out of her limbs. She sank to her knees beside the bed. Her jaw worked several times before any sound came out. "Jack, I…"

He shook his head from side to side. "No, shhh, I forgive you."

She didn't ask how he knew and she certainly respected and cared for him too much to deny it to his face.

All along Jack had known. He knew she had defiled their marriage bed. He knew she didn't love him the way he loved her. Her heart belonged to another man. And worst of all, he knew the only child in the family to carry on the Blackwood name didn't belong to him.

Abby's heart filled with loathing for herself. Not only had she been unable to love this admirable man, he had spent his life loving and nurturing another man's son.

Why hadn't he ever thrown it up in her face? Why hadn't he called her terrible names and publicly humiliated her like she deserved? Why hadn't he rejected Eric and shown more attention to his daughters? The fact that he hadn't, that he was too good for such behavior, even though she would have deserved every bit of it, made her feel that much worse.

*I've already forgiven you, Daughter, long ago. Forgive yourself.*

The still small voice speaking in her spirit was as clear as if spoken aloud. Her Heavenly Father had forgiven her for the adultery she committed with Noel Wyatt twenty years ago just like Jack said the night of the accident. She had sought God with a broken and contrite spirit, and found Him at her altar of prayer. By His grace she was forgiven.

But not for this; not for hurting Jack. She had resolutely held onto the love she had for Noel Wyatt and cherished the memories of him in her heart, and all the time denied the man who deserved it most, her own husband. She sent a good, honest, God-fearing man to his grave without ever returning the love he so freely gave. Jack knew his only son belonged to another man; he must have suffered immensely. She could never forgive herself for hurting Jack so badly, how could she expect God to?

She deserved stoning, not mercy.

*I've already forgiven you, Daughter, at the time of your repentance. Forgive yourself.*

Jack had told her the same thing, but it wasn't that easy. How could she possibly love herself after the way she'd hurt him? She would never be worthy of God's mercy. She was a Jezebel; the worst of the worst. She looked down at the passage from Proverbs again. God could never accept someone like her into His Heavenly Kingdom when His own word condemned her.

Eric had been in his room all evening. Usually he came downstairs to see if she needed anything or just to keep her company but not tonight. His devastation over losing Jamie didn't concern her. He was young; he would get over it. What worried her were the questions he'd asked earlier.

Jack must have said something to him the night of the accident, she reasoned. He must've told him the truth. He looked up at the tall, dark-haired young man, so different from himself, and said; "I know you're not my son, Eric. You've never been good enough to be my son. You were conceived in sin. I don't know where you came from, but you're no part of me."

Abby shook her head. Jack never would have said anything like that but he may as well have because now the boy knew. He shared his mother's shame and soon he would want details. He had already asked. Before long, she would be unable to dodge his questions. He would want the whole story. She shuddered to think what would happen when all of Jenna's Creek knew what she did. Her church family would look down on her, no matter how much they spoke of forgiveness. People were people; they liked to talk and loved to remember indiscretions. Her daughters would be ashamed of her. Her innocent grandchildren would be so confused; they wouldn't understand why everyone suddenly hated their grandmother. And Eric, the fruit of her iniquity, would turn his back on her too.

Until then she would hold on tight savoring every moment, thankful that Jamie Steele no longer stood between them. And she would keep on hating herself for the loathsome creature she was.

Jamie didn't say anything to anyone about Jason's proposal. She went straight to her room and lay across her bed to think. A part of her was breathless with anticipation over a new life in California; a new campus, a world of possibilities she hadn't even imagined. Anything could happen out there. Best of all she'd be with Jason, her first love. She laid a finger against her lips and relived the kiss on the front porch. He was as sweet and caring as ever. He would make a wonderful husband. He would never do anything to hurt her the way her dad had hurt her mom. He loved her and eventually she would grow to love him as much as she thought she did two years ago.

In time, her heart would stop aching for Eric Blackwood.

Love wasn't the most important part of a marriage anyway, was it? Plenty of people lived their entire lives without it. Just like Grandma Cory and Grandpa Harlan. They loved and cared for one another, but their relationship had been more caregiver-patient than husband and wife for as long as she could remember. Grandma didn't seem to miss the romance and companionship of a more conventional marriage and Jamie was certain she didn't regret one moment of her life with Grandpa.

What about all those arranged marriages in other cultures? Those couples were oftentimes complete strangers when their families or governments put them together. They learned to make things work. Jason was better than a stranger. He was wonderful, funny, caring; a solid Christian man. He'd be a good father to their children. He would even understand if she decided against children, unlike Eric who wanted a big family. Jason was sensible and intelligent; he'd always provide her with a good living. He was too conscientious to ever consider straying.

No, her heart didn't go crazy inside her chest the way it did when Eric spoke her name, but that was kids' stuff. That went away after a few years of marriage anyway. Real wives didn't go all giddy with excitement whenever they heard their husband's car in the driveway, or call out his name when they were alone just to hear the sound of it on their lips. According to the shows Grandpa Harlan watched on television, marriage was a prison, a ball and chain, a killer of passion and excitement. Even if she had married Eric, they would've turned into a bored, frustrated married couple by the time the first baby came, just like on TV. Marriages lacked passion, romance, and butterflies in the stomach. That stuff only existed in those trashy romance novels Grandma Cory didn't allow in the house, and even then it never occurred between married people.

Eric.

No, she was through wasting her time on him. So what if he was the one to set her pulse racing. He hated her, remember? He didn't want to see her face again.

*Eric is the one you love.*

It doesn't matter who I love, he doesn't love me back. He doesn't want me, Jason does. Jason came all the way from California to ask me to marry him; now that's romantic. That's the stuff trashy romance novels are made of. Jason wants me in his life, Eric doesn't.

*Eric is the one you love.*

Jamie undressed and climbed into her pajamas. As of this minute, she'd start following her head instead of her heart. Her heart couldn't be trusted. She turned off the light and stared at the twinkling stars outside her window and wondered if she could see them over the city's lights in San Francisco.

Eric had been lying in his bed for nearly an hour, unable to sleep. With an anxious groan, he sat up and leaned his weight on one elbow and stared at the multitude of stars outside his window.

He'd been sleeping a lot the past couple of months; more than when he was in grade school and Mom made him go to bed at eight-thirty on school nights. Sleep offered a solace he couldn't find anywhere else. Escape from his mother's woeful expressions; escape from the question of his paternity; escape from the oppressive mantle that hung over the house; and especially escape from the void in his heart caused by Jamie's absence. Now even the peace of sleep eluded him.

Had he actually told Jamie he didn't want to see her again? That couldn't have been him. Surely she knew he didn't mean it; that he was talking out of his head. But maybe he did mean it. She was acting so unreasonable, expecting him to marry her when he was experiencing the most devastating season of his life.

*When did Jamie say she expected a proposal from you?*

Eric wrinkled his forehead and wondered where that thought came from. Of course she expected him to marry her; it was what all women expected sooner or later. If you dated exclusively for more than three months and talked about the future and what kind of parent you imagined yourself being, the woman automatically assumed she was the one you'd be doing all that with, even if you never said as much.

*She is the one you pictured yourself with.*

Not necessarily.

*You bought the ring.*

But she had no right to assume—

*You're the one making assumptions.*

Eric swung his legs over the side of the bed and went to the window. He leaned his shoulder against the frame and stared across the tree-lined street at the houses opposite his; houses he had spent his lifetime staring at from this upstairs window. He knew all the inhabitants. He knew the old folks whose kids never came to visit anymore; he knew which ones were widowed and whose husband went out to buy a pack of cigarettes in 1966 and never came back. He knew the Blanchards were the ones who fought the loudest, threw things when they got mad, had the cops called at least once a summer for somebody smacking somebody, or playing their music too loud when their friends came over on their noisy motorcycles, rattling the windows of all the houses on the block. He knew the Millers were schoolteachers and took their kids on educational vacations to places like Gettysburg and Mount Rushmore every summer. He knew the Stanforths acted all friendly and civil to your face, but behind your back they'd talk about you all over town and complain if you didn't keep your grass mowed or your kids' bikes picked up off the sidewalk.

He had never known any life other than this one inside the second house on the left from the corner, the white two-story between the VanZants on the left and the Gibsons on the right, his parents' house—207 East Mulberry. These days though, he felt like a stranger. He saw it in his mother's face when he told her he didn't look like the Blackwoods. He was right; she knew he was right. She tried to distract him by telling him he looked like her side of the family, but that wasn't true either. He was a stranger that didn't belong here; maybe he didn't belong anywhere.

He went back to the bed and sat down on the edge. He put his elbows on his bare knees and leaned forward, cupping his chin in his palms.

*Go to Jamie. She needs you. You need her.*

Seeing Jamie wouldn't solve anything. It would make him feel that much more like an imposter, a pretender. He didn't think he loved her anymore. She didn't understand how much his mother needed him right now. How could he love someone as selfish and manipulating as she?

*When did she ever manipulate you?*

She manipulated me when she made me fall in love with her. She tricked me; she knew I would be defenseless against her womanly wiles and would spend every penny I had on that ring. Dad thought marrying her was a great idea, but he would. He was weak too, bewitched by a woman himself. Mom, on the other hand, had seen right through her. She had been against me making a snap decision from the beginning but I wouldn't listen. I let my hormones, youthful enthusiasm, or whatever it was cause me to fall for Jamie with her huge brown eyes and silly smile. She knew how to look up at me from under those dark lashes and whisper my name and make me feel like I could...

No, I'm not thinking about that right now. I'm not thinking about her soft voice in my ear or her fingers in my hair. That's how she tried to trap me in the first place. It's a good thing I got away from her when I did.

*She never tried to trap you.*

She got me to buy that ring, didn't she? She got me to spend all the money that I could have used for a new car or even a down payment on a house someday.

*What need do you have of a house? You're going to live here forever with your mother, aren't you?*

"Shut up," Eric said aloud, straightening up and directing his words at his reflected image in the darkened window looking out onto the street. "Get off my back."

He shook his head and rubbed a shaky hand across his bristled chin. He was losing it; talking to himself in the middle of the night. He checked the clock on the nightstand by his bed. Nine-fifty, when did he start thinking nine-fifty was the middle of the night? He stood up and pulled on a pair of long cotton pajama bottoms over his boxer shorts. He had to get out of this room; he had to hear the sound of another human voice before he totally went out of his mind.

He could call Karen. No, she'd nag him about the way he was treating Jamie or his decision to stay home from school this fall. Christy, no, she'd tell him to shave, clean himself up, and get a job. Maybe there was something on television worth watching; not likely, but at least the television didn't talk back. Best of all, he could watch it all night and never be forced to think about anything.

❧

"Uncle Eric, guess what's they're doing tonight at the fair-grounds?" Karen's four-year-old daughter, Rebecca asked breathlessly. Before he had time to offer a greeting, let alone guess, she rushed on, "They're having the fireworks. The fire department is going to be there and—and everything cause it's really danger-ous—and—and last year Christopher said—he said last year one of the rockets shot up in the air but then it—it had a accident or something and—it—it landed on a—a car and this little girl—she got caught on fire. So this year they're making the fire department be there so if—if she gets caught on fire again—they can put her out."

Eric pressed his lips together to suppress a chuckle even though Rebecca couldn't see his face through the telephone lines. "Christopher told you that, huh?"

"Yeah," she replied, still breathless and excited. "He said she had long red hair like me and freckles and she was even—she was wearing a red, white, and blue dress like—like the one I'm gonna wear tonight. I'm not a-scared though like I—I was last year, 'cause I'm four now and—and I—I'm not a baby anymore even though Christopher says I am. I'm not a baby, am I, Uncle Eric?"

"No, sweetheart, you're not a baby. You're a big girl; big enough to know when your brother's pulling your leg. No little girl got hit by a rocket and caught fire last year. I'm sure if she did, they would've said something about it in the paper."

"You think so?"

"Yeah, I'm pretty sure I would've heard about it."

"Maybe—maybe it was a secret. They—they didn't want to scare the other little girls and their mommies and their daddies—so—so they didn't tell nobody."

"Maybe," Eric said, diplomatically, "but I still think Christopher was just teasing you. He doesn't know yet what a big girl you are, and how you don't pay any attention to his stories anymore."

"Oh, I don't, Uncle Eric," she assured him, "'Cause he's a big ol' story teller—and I don't b'lieve nothing he says no more."

"I think that's a good idea, Beck. Whenever he tells you some-thing like that, and you wonder if it's true or not, you come ask your old uncle Eric, and I'll tell you if you need to be worried or not."

"Okay," she said with a giggle. Eric could tell she was covering her mouth with her hand, "'Cause you and me is buddies, ain't we, Uncle Eric? We're a team."

"Yeah, Beck, we're a team."

"Well, will you come with me to the fireworks tonight then? Just in case that little girl's there—and—and a rocket has another ac—accident—and—you can push me out of the way—or something, so it won't hit me and catch me on fire. Okay?"

Eric's light mood and the smile on his face—his first genuine smile in a long time —faded instantly. "Well, I wasn't planning on going anywhere tonight, honey. I'm a little tired, and I thought I'd just stay here with Grandma."

"That's what Mommy said you'd say. You never come over no more. You never play with me." Her tiny voice, only moments ago filled with excitement over her story, now quaked with impending tears. "I don't think—you—you even wanna be on my team no more."

Now tears stung Eric's eyes. It broke his heart to know he was hurting his niece. He always had a soft spot in his heart for the little green-eyed sprite. She could talk him into doing things that would embarrass the life out of him if anybody ever found out. Things like throwing a blanket over his head, chasing her through the house making scary monster noises, or lying prone on the floor—the victim of a grizzly bear attack—while she and Christopher stitched up his wounds with imaginary, invisible, magic thread.

"Now, Beck," he began. "We're still a team, you know that. You're my best girl. I do want to come over and play with you, but I've been busy lately."

"Huh, uh," she declared. "Mommy and Daddy said you're just feeling sorry—for –for—well, I forget what for, but you're just feeling sorry—and—and that's why you don't come over no more. That's why Mommy said for me to call and ask you to…to go to the fireworks. She said if—if I called and asked—you'd say yes. But you—you didn't say yes," her tiny voice quaked again, "cause I'm not your girl no more."

Her tears erupted. Even in his anger at Karen for coaxing her into making this little plea, Eric still felt about two inches tall. "Rebecca—Becky, please, honey, don't cry." All along he thought his niece had called on her own, to invite him to the fireworks. She probably did want him there, but her mother put the thought into her head. If he knew his sister, she was probably standing behind Rebecca right now, poking her with a pin to keep the tears flowing.

"Becky, stop crying," he said a little more forcefully. "Put your Mommy on the phone."

"She's busy," she said through the tears that were beginning to subside.

"Rebecca Abigail, let me talk to your mother."

"You're mean, Uncle Eric. I don't wanna talk to you no more." The connection was broken.

Eric's knuckles had gone white from gripping the phone so tightly. He placed it in the cradle and immediately picked it up again. He dialed the familiar number and waited through three rings before Karen picked up.

"Hello?"

"Karen, I—"

"What in the world did you say to Rebecca?" she demanded. "She's sitting here bawling her eyes out, saying something about you not liking her anymore; that you don't care if she catches on *fire*. For heaven's sake, Eric, what a thing to say to a little girl."

"I didn't say anything like that." He started to explain until he remembered he hadn't done anything wrong. "I don't appreciate you using your daughter to get to me. Having her call me up like that; that was dirty, Karen."

"Well, maybe it was," she admitted, "but she's been hounding me all week, wanting to know if Uncle Eric is going to take her to the fireworks. I knew if I called, you'd say no flat out. I told her if she wanted you to go so badly, she could call you herself."

He wanted to nurse his anger a little longer and get a few more barbs in, but all he could think of was his niece crying in the background. "Is she all right?"

"Yes, she's fine. Her favorite cartoon starts in a few minutes, and she'll forget all about it."

"That's comforting."

"She's four, Eric, but she still wants you to go. So does Christopher. He's just not as enamored with his Uncle Eric as Rebecca is." The irritation slowly worked its way out of her voice. "Eric," she said gently, "why don't you go with us tonight? It's the Bicentennial, for pity's sake. I know Mom isn't interested. She's never liked those kinds of things, but you always have. It would mean so much to the kids, to me too. You haven't even seen the baby in weeks. He's starting to talk," she added hopefully.

Jabber, she meant. Why did mothers always insist their fifteen-month old babies could talk when they were only making noise? "Like I told Beck, I don't feel like going anywhere tonight."

"Fine," she snapped at his weak excuse. "Don't do anybody any favors. Sit in that house and rot for all I care." The phone went dead in Eric's hand again, without tears this time, but feelings had been hurt just the same.

Karen *did* care if Eric rotted in that house, but she wasn't about to call back and tell him so. He needed to apologize, not her. Just because Rebecca seemed to have temporarily forgotten how badly she wanted him to take her to the fireworks, it didn't mean she was over him no longer treating her like 'his girl'. Uncle Eric was the greatest thing in her book since sliced bread and it rankled Karen to know his recent behavior hurt her.

She wished their father were here to talk to Eric. He could always get through to him, but of course, if Jack were here, Eric wouldn't be going through whatever it was he was going through. Tears stung Karen's eyes at the injustice of it all. She missed her father, she missed her brother; she wished her mother would stop feeling sorry for herself and feeding off Eric's sense of responsibility. That was the problem in a nutshell. Eric wanted to take care of his mother, to ease her pain, to fill his father's shoes. No matter how hard he tried, he could never do it so why did Abby encourage him to try?

If she had time this afternoon after Roger got home from work—between getting the kids ready for the fireworks and fixing supper and getting the baby down for a nap— she'd go over there and try one more time to talk some sense into her mother's head. But every time she tried to broach the subject, it came out sounding like she was insensitive, like she expected her mother to get over her husband's death in an amount of time convenient to the rest of the family. None of them expected that. Karen just wanted her to set Eric free so he could face his own grief and not be responsible for hers.

Karen sighed and went into the living room to turn on the television. "Knock off that crying, Rebecca Abigail, or you won't be watching Scooby Doo," she called in irritation to her daughter and immediately wished she were a more patient person.

As expected, the tears stopped flowing, and Rebecca and Christopher raced into the living room, cheering wildly, to settle on pillows on the floor in front of the television. "Don't sit so close," she admonished half-heartedly as she headed for the kitchen to wash up the lunch dishes. "After your show is over, you're both taking naps."

"Okay, Mommy," they chorused, their enraptured green eyes never leaving the screen.

Jason drove back to Cleveland Monday night, July fifth. He invited Jamie to see the fireworks on the fourth, but she begged off, claiming she had a headache. Actually she didn't want to run into Eric. Not because he would see her with Jason and put them both in a potentially embarrassing situation, but simply because she wasn't ready to see his face. If she did, she couldn't guarantee she wouldn't break down and cry in front of the whole county, Jason included.

Jason told her before he left he wanted to give her plenty of time to think about his offer; he didn't want to pressure her into uprooting her entire life if it wasn't what she really wanted. He'd be in Cleveland till the end of August. She could go to San Francisco with him then or wait as long as Labor Day weekend. By then her mind would have to be made up and arrangements made for the transfer from Ohio University to Stanford or another school of her choice in the San Francisco area. If she waited till the last minute, they would have to get married out there since there was no way he could afford to fly back for a wedding. It was up to her, he assured her; he had already made his desires known.

"I'll be thinking of you every minute, Jamie, and waiting to hear from you. I hope you decide to come with me, but if you don't I'll understand. I love you. I want you to do whatever makes you happy."

Good old understanding Jason. Her decision would have been easier if he had fallen down on his knees and begged her to say yes; that he would curl up and die if she turned him down; that she was his reason for living, his everything, his one and only. Instead he told her that whatever her decision, he would understand.

Passionate, no—romantic, no—understanding, yes.

She watched him drive away, down Betterman Road, a five-hour trip to Cleveland ahead of him, and thought how sweet it was of him to come all this way to see her. That was romantic, wasn't it? Maybe so, but it had also been a practical choice. He planned to see his father anyway. He was able to visit his ailing father and propose marriage to his lady fair at the same time; killing two birds with one stone.

Tuesday morning, Jamie pushed aside her indecision about Jason and the aching void in her heart caused by Eric's absence. She clocked in at the drugstore twenty minutes before opening and went to the safe in Noel's office for the money necessary to prepare her cash register drawer for business. As usual for that hour of the day, Noel occupied the high-backed leather office chair behind his desk.

"Morning, Noel," she said, going straight for the safe. The small metal door was open, and the pouch from the bank was ready and waiting for her inside. Each bag was marked with a scrap of memo pad taped on, a name scrawled across the front for whichever register the money was supposed to go into. Noel prepared the bags the night before, counting out the right amount of cash and labeling the bag for the three registers that would open the following morning. Paige's bag was already missing. She always arrived first. Sheila's lay next to Jamie's. Sheila was the last to get to the store every morning. She had three kids and a husband who wasn't much help around the house, so she was always behind schedule.

"Morning, Jamie, how are things?"

"Fine," she said, removing the pouch from the safe.

"Did you see Jason off last night?"

"Yes, he's back in Cleveland I'm sure by now, working his fingers to the bone."

Noel leaned the chair back on its springs and laced his fingers behind his head. He smiled, always having a soft spot for Jason. "Yes, he's a boy after my own heart. He'll be working up until they lay him in the ground."

A typical Noel Wyatt comment; those were the types of people he admired, the ones who worked themselves to death, just like he planned to do.

"Are you still seeing Eric Blackwood?"

Jamie blanched, immediately filled with guilt. She never had gotten around to saying anything to Jason about Eric. She didn't know why. He would've understood. He would've said it was only natural that she dated other people while he was in California. He wouldn't have experienced one pang of jealousy. Jason never got jealous. He understood.

"No, not exactly," she mumbled to Noel. "He's been spending a lot of time with his mother since his father..."

Her voice trailed off. Now, she really sounded horrible. Noel probably thought she went from man to man looking for the one who could show her the best time. She didn't have time for one who may be suffering from some sort of tragedy.

"Yes, so I hear," he said. "How's Mrs. Blackwood getting along, do you know?"

He knew she hadn't told Jason about Eric, guilt was written

all over her face. Why else would he look at her so strangely? Or maybe he knew Eric had dumped her, and she hooked up with Jason on the rebound. She was a fickle two-timer and Noel could see right through her.

"She's having a pretty rough time of it, I expect," she said vaguely, turning the money pouch over and over in her hands. "I haven't talked to her for a while since Eric and I aren't...I haven't been to the house in a long time," she finished lamely.

Noel leaned forward in his chair and put his elbows on the desk, resting his chin in the palms of his hands. Jamie frowned and tried not to stare, wondering who he reminded her of when he did that. It was like when she watched a movie and spent the whole time trying to remember in what other role she had seen the actor who played the leading man's best friend.

"I should have sent flowers," he mused aloud. "I thought about it, but it wouldn't have looked right." Footsteps sounded on the stairs. Sheila had arrived to get her money pouch. That meant it was almost time to open the store. Noel looked up suddenly, almost startled to see Jamie still in the room. "Well, um, give them my regards, would you?" he asked. "The next time you see them."

Wasn't he paying attention? She just said she wasn't seeing Eric anymore and hadn't been to the house in a long time. She nodded her acquiescence and squeezed past Sheila in the doorway. Noel was obviously disgusted at the way she led Jason on like she had, not even explaining to him the seriousness of her relationship with Eric. He would probably get on the phone today and call him in Cleveland and tell him what a two-timing hussy Jamie Steele had become.

Noel sat back in his leather chair and stared at the closed door Sheila had just gone out of, his mind a thousand miles away. As usual these days since hearing of Jack Blackwood's death, his thoughts were on Abby and Eric. He wished for the thousandth time he could do something to comfort them. He loved Abby, cared deeply for her feelings, and suffered because he knew she was suffering. He loved Eric because he was his son, but in actuality he knew practically nothing about the boy. Until he won the Benjamin F. Wyatt Memorial Scholarship for Science during his senior year of high school, they had never been introduced. They had never spoken on a familiar level before he came to work at the drugstore, and Noel made sure those occasions were kept to a minimum.

He hated to use Jamie to get information about Abby and Eric, but his curiosity got the better of him these days; must be his age.

Being in Eric's presence made him incredibly nervous. He was his son; he wanted to talk to him about any potential problems in school, his apparent affection for Jamie Steele, his plans for the future, how he planned to support a wife and kids; all the fatherly stuff that he had been unable to ask. Even now he couldn't ask. Eric belonged to Jack Blackwood, regardless of biology. Jack's death hadn't changed anything. He still had no claim to the young man he fathered.

He used to think of Jason Collier as a son; he had dreamed of training him to take over the business someday. Jason had a head for it; he was a natural businessman but his dreams were in the courtroom, not behind a pharmacy counter. Noel fought his own disappointment when Jason made his intentions known. He had almost asked him if he wouldn't rather consider medical school. But he didn't believe in trying to manipulate other people's lives, even if he felt his way was best. So Noel did what he could, helped him fill out scholarship applications, wrote recommendation letters, and offered his advice on college entrance interviews.

Noel didn't mention Eric when Jason stopped by Monday afternoon on his way out of town, happy as a clam, and announced he had proposed to Jamie. The girl could do that herself.

"I told her to think about it," Jason explained, looking from Noel to Lucinda for confirmation that he'd done the right thing. "We have to get this thing done before classes start at Stanford. I sure can't take her out there without marrying her first."

After Jason left for Cleveland, Lucinda turned to her son and asked, "Why so pensive, Noel? I thought you'd be happy for Jason and Jamie."

"I'm just wondering what's become of Eric Blackwood," he said.

Lucinda furrowed her brow and stared hard at him. Noel was sure she had figured out his relationship with Eric two years ago, but she never admitted as much. "What about Eric Blackwood?" she asked.

"He and Jamie have become quite an item the past year or so. I thought the two of them were getting serious."

"Well, Jamie has a right to marry whomever she chooses."

"I know, Mother. I'm just saying she was seeing Eric until—until recently and suddenly she's considering a proposal from Jason. I'd hate to think she's on the rebound from Eric and would end up hurting Jason."

"And I hate to think you've got nothing more important to do at your age than worry about the love lives of your employees."

"Jamie and Jason are more than employees, you know that."

She narrowed her eyes and scrutinized him over the rim of her coffee cup. "And what about Eric, what is he to you?"

Noel's lips parted, and he almost spilled the truth. It would feel so good to speak the words aloud. *"I'm in love with Abigail Blackwood, Mother. I always have been, and Eric is our son."*

If only things had been different; if only he had made his true feelings known to Abby when he first realized them himself; if only he had asked her to marry him back during the war before she married Jack. They had both lived to regret his sluggishness, even giving into the ill-fated affair that resulted in Eric's conception.

That was ancient history. Abby was Jack's wife—his widow now—and by all appearances had been happily married. Simply because Jack was gone, nothing would change. Noel would go home to his big empty house on Bryton Avenue and sit in front of the cold fireplace and read the Wall Street Journal. He'd prepare a sandwich or some such thing for his dinner and eat it in the living room. On Sundays he would eat at his mother's house after church as he'd done since the collapse of his marriage to Myra Curtsinger.

Noel had just turned sixty, his beloved mother was ninety-two; how much longer would his life go on as it always had? When

Lucinda Wyatt gave in to old age, his last remaining relative in the area would be gone. Then what? His sisters lived on opposite ends of the country with their own families and grandchildren and great-grandchildren. Noel was the only one without anyone behind him; the last of the great Wyatt clan that once populated the county. He would go to the grave without a son to carry on the family name, without grandchildren to bounce on his knee and tell stories of all the Wyatts who had gone on before them.

Noel hated it when his mind dwelled on such things. It was a pointless, self-pitying pursuit. His mortal life was winding down. He might hang on another twenty years or so. His physician, barely out of his twenties—the injustice of that was overwhelming—said he had the health of a man half his age. Noel doubted the validity in that statement. He probably said that to all the old codgers who clogged up his daily roster; but on the off chance the gum-cracking doc was right and he did live to be eighty or so, what good would it do anybody? He wouldn't make any medical breakthroughs to benefit mankind. He wouldn't run for office or invent an alternative fuel source rendering the oil barons of OPEC obsolete. He would continue to shuffle around the house on Bryton Avenue, run the drugstore until his old bones wouldn't let him out of bed, and eventually pass away—preferably in his sleep.

He slapped the desk and stood up with a disgusted grunt at himself. The store was opening below him. In a moment, the phone behind the pharmacy counter would ring, and some doctor would call in a prescription for a patient. He had more important matters that demanded his attention than wishing his life had gone differently. He needed to find a pharmacy assistant to take Noreen Trimble's place. Angie's classes would be over soon, and she would move on to another store where she wasn't just someone's assistant. Then he would be alone behind the counter again.

In his heart of hearts, Noel knew why he was dragging his feet at finding someone else. Not only would he be accepting the fact that Noreen was imprisoned for a murder he believed she hadn't meant to commit, and not coming back, he harbored a secret desire that Eric would someday take his place behind the pharmacy counter.

When he learned Eric had majored in microbiology, his chest had swelled with pride. Like father, like son. If he could only convince the boy to go on to graduate school, he would have the proper training to take Noel's place. Noel could retire, spend a few winters on a beach somewhere with the knowledge that all was well back home because his own son was minding the store.

Noel shook his head. None of that was ever going to happen. He didn't like the beach, he didn't know how to relax, and regardless of his fantasies of the father/son relationship he imagined cultivating with Eric, it was never going to happen. He would die without an heir to leave his business to.

Everything could have been so different, if only…

# Chapter Eighteen

Cory Steele placed the clean spoons in the drawer and slid it shut with a bang of her hip; so much to do and such a short time in which to get it done. The lunch dishes had just now been put away. Normally she put them away as soon as she finished them, but today didn't seem to be a day for getting much accomplished. Too much else required her attention without worrying about clearing off the countertops. Some things had to wait these days. Dinner simmered in the stew pot on the stove. At least that job was done and out of the way.

Poor Jamie; Cory didn't want her to come home from work tonight to a bunch of farm chores. The girl had enough on her plate right now. She had been moping around the house since the first of July when she had her big blow-up with the Blackwood boy. Jason's sudden appearance on their doorstep had perked her up for a day or two, but now her hang-dog expression grew more forlorn every day and Cassie's constant barrage of questions didn't help.

*"What's up with Jason showing up out of the blue like he did?"*

*"Where's Eric been lately? Aren't you seeing him anymore?"*

*"Is Jason going back to California in the fall? Is he still in love with you?*

*"So who are you dating now, Eric or Jason? You'd better make up your mind. I don't know which one I'm rooting for. Eric is gorgeous, but Jason is so sweet. He's like a big brother to me already."*

Cory didn't miss the melancholy glaze that settled over Jamie's expression every time Cassie got to going. The poor girl was hurting, and she didn't have an inkling of what to do about it.

Her mood even affected Harlan who seldom noticed anything going on around him. The doctor's told her his decline would quicken as he neared the end. She could see it so plainly now that Jamie didn't live at home much of the year. Whether with Jamie's departure, the passage of time, or his advancing age Harlan was slipping away. He was losing weight, interacting less with the family, sleeping more, and spending nearly every waking minute in front of the television.

The swish, swish of a broom across the linoleum caused Cory to turn her head in surprise. The end of the broom entered the kitchen first, followed by Harlan who pushed an ever-increasing amount of dirt ahead of him. Even before he stopped doing chores, he never swept the floor unless Jamie could coax him into helping her with some light housekeeping.

He didn't look up from his work or acknowledge Cory's presence as he moved across the faded kitchen floor. He reached under the kitchen table to retrieve an errant dust bunny and scraped the broom along the chipped baseboards, going through all the motions Cory herself would do had she been behind the broom. After several moments of meticulous sweeping, Harlan moved to the center of the floor and swept the dirt into a tidy pile. He snapped the dustpan off the side of the broom and bent over to collect his pile of dirt. He moved the dustpan back several times on the floor, eliminating the line of dirt between the floor and the dustpan as he went. With careful precision he straightened up, the dustpan in one hand, broom in the other. He leaned the broom against a kitchen chair and approached the stove. He removed the lid from the pot of simmering stew and dumped the contents of the dustpan into the pot. Carefully, to escape the rising steam, he replaced the lid on the pot, picked up the broom from where it rested against the chair, and carried it and the dustpan from the room.

Cory's arms dropped to her sides. Her jaw dropped open in disbelief. Her head pivoted from the stew pot, to the kitchen door her husband had just gone out of, and back again. From outside the kitchen window she could hear Cassie's melodious voice singing Church in the Wildwood as she headed to the vegetable garden with the hoe.

There was so much yet to do before nightfall. She let out a breath of exasperation and turned off the heat under the stew pot. If memory served her correctly, there was a chunk of leftover ham in the refrigerator. She headed to the pantry to see if there were enough potatoes she could fry up for dinner and add to it.

The door swung open to reveal the diminutive Lucinda Wyatt on the other side. A welcoming smile split her lined face. Her once dark hair, now completely white, lay in neat pin curls all over her head. She held out a tiny fragile hand and ushered her guest inside the cool interior of the house. "Hello, dear, I'm so glad you could make it. I haven't seen you in forever."

"It has been a long time," Jamie said in agreement. She set her purse and car keys on the little table inside the foyer. She pulled her shirt away from her skin and fanned herself with the fabric. Outside the house, the temperature nudged its way toward the upper nineties. If she went to California with Jason, she certainly wouldn't miss the muggy Ohio summers.

Lucinda led her into a sunny sitting room to the left of the foyer. She settled herself on a fragile looking settee and motioned for Jamie to take a seat across from her. "We had a nice visit with Jason a couple of weeks ago," she said without preamble, and then continued on before Jamie could respond. A typical Wyatt trait; they didn't intend to be rude; they were just always in a rush for information. Jamie quickly discovered one had to talk fast around here in order to get in on the conversation. "It was so good to see him again. California seems to agree with him."

"Yes, from what I gather, he's ready to make it his permanent home."

"That's fine for him, I suppose, but I hate to think I'll never see him again. My daughter Genevieve has lived in Pasadena for thirty years. I don't imagine she'd dream of coming back."

"No, I suppose not."

Jamie could see the gears turning in the old woman's head. She tried to think of something to say, before Lucinda had a chance to bring up the real reason of why she'd summoned her this afternoon. She was pretty sure she knew, especially since she asked about Jason right off.

Lucinda clasped her hands together and leaned forward. Jamie braced herself. "How does your family feel about him asking you to move across the country?"

For once in her life, Lucinda Wyatt stopped talking and studied Jamie with uncharacteristic patience.

Jamie felt the color drain from her face. So Lucinda and Noel knew about Jason's proposal. She realized she was hoping no one ever found out; that she wouldn't be forced into making a decision. "Um, well, I haven't exactly told anyone about—his offer," she stammered. "I didn't know he mentioned it either."

"I didn't think you had." Lucinda stood up and moved to where Jamie sat. She settled herself on the sofa beside her. "Don't worry I'm pretty sure he only told Noel and me. You know how Jason is; he doesn't talk about his personal life except to those he knows will be discreet."

"There's no need to be discreet." Jamie heard the crack in her voice, but raised her chin and continued. "I don't care who knows."

Lucinda put her arm around Jamie's shoulder. "Then why haven't you told your family?"

Jamie shrugged. She sniffed and wiped her nose on the back of her hand. The cool air inside the house was making her nose run. "I know they'll be thrilled."

Lucinda took a tissue out of a box on the end table and stuffed it into Jamie's hand. "Then whatever is the matter?"

"Nothing," Jamie said, dabbing at the end of her nose. "Everything's fine. His proposal couldn't have come at a better time."

"Oh? And why is that?"

"Well, what I meant was…" Jamie had no idea what she meant.

Was she actually considering Jason's proposal simply because it was keeping her mind off the terrible void in her heart over Eric? Surely she wasn't that superficial.

Lucinda studied her for a moment longer, and then spoke up. "Jason was as pleased as punch when he told us he asked you to marry him. You, on the other hand, look like you've lost your best friend."

Jamie forced a smile. "No, I'm fine. I'm very happy. All I've been thinking about the past two weeks is living in California. You're right, it'll be very exciting." She almost believed it.

Lucinda squeezed Jamie's shoulder and pulled her against her. "Oh, Jamie, please tell me what's bothering you. You mustn't try to convince me of your happiness when you can't even convince yourself."

Jamie looked into Lucinda's face. She hadn't realized her emotions were so close to the surface that anyone with an observing eye could read them. "I haven't decided what I'm going to do yet," she admitted. "I'm flattered that Jason came all the way from California to see me. I never expected it. And we had a wonderful weekend together."

"So, what's the problem?"

"How do you know if you love someone?" she blurted out. "I mean, if you know you used to, but then you don't see them for a long time. Then you meet someone else who you think you might be in love with. But something happens, and you can't be with that person anymore. Wouldn't it be better to go with the first one, who at least loves you and is willing to cross a thousand oceans to be with you? What if you wait for the other one, but he never comes back? Then your only chance for happiness is gone."

"Jamie, honey, how old are you now, twenty? You can't possibly believe this is your only chance at happiness?"

"I don't know, maybe. I believe God has a purpose for my life, and maybe this is it. To marry Jason and move to California and have a wonderful life."

"If that's true, why are you so miserable?" Lucinda studied Jamie's face for a moment before continuing. "I believe God has a purpose for you, too; but I also believe He knows what He's doing. Like it or not, Jamie, you're the type of person who'll probably never live more than a hundred miles from where you were born. Now why would God create that in you and then uproot you and send you across the country?"

"Maybe once I got used to it, I'd love it. I've never been anywhere before, so I don't know what I'd like. Maybe God wants me to try new experiences."

"Possibly, and it's also possible that you aren't even in love with Jason anymore. You could be ideally suited for California, but miserable because you're with a man you don't love."

"But Jason is so right for me. We have everything in common. I know we'd be happy together. Everything with him is so easy."

Lucinda laughed and then checked herself apologetically. "Jamie, sweetie who ever said love is easy? It isn't. If memory serves me correctly, it's exciting. It's exhilarating. It's worth the effort you put into it, but it's never easy."

If possible, Jamie looked even glummer. "Oh, sweetheart, don't worry. You'll be fine. You'll make the right decision. Just keep praying about it. Please, please, don't make any decision in haste. I'll be praying for you too. Take your time, listen for the Lord's leading, and…" she put her hand on Jamie's knee, "don't be afraid to listen to your heart. You don't fall in love with someone because he's right for you. Let your heart show the right way. Even if it's the hardest thing you ever have to do, it will pay off in the end."

Mrs. Wyatt stood up. "Come in here, dear. I have something I want to give you."

Jamie followed Mrs. Wyatt into a large bedroom off the main hallway. The old woman hit the light switch by the door and filled the cavernous room with light. A walnut four-poster bed occupied the center of the room. A star quilt done in ecru, multiple shades of blues, and red covered its expanse. A wardrobe stood sentinel near the bed along with a dresser and jewelry armoire. A free standing mirror and a quilt rack stood on opposite sides of the closet door; each a heavy piece created from the same dark walnut.

Jamie stepped immediately toward the bed and leaned over the magnificent quilt. "Oh, Mrs. Wyatt, it's beautiful. I've never seen anything like it." She kept her hands at her sides although they longed to reach out and touch the immaculate hand stitching.

"Thank you, dear. My mother helped me stitch this quilt the year before she died. She would come over nearly every afternoon and we worked on it together." Mrs. Wyatt laid a reverent hand on the fabric as she remembered. "She was a wonderful quilter. She taught me and my sister, but of course our talents never matched hers. She won nearly every competition she ever entered. There are several pieces around here that she did, but this is my favorite. The year we worked on this, she was in a great deal of pain from her arthritis, but she wouldn't stop. After she passed away the following spring, I realized why it was so important to her to see it finished. My girls, Genevieve and Gwen, argue good naturedly, of course, over which of them is going to get it after I'm gone, but I just tell them I'm not leaving."

Jamie leaned further out over the bed, her eyes hungrily absorbing the colors and intricate pattern. The quilt and story of Mrs. Wyatt's daughters fighting over it, made her miss her own mother. What she wouldn't give for a similar tangible link between Nancy, Cassie, and herself.

Mrs. Wyatt moved to the cedar chest that stood in contrast against the foot of the walnut bed, and opened the lid. The pungent scent of cedar reminded Jamie of the bottomless closet in Grandma Cory's bedroom. Mrs. Wyatt pulled out a quilt done in pale yellows and every shade of blue from robin's egg to royal.

She opened it carefully to display the design. "This pattern is called a log cabin. I want you to have it."

"Oh, no, I couldn't," Jamie protested weakly, wanting nothing more than to snatch the quilt out of her arms.

"You have to take it. You wouldn't want to hurt my feelings, would you?"

Jamie allowed it to be pushed into her arms, and she looked down admiringly.

"I made this one myself after Mother passed away. It's been in this trunk for close to twenty years. I don't quilt like I used to. Arthritis is the thief of many an old woman's pleasures. But I've always loved this pattern and what it symbolizes. The dark and light contrasting colors represent the walls of the home. See the little patch of red in the center of each square. It represents the heart; the center. Whether you spend your life in a trailer park outside Jenna's Creek with five kids, or alone in a chateau in the Swiss Alps, you, as the woman, will create the heart of your home.

"If you ever have children, no matter how old they get or how far they roam, they'll always think of you as the center of the family. They'll love their father, but when they come home, it'll be to see Mother. We are the nurturers, the teachers, the souls of the world whether we have children or not. No matter whom you decide to spend your life with, or even not with, you'll be the center of your home. I want this quilt to remind you of that."

Jamie tucked the quilt under one arm and put the other around Mrs. Wyatt. "I'll remember," she whispered, her chest full. "And I'll remember you understanding me even when I don't understand myself."

Lucinda hugged her back. "You're a lot smarter than you give yourself credit for. You'll do the right thing, dear, don't worry about that."

The two women turned toward the door. Jamie noticed for the first time a photograph hanging on the wall of a dark-haired young man in a baseball uniform. He stood atop a pitcher's mound, posed and ready to release a pitch, his weight on his back leg with the other cocked in front of him, both hands clutching a baseball at his waist. She drew back puzzled, and didn't miss the reaction from Mrs. Wyatt out of the corner of her eye.

Why did she have the feeling she had seen this picture before? "Who..." She narrowed her eyes and stepped closer to examine the picture. Though outdated and captured in black and white, the uniform was still easily recognizable as belonging to the South Auburn High School Cyclones. Dark, unruly hair stuck out from under the striped baseball cap framing a handsomely, familiar face. "That looks like..." Her voice trailed off again. "Oh, my, that's Noel, isn't it?"

"Yes," Mrs. Wyatt said, stepping up beside her and smiling at the picture. "That's my boy, my baseball star, hasn't changed a bit—at least not to these tired old eyes."

"You know, he really hasn't changed," Jamie agreed, still studying the photograph. "Those eyes are the giveaway, and that square chin. Look at that thick dark hair, so much of it. If it wasn't for the little bit of gray he has now..." She took a step back from the picture and cocked her head thoughtfully; definitely Noel, yet reminiscent of someone else. She had seen the face in this picture somewhere before; not the face of the current Noel Wyatt, graying, softened by age, but someone else with the same face, dressed in the same green and white baseball uniform.

# Chapter Nineteen

Abigail Blackwood dabbed mascara on her dark lashes. Other than the occasional use of foundation and a touch of lipstick—usually on her way to church on Sundays— she wasn't the make-up type. She supposed it was a holdover from growing up a tomboy under three older brothers. To this day, she wasn't one of those women who obsessed about her looks; getting wrinkles, counting gray hairs, or worrying as her hips expanded. Her figure had held out reasonably well, considering her love for brownies, cheesecake, and the fact she'd given birth four times. If that didn't give her the right to wear her comfortable size twelve's with no concern for what the world thought about her virtually nonexistent waistline, what did?

At the present time, her size twelve slacks hung on her gaunt frame. She figured she'd lost fifteen pounds or so since April, but she had no intention of going out and buying smaller clothes. Her appetite would someday return, and she'd go back to the weight she'd maintained since the girls were in grade school.

Her ashen complexion and hollowed out cheeks caused by the drastic weight loss, depression, and a summer spent almost exclusively indoors, did concern her. For all her nagging, Karen had a point when she suggested Abby get outside occasionally and see the sun shining. Her recent lifestyle changes weren't doing her health any good.

This morning was one of those unavoidable trips downtown. There were several stops to make and things to take care of, hence the mascara. She'd hate to run into any small children and scare the life out of them with her haggard, unmade up face.

Her first stop was the bank to transfer money from savings into the checking account where the check from Jack's life insurance policy had been deposited. She hadn't touched the money since paying off his funeral, but some upcoming household expenses required extra cash. She hated doing it. She and Jack never touched their savings, even with Eric in college. Their money had been budgeted so that his weekly paychecks took care of all their needs. She never had to get a part-time job to help out, they didn't dip into savings when taxes or house insurance was due; they just tightened their belts and made his check go a little farther. Now that he was gone and the weekly deposits into the family coffers had stopped, she was forced to make some serious changes. She wasn't hurting for money by any means; Jack had taken care of everything, just in case, but she didn't want an unforeseen future event to wipe out what she had. She was alone now—practically unskilled in the eyes of the working world—facing another eight and a half years before eligible to draw social security from Jack's account.

Social security! Was she that old? Was that all she had to look forward to the last half of her life? Sitting at home waiting for the mailman to deliver her monthly check until her body gave out? With her luck, she'd live forever.

She was barely in her fifties. What in the world was she going to do with the twenty or thirty years she had left? She'd never seriously considered a job outside her home. She'd always had one; wife and mother, more than enough to keep her busy and fulfilled.

Not now. Now it was just her and Eric. She was far from busy these days; most of her hours were spent in bed or in front of the TV. As far as fulfillment...she hadn't given that concept any thought before. Women of her generation didn't worry about being fulfilled, they just did what was expected of them; played the role of cook, housekeeper, and now, doting grandmother, and that was that. Fulfillment was for younger women—the bra burners—searching for happiness outside the home. Abby never considered burning her brassiere. She wasn't a rocket scientist, but she understood the laws of gravity.

Abby's fulfillment had always been found in the bosom of her family. A pang of guilt assailed her when she thought of how she'd forsaken her three little grandchildren lately. Roger or Karen brought them over to visit periodically, but Karen was irritated with her and had stopped coming by as often. Maybe after the bank, the grocery store, the church to drop off two cherry pies she'd baked for an upcoming bake sale, and filling the car up with gas, she'd stop in to see them. That would be a pleasant surprise. If Roger was home, she could get him to look at the Buick, and see if he could figure out the source of a pinging noise coming from underneath the hood. On second thought, she'd ask the man at the service station to do it. He'd charge an arm and a leg, but it wasn't fair to keep bothering Roger with every little thing that came up.

After a quick trip through the grocery store, Abby turned the car down a back street and pulled into the parking lot of the feed and grain. The place was deserted. Old Mr. Davenport would get her in and out in short order. This used to be Jack's errand. He would come in on the odd Saturday whenever she needed fertilizer for the garden. Now, like everything else, the task was left to her. That's why she'd come today instead of a Saturday when the parking lot was packed with farmers from every size farm in the county, most with their trucks pulled up alongside the grain elevators, jawing with one another while Mr. Davenport's hired help filled their orders. Some just stopped in for dog food or grass seed and made a morning of it; even the women who came in their beat up pick-up trucks with their hair pulled back tight against their heads, wearing their husbands' cast-off overalls intimidated Abby. Many of these farm women chewed tobacco like their men folk, could lift a hay bale or a new calf as easily as she could a toddler, and cuss a blue streak if they thought Mr. Davenport was weighing a little light on the scales.

Inside, the heavy smell of grain and dust that covered every surface, including Mr. Davenport, greeted her. He got up from his stool behind the dusty counter and gave her a gap-toothed smile.

"Morning, Mrs. Blackwood." One thing about Old Mr. Davenport; even though he was on the wrong side of eighty, he could remember the name of every customer he had, even ones like her who he only saw once in a blue moon. "I'm awful sorry to hear about Jack."

"Thank you, Mr. Davenport," she mumbled, careful not to bump up against anything and cover her outfit with a fine layer of feed and grain residue. She still had to drop her pies off at the church.

"He was a good feller, he was," the wrinkled proprietor continued. "I always appreciated him doing business here. I know he could've bought his fertilizer at that new farm supply store in Blanton; lots a folks doing that nowadays. Won't be long, a feller like me'll be run plumb outta business."

Abby hadn't really thought about it before, but Mr. Davenport obviously had. Supermarkets and auto supply store chains were springing up everywhere, even here in Auburn County. It had to be a major concern for small operations like Mr. Davenport's. Certainly there would always be a need for a feed and grain though. Where else could people go for feed for their livestock? She was sure he had no cause for alarm.

She thought of Noel and his drugstore. How long could he compete if one of those nationwide retail drugstore chains moved into the county? Wyatt's Drugstore was an institution in Jenna's Creek. Would the community ever decide to chuck his personal service in order to save a few pennies on a can of deodorant?

She turned her attention back to the business at hand. "That's what I'm here for today, fertilizer. I only need one fifty-pound bag. My garden isn't as big as usual this year," she added in explanation.

"Sure." He nodded and headed out the door she had just come in. He hefted a bag from a mountainous pile outside the front door onto a dolly as if it was filled with feathers and steered it down the ramp to her waiting car. She realized she'd need Eric to unload it from the trunk when she got home.

Mr. Davenport added the tax to her total in his head. She used the hood of the Buick as a desk while she wrote her check. She thanked him and climbed into the car. "You take care of yourself, now, Mrs. Blackwood," Mr. Davenport told her. "If there's anything you'd be needin'…"

Abby nodded and lifted her hand as she dropped the car into reverse. "Thank you, Mr. Davenport," she called out the open window and let the car back into a wide arc across the empty lot away from him. She hoped his eighty-year-old ears wouldn't hear the pinging under the hood and offer to take a look at it for her.

She straightened the wheel and bumped across the long abandoned railroad tracks that once brought grain to fill the elevators about the time Old Man Davenport was a boy in short pants. She saw a car approaching on the street. As it drew abreast of the Buick, it slowed down. The woman inside the car twisted her neck in Abby's direction and brought her car to almost a complete halt. Abby didn't recognize the driver and waited patiently for the car to pass so she could pull onto the street. At the last minute, the car made a sharp right and pulled into the lot beside her.

Abby used the button to lower the power windows on the passenger side of the car. When Jack bought the car three years ago, she thought power windows were an unnecessary extravagance, but now she couldn't imagine doing without them. They sure made life easier.

She was taken aback when she noticed the stern look on the other woman's face; a face she vaguely recalled from somewhere. She smiled anyway and leaned forward to turn down the volume on the radio.

The woman barely took the time to put her car into park before she started talking, her voice raised over the sounds of the two cars' engines, her face flushed with repressed anger. "I think it's a shame you bringing that boy of yours into the drugstore like you did, flaunting your indiscretion under good people's noses."

"Her boy", "the drugstore", "indiscretion," what was this woman talking about? Who was she? Suddenly it hit her, Paige Trotter, who worked behind the cash register at Wyatt's drugstore. She had seen her on the few occasions she had stopped in to pick up something. Eric had mentioned the sour-faced thing throwing a barb at him every now and then after he went to work there. Abby had never given her a moments thought before now.

In horror, she suddenly realized this creature somehow knew about her and Noel. Impossible, no one knew. It happened over twenty years ago. Anyone who may have seen Abby in Noel's car back then or behaving in a mysterious manner would have forgotten about it by now. If rumors had been circulating, it would've been all over town in no time. People in a small town didn't let something as good as an illicit romance go by without plenty of gossip and finger pointing. She glanced in her rearview mirror and saw that Mr. Davenport had disappeared back inside the feed and grain. Good. She didn't want him to witness her humiliation.

Abby managed to keep her face devoid of emotion and her voice even. "I don't know what you're talking about. I don't even know you. I can't imagine how you know me."

A sneer pulled the woman's lips into a mirthless grin. "I know you, all right, and I know all about how you got that boy of yours a job at the drugstore." She paused a moment for her words to sink in. "You and Noel Wyatt think you're so clever. You think you've got everybody fooled. Well, you don't. I know what you're up to, and it just ain't right."

The woman wasn't making any sense. Abby was beginning to wonder if she was even talking about Eric's paternity. "Just what is it you think we're up to?" she asked.

"I've dedicated my whole life to Noel and that lousy drugstore," Paige growled, "and for what? So my nephew, Calvin, could graduate and get a job behind the counter as his assistant. Everything was working out perfectly too. I knew God had a hand in it when Noreen Trimble went to prison two years ago, and the position opened up."

Abby's mind went back to the discovery of Sally Blake's body—missing for more than twenty-five years—in an abandoned well and Noreen's confession that she had killed Sally in self defense. She doubted the logic in a merciful God sending someone to prison so a young man could have the job he wanted.

"I wasn't too worried when Noel hired Angie to take Noreen Trimble's place," Paige continued her litany. "We all knew she was just temporary until someone with Calvin's qualifications could get out of school. Noel can't live forever, and if Calvin plays his cards right, he'll be set for life."

Abby's impatience got the better of her. "I still don't know what any of this has to do with me or my son," she interjected. "I don't know anything about your nephew. If you've got a beef with Noel for not hiring Calvin, I suggest you take it up with him."

"Ha! You sure are a prissy one, ain't ya? That figures. Well, you can deny it all you want, but I know why Eric's at the drugstore. He's come to take Calvin's position."

Paige's face was turning an angry shade of red. Abby wondered how stable she was. She considered hitting the button to return the power window to its closed position and driving away.

"Calvin deserves that job," Paige sputtered. "I've given Noel my whole life, and I deserve something out of it. Not you and your bastard son."

So Paige did know about Eric. How? The physical resemblance, of course; it was amazing more people hadn't figured it out before now. Utilizing a control she didn't know she had, Abby kept her expression neutral.

"You trapped Noel, you little floozy," Paige went on. "You knew all along what you were doing, and now everything's just falling into place for you, isn't it?" Her voice rose even higher, drowning out the sound of Abby's overheated engine growing tired of idling. "Let me tell you, I'll ruin the both of you before I let that smart-aleck son of yours come in and ruin Calvin's future. I'll tell the whole town what you two did. What will that fancy church of yours think of you then; what about all those nice neighbors you got, and Noel's fancy-schmancy country club friends?" Paige threw back her head and barked out a humorless laugh. "Oh, how the mighty have fallen. You tell Noel that for me, okay?"

"Why don't you tell him yourself," Abby snapped back. She didn't appreciate being threatened by this two-bit thug, even if her threats did go through her veins like ice water. "Noel doesn't owe you or your nephew anything. He's given you a paycheck all those years, hasn't he? That's all he owes you. If you've got a problem with the arrangement, why don't you go work somewhere else?"

"Yeah, just what I figured. Take up for your boyfriend."

"I'm through listening to this," Abby exclaimed, her quaking voice betraying the calm demeanor she tried to present. "None of this involves me or my son. I suggest you leave the two of us out of your personal problems with your boss."

She hit the button on her door, and the passenger window began its slow assent. Not in time to shut out Paige's parting comment. "It's about to become your problem, honey, when I tell everybody in Jenna's Creek what I know…"

Abby dropped the car into drive and hit the gas. She turned the car north instead of south. Her hands trembled against the steering wheel, and the blood drained from her face. She couldn't very well deliver her pies for the church bake sale now. She'd call Karen from the house and tell her to come pick them up. Karen would be irritated that she hadn't delivered them herself, but she'd never wanted to bake the pies in the first place. Karen had signed her name to the volunteer list on the bulletin board at church without asking her. Typical, someone was always trying to control her life by one means or another.

On shaky legs that threatened to give way under her, Abby carried the groceries and carefully wrapped pies into the house. She set the pies on the table and the groceries on the counter. She reached into the first bag and drew out a can of peas. She stared down at the label without really seeing it, and then turned her eyes to the phone. She should call Noel. She should explain to him what was going through Paige's twisted mind. She was sure he had no idea. She should at least let him know what was coming; warn him ahead of time. What would she say?

"The whole town is about to find out about our twenty-two-year-old tryst through a disgruntled employee of yours; either hire her nephew or our cover is blown, buddy."

She set the can of peas on the countertop and pulled out three more. What had she been thinking? She and Eric didn't even like canned peas. She only fixed them for Jack; they were his favorite…

What was she going to do? She wanted to talk to someone. She felt an irresistible urge to confide in someone, bare her soul. She hadn't done it in so long, she didn't know if she remembered how. She didn't have many close friends in whom she could confide. With all her secrets, she never felt worthy of friendship. How could she ask another woman to confide in her when she would never be able to do the same? If they found out what she did, they would hate her. She was a hypocrite; a Jezebel. The women at her church were too good for her. They would never understand her sins. Who would?

*I have forgiven you, Daughter. Forgive yourself.*

The woman in the Bible, caught in the very act of adultery, had been forgiven by Christ. *"Neither do I condemn thee,"* he had said. *"Go and sin no more."*

Forgiveness for adultery maybe, but Abby wouldn't fool herself into thinking she was forgiven for what she did to Jack. She ruined his life. Because of her sinfulness, she had stolen his chance at happiness. Worst of all, he'd known all along Eric wasn't his son. Yes, God could forgive her for committing adultery, but He wouldn't forgive her for hurting Jack. Neither would anyone else. They would see her for what she was; weak, sinful, tainted. No amount of forgiveness could erase what she'd done, the lives she'd destroyed.

Paige was right. Her church friends would turn their backs on her along with the neighbors. How they would whisper about her behind their closed doors. She could feel their stares already and see their pointing fingers. All these years she had put on a front of being some kind of virtuous woman, and now they would know what she truly was.

She covered her mouth with her hand when she realized the shame her children would go through. She had raised them to be good; to obey the commandments, to always tell the truth. They would discover she was the worst of sinners. She had broken their father's heart with her indiscretions and her inability to love him while the love for another man burned in her heart. They would hate her and she would deserve it.

Fortunately she didn't have to call Karen. Eric was in the family room in front of the television when she got home and readily agreed to deliver the pies to the church after she gave him some lame excuse about not feeling well enough to deliver them herself. He gave her a weird look but, of course, didn't question her. He was used to her headaches by now. Since his questions last month, anytime he came near with a look on his face like he was even thinking about discussing something important, she claimed she didn't feel well and fled to her room. She didn't know how much longer she could keep avoiding someone who lived under the same roof, but she wasn't ready to face his questions, not even with Paige Trotter making threats.

After he piled the pies safely in the back seat of his car and drove away, Abby paced the floor, first trying her hand at straightening the living room, and then reading a paperback that had been lying around the house for months. Neither plan was accomplished. She couldn't get her mind off Paige Trotter. She had been so careful for so long. No one had found out her sin, no one except the Lord who knew all.

She had spent her life paying for the crime of loving a man other than her husband. Now her entire family was going to be ripped apart because of one woman's twisted quest for vengeance, for a wrong that had not even been committed against her. Maybe she could go to Paige and reason with her. She could point out that Eric wasn't even working at the drugstore anymore. He was not standing between her nephew and the position of Noel's assistant. Abby would tell her she never wanted him working there in the first place. Maybe then Paige would agree to keep what she knew to herself.

No, that wouldn't happen. For one thing, Paige Trotter didn't seem like the type who could be reasoned with and if she had figured out Eric's paternity, it would only be a matter of time before someone else did too—like Eric. He knew she wasn't being honest about his paternity, and sooner or later he would take a close look at Noel Wyatt's face and figure it all out on his own.

Why did this have to be happening after all this time? Why couldn't her terrible sin remain a secret like it had for the past twenty-one years?

A scripture popped into her head. "*For there is nothing covered, that shall not be revealed; neither hid, that shall not be known.*"

She was only kidding herself to think she could commit such an act as adultery and it never come back to haunt her. *Why, Lord; why now?* Her spirit cried. *You've already forgiven me. You've cast it into the sea of forgetfulness. Why do I have to face it all over again?*

The only answer she received was silence and heaviness in her spirit. "*Nothing is covered that shall not be revealed.*" The closest Bible was the one in Jack's study. She hurried down the hallway and into the small room. From the bookshelves lining one wall, she took down the huge family Bible, the one where she recorded all the births, deaths, and marriages that had taken place in her family since she and Jack married in 1944. Other than the recordings, the Bible was seldom used. It was too large and cumbersome for personal studying or taking to church. The grandchildren used to like to climb into her or Jack's lap and look at the beautiful illustrations, and listen to the stories that went with them.

A pang of loneliness stabbed at Abby's heart. That hadn't happened in over three months. How long had it been since the grandchildren came over to spend the night? How long had it been since she held one of them in her lap? Now when Karen or Roger dragged them over for a short visit, they sat close to their parents and looked aimlessly around the house, probably wondering when Grandpa was coming back. Jack was always the fun one. He gave them horsey rides on his back, pushed them on the tire swing out back, and drove them to the Dairy Queen for a dilly bar. She was the one in the kitchen getting dinner on the table or baking cookies for when their fun with Grandpa was over.

Her eyes smarted and a tear rolled down her cheek. Little Alex didn't even come to her anymore when she held out her arms to him. She couldn't expect him to; he was sixteen-months-old, and she was virtually a stranger to him. But it still broke her heart to see him cringe against Roger's shoulder whenever she came into the room.

Even Christopher and Rebecca got that trapped, lonesome look on their faces every time they came over. Uncle Eric wasn't fun anymore either. This wasn't a house; it was a tomb, a shrine for their deceased Grandpa.

The crisp pages of the family Bible fell open to the record-ings pages. The last death recorded was that of her father's four years earlier. She hadn't gotten around to recording Jack's yet. She couldn't bring herself to do it. It made everything so—final. She reached out and let her hand smooth over the faded ink of the last entry. She wouldn't record it today either; someday, soon.

"Oh, Jack," she traced the line where his name would soon be written, "I'm sorry, dear," she said aloud. "I should've made you happier. I do love you." The admission caused her voice to crack and fresh tears to spill down her cheeks. "I miss you so much. We all do. What are the grandkids going to do without you? What will any of us do?"

With a belabored sigh, she turned the heavy book over and turned from the back cover to the New Testament. The scripture she wanted was somewhere in the four gospels, probably several of them. Matthew, no Luke; she turned to the familiar book and began scanning pages. It had been a long time since she spent any serious time in Bible study, since April to be exact. She'd been too busy the past three and a half months feeling sorry for herself to read Scripture.

Chapter twelve; her finger slid down the page and came to a stop. Verse two. Jesus was talking to the multitude about the Pharisees' hypocrisy. *"For there is nothing covered, that shall not be revealed; neither hid, that shall not be known. Therefore whatso-*

*ever ye have spoken in darkness shall be heard in the light; and that which ye have spoken in the ear in closets shall be proclaimed upon the housetops."*

Abby gulped in shame. How many times had she opened her mouth and said something in haste that would bring shame if shouted from the rooftops? She imagined the hurt feelings or bitterness caused by her careless words if the person she was talking about ever overheard them.

Before she could repent for letting her tongue work before her spirit had a chance to bring it under subjection, she continued reading. *"And I say unto you my friends, be not afraid of them that kill the body, and after that have no more that they can do. But I will forewarn you whom ye shall fear: Fear him, which after he hath killed hath power to cast into hell; yea, I say unto you, Fear him."*—*f*ear Him.

She had done a terrible thing by having an affair with Noel Wyatt twenty-two years ago. She never should have allowed herself to be drawn into the situation in the first place, but it had happened. Eric's birth had been a direct result of that transgression; Eric, whom she loved more than her own flesh. Her selfish actions had hurt Eric, they'd hurt Jack and the three little girls she had at home, they had even hurt Noel—and all that concerned her was the embarrassment and shame she would suffer if Paige Trotter shouted her transgression from the rooftops.

Paige's threats shouldn't have come as a surprise. Jesus himself warned her of what would happen with something done in secret. If she had meditated on His Word back then instead of giving into the desires of the flesh, she could have avoided this present grief. But it was too late for that. She had sinned. God's grace had forgiven her, but she still had to live with the consequences of her actions.

Either by Paige, someone else, or her own admission, her evil deeds would be shouted from the rooftops. It was going to happen. Her family would find out the same as Jack had years ago. The good people of Jenna's Creek would know. Noel's business could suffer. Everyone involved would suffer.

Abby's forehead dropped onto the thick volume, and her body was wracked with sobs. *But, Lord, why should Eric have to suffer? It was Noel's and my fault. Do whatever you will to us, but not Eric. I don't want people laughing at him. I don't want them pointing. Most of all, oh dear God, I don't want him to hate me. I know what will happen when he finds out. He'll hate me and I'll lose him.*

Eric pulled into the gas station and got out. Bruce Hemming threw open the glass door and started toward him. "Hey, Eric, fill 'er up?"

"No, Bruce, I got it." He removed the gas cap and stuck the nozzle into the tank.

Bruce took a shop rag from his back pocket and wiped at the black grease on his hands. "How's everything going, buddy?" he asked. "Don't see much of you around."

Bruce had graduated a year ahead of Eric from South Auburn High School, but they had played on many of the same sports teams. Bruce had been one of the fastest runners the track team ever produced. Everybody thought he would get an athletic scholarship and go to college, but he had other plans. Upon graduation, he started working for his old man at the service station. Now he worked on engines, changed old ladies' oil, and pumped gas for a living. He married his high school sweetheart, and they already had two kids.

"Oh, I'm around," Eric said with a half-smile. "Don't get out of the house much. Mom's not doing so good since—since Dad died."

Bruce scrubbed anxiously at his hands with the rag. "Hey, man, I heard about that. I'm real sorry."

"Yeah, thanks." The counter dinged up to the five-dollar mark and Eric removed the nozzle from the tank. It would probably hold another dollar or two, but a five was all he had. He'd have to hit Mom up for a couple of bucks. He opened his wallet toward himself so Bruce wouldn't see how empty it was, and removed the five.

Bruce stuffed the wrinkled bill into his shirt pocket. "So what are you up to? Still going to college?"

"Uh, yeah, I'm out for the summer." Eric didn't want to admit he wasn't planning on going back any time soon.

"Where ya working? Last I heard you were over at Wyatt's Drugstore. Man, you always did have it made."

Eric chuckled and broke eye contact. Lying made him uncomfortable. "Yeah, got it made." He opened the car door and stuck one leg inside. "Hey, listen, Bruce, it was good talking to you. Tell Cathy I said hi."

"Sure will."

Bruce stepped away as Eric put the car in gear. Through the rearview mirror, Eric saw him shake his head and head back into the building. *What a loser*, he was probably thinking. *No job, no woman, just sits around that house all day with his mother; another Norman Bates in training.*

Eric mashed down on the gas pedal and spun out of the lot onto the street. Who cared what a jerk like Bruce Hemming thought of him? His life hadn't turned out so hot either; stuck in a smelly garage all day working for his old man and going home to a fast-fading, ex-homecoming queen and two squalling kids.

*At least Bruce is doing what he always wanted to do. He has no reason to be ashamed of the man looking back at him in the mirror.*

Who asked you? Eric screamed at the voice in his head as he turned the car toward home.

For the past month, since his break up with Jamie, Eric nursed his anger toward her to keep from thinking too much on his father's last words or what they could have meant. He convinced himself Jack was talking out of his head when he said he couldn't have loved him anymore if he'd' been his own son. Talking to Bruce brought it all back.

Several times since that night, he tried to approach his mother to talk about it. He wanted to tell her point blank what Dad said and ask if she had any idea what it meant. But each time he got his nerve up she claimed she had another headache. She needed to see a doctor about them, but he knew if he suggested it, she would just get upset again.

If he wasn't Jack Blackwood's son, who was he? Where had he come from? Had his parents adopted him as an infant and decided not to tell him? That would explain the six years age difference

between him and Christy. It would explain how a family with
three petite, red-haired daughters ended up with him; dark, ruddy,
square-shouldered, and towering above the rest of them.

Why hadn't they told him? Did they think he couldn't handle
it? What about his sisters, did any of them know about the adoption? Karen was ten-years-old when he was born, not totally unaware of where babies came from. Surely she would have noticed
when her slim, athletic mother brought home a baby boy one day,
claiming he was her new baby brother. Abby and Jack couldn't
have fooled the girls, especially not Karen. There would've been
some explanation about where this little bundle came from.

The house was quiet when he got inside. He found his mother
sitting in the family room, the TV on but the sound turned down
so low he doubted she could hear it.

"Mom, is everything all right?"

Her head snapped toward him and he cursed himself for star-
tling her. He could tell she'd been crying. "Hello, dear, I didn't hear
you come in. Did you get the pies dropped off all right?"

"Yeah, no problem, Sister Thompson said to tell you thanks.
She says you always make the best pies; they're sure to bring a lot
of money."

"That's nice." Abby pulled herself up off the couch. "Are you
hungry?" She glanced at the clock over the mantle. "Oh, dear, I
didn't realize it's so late. We missed lunch."

"Don't worry about it. I'll fix me a sandwich later."

She moved over to him and reached up to pat his cheek. "You're
a good boy, Eric. I love you."

"I love you too, Mom."

"If you don't mind, I think I'll go lay down for awhile."

"Sure, Mom," Eric watched her move slowly from the room
and head upstairs. If he didn't know better, he would think he was
watching an eighty-year-old woman.

*What's happening, Mom? How long are we going to live like this?*

He thought of Bruce again, his wife, and two kids. Maybe he
was stuck in a dead end job that he would grow to resent. Maybe
he sometimes wished he was back in high school, running the 440,

and hearing the crowd cheer him on. But at least he didn't have to go to his mother every time he needed gas money. He had a reason to pull himself out of bed in the morning and lay down again each night worn out from an honest day's work.

Eric headed for the kitchen to fix something to eat, even though he wasn't hungry, determined to dispel the doom and gloom that had settled over him. Something had to change; if not, Mom would follow Dad to the grave within a few years. She had every right to mourn, but it had gone beyond that. While she wasted away in front of him, he did nothing to stop it.

His reason for getting up in the morning had become more of a crutch—an excuse than anything else. Abby still needed him, but surely he could find a way to support her without avoiding his own life.

# Chapter Twenty

"You're up early," Abby said to Eric the next morning when she found him in the kitchen fully dressed, a bowl of over-cooked oatmeal in front of him.

He stared into the bowl, as though afraid to face her. Her stomach plummeted. She dreaded that look. It reminded her of when he was a kid and got caught doing something he knew would warrant punishment.

"I'm going to the drugstore this morning to see if Noel has room for me," he said in a small voice.

She grabbed hold of the counter to steady herself. The drug-store—that was the last place she wanted him to go, especially now! What if Paige Trotter jumped him with what she knew the instant he walked through the door? "What—why?" She responded.

He ducked his head again. "I've been thinking—I don't like not having any money in my pocket. I need to be doing something for myself."

"Oh, honey." She reached for her pocketbook on top of the refrigerator. "How much do you need?"

"No, Mom, that's what I'm talking about. I'm not a kid. I should be working, at least a little."

"But it isn't necessary. Any time you need money, just ask."

"I'm tired of asking you for money. I'm just going to work part-time until I find something else."

"Eric, I need you here. There's work in the garden, and the

garage could use a coat of paint. I was thinking of asking Roger about roofing the shed."

"All that stuff can be done some weekend. I'm not planning on leaving you here alone. I just want to get back to work. I'm beginning to feel like a totally useless member of society."

"Well, I don't know what brought all this on, but I think it's ridiculous. You're taking care of your mother. What could be nobler for a young man to do?"

He showed no signs of backing down. "Mom, please. I'll still be home more often than not. It's no big deal."

*Tell him. Tell him right now before he goes to the drugstore and hears it from Paige Trotter.*

"If you really feel like you have to work, why don't you go to the unemployment office and see what they can do for you? There's no need to waste your time at the drugstore. What if you run into…" she left the sentence hanging intentionally. He would know whom she meant.

A shadow passed over his handsome features. "It doesn't matter if I run into Jamie. It's not like I've been going out of my way to avoid her." Both of them recognized the lie. "Noel's been good to me, and I plan to do right by him at least till I find something more steady."

There was no point talking to him when he got this way. Stubborn as the day was long. Just like his…

"Fine, do what you think you need to do."

Jamie stood behind the cash register, a bemused expression on her face as she waited for the elderly couple in front of her to pay for their purchases. They were too busy bantering back and forth with each other over the name of the Channel 12 weatherman to pay any attention to her. She had already repeated the amount owed twice, but they weren't listening. Finally she got their attention long enough to complete the transaction before they moved toward the door, still adamantly disagreeing over the weatherman's identity.

She heard Paige humph beside her. The older woman seldom said two words to her all day. "Can you believe those two?" Paige mumbled with a wag of her head toward the door when Jamie turned to face her. "They'll argue about that the rest of the day."

"At least they're talking," Jamie said. "That's how they communicate."

Paige huffed again. "Is that what they teach you at that fancy college?"

"No," Jamie said, refusing to take offense. "It's what I think from watching people. They're probably all each other have left in the world and if they want to debate about the Channel 12 weatherman, at least it keeps them from wondering why the kids don't call. I think its darling."

"You would," Paige muttered under her breath as she rang up a teen magazine a young girl dropped on the counter.

Jamie smiled to herself and straightened the paper bags under the counter while waiting for another customer. Disliking the entire world was Paige's way of communicating. There had to be a softness in her somewhere that no one had bothered to look for before. She had determined to find it when she got promoted to working the cash register next to her two summers ago. Unfortunately, her goal still eluded her.

She looked up from the bags and saw the girl with the magazine was gone. Paige had one hand planted on the counter, the other clenched into a fist and resting on her hip, while staring a hole through her.

"What are you smiling about?" Paige asked with a sneer.

"That old couple; they're probably in their car right now on their way home still arguing about that weatherman. If he only knew the trouble he caused..." She ended the thought with a chuckle.

Paige's sneer deepened. "You find humor in the oddest places. I don't see what you've got to be so happy about all the time. Are you ever in a bad mood?"

Jamie immediately thought of the long summer without Eric. Her mood had been anything but good. She was glad though, it hadn't been obvious to the people she worked with. She thought of Jason waiting for her in Cleveland; of Grandma Cory and Cassie who had worried about her ever since she broke up with Eric; of Mrs. Wyatt who reminded her to pray and listen to her heart.

"I have too much to be thankful for to waste my time being in a bad mood," she said to Paige with an easy smile.

"Like what, that drunken father of yours or your crazy grandpa?"

The smile on Jamie's face became a little strained. Paige kept abreast of all the negative gossip in town and used every opportunity to throw it back in the victim's face.

"I am thankful for the lessons my dad taught me, although maybe indirectly. And my Grandpa Harlan is the sweetest, most gentle person God ever put on this earth." Her smile was genuine now. She meant every word she said. "I'm thankful for my grandparents taking me and my sister in when my parents couldn't take care of us. And most of all, my Heavenly Father—"

"Okay, okay," Paige cut her off with a raised hand. "I get it. You're thankful." She rolled her eyes. "I guess you're thankful for that boyfriend of yours too."

Jamie's heart skipped a beat, and she wondered which one Paige was referring to and why.

Paige brightened, pleased she had finally elicited a reaction. "What's everybody in town gonna think when they find out about his rich daddy." At Jamie's confused expression, Paige hurried on, a delighted smile on her face. "Yeah, pretty soon everybody's gonna know what happened all those years ago." She shook her head distastefully. "The two of them thinking they could carry on that way and nobody'd be the wiser. Of course you and him'll have it made, all that money, you'll be sittin' pretty, won't ya?"

The last thing Jamie wanted to do was let her curiosity show and ask what she was talking about. She still couldn't tell if Paige meant Jason or Eric. Jason's father had health problems, and she was pretty sure he didn't have any money. Maybe he had cheated the Workers' Compensation people out of a large sum, and it was about to come to light. As far as Eric's family having money, she knew his mother had received an insurance settlement, but she doubted it was enough to make her rich.

"I'm sure I don't know what you're talking about." She picked up the feather duster beside the register and began to dust off the packs of cigarettes on the shelves above her head.

"Yeah, I'll bet."

Jamie was glad to see several customers approach the cash registers. Hopefully the distraction would make Paige forget whatever she was driving at. At that moment, the bell over the store's main entrance jangled. Jamie glanced up, and her heart leaped into her throat as Eric strolled in. Eric—what was he doing here? Was he looking to get his job back or just running an errand? If so, she hoped he wouldn't come to her register. She didn't think she could bear standing so close to him, hearing his voice, dropping money into his outstretched hand. She hadn't laid eyes on him since they broke up the first of July. Out of the corner of her eye, she saw Paige square her shoulders.

"Well, speak of the devil."

At least now she knew whom the woman had been talking about.

As Jamie waited on the elderly gentleman who had stopped at her register, she glanced over his shoulder to see which way Eric was headed. She wished he hadn't come in; she wouldn't be able to think clearly as long as he was here. He looked up and caught her eye. Jamie broke eye contact first and reminded herself to breathe. When the customer moved away, she grabbed the feather duster again and swept vigorously at the cigarette display above her head. A cloud of dust drifted down, making her cough.

"I can't say I'm surprised to see him here," Paige said, interrupting Jamie's thoughts.

"What? Jamie responded, trying to make sense of Paige's ramblings—who?"

Paige pursed her lips and nodded her head in Eric's direction, "Lover-boy. I guess you'll find out soon enough." She arched her eyebrows, "If you don't know already."

Jamie ignored the knowing look and attacked the displays of

batteries and film behind her with the feather duster. She didn't
particularly care about what Paige was getting at, as long as Eric
didn't come over and talk to her. Even if she decided against going
to California with Jason, she was through with Eric Blackwood.
Nothing could make her change her mind—not even seeing him
in his blue jeans and pressed shirt, his hair doing that little flip over
his left eyebrow.

🐚

Eric stopped in front of the pharmacy counter and waited for
Noel to finish with a prescription. Noel looked up from his work
and smiled in greeting. Eric nodded back and a shock of dark
hair fell haphazardly over his left eye. When his left hand moved
automatically upward to push it back into place, he saw recogni-
tion flash across Noel's face. He lowered his hand back to his side,
although he had no idea what the look meant or why it made him
uncomfortable.

Noel finished counting out the medication for a viral infection,
careful not to look up again. Too many times since he hired Eric
he caught himself watching him, a flood of love and parental pride
engulfing him, so much that he feared someone would see it on
his face. Every time he saw the boy their resemblances smacked
him in the face, from the stubborn cowlick, to his broad shoulders,
to the reputation of his slider on the pitcher's mound. Fortunately,
they were aging at the same rate so they would never look exactly
alike; but how much longer before someone noticed the similarities, especially with the two of them standing side by side in the
drugstore?

He pushed the thoughts out of his head and bagged the vial of
medication, then slipped it into the proper alphabetically marked
slot. He moved to where Eric waited, his lean frame against the
counter, his arms crossed carelessly over his chest, his eyes riv-
eted to the front of the store. Noel followed his gaze and saw
Jamie Steele waiting on a customer. She threw back her head and
laughed in response to something the young man said as she slid
his purchases into a narrow drugstore bag.

He wanted to shove Eric away from the counter and say, "*Go get her, Son. Tell her how you feel, or you're going to mess around and lose her forever. You'll end up a lonely old man; the only woman you ever loved married to someone else. Take it from someone who knows.*"

"Morning, Eric, what can I do for you?"

Eric tore his eyes away from the front of the store and looked at Noel. He cleared his throat nervously. "I know I kind of left you high and dry a while back, and I understand if you don't need me…"

"Are you ready to come back to work?"

Eric smiled with relief, "Yes."

"Are you sure?"

He nodded. "Yeah, I've been sitting around the house too long. I should tell you though, Mom isn't doing so great, so this may have to be on a trial basis."

Noel wanted to tell him the best thing he could do for his mother was let her stand on her own two feet, but it wasn't his place. "Sure, I understand. We'll play it by ear. When can you start?"

"As soon as you need me," Eric replied enthusiastically.

"How about right now?" Noel asked as he walked around the pharmacy counter and headed toward the back of the store. Eric fell into step beside him. "We're understaffed right now, so I can put you to work this morning." He opened the door to the stockroom and stepped aside to allow Eric in ahead of him.

Two young people Eric recognized from earlier in the year were hard at work on a shipment that had just been delivered. "Heads up," Noel called announcing his arrival as if to instill fear in his employees. No chance of that happening. Noel Wyatt was arguably the easiest boss in the county to work for. He was fair, impartial, and friendly. He expected a lot, but gave the same in return.

"Got another pair of hands for you today," he told them as they looked up at the interruption. "I expect you to be done in half the time with Eric here to help. That'll leave you plenty of time to strip down the shelves in automotive and give them a good scrubbing before we close for the day." He finished with a smile and backed out of the stockroom, relishing in the distasteful looks that followed him. Everybody hated to clean automotive, the smallest department he had. Located in a corner at the back of the store, it carried an assortment of spark plugs, oil filters, windshield wipers, and the like, and got the dirtiest and most disorganized in the shortest amount of time. Those farmers always managed to get grease and field dirt all over everything they touched every time they came to town. That would break Eric in right and prove to himself he wasn't demonstrating nepotism in his job disbursement.

# Chapter Twenty-one

Eric worked at the drugstore the next three days. Although he stayed busy he couldn't see where they were under-staffed, and realized Noel probably put him to work out of pure Christian charity. While he hated for Noel to think Jack left his family in financial straits, he was thankful to be doing something besides sitting at home. Most of his shift was spent in the stockroom or somewhere out on the floor, scrubbing shelves or mopping remote corners of the building. Whether Noel had intended it or not the mindless work was good for him. He could heft the mop bucket back and forth, attack the ceiling for cobwebs, and wear himself out completely without thinking. By the end of his eight-hour shift, he was tired. He would drag himself home, unaccustomed to the physical labor, and fall onto the couch where he'd watch TV the rest of the evening—another mindless pursuit.

Not thinking about Jamie wasn't as easy. Every morning when he walked into the store, she was the first thing he saw. Try as he might, his eyes automatically went to the second register, seeking her out. The first two days, he averted his eyes and tried not to look like he was looking. By the third day, he convinced himself he was being ridiculous and greeted her with a polite nod as he walked past. No reason why he couldn't be civil. He still had feelings for her, even if it was best that those feelings be ignored for the time being. His focus was his mother, she still needed him. He already felt lousy enough for leaving her home alone all day so he could go back to work.

After three days of work, he had his first day off. He promised Abby it was only a part time job; at least until something better came along. He awoke before eight, dressed, and went downstairs. Abby had disappeared outside before it got too hot, her gardening gloves in one hand and a spade in the other. Belatedly she had developed an interest in her garden, and spent hours toiling in the soil, trying to revive the withered perennials that came up every year, whether she paid attention to them or not. There wasn't much she could do this late in the season other than keep the weeds at bay, so she attacked them with fervor every morning.

Eric checked out the back door to make sure she was busy, and then hurried through the house to Jack's study. He had wanted to go through Jack's personal papers since he first considered the possibility he might be adopted. He turned on the small television in case his mother walked in unexpectedly. She would just think he was watching TV in the quiet, darkened room like he often did these days.

The den was more of a small room off the foyer where his dad went for privacy rather than an actual study where important matters were tended. Everyone in the family used the den—the girls for homework and illicit phone calls to boyfriends, Jack and Eric for watching college football on Saturdays when the girls were making too much noise in the rest of the house.

Bookshelves, installed by Jack twenty years ago, lined one wall and were filled with Little Golden Books, study Bibles, cheesy romance novels, and Chilton's car repair manuals for makes and models they no longer owned; something for everyone. The two outside walls had large, paned windows overlooking the front and east side of the house, but the dark-paneled room with its heavy drapes stayed cool and dark. Abby had strategically placed floor and table lamps throughout the room so any past time could be comfortably pursued. Eric remembered how years ago he'd find his parents in here, his father on the small loveseat with the daily paper and his mother close by, crocheting a baby afghan for an expectant mother at church or a colorful scarf for one of the girls.

Pushing those thoughts aside, he moved straight to the desk and pulled open the deep drawer on the left hand side; the one with the lock that hadn't been used since the key disappeared sometime in the early sixties. He rummaged through the drawer's contents, looking for a folder or something that might hold important papers. Jack wasn't the most organized person on the planet and unfortunately, he kept all the family records. Eric remembered seeing his birth certificate several years ago when he went to apply for a drivers' license. It looked official, but he was pretty sure a new birth certificate was issued when a child was adopted with the new parents' names in all the appropriate spaces. He wondered if an old birth certificate still existed or perhaps correspondence from a state children's agency. Even a mysteriously written, canceled check to an unknown attorney would make him think he was on the right track.

He easily found everything he was *not* looking for; packets of old school photographs taken in elementary school that had not been passed out to grandparents. Jack loved pictures of the kids and always bought the largest package available, consequently running out of relatives before running out of pictures. The halls and stairway were lined with decades of smiling offspring; goofy gap-toothed grins, crooked bangs, and tons of freckles that seemed to multiply under the camera's lens—with the exception of Eric, of course, whose nose was freckle-free.

He located insurance forms, warranties for the hot water heater and the furnace, car titles for the truck and the Buick; everything but what he wanted. He slammed the drawer shut and slid open the next one; old water bills, bank passbooks, all marked in Jack's nearly illegible scribbling. Even that didn't resemble his own.

"Eric." His mother's voice came from the back of the house. "Are you up yet?"

It was after nine o'clock, of course he was up. What a sad state of affairs that she didn't know if he'd be out of bed at this hour. Before his father died, she would've been pounding on his door by eight demanding he get his lazy carcass out of bed and make use of the daylight.

"In here, Mom," he called back, sliding the drawer shut as quietly as possible and settling onto the dark leather loveseat in front of the TV.

She appeared in the doorway. "I thought I heard you moving around." She glanced at the desk and then at him, her eyes accusing. "Were you looking for something?"

He shook his head absently, still looking in the direction of the TV. Out of the corner of his eye, he saw her look again toward the desk. "Well, okay then. Are you hungry?"

"No, I'm fine." He got up and switched off the set. "Is it dry enough outside to start the mower? I thought I'd get at the backyard before it gets too hot."

"Oh, I'd appreciate that. It's supposed to rain this weekend, and the yard's pretty shaggy. You know how your dad hates…" Her voice trailed off, and her face filled with pain.

Eric moved to her side, "Mom?"

She waved him away with a flick of her hand. "It's already getting hot. If you're going to mow, you better get started."

Eric wished she would say something, anything, about how she was feeling. Whenever Jack's name came up, whether by accident or intent, she clammed up. It wasn't good for her to keep silent, but he guessed she would talk when she was ready.

He walked past her and headed down the hall to the back door. He needed to check the oil and maybe sharpen the blades before starting the mower. That would keep him busy the rest of the morning. Too busy to think about what he hadn't found in Jack's desk.

Abby waited until the kitchen door slammed shut behind Eric before going to the desk in the den. She opened the drawers one at a time and glanced inside to see if anything was out of place. It was difficult to tell; Jack, a habitual pack rat, always threw everything in with no rhyme or reason. She would get around to straightening it out one of these days.

Eric had been looking for something even if she couldn't find evidence of his snooping; probably something to confirm his suspicions about his father. Every day this week when he left for work at the drugstore, she paced through the house until he returned, bracing herself for the big blow-up, the one that would come when Paige Trotter told him about his real father. Every afternoon he returned, told her how his day went, how beat he was, and asked what there was to eat. Nothing was ever said about Paige. No shame or disgust showed on his face. No vicious names were hurled. So far, for whatever reason, Paige kept her mouth shut, and Eric still didn't know anything.

The anticipation of what she knew was coming was almost more than she could take. How much longer? When would the bomb drop? She almost preferred Eric's reaction to the waiting.

What would he think if she went outside right now where he was in front of the shed loosening the bolts that held the lawn mower blades in place and spilled the whole story? *Your mother is a Jezebel, Eric, not worthy of your father. She had an affair. You are a result of that affair; a result of her sin. You know your real father, Eric—he's your boss at the drugstore. Even though Jack Blackwood was a wonderful husband and provider, he wasn't what your mother wanted so she rushed into the arms of another man. She begged God's forgiveness before you were born, but her sin was too great to be blotted out. She sinned against the most wonderful man in Jenna's Creek. She hurt him and somehow he found out. He went to his grave knowing the son he loved so much wasn't his. For that, God will never forgive her.*

Abby gripped the sides of the desk, her insides as jumbled as the contents of the desk drawers. He would be disgusted, infuriated, repulsed. He would never be able to look at her again. She would lose the love of the person who mattered most to her.

*Tell him the truth, Abby. Tell him before he hears it from someone else.*

She shook her head and slammed the desk drawer closed. No, she couldn't take the risk. Eric could never know of her infidelity.

*Tell him. He deserves the truth.*

I'll lose him. He won't love me anymore, she cried out in her spirit. She sat down hard on the loveseat and dropped her head into her hands. How could she bear him looking at her with disgust and shame in his eyes? What if he left? What would she do if he moved out and never came back?

"Eric?" Roger straightened up from under the hood of his car and wiped grease off his hands with an old rag. "I thought I heard your old heap pull up. What brings you around?"

"I was hoping to talk to Karen. Is she home?"

"You know she is," Roger replied with a wag of his head toward the house. "She's cleaning blackberries to cook up for jelly while the kids are taking their naps. I'll bet she'd love some help."

"I guess that wouldn't kill me. Oh, and by the way, when you get a free afternoon, I need you to come to the house and show me how to re-plaster the wall in my bedroom."

"What happened to the wall in your bedroom?"

"I'll explain later." Eric headed into the house. Cutting the grass hadn't had the affect he'd been hoping for. Rather than keeping him too busy to think about his father's last words to him and his mother's reaction to his questions, his mind fixated on the notion that he was adopted. It was the only logical solution. It made perfect sense. Just because he didn't find any evidence in Jack's desk didn't mean a thing. No evidence might exist after all this time, especially if his parents didn't want him to know the truth.

He wouldn't get anything out of Abby, at least not now. She was too fragile. He couldn't stand the trapped look on her face every time he went near her, the terror in her eyes of demands he might make.

That left Karen; ten-years old at the time of his birth, he stood a better chance getting information from her. He didn't expect her to know details, but surely she knew enough to confirm his suspicions.

That's all he wanted right now, confirmation.

"Hey, Sis," he said, stepping inside the kitchen. "Need any help?"

Karen spun around, nearly dropping the glass bowl of blackberries in her hands. "Eric! What are you doing here?" She set the bowl down, shook the water off her hands, and rushed forward to hug him.

"Easy now, Sis," he said laughing and hugging her back. "It hasn't been that long since I've dropped by, has it?"

She released him and gave him a playful smack on the chest. "You know the answer to that, wise guy. Why are you here? Is Mom okay?"

"She's fine. Does something have to be wrong for me to come see my favorite sister?"

"You're kidding, right?" She arched her eyebrows skeptically, before going back to the bowl of blackberries. "The kids are asleep right now, but they'll be thrilled to see you. Can you stay for supper?"

"Maybe, but I want to talk to you about something first. You may not want me to stay after that."

She dumped the berries into a colander in the sink and turned to face him. "I knew you came here for something."

Eric stared at the floor for a moment, taken aback by her strong reaction. Finally he found the nerve to look up. "Karen, I'm sorry. I know I've been a jerk lately but I just did what I thought I needed to do."

She crossed her arms over her chest and waited, her expression softening slightly.

"I don't know exactly the best way to say this," Eric went on, encouraged that she wasn't going to lecture him. "I guess it's like ripping off a band-aid. It's better to give it a good yank and get it over with it."

She cocked her head expectantly.

He didn't know what she was expecting to hear; probably something in defense of his decision to quit college, or the way he hadn't left the house for more than a few hours at a time since last spring. No matter how he asked, his question was sure to throw her for a loop. "Do you remember when Mom and Dad brought me home from the hospital?"

"Huh?" Her arms dropped to her sides, "When? Do you mean after you had all those tests in Columbus a couple years ago?"

"No, not then. When I was born."

"When you were born? What does that have to do with anything?"

"Please, Karen, just tell me. Do you remember anything about it?"

"I don't know. I guess so."

"Who did you stay with when Mom was in the hospital?"

"Probably Grandma Frasier, Grandma Blackwood still had kids of her own living at home. No, wait a minute, that's not right. Grandma Frasier came to the house. It was easier that way. She stayed a few days so she could fix supper every night for Dad when he got home from visiting you and Mom at the hospital, and we girls didn't have to miss any school."

"So you do remember?"

"Yeah, I was ten-years old. I remember being really mad because I wanted to miss school, but Dad wouldn't let us."

"What do you remember about the day they brought me home?"

She cocked her head and pursed her lips, searching her memory for specifics. "Well, I remember me, Elaine, and Christy decided it wasn't all that great having a little brother. All the relatives came to the house and made over you like they'd never seen a little boy before. It was irritating, the way they went on and on."

"And you remember Mom being pregnant?"

"What? Of course, she was pregnant. Haven't they got to the part yet at college about where babies come from?" She stopped talking and her eyes narrowed. "What's all this about, Eric? I'm sure you and Mom haven't been sitting over there looking at baby pictures, and you decided you wanted an objective opinion. What's going on?"

Eric sank into a kitchen chair, feeling like someone had let the air out of him. He expected Karen to confirm his suspicions. Now he was more confused than ever. She had no reason to lie to him. She was telling him exactly what she remembered from those days, right down to the sibling rivalry of finally having a brother.

"I can't say, Karen. I really can't, not right now."

She moved to the table and stood over him. She put her hand on his forehead and ran it back through his hair. "Eric, are you sure everything's all right?"

He looked up into his sister's concerned, green eyes and saw a stranger looking back at him. Who was this woman? Who was *he*? Suddenly the kitchen felt stuffy and confining. He needed to get out of here. He needed to talk to someone who would understand, who would let him talk without passing judgment, someone...

"Karen, I gotta go," he said, shaking her hand off his head and standing up. "I need to..." His voice trailed off. He wasn't sure what he needed.

"Eric, don't leave. I thought you were going to stay for dinner." She watched helplessly as he strode toward the door. "The kids'll want to see you. It's been such a long time."

Facing the screen door he gave her a little wave without turning around. "Tell 'em I'll be back. I promise. I—I gotta go." He hurried out the door before she could say anything else.

With no conscious thought, Eric backed out of Karen and Roger's driveway and headed east out of town. He drove straight through Jenna's Creek's business district barely aware of sitting through traffic lights waiting for the signal to turn green. When a carload of teenagers turned in front of him at the Myles and Munroe intersection, he stomped on the brake pedal to avoid a collision, and then moved on, unaffected. Past the city limits sign, he turned off the new highway and onto Betterman Road. Within two minutes he was pulling his car into the Steele driveway.

# Chapter Twenty-two

Cassie was crouched in the flowerbed alongside the house, pulling weeds from among the groupings. At the sound of Eric's car in the driveway, she straightened, put one hand to the small of her back, and pushed her rich, auburn hair away from her face with the other. She's growing up, Eric thought as he brought the car to a stop within a few feet of her. With her looks and saucy attitude, there was nothing she couldn't get some poor schmuck to do.

He climbed out of the car and headed toward her.

"Well look what the cat dragged in," she said in mock disbelief. "It's about time."

"Is Jamie around?" Eric asked, ignoring her disdain. He guessed he deserved it.

She tilted her head and gazed up at him out of the corner of an exotic hazel eye. "It depends."

"On what?"

"On you, Eric," she said. Pulling herself up to her full five feet and six or so inches of height, she stepped gingerly over a cluster of flowers to stand in front of him. She'd gotten taller over the summer. He wondered if she'd passed Jamie up yet. Unlike Jamie who stumbled through life with the grace of an offensive lineman, Cassie carried herself with the confidence and poise of a model. He thought again of the poor schmuck—more than one, most likely—who would make the mistake of falling in love with her.

"My sister isn't going to sit around here her whole life waiting on you," she was saying. "Maybe she's too polite to point it out, but you're not the only pebble on the beach."

"I never thought I was."

"You think you can have any girl you want, don't you; with that gorgeous dark hair and big blue eyes?" He wasn't sure if she was trying to insult him or not. "Well, not my sister. She has options, you know."

Eric opened his mouth to tell her he wasn't here to force Jamie into any kind of commitment. The familiar squeak of the back screen door stopped him before he could utter the first syllable. He turned and saw Jamie on the edge of the porch, her cheeks flushed and short dark hair—highlighted from the summer sun and slightly damp with perspiration—hanging loose around her face. She had obviously been in the middle of some household chore inside the hot farmhouse. She wore a man's shirt, with the sleeves rolled up and the tail knotted at the waist, and a pair of bleach-spotted, cut-off blue jeans that exposed her long slender, tanned legs. She wiped a droplet of sweat from her forehead with the back of her arm, leaving a dirty smudge in its place.

He had never seen her looking more beautiful.

"Jamie," he said taking a step toward her.

"Hi." Self-consciously, she tucked an errant strand of hair behind one ear and wiped at the smudge on her forehead.

Cassie put her hands on her hips and looked from one of them to the other. "Jamie, you've got the worst timing. I had him this close to admitting what a jerk he's been lately."

"Thanks, Cassie," Jamie said, keeping her eyes on Eric, as if she thought he might vanish into thin air any minute. "I think I can handle it from here."

Cassie gave an exaggerated sigh and slapped the dirt from her hands onto the seat of her pants. "Sure, fine, you take care of it." She started toward the front of the house, but mumbled under her breath loud enough for Eric to hear. "Don't forget to ask the weasel where he's been all summer."

Eric didn't particularly care about Cassie's opinion of him at the moment. His attention was focused on Jamie. He searched his mind for what had brought him here in the first place. Something he tried to talk over with Karen, but knew she wouldn't understand. The only person who ever understood him was a few steps away on the back porch, reeking of ammonia and floor cleaner.

He was no longer bothered with questions of his paternity. It didn't matter what his dad had said or what his mom had not. All that mattered was getting closer to Jamie.

He took a tentative step closer to where she stood on the porch, her elevated position making her a few inches taller than him. She was so beautiful. How had he forgotten that? She hesitated only a moment before stepping off the end of the porch. He took another step. All he wanted was to take her in his arms; feel her body against his, breathe in the fragrance of her hair, her skin, tell her what a fool he'd been, and how much he missed her.

In a moment she stood right in front of him, the top of her head coming to his chin. Like he thought, Cassie had outgrown her. She tilted her head back and looked into his eyes. His tenuous resolve collapsed. Slowly, he wrapped his arms around her, drawing her against him. She didn't resist. He tangled his hand in the hair at the back of her head and pressed her cheek to his. His eyes filled with tears. She felt so good, so natural. This is where she belonged. Had he gone a whole summer without realizing it?

Slowly he relaxed his hold on her and looked down into her brown eyes.

She took a half a step back and gazed up at him. "Why are you here, Eric?" Her expression was guarded, cautious.

"I don't know," he murmured and tightened his grip on her again. "I—I had to talk to someone…"

She stiffened and pulled back, "About what?"

*Here it comes*, he thought, *the rejection, the demand for an explanation.* A lump the size of a baseball settled in his throat. Why did she have to be so beautiful? Why couldn't he remember what they'd fought about in the church parking lot last month? He swallowed hard, but the lump doubled in size. He shrugged helplessly and murmured the only words·that came to him. "I'm sorry."

She stepped completely out of his grasp and stared unseeingly at his car parked in the driveway, her own emotions threatening to erupt.

He had to say or do something before she politely, or not so politely, asked him to leave. "Can we go for a walk or something; to talk?"

She shrugged and moved wordlessly off in the direction of the barn. He followed one step behind, almost nervous about seeing her again. They reached the metal gate next to the barn and climbed over. In the late afternoon, the barnyard was quiet. The cows would come in from the field before long for the evening milking. She would be too busy to talk then. He had to get everything out that he needed to tell her.

At least her reception wasn't as hostile as Cassie's, for that he was thankful. She had let him embrace her. She had held onto him too, if not as tightly. She was willing to listen to what he came to say.

They made their way through the field and down the hill, along the worn path to the pond. Jamie stopped at the water's edge and sat down on a bench fashioned from two split logs butted against each other and held together with several long rusty bolts. Eric sat down beside her. She stared out over the cattails growing thick along the bank.

Encouraged that she hadn't yet yelled at him or punched him in the nose, he spoke. "The last time I saw you, I said some horrible things. I was angry. You were angry. I'm sure what I meant to say got blown out of proportion."

She kept watching the cattails stirring gently in the slight breeze that moved over the water.

"I'm sorry, Jamie, I really am," he continued. "I never should have let my temper get away from me like that. I'm supposed to be a child of the King, and I sure haven't been acting like it lately." She didn't respond so he kept talking. "It isn't just the way I've been shutting everybody out either, I haven't opened my Bible in weeks. No, it's been longer than that. I don't think I've really prayed since that night at the hospital."

Jamie spoke up, her eyes still on the cattails. "Kerry Hollister stopped by the drugstore a couple of weeks ago and asked how you were doing. She told me you haven't been to any church functions all summer."

"She's right. I haven't felt like facing anybody."

"I'm the one who's sorry, Eric. I should understand better than anybody what you've been going through. When Mom died I didn't want to see or speak to anyone either. I didn't want to be around people who were smiling and having a good time. I was so miserable, I thought they had some nerve being so happy. Then when Dad died, I was angry and miserable for a whole different set of reasons."

How could he explain his reasons for shutting himself off from everyone and everything he cared about? He wasn't sure he could explain it to himself. Like what she went through after her parents' deaths, he hadn't wanted to be around anyone who couldn't understand his suffering, but it was more than that. He had promised his dad he wouldn't begrudge Abby's need to lean on him.

Worst of all, was Jack's final message to him. *"I couldn't have loved you anymore if you'd been my own son."* While he should be mourning his father, all he could think of was what those last words implied.

She had stopped talking, and her eyes searched his face. "Eric, what did you come here to talk about? I'm trying to understand, I really am, but how can I know what you're going through if you won't talk to me."

When did she get so good at reading his mind?

Jamie shifted her weight on the narrow wooden seat and waited for him to speak. She had been more than a little surprised to see his car pull up outside the house a few minutes ago. She'd about given up on that happening again. When she went out to the porch, she didn't know what to expect. Had he come to scream at her some more, or did he have reconciliation on his mind? So far, there'd been no yelling so what was he doing here?

"There's a lot going on at the house right now," he began. He stood up, jammed his fists into his pockets, and stared at the sun reflecting off the murky water. "Mom's not doing well at all. She started working in her gardens again, so that's a good sign, but I don't know." He shook his head despairingly, glanced in Jamie's direction, and then back at the water. "She just—she's so nervous. She follows me around the house, asking me what I'm doing all the time. If she isn't doing that, she's in her room resting from a headache. She never wants me to go anywhere. She doesn't come right out and say it, but I can hear it in her voice that she wants me with her; it's like she's afraid of something. She isn't pleased at all that I've gone back to work. Now she's kind of giving me the silent treatment."

"It's only natural, Eric. In the back of her mind, she's probably afraid something will happen to you like it did your dad."

He shook his head again. "It's more than that. I think she's afraid I'll stop loving her."

"Why would she think that?"

He didn't answer for a long time. He removed his hands from his pockets and turned toward her. He took her hands in his and pulled her to her feet.

He was quiet for a moment as he stared into her eyes. "I haven't been coming around because I've been mad at you. I convinced myself that a big part of my misery was your fault. That you've been trying to force me into something I couldn't handle right now. It's like I thought I had to choose between you and Mom. I guess I figured she needed me more."

She pulled her hands away from his. "No one ever expected you to choose between me and your mom."

"I know, I know. You're sister's right, I am a jerk."

"I never tried to force you into a proposal either. You were the one who brought that up." She looked away, unshed tears stinging her eyelids.

"I know. I was completely wrong. I came here tonight to talk to you about what's been bothering me about Mom, but all I want to do now is convince you to forgive me. I shouldn't have blamed you for my pain. It had nothing to do with you. I wasn't thinking straight. I guess I had to be mad at somebody so I wouldn't be mad at Dad for dying."

"Oh, Eric," she said as she moved closer.

He reached out and touched her cheek. "Jamie, I'm sorry. I don't want things to go on like this. It's been tearing me up seeing you in the store all week. I try to ignore you, but you're all I think about." He caressed her cheek. "I've missed you so much."

She allowed him to ease her back into his arms. "I've missed you too," she said breathlessly. "Since our fight in the church parking lot, I've been so mad at you at times I just wanted to tear your head off. Then other times I can't think of anything except how badly I want to see you again. I'm sorry. I should've been more understanding to your situation. Grandma Cory tried to tell me, but I wanted to be mad."

He gave her the first smile she'd seen on his face in a long time. "So, you don't want to rip my head off anymore?"

"Well, only once in a while."

He smiled. She smiled and sniffed back a tear. He pushed a strand of hair behind her ear. She tightened her hold around his waist. He pulled her closer. Their noses met then their lips. Eric put his hands on either side of her face as he held her face against his. Jamie moved her mouth against his and struggled to still the longing rising up in her heart.

Always before they limited physical contact to hand holding and a goodnight kiss. They decided early in their relationship that extended physical contact would only lead to problems neither of them wanted right now.

Eric's arms moved around her again, drawing her even closer. She was acutely aware of his body against her. She knew she should push him away, but her body wasn't listening to her head. She arched her back to get closer, and a tiny moan of pleasure escaped her lips.

*Be still, and know that I am God.*

She barely heard the still, small voice over the pounding of her heart, but she heard it just the same.

This was so different than the kiss she shared with Jason. In Jason's arms, she found familiarity and comfort. With Eric, it was passion, hunger…

They had to stop. This could not continue, not if she wanted to maintain every value and belief she held dear. Eric pulled her closer still. Uncle Justin's comfortable, old work shirt rode up around her waist. She felt Eric's hand on the bare skin of her back

Fighting against every fiber of her fleshly being, she put her hands on his chest and pushed him away. "Eric, stop," she gasped.

He stepped back, and his arms fell to his side. "Man, I'm sorry. I shouldn't have—I just missed you so much…"

If she had to stand there much longer, watching his lips move, she didn't know how she could be expected to control herself. "Please, stop talking." Her knees wobbly, she sank onto the bench and clasped her trembling hands in her lap. "I don't think that's what you came here to do."

He sat down beside her, leaving a foot of space between them. "No, it wasn't, but I won't say I hated it."

"Eric, please."

"I know. I'm sorry." The smile on his face disappeared, and he ran both hands through his hair. "I do have something I want to talk about; something that's been bothering me for a long time. I was at Karen's today, hoping she could clear some things up, but all of a sudden I knew I had to talk to you. I couldn't get here fast enough. Like I said earlier, a lot's been going on, and I don't know what to think."

"About what?"

"I want to go back to school," he announced and Jamie felt a surge of hope, "but I'm afraid to leave Mom alone. She's never been by herself, and I don't know if she can handle it. I feel like I'm deserting her. You should have seen her face the other morning when I told her I was going back to work. I think something happened a long time ago that she doesn't want me to find out about. If I leave now, she's gonna think I'm leaving because of that and not because I just want to graduate when I'm supposed to."

"Eric, what is it you think happened?"

"I don't know." He turned toward her, his expression anxious. "I just know it's eating her up inside."

"Can't you talk to her about it? She'll feel better if she doesn't think she has to keep protecting you."

"It's not that simple. You should see the way she's acting. She isn't going to open up because I tell her I'm a big boy, and I can handle it."

"You have no idea what it is?"

He was silent for a long time.

"Eric?"

"My dad told me something that night in the hospital after his accident. Do you remember when Mom told me he wanted to see me? At first I thought he was confused by the medication or something, but since then I've been giving it a lot of thought and some things don't add up."

"What things?"

"Like the fact that I don't look like anybody in my family."

He kept his eyes on his hands clenched tightly in his lap. Jamie felt her heart rate pick up again. What was going on? His prolonged silence worried her. "Eric, what did he say to you?"

"He said he couldn't have loved me anymore if I had been his own son."

Her brow knitted together in confusion.

"I'm not his son, Jamie," he said to clarify. "I'm not a Blackwood."

"You were adopted?"

"I thought so, but I talked to Karen today. She was ten when I was born. She remembers Mom and Dad bringing me home from the hospital. She remembers Mom being pregnant. She wouldn't lie, even if they told her to back then. She's not capable of that."

"If you know you weren't adopted, then what are you getting at?"

"Aren't you listening? My dad said he loved me like his own son. That means he knew I wasn't his biological son, but Karen remembers Mom being pregnant. Mom had a baby that didn't belong to my father—me."

"But—wait a minute you've got to be jumping to conclusions. What if your parents went to the hospital to have their baby and— it died or something? Then they met a young girl who was giving up her baby for adoption or the babies got mixed up; maybe that's what happened."

"Or maybe my mom was cheating on Dad and I'm the mail-man's kid."

Jamie had to admit his crudely put version was more plausible than a hospital conspiracy. "You've got to talk to your mother, Eric. You can't keep torturing yourself with possibilities when there could be a simple explanation."

"And what if it happened the way I think it did? How in the world do I ask my church-going, Bible-believing mother if she committed adultery? Just the words coming out of my mouth would kill her, whether they're true or not."

Jamie stared out across the water. She could think of nothing more to say. If his suspicions were right, what good could be gained by having Abby relive an apparently painful past?

# Chapter Twenty-three

"So, what was Eric doing here last night?"

Cassie barged into Jamie's room while she got ready for work and threw herself across the neatly made bed. Jamie turned halfway around in her seat in front of the mirror and scowled at the wrinkles in the flower print spread. Cassie saw the scowl and half-heartedly smoothed her hand across the worst of the wrinkles. She never understood why Jamie freaked out over a neatly made bed. All Grandma Cory expected was that their beds be made as soon as they rolled out of them; she never said they had to be perfect.

"You two were outside talking an awfully long time," she continued, turning her attention back to Jamie. "Does that mean you made up with the rat?"

Jamie shrugged noncommittally and turned back to the mirror to apply her eye shadow; just a touch to bring out the flecks of color in her deep brown eyes. "Maybe, and he's not a rat."

She saw Cassie roll her eyes in the mirror's reflection. "Yeah, well, if you say so. Just explain what maybe means?" She sat up on the bed and threw her legs over the side, leaving an ocean of wrinkles in her wake. "What about Jason? Remember him? Does he even know about Eric? Does Eric know about him?"

Jamie sighed and snapped the lid closed on the container of four coordinating eye shadows guaranteed to accentuate brown eyes. No, Jason's name hadn't come up last night. She spun around in her seat and gave Cassie her full attention. "It's none of your business."

"That's what I thought," Cassie squealed triumphantly. "You're a two-timer."

"I'm not a two-timer. I can't believe you're even interested. I've had a total of two boyfriends in my entire life, and you never cared before."

"Exactly, suddenly your incredibly boring love life has turned into a soap opera, and you're not keeping me up to speed. Until I turn sixteen next month and am allowed to date myself, I'm forced to live vicariously through you. Come on, Jamie, what gives? What's going on?"

Jamie groaned, put her elbow on the dresser, and rested her chin in her hand. She didn't even think about Jason last night while she was drifting off to sleep, her mind joyfully occupied with the memory of Eric's arms around her. Now reality crashed down around her. She hadn't wanted to think about it before, but now she had no choice. What *was* she going to do about Jason?

"No," she said in response to Cassie's earlier question, "Jason doesn't know about Eric, and Eric doesn't know about him."

"Oh, my gosh!" Cassie's hazel eyes snapped with excitement. "What are you going to do? You realize Jason is up there in Cleveland probably wasting all his free time mooning over you while you're down here smooching by the pond with another guy."

"Cassie, that's not exactly what's going on." Jamie kept her voice level, all the while praying her impressionable, little sister hadn't witnessed the passionate embrace she and Eric shared. The blood rushed to her face, and she turned hastily back to the mirror.

She could tell by the look on her face, Cassie wasn't buying her innocent act. "Then tell me what is going on. Grandma Cory and I were talking last night while you and Eric were off doing heaven only knows what. We're worried you may not know what you're getting yourself into."

"Oh, is that right." At twenty-years-old, she didn't need her grandma and sister discussing her love life behind her back. But then again, she couldn't really blame them. Her recent behavior was a wee bit out of character for her. She was always the levelheaded one in the family, more like Grandma Cory and Uncle Justin than she cared to admit. She thought things through, never acted impulsively; a look-before-you-leap type of personality. From their point of view, it probably did look as if she didn't know what she was doing; getting seriously involved with Eric, then refusing to speak his name, spending time with Jason and contemplating a mystery announcement, only to spend last night with Eric again. Her family probably thought an invasion of the body snatchers had occurred in their own home and she had been replaced by a pod person who looked like her and talked like her, but wasn't the real Jamie.

"I love Eric," she said simply, choosing not to torture Cassie anymore by beating around the bush. "I've loved him for a long time. We had a serious fight the first of July, and said some things we probably shouldn't have." At Cassie's questioning expression, she elaborated. "Like, 'I hate you, you dirty rotten creep. I never want to see you again.' Something like that; it was more my fault than his. I wasn't as patient and understanding as I could have been with what he was going through with his Dad dying and everything. I thought it was over between us and I'd never see him again. Then that very night, Jason came home."

"And swept you off your feet with an old, but not forgotten love," Cassie added dreamily.

"Sort of, he's coming back at the end of the summer, and he wants to get married."

Cassie's eyes grew to the size of dinner plates, "To you?"

"Yes, to me. Who else?"

"But what about Stanford, I thought he was going to law school?"

"He still is. He wants me to transfer from Ohio University, and the two of us go to California as husband and wife."

"Oh, my gosh, how exciting!" Then her face fell. "And you said 'no'."

"Not yet, I told him I'd think about it."

"Wow! Jamie, I can't believe it. You are a two-timer," she shrieked with real pride in her voice. "I didn't know you had it in you. But what about Eric, I thought you said you loved him?"

"If you'd let me finish..." Jamie admonished.

Cassie clamped her lips together and slid her hands under her thighs, determined not to interrupt again.

"I was seriously considering going to California with Jason," Jamie continued. "Everything he said made perfect sense. I really care about him. He's wonderful and caring, and he'd be the perfect husband for the right woman, but I don't think caring for someone is enough of a reason to get married."

"And when did you figure that out, when Eric laid the old lip lock on you?"

Jamie blanched, shamefaced. Cassie's comment wasn't too far off the mark. "Maybe that's what clinched it," she admitted. "I thought maybe God sent Jason back when He did because it was over between me and Eric. But deep down, I knew I couldn't marry someone who didn't make me melt when he came into a room. I guess that's why I didn't answer Jason when he asked me over July fourth weekend."

"But *California*, oh, Jamie, that'd be so exciting!"

"Not for me. I love it here." Jamie ignored Cassie's nose wrinkled in distaste. "This is my home, and I don't want to have a life anywhere else."

"And of course, this is where Eric's at," Cassie added.

"Yes." Jamie picked up her brush and moved it through her hair, staring at her reflection in the mirror. After a few moments, she forced her gaze back to Cassie. "But that's not the only reason. I don't even know if Eric feels the same way about me that he did before—before his dad died. Last night we really didn't talk about it. We just talked about all this other stuff, but being around him..." Jamie couldn't keep a wistful sigh from escaping her throat. "After seeing him last night I knew for sure I couldn't marry Jason. It wouldn't be fair to him or me. I love Eric. I love OU. I want to stay here."

Cassie wasn't interested in letting the conversation turn to

Jamie's college career. She only wanted to hear about love. "Does this mean you're going to marry Eric?"

Jamie shrugged. "I told you I don't know if he still loves me." She thought of the kiss last night and wondered for the first time if it had been prompted by love or desperation. "Since his dad died, things have been upside down," she said. "Everything's changed."

Cassie groaned dramatically and fell back onto the bedspread. "So you're turning down Jason and California for someone who may not even love you anymore."

"That's not the point, Cass. I'm turning down Jason and California for myself. If Eric loves me and wants to marry me, well, that's great, but for now, I have to think about what I want. I'm not going to marry a man simply because I might not get another chance at love." She smiled to herself when she realized how much she sounded like Lucinda Wyatt.

"Jamie, I don't understand you," Cassie said, sitting up in the bed. "What if you turn down Jason and stay here, and it never works out between you and Eric. You could've had such an exciting life in California. Instead you'll end up wasting your life in boring old Jenna's Creek, just like Grandma Cory and poor Aunt Marty."

"Neither of them thinks their lives have been wasted."

"That's because they don't know any better. They've never been outside the county. You have, you're getting an education, and you're going to let it go to waste here."

"Oh, Cassie, that's silly. My career won't be wasted no matter where I live. I'm sorry, a small town may seem boring to you, but it has its charm. I wouldn't want to live anywhere else."

Cassie groaned again and rolled her eyes toward the ceiling, "Boooring."

"Maybe, but no one has ever accused me of being exciting," Jamie reminded her.

"You've got a point."

"Did you come in here to insult me?" Her voice was indignant, but her eyes glinted with playfulness.

"No," Cassie answered. "You're pretty cool—sometimes. I just hope you don't end up regretting giving Jason the old heave-ho. He's a sweetheart and for some reason, he's crazy about you. But then again, I saw the look on Eric's face last night when you came out on the porch. Man, it was pathetic. He looked like a lovesick puppy. I don't think you have to worry too much about him not loving you anymore."

Jamie grinned and felt her face flush. "I hope you're right."

Cassie stood up and moved to the stool where Jamie sat. "Now you're the one who looks pathetic. I guess if you love the guy that much, you couldn't really go to California with someone else." She leaned over and put her arms around Jamie's neck. She looked at her face in the mirror's reflection. "I love you, Sis. I want everything to end up the way you want. Even if that means spending your life here in Jenna's Creek changing diapers for Eric Blackwood's kids." She loosened her arms and moved toward the door.

"Cassie," Jamie said, stopping her just as she put her hand on the doorknob.

"Yeah," Cassie looked at her over her shoulder.

"I love you, too."

Cassie wrinkled her nose as she opened the door, "Yeah, whatever."

After Cassie was gone, Jamie turned back to the mirror. If she didn't finish getting ready for work, she was going to be late. For the first time in her working career, she didn't care. She couldn't get the image out of her head of changing diapers for hers and Eric's babies. Cassie was right; she was pathetic. She didn't even like babies.

It felt good to be out of the house, even if he was up to his elbows in grease and grime in the automotive department. Today though, his mind had a hard time focusing on the job at hand. Eric couldn't get Jamie's smiling brown eyes out of his head. Her shift would be over a few hours before his and their lunch hours did not coincide, so he wouldn't see her again in the store for the rest of the day. That didn't stop his mind from working overtime on her sweet face and lilting voice. By the time his shift ended, he knew what he had to do.

Last winter his dad had been pleased with his intentions to propose to Jamie while his mother was more hesitant. "Why do you have to get married now?" she had asked with Jack by her side. "Why not wait until you both graduate? If she's the one for you, what difference will a few years of waiting make?"

Couldn't she see a few more years away from Jamie would kill him? He wanted to be with her right now, this very minute. If she'd agree to running away with him tonight and eloping, he would gas up the car and leave the ladder leaning against the side of the farmhouse on Betterman Road.

He blushed with shame at the thoughts of what could have happened last night when he held Jamie in his arms. For the first time in months, he hadn't fallen asleep wondering about the secret his parents had kept from him. He was too busy repenting for his careless actions and deeds. He had sinned in his heart, if not in body. Yes he loved her, mind, body, and soul, just as God had designed in the beginning. And he wanted her—desperately. Their relationship had remained chaste so far, but he didn't know how strong he'd be if another opportunity like last night was presented again.

Raging hormones wasn't a reason for speeding along a marriage, but after last night, he was having a hard time thinking of anything else. He loved Jamie; he wanted to spend the rest of his life with her and he planned on proposing by the end of the week. Enjoying her completely after their union was sanctified before God was just an added perk he couldn't keep out of his mind.

He knew without looking the engagement ring would not be in his sock drawer. The wall and the busted drawer still bore the scars of the temper tantrum he threw the day of the fight in the church parking lot. He had jammed the drawer back together with the heel of his hand, but it still stuck on the drawer guide every time he forgot and opened it too quickly. The wall needed to be patched and repainted, something else he'd have to take care of one of these days.

As far as the ring and the velvet box, he had no idea what had become of them. After putting the drawer back together as best he could and crawling around the room on his hands and knees to retrieve socks and underwear, he had been in no mood to look for the ring and box. Stupid, stupid, stupid, he condemned himself, and shot a hand through his thick dark hair.

He turned toward the hole in the wall, the direction he'd been facing when he threw the tiny, velvet box and tried to reconstruct the crime in his head. He remembered hearing the ring roll across the hardwood floor until the wall or a piece of furniture had brought its journey to an abrupt end. That meant the ring was now free from the box somewhere in the room, unless it had dropped through a heating vent in the floor—great. He dropped to his hands and knees and crawled along the baseboards. From the amount of dust bunnies clinging to the knees of his trousers he didn't have to worry that the ring—which had cost him more than he made at the drugstore all summer—had been swept up and thrown away. The floor hadn't been acquainted with a broom in quite some time.

"Lose something, dear," his mother asked from the doorway.

Eric sat back on his haunches and rested his hands on his thighs. He hadn't wanted her to find out his plans like this. He wanted to sit her down with a cup of hot tea and tell her calmly and rationally that he planned to ask Jamie to marry him. Of course it'd be easier if they eloped first and he called her afterwards from the state line.

"A ring," he answered simply.

A shadow passed over her tired features.

Those elopement plans were sounding better and better all the time.

"What kind of ring?" Suspicion edged her voice.

It was too late to turn back now, "An engagement ring."

The shadow further darkened her features. "Engagement ring; you never told me you were buying a ring. When did this happen?"

He got to his feet and brushed a fine layer of dust from his knees. "I told you and Dad last February I wanted to get married. I've had the ring since around then. With everything that happened, my plans got put on hold."

"Why are you looking around on the floor? Surely you didn't leave it lying around to get lost if it meant so much to you." She walked the rest of the way into the room and glanced around the baseboards. He hoped she wouldn't spot it immediately and make him look like an even bigger fool for overlooking it when it was in plain sight.

"We had a big fight one day, and I kind of threw it across the room."

"Oh, yes, I remember; the day you busted a hole in the wall, which you've never fixed, by the way."

He ducked his head in shame at the accusatory tone in her voice. He swallowed hard and braced himself. He wasn't going to let her get his mind off the matter at hand. "Well, I need the ring now. I don't want to ask Jamie to marry me without it."

Abby's face went white and her jaw dropped open. "You're going to propose? You don't even have a real job."

"Yes, I do. At least until I go back to school. I'm asking her this weekend, but I promise, Mom, we won't get married before I graduate next summer unless she wants to. I don't care anymore. I love Jamie, and whatever it takes to make her happy, I'm gonna do it."

"You're going back to school too, then? When were you planning on telling me all these life changing decisions of yours, Eric? You used to ask my opinion about what to wear when you got your class pictures taken. Now you're going back to school and getting married without even mentioning either one to me."

Eric took a step toward her. "I've been afraid to tell you anything lately, Mom. You know how I feel about Jamie. You also know I haven't had anything to do with her since April and you haven't even asked why. You act like you're relieved she's out of my life."

A blush crept into her cheeks, confirming his accusations. He hurried on before he could loose his nerve. "You've also known since I was a kid that I wanted a college degree. When I told you I wasn't going back to school, you didn't try to talk me out of it, even though I only have one year left. Before Dad died, you would've knocked me over the head if I mentioned dropping out. I guess you'd rather I live in this house forever and take care of you and grow old working in the stockroom at that drugstore. Dad would be disgusted at the way both of us have been acting. I still miss him, but I've got to get on with my life and so do you."

"I know you want to get on with your life but how do you plan to support a wife, and maybe children, if you're both still in school? You've given this so much thought, explain that one to me."

"Mom, this isn't about getting married and going to school. I'm trying to tell you we can't keep living like this; stuck in this house, afraid to see daylight. I love Dad and I love you, but this isn't healthy. You know it's not."

Tears appeared in Abby's eyes. She put her hand to her brow as if in pain. "You're right, Eric. I've been keeping you here the past five months because I was afraid to be alone. I wasn't ready to face life without your dad."

"None of us were ready."

She went on as if she didn't hear him. "It's not as simple as just getting on with our lives. There are things you don't know."

A muscle twitched in Eric's jaw. "Then tell me, Mom. Help me understand. Whatever it is, you've got to let me help you through it."

She looked down at the floor and shook her head. "You're the most important thing in my life. I couldn't lose you."

"Why do you think you'd lose me? Not because I'm getting married. Stop treating me like a dumb kid. Tell me what's worrying you."

For a moment her face crumpled. She was either going to spill the whole story, or she was dangerously close to tears. He didn't know which one he was more prepared to handle. Then she clenched her teeth and lifted her chin defiantly. "The only thing bothering me is what's always bothered me. You are obviously still too immature to get married; crawling around on the floor looking for a ring you threw away in the height of a temper tantrum. Is that the action of a man prepared for the responsibility of marriage? You're proving that I was right from the beginning. You're letting your hormones make your decisions instead of your head. Don't think I don't know where you were last night. It doesn't take a genius to figure out what's got you all fired up about finding that ring all of a sudden. Getting married now in the state you're in would only be a mistake."

"The state I'm in? What state is that, love; since when is getting married because you're in love a mistake?" Eric shook his head. "Mom, you're not making any sense. Everybody else has expected Jamie and me to get married even without our talking about it. They can see it a mile away, everybody except you. Why, what have you got against her? What have you got against me being happy?"

"I am trying to preserve your happiness, Eric," she exclaimed. She took a deep breath and heaved her shoulders, struggling to bring herself under control. "I know what happens when people give in to their emotions and act without thinking something through; that's what I see you doing with Jamie. All I'm asking is that you *think*. Use your head. *Think* about where you'll live; *think* about all the responsibility of keeping a wife happy; *think* about where the money will come from if you suddenly find yourselves with a baby on the way. If the two of you are really in love and you want to get married someday that's great, more power to you. But I can't agree to this until you've spent some time thinking and praying about it. I still stand behind what I said last February. If you go against my wishes and get married, I won't be offering you any help."

Eric stared at her dumbfounded. Wasn't she the pot calling the kettle black, accusing him of thinking with his emotions instead of his head? So what if he went to see Jamie last night, at least he wasn't married to someone else at the time. It took every ounce of control and respect for his mother that he possessed not to say it out loud.

"I haven't asked you for any help, Mom," he hissed through

clenched teeth. "And believe me, I won't. I'd rather Jamie and I live on the streets than come to you for anything."

"Oh, my, isn't that a mature statement."

What had happened to his mother? When had she become this bitter, vindictive person standing before him accusing him of things that were none of her business? This was his life; he had a right to live it any way he saw fit. If he wanted to get married to the woman he loved she had no right to second guess him. Yes, he understood that she wanted the best for him, but he was beginning to wonder if all she was thinking about now was what was best for her.

With purposeful strides, he stepped to the busted dresser and yanked open the drawer. As usual, it caught halfway open and wedged itself at an awkward angle. He didn't turn around to see the smug look that most certainly covered her face. He dug inside and removed a few pairs of underwear and socks. He shoved at the uncooperative drawer and managed to close it an inch or two before it stuck even harder. Ignoring it, he reached for the next drawer, which slid open smoothly.

"What are you doing?" she asked from behind him.

"Getting a few things together," he answered as he removed a couple of t-shirts and a pair of shorts before slamming that drawer back into place.

"What for? Where are you going?"

He tossed the clothes on the bed and moved to the closet. "I don't know, maybe Jamie and I can get an apartment together without getting married. Will that make you happy?"

"Don't you dare talk to me like that in my house," she hurried up behind him, and put her hand on his arm as he flung open the closet door. She pulled him around to face her. "You're not leaving this house, young man. We're not through talking."

Eric jerked away from her and turned back to the closet. Abby's mouth dropped open. Eric had never openly defied her in all his twenty-two years of living. He averted his eyes, a little shocked himself at his behavior, and tossed a suitcase onto the bed beside the clothes.

"Did you hear me, Eric Blackwood?" Desperation was evident in her voice. "You're not going anywhere. I'm still you're mother, and you'll do what I say."

He turned around from the closet door to face her, two shirts still on their hangers in one hand and a pair of jeans in the other. "No, Mom, not this time." He wanted to say more. He wanted to tell her that he was a grown man and she needed to accept that, he was no longer a little boy she could bend to her will—but he didn't. Too much had been said already.

He unzipped the suitcase. Without a word, he hurriedly stuffed the small amount of clothes into the bag and zipped it up. Then he remembered all the stuff he needed out of the bathroom. When he got back, his hands full of hair care products, shaving cream, a razor, and two bottles of medication, Abby stood in the same spot as when he left the room. From the look on her face, she had no idea what to expect from him next.

He brushed past her and unzipped the bag just enough to shove his toiletries inside. When all was finished, he set the bag up on its end and gripped the handle. Only then did he look at her. "I'm spending the night at Karen's. Don't call." He started out of the room.

"But Eric…" she sounded so distraught, so lost. He stopped, but didn't turn around. "What about the ring?" she asked. "Does this mean you aren't going to ask Jamie to marry you?"

"I'm still asking her, Mom. I'll just have to put it off for a day or two."

He half expected her to follow him downstairs. He listened, but didn't hear her leave his room. Without a backwards glance, he let himself out the front door and hurried down the walk to his car.

Abby stood in the middle of Eric's room and listened as the four-cylinder engine in his little car sprang to life. The car slipped into gear, backed out of the driveway and drove off. He didn't let the engine warm up as usual. Jack always told him, even in warm weather, he needed to wait a full minute for the oil to lubricate the motor; he never listened, too impatient, too many things to do. She could hear the complaint of the engine, before it turned the corner, where it was absorbed into the neighborhood's night sounds.

She thought about crying, but she'd done so much of that lately. It never accomplished anything anyway. She considered screaming and throwing something against the wall as Eric had done a month ago. That might bring a moment of satisfaction. She thought about calling Karen and telling her Eric was on his way and when he got there, she could tell him to just turn himself around and come back home. His mother was not through with him.

With the weight of despair settling into her chest, she left the room and went downstairs to the kitchen. She wouldn't cry, she wouldn't throw things, or scream. She wouldn't call Karen and demand she send Eric home. He was a grown man. He couldn't be forced to do something he didn't want to do. He might obey her out of respect for her authority, but the days were gone when she forced him into compliance.

She turned on the flame under the teakettle and went to the cabinet for her favorite cup. Tiny cracks in the porcelain splayed across the rim from the years of daily use. Every year or so one of the kids would get her a new cup along with a selection of flavored teas and a devotional book or daily planner for Mother's Day or Christmas. She enjoyed the teas, reading the devotions, and used the planner, but the cups were put away in the cabinet and seldom used. Somehow her soothing brews always tasted better out of her own cup.

She sank into a kitchen chair and waited for the water to boil. What had happened upstairs? How had she lost control of the situation like that? When had she lost control of Eric? She wasn't accustomed to flagrant disobedience or dismissal. She ruled this place and everybody knew it, no matter how often over the years she insisted that Jack wore the pants in the family. Now she understood how Karen got to be so bossy and expected to be obeyed instantly with no questions asked; like mother, like daughter.

She rested her chin in the palm of her hand and watched the stove element turn bright red under the teakettle. "Oh, Jack," she said aloud with a sigh. "I would've handled things so much better tonight if you'd been here to keep me in check."

She missed her husband more than she ever dreamed possible. Not for the children and all they had lost by his early death, but for herself. She never thought his passing would leave such a void in her life. She missed the sound of his footsteps on the back porch when he came home from work. She missed preparing big dinners for her hungry husband and sitting across the table from him, listening to him carry on about his day. She used to get tired of listening to him talk about who did what to whom at the plant but she listened attentively, knowing it was his way of unwinding from a long day of working for people who didn't treat their employees very well.

Now the dinners she prepared weren't dinners at all. Eric never had much to say, and she had no appetite or desire to cook, so the two of them often ended up eating soup and sandwiches at the kitchen table. What she wouldn't give to hear Jack grumble about the boss breathing down his neck and the cut backs in health care benefits.

Now that his absence in the house was dismally apparent, she realized how much of a friend and confidante he had become over the past thirty years. Even though their relationship lacked the passion and fire of many of their married friends, she could tell him anything. He laughed at her jokes and she enjoyed his, they each understood the other's little idiosyncrasies, and of course, there were the children to bond them together.

She had grown used to Jack during their years together even if she had been unable to give him her heart. For the most part their life had been a good one. Jack was always good to her and the children, never giving her a moment of grief. He was a good man. It wasn't his fault she couldn't love him. He had done everything within his power to please her. Now he was gone and her only regret was she hadn't been the wife he deserved.

"Now I've lost Eric, too," she said to the teakettle.

It hissed softly in reply, steam appearing through the tiny opening on top.

*Call Karen's. He's probably there by now. You can apologize.*

What did she possibly have to apologize for? She hadn't done anything wrong. He was the one behaving irrationally. He didn't have a full-time job or a place to live. He couldn't afford a wife. What was he thinking? She was simply sparing him untold pain down the road.

*Call him. You need to tell him the truth. All your children deserve the truth.*

The teakettle let out a shriek and Abby jumped, startled by the noise. The shriek turned into a steady whistle that went straight through her head. She hurried to the stove and removed the kettle from the heat. Why was she boiling water? She didn't want tea; she was jumpy enough already.

How could she tell Eric and the girls the truth? They would never forgive her. Eric was gone. If he even suspected what she'd done, he would never come back.

*He already suspects.*

No, impossible! He can't know.

*Someone will tell him. Wouldn't you rather he heard it from you?*

I would rather he not hear it at all; what purpose would it serve?

*You have already been forgiven, Daughter. Forgive yourself.*

I can't forgive myself. I've made too big a mess of things.

*Too big for Me?*

Abby sat back down in her chair, propped her elbows on the table, and put her head in her hands.

*I've already forgiven you, Daughter. Forgive yourself.*

I can't forgive myself, Lord. I've done too much damage. I hurt Jack. When the kids find out, it'll hurt them too. What about Mother Blackwood? She's lost her son; I can't take her only grandson away from her, too. I've made too much of a mess of things. I just have to hope no one ever finds out the truth.

*Eric suspects the truth.*

I'll convince him he's wrong. I'll...

*You'll do what?*

I'll...

*You'll lie to him?*

Yes, it'll be for his good. The truth will only hurt him.

*Read My Word.*

Abby stood up and went to the cabinet. She got a teabag from the canister and set it into her cup. Carefully, she poured steaming water from the kettle over the teabag. She knew now what she would do. The tea that she didn't really want would settle her shattered nerves and help her come up with a logical answer to Eric's questions, even if only temporarily. She would even have an answer in reserve in case Paige Trotter had already put her poison into the boy's head. The one thing she *wouldn't* do was read the Bible. Her mind was too concerned with saving her family.

# Chapter Twenty-four

Eric had every intention of going straight to Karen's house. He wasn't in any state to see or talk to anyone right away. Karen would take one look at his face and the hastily packed bag in his hand, and she'd know not to ask any questions. But just before turning south on Highway 35 outside of town, he made a right instead and headed west to Betterman Road. Even if he didn't say a word about why he left his mother's house tonight, he needed to see Jamie.

Jamie sat at her desk and stared at the black and white kittens frolicking across the top of the sheet of stationery in front of her. All day long she had gone over what she would write in her head. Even in her imagination, she couldn't come up with an appropriate opening line. The kittens across the top of the page didn't help. Frolicking felines brought to mind carefree days, sunny skies, and that everything was right with the world; not *'Thanks, but no thanks to your marriage proposal. You're a great guy, just not the one for me.'* She wondered if Hallmark sold stationery with a skull and cross-bones motif more befitting the contents of the letter, or perhaps a stick of dynamite with a lit fuse protruding from a Valentine heart. How about that? At least then Jason could see it coming.

She held the pen—her poison pen—poised over the paper as she had for the past twenty minutes, waiting for inspiration on how to tell one of the sweetest people alive she had no desire to spend the rest of her life married to him. Nothing she had come up with so far was suitable. Even writing a letter seemed cruel and heartless. This was something that should be done face to face not via a whimsical frolicking kitten greeting, but Jason was in Cleveland and she was here in Jenna's Creek. She wouldn't be seeing him until the end of the summer when he returned for the answer to his marriage proposal. It would be extremely unfair to wait until then and say, 'Oh, by the way, I decided a few weeks ago I didn't want to marry you, but thanks for asking. See ya.'

This would be a lot easier if she didn't care so much for him. He was a wonderful person and he would make someone a great husband someday. It was the best thing for both of them, she told herself for the thousandth time. He would only regret it later if she married him when her heart wasn't totally his. Even if nothing became of her relationship with Eric, she couldn't move to California. She cared for Jason, but she didn't love him. She couldn't marry a man she didn't love more than anything this side of heaven. It wouldn't be fair to either of them.

She pushed the stationery with the black and white kittens aside and pulled a spiral-bound notebook out of the desk drawer. She flipped back the cover, clicked the button on the top of the pen, exposing the point; *Dear Jason...*

"Jamie," Grandma Cory's voice called from the bottom of the stairs. "Eric's here."

Jamie's heart skipped a beat—*Eric.* Just the sound of his name brought a flush to her cheeks. Whether this euphoria was an illusion that would disappear after a few months of marriage like TV and magazines warned she didn't know, but she was prepared to take her chances. She would never consider spending the rest of her life with anyone who didn't set her heart to racing the way Eric did.

She turned the notebook upside down and set the pen on top of it. She glanced at herself in the mirror and combed her hair away from her face with trembling fingers. She took a deep breath and headed down the stairs, the letter to Jason forgotten.

Halfway down the stairs she saw him waiting by the front door, hands shoved deep into his pockets as he gazed forlornly around the living room. At the sound of her footsteps on the stairs, he looked up at her. He smiled tentatively and moved to the foot of the stairs. His expression caused her heart to sink. Oh, no, what now? Had he taken her advice and talked to his mother, and things had gone as badly as he feared, or was he here to break up with her—again? Even though Cassie, the resident expert on matters of the heart, had assured her Eric was as crazy over her as she was over him, the look on his face right now could only mean bad news.

"Hi, Eric," she said, trying to sound nonchalant. If he were here to break up, she wouldn't let him see it was killing her. She reached the bottom stair and stopped. From her elevated level, they were the same height. "I didn't expect to see you tonight."

"I know," he said. "Sorry about it being so late. It's not a problem, is it?" He looked toward the kitchen where they could hear Grandma Cory puttering around.

"Oh, no, it's no problem."

"I'm on my way to Karen's. Mom and I had a huge fight."

"Eric, I'm so sorry."

Eric stared at his feet, oblivious to her inner turmoil. "Maybe it was a long time coming."

She touched his arm. "Are you okay?"

"I don't know—I guess."

"Do you feel like talking?"

For the first time since she reached the bottom stair, he leveled his gaze at her. "I haven't decided yet."

She offered an encouraging smile. "Want to go sit on the porch swing?"

He nodded and took her hand. Outside, they settled themselves side by side in the old porch swing. They sat in silence and stared across the fields on the other side of the road. Jamie tried not to speculate what the fight might have been about. He would talk when he was ready.

They sat for nearly twenty minutes before he started talking.

"I don't know if my relationship will ever be the same with Mom again. Before Dad died I could talk to her about anything;

she was really cool. Now I can't open my mouth, especially if it's something important."

Jamie waited for him to go on, but he didn't. "I'm sure things will get back to normal between the two of you someday. She just needs more time."

"I'm beginning to wonder about that."

"What do you mean?"

"I don't know what was normal for her. I doubt any of us knew her like we thought we did, even Dad. Maybe he was the stabilizer of the family and now that he's gone, she's falling apart."

"Your mom doesn't seem like an unstable person, Eric. She's been through a traumatic experience. Anyone would—"

"No, anyone wouldn't," he interjected. "I know it's been hard on her. I'm not saying it hasn't." He ran a hand through his thick dark hair. "I think I may have been on the right track the other night."

He didn't have to explain what he meant. Jack's last words to him filled Jamie's head. *I couldn't have loved you anymore if you'd been my own son.*

"And?" she gently prodded.

"Mom said tonight there were things I didn't know. When I asked her to explain, she clammed up and then started yelling about something totally different. I think it's just like I thought. She had an affair, and my birth was a result of it."

Jamie turned in the swing to look at him. "Eric, are you sure you're not jumping to conclusions?"

"What choice do I have?" he said angrily. He took a deep breath and started over, his voice softer. "She won't talk to me, not about anything. It's like I lost both my parents last spring. Dad's dead and Mom's not who I thought she was."

"She's still you're mother."

"No," the determination in his voice startled her, "not if she did what I think she did."

"You don't mean that."

"Yes I do. I mean every word of it. If what I think is true, she's done nothing but lie to me and our whole family all my life. Dad knew about it, that's the worst part. He knew all along and still treated me like I was the best thing that ever happened to him. How could a man do that for another man's kid? That says a lot about who my old man was. It also says a lot about Mom. If she did something like that to Dad, I don't know what to think of her."

"Eric, you mustn't—"

"I mustn't what? Blame her for what she did to Dad; all the heartache she put him through? If it's true, Jamie, I can't forgive her. There's no way I can look at her the same way again."

Jamie put her hand over his and squeezed. She wanted to tell him he was wrong, that Abby was still his mother no matter what she may or may not have done in the past. Jamie knew all too well the miry clay of unforgiveness. She had felt the same way about her own dad for the abuse he had directed at her mother. After his death, he couldn't admit his mistakes and seek her forgiveness but she had to forgive him just the same. Not only did her salvation depend on it, but also her peace of mind.

She kept her thoughts to herself. Eric wasn't in any frame of mind to listen to her tonight. Later, after he had time to think and sort out his feelings, she would offer her advice.

The gray dawn seeping in through the half-drawn Venetian blinds brought Abby Blackwood to a gradual state of wakefulness. She rolled away from the window and winced as a fierce pain shot through her temple. She had used a headache so many times in the past five months as an excuse to get away from an uncomfortable situation, she wondered if God put this one on her as a lesson in honesty. No, this wasn't punishment, simply the result of a terrible night's sleep.

She forced herself to a seated position and swung her legs off the edge of the bed. She needed something for the pain. Last night—actually this morning—at around two a.m. when sleep refused to come, she considered taking one of her leftover sleeping pills the doctor had given her to get through those first days without Jack, but she refrained. She wanted to hear Eric in case he came home during the night. She had slept fitfully without the aid of the pill, and awoke at every sound.

Eric didn't come home.

She wondered if he ever would.

She got to her feet and shuffled across the hardwood floor to the hallway. She hoped she'd find something strong in the medicine cabinet for this headache. It reminded her of the sinus headaches she used to get.

Once again, as was so often these days, her headache reminded her of Jack. August was her worst month for allergies. It had been that way since she was a child, but back then, she didn't know anything about allergies. She suffered in silence through the headaches and the drippy nose as only a kid could, and learned to live with them. In her twenties and thirties, the allergies worsened. Relief came only after the first hard frost of September. She always prayed for an early one. The best thing about turning forty was that the severity of her allergies seemed to lessen with age.

In those early years of married life Jack did everything he could to ease her suffering. He bought every remedy on the market. He made countless trips to the bathroom to rewet warm rags for her forehead. He dimmed the lights and herded the girls to the other end of the house so she could rest.

Oh, Jack, you deserved so much better than me.

*I have already forgiven you, Daughter. Forgive yourself.*

Abby turned on the bathroom light and shut out the voice in her head. She wouldn't fool herself into thinking she was forgiven when her head knew it wasn't possible. She was guilty.

No pain relievers in the medicine cabinet. Eric had taken several bottles of medication with him last night, presumably the headache medicine too. She might find something downstairs. She went back to her room, slipped on her bathrobe, and headed downstairs. The house was so quiet. This was the first time in more years than she cared to remember that she was the only person here. When the kids were little and their needs overwhelmed her, she thought they would never grow up. There was always some sort of tragedy or mayhem going on; running here, going there, never a moment's peace. Now suddenly, in the blink of an eye, she was alone.

A search of the downstairs medicine cabinet turned up nothing. *Even an outdated individual packet of Bayer like they sell at the convenience store would do the trick*, she thought as she moved toward the kitchen. Unfortunately, the kitchen cabinets revealed the same. She would have to endure the pain until one of the stores opened downtown.

The best room downstairs for a headache was Jack's study, with its heavy drapes and cool interior. She took a couple of pillows from the sofa in the family room and headed down the hallway. She tried not to think of Eric as she plumped the pillows into place on one end of the loveseat and situated herself. She kept the door open in case he came in. This would be the first room he'd pass on his way into the house. She lay back against the pillows and closed her eyes. The tension behind her eyes lessened immediately. Good, maybe she'd fall asleep. That would be better for her headache than anything.

Before she could relax, her brain started going over the fight last night. Why couldn't Eric see reason? He had no business getting married or going back to school, for that matter. What was he thinking?

*He's in love.*

What does the boy know about love? He's too young.

*You were younger than he is now when you fell in love.*

Yeah, and look at the mess I made.

*Tell him the truth.*

The truth won't change anything.

*Do you want him to hear it from someone else?*

Her inner monologue was getting her nowhere. She readjusted her pillows. As soon as she closed her eyes, the voices were back, arguing back and forth, making sleep impossible. Abby sat up and flipped on the lamp next to the loveseat. The first thing she saw was the thick family Bible she had left sitting on the sofa table the other day. She remembered last night when she had been prompted to read the Bible but hadn't. She did that a lot lately; ignored her spirit's urging to turn to Scripture. Her entire adult life, she had found peace and strength within the worn leather covers of her Bible. Why was it, now when she needed it more than ever, she repeatedly turned away?

She turned the heavy book around to face her and opened it. The silk ribbon still marked the twelfth chapter of Luke.

*"For there is nothing covered that shall not be revealed; neither hid, that shall not be known."*

She sighed and pushed down the heaviness rising in her throat.

*"But I say unto you my friends,"* she read on in verse four, *"be not afraid of them that kill the body, and after that have no more that they can do. But I will forewarn you whom ye shall fear; Fear him which after he hath killed hath power to cast into hell; yea, I say unto you, Fear him."*

What if Eric won't forgive me? What if he stays at Karen's and never speaks to me again? She waited in the silent room, but heard no answer. The gentle ticking of the clock on the mantle seemed to rise in volume as seconds ticked by.

My actions have hurt too many people; Eric, the girls, Mother Blackwood, and Jack's dad. They'll never speak to me again when they find out. They won't be able to stand the sight of me.

*"But I say unto you my friends, be not afraid of them that kill the body, and after that have no more that they can do."*

They're my family I don't want to disappoint them.

Abby lowered the heavy volume to her lap and stared at the opposite wall. The lies she thought up last night to satisfy Eric's questions pressed in on her. She couldn't keep up this juggling act, it was too hard; a burden she could no longer bear.

*How much longer, Daughter? I have already forgiven you. Forgive yourself.*

Could she? Was it possible after all this time?

*Trust Me.*

Was it possible? After everything she'd done, after the im-measurable pain she'd caused Jack and the immeasurable pain she would cause her family when they discovered her indiscretions, was it possible God had already forgiven her? Was there a place awaiting her in His kingdom? She clasped her hand over her mouth.

*Oh, Jack, are you waiting there for me?*

She blinked away her tears and tried to focus on the words of the Bible in her lap. Without her reading glasses, she could barely decipher a word, but it didn't matter, she knew them by heart. "*But I say unto you my friends...*" A peace rose up inside of her. For the first time in a long time, the fear began to subside.

Jesus loved her, she realized. Even in the midst of a stern warning about fearing the One who could send her to hell, He had called her *my friend*. Regardless of her actions or how unworthy she was of His love, He considered her a friend.

*Oh, Jesus, You've got to help me through this. I'm so afraid I'll lose my entire family. None of them will want anything to do with me when they find out what I've done. But I'll trust You, Lord. I've been so hard-headed and so wrapped up in myself, I don't know how You've put up with me. I didn't listen to You twenty-two years ago. I went ahead and did what I wanted and now I'm paying the price. But I know You'll be here with me in whatever lies ahead. No matter how anyone else reacts to what I have to tell them, You are the only One who matters. You have forgiven me. I'm not that adulterous woman anymore. If my family turns their backs on me, I won't be alone. I know You'll still consider me Your friend.*

She set the Bible aside and sank to her knees in front of the loveseat. She raised her hands heavenward and let the tears of gratitude and repentance flow freely down her cheeks. Her sins would become known, Eric would learn who his real father was, and her daughters would either hate her or forgive her; that would be between them and God. She wasn't afraid anymore. She wasn't alone.

# Chapter Twenty-five

"Eric, that was Mom on the phone again. How long are you going to keep dodging her?"

Eric lay on the floor of Karen and Roger's living room, propped up on one elbow, his long legs stretched out in front of him, a niece and nephew on either side with a game of Trouble between them. He looked up at his sister from his semi-reclined position and shrugged.

Rebecca nudged his shoulder, "Your turn, Uncle Eric."

He looked back at the game and pressed down on the popper.

"Three!" Christopher exclaimed. "Ha, ha, he landed on you, Rebecca."

"Did not?" Rebecca cried. "See, Uncle Eric, you can move this man if you want. Then you'll be closer to home. You don't have to land on me, do ya?"

"Eric, did you hear what I said?" Karen asked from the doorway.

"You have to move that man, Uncle Eric," Christopher said. "You can't move the other one cause then you'll land on yourself. You ain't allowed to land on yourself."

"He can if he wants to, can't you, Uncle Eric.? You can land on yourself."

"Nuh uh, that's stupid," Christopher stated. "You don't land on yourself. He has to land on you." He put his fingers around the playing peg in question.

"No!" Rebecca put her fingers over her brother's and squeezed until her knuckles turned white. "Move your other man, Uncle Eric. Pleeeeze."

"Ow!" Christopher yelped, "Let go."

"You let go! Uncle Eric, Christopher's cheating! He can't move for you."

Karen moved across the carpet and scooped up the game. "All right, all right, that's enough playing for one day."

"Mom, Christopher's cheating."

"Rebecca doesn't know the rules. You can't land on yourself."

"Yes, you can, Cheater!" She curled her hand into a fist and drew back for a swing.

Christopher thrust his chin forward, ready for the hit. "Stupid!"

Eric pulled himself into a sitting position, out of the line of fire.

"All right, I've heard enough out of both of you." Karen set the game on the table, her hands on her hips, and glowered down at them. "Go upstairs and play nicely, or I'll put you down for a nap."

"I'm too big for naps," Christopher cried indignantly.

"Me too," Rebecca chimed in.

"Not if you're going to fight over a game. Now, get upstairs, and don't let me hear a word out of either of you."

Their grumbling wisely turned inward, the two red-headed youngsters scrambled up off the floor and tore up the stairs. After their footsteps receded to silence, Karen turned her attention to Eric still seated on the floor. "Now, as for you…"

"Do I have to take a nap too?" he asked as he got to his feet.

"No, you get to explain why you're avoiding Mom. I'm thrilled you're here spending time with the kids, but it's been three days, and all I know is Mom keeps calling and you won't go to the phone."

"It's nothing. I don't want to talk about it." He switched on the television set and reached for the TV guide.

"Fine, well as long as you're here, Christopher and Rebecca

have dentist appointments this afternoon. You can stay here with Alex while I take them."

Eric didn't like the idea of changing diapers. "How about I take them and you stay here with Alex?"

"Good idea. But it's only fair to warn you, the last time we went Christopher bit the dentist and Rebecca cried so hard she threw up all over herself."

"Yeah, like I said," Eric said, his eyes glued to the television screen, "you take the kids to the dentist, and I'll stay here with Alex."

Jamie gazed around the room, her eyes wide. "The house is so quiet. Where is everybody?"

Eric grinned. "Karen took the kids to the dentist. It's just me and Alex."

Jamie cautiously approached the playpen and studied the toddler. Her only exposure to babies had been at church where they cried and fretted and basically made a nuisance of themselves. This one appeared harmless. Alex gazed up at her, his chubby fists clutching the railing, his gaze solemn, apparently as apprehensive about her as she was him. "Does he stay in that thing all day?" she asked.

Eric chuckled and leaned over the playpen. He grunted as he lifted Alex out. He was a hefty load. "Don't worry, Jamie, he won't bite."

Jamie backed away, her hands raised in front of her in mock horror as Eric held the baby out to her. "Can you guarantee that?"

"I guess not. Although in his defense I must say he's the most mild mannered of Karen's kids. He must take after Roger." Eric turned the baby around to look him in the face. "Yeah, we've been having a nice quiet afternoon watching the ball game, haven't we, big guy?"

Jamie was through kidding around. When Eric called her earlier that day at the drugstore and asked if she wanted to stop by after work, she decided she would force him to make a decision about the situation with Abby. "Have you talked to your mom yet?"

Eric turned away and lowered Alex into the playpen. "This little guy keeps me too busy, don't ya, Tiger?"

"Eric, you should talk to her."

"You sound like Karen."

"Maybe she's right."

"Nah, are you hungry? I fixed me and Alex some macaroni and cheese for lunch. There's some left."

Alex stuck a fist in his mouth and studied Jamie warily over the top rail of the playpen, then he plopped down on his bottom and fumbled for a plastic elephant, which he promptly crammed into his mouth.

Jamie opened her mouth to speak, but Eric cut her off. "Let's not talk about that right now. We've been having a nice peaceful afternoon," he glanced at the clock on the mantle, "and that'll end soon enough. Got any ideas on how to kill thirty minutes before the troops return?"

Jamie shook her head. If he didn't want to talk, she couldn't force him, but he would have to face his mother eventually.

"Wanna watch TV?" he suggested.

"No." It came out more firmly than she intended. He tilted his head questioningly, and a shock of dark hair fell over his left eye. "Eric, you invited me over here," she reminded him, "certainly you had something in mind?"

"Only what always comes to mind when I see you."

"Eric!"

"That's not what I meant," he said with a sly smile. "You always have your mind in the gutter."

"Then what did you mean?"

"Later," he replied vaguely. He reached out and took her hand. "Come over here, and sit with me on the couch. If we're real quiet, Alex'll fall asleep. Hopefully, he'll stay that way until his mother gets here."

"I thought you said he's no trouble."

"He's not, but even the best natured babies are better asleep."

Eric sat down on the couch and pulled Jamie down beside him. She took a copy of a woman's magazine off the coffee table and absently leafed through it. "How long are you planning on staying here?" she asked innocently.

"On the couch?"

"Funny," she said and flipped another page. "Classes start in three weeks. Are you ready to go back to school?"

"Just about, I need to get hold of the guys I roomed with last year, and see if they still got room for me in the apartment."

She lowered the magazine. "Well, I hope you're not planning on turning this apartment into some sort of den of iniquity."

"Why else would I have one?"

She slapped his arm with a corner of the magazine. "You are a laugh riot today."

"You're welcome to come over every night and make sure I'm behaving myself."

"I might do that."

He snatched the magazine out of her hands and threw it over her shoulder. He grabbed her by the arms and pulled her against him, "Promise?"

"You'd better behave yourself," she warned him playfully as she snuggled against his chest. "We have an audience, little Alex may tell his mother what the babysitter was up to while she was away."

"Don't worry about Alex. We've got this little deal worked out. I don't tell on him for skipping his nap, and he doesn't tell on me for seducing unexpected visitors."

"So, I'm not the first?" she looked over at the playpen. "Go ahead, you can tell me, Alex. I'll protect you."

"Don't breathe a word, Alex."

Alex sighed disinterestedly and lay down, a stuffed animal becoming an impromptu pillow.

"See what I mean?" Eric said. "He knows how to keep a secret."

"I bet I could get it out of you." Jamie rose up on her knees and put her hands around his throat. "Now talk. Who else has been here?" She pushed him back until he was flat on the couch with her straddling his waist.

Eric grabbed her wrists. "I'll never talk." With one quick jerk, he pulled her hands away from his throat and rolled her over. They fell off the couch together, Jamie on the bottom, wedged between the couch and the coffee table. "Now, who's in charge?" he said barely able to keep a straight face.

"Just because you outweigh me doesn't mean you have the upper hand."

"Oh, really?" he said. Still holding her wrists, he pinned her arms against the carpet and nuzzled her neck. He raised his head and looked down at her. "You seem to have gotten yourself into a fine pickle, Miss Steele. Care to tell me how you plan to get out of it."

"I have my ways."

"Such as?" He nipped her chin with his teeth and then moved around to her ear.

She twisted her head to the side. "Eric, stop! You're tickling me. I can't breathe."

Eric raised himself up a fraction of an inch and let go of her wrists. He started to say something, but didn't. He regarded her with his fathomless blue eyes, first looking into her eyes and then studying the curve of her mouth. "Jamie," he murmured before lowering his mouth to hers.

Jamie forgot about the hard floor beneath her and the cramped space between the coffee table and the couch. She put her arms around his neck and pulled him closer. She forgot about the kiss at the pond that almost got out of control. She forgot about Alex drifting off to sleep in the playpen ten feet away, and the fact that Karen and the kids would be home any minute. All she knew was that she wanted Eric to keep kissing her.

"Jamie," he breathed, lifting his mouth off hers to take a breath. "I love you." He put one hand underneath the small of her back and lifted her to him.

Her hands tangled in his hair. "Oh, Eric, I love you."

He shifted his weight and cupped her chin with one hand. He kissed the side of her mouth, her chin, her neck. He propped himself up on one elbow. As he lifted his head to kiss the other side of her face, he hit the bottom corner of the coffee table with a wood splintering crack. He yelped in pain and jumped up on his knees. "Ah, man," he said, rubbing the back of his head with his hand.

Jamie sat up. "Are you all right?" She put her hand over his. "Are you bleeding?"

He pulled his hand away and looked at it. "No, I don't think so. But I'm gonna have a nasty goose egg back there."

Jamie scrambled to her feet. "I'll get some ice."

"No, it's all right," he resisted feebly, but she had already disappeared into the kitchen. When she returned, Eric was on the edge of the couch, one hand over his wound. He looked up and smiled as she applied the bundle of ice secured in a paper towel. "I think maybe someone was trying to get our attention."

Jamie sat down next to him to hold the paper towel in place. "It's a good thing. I don't think either of us can be trusted."

He reached out and grasped her free hand. "Jamie, I'm sorry. I can't seem to stop acting like a jerk around you lately."

"It's my fault. I shouldn't have started goofing off in the first place. We've got to keep this stuff from happening."

"I know."

"No, I mean it, Eric," she said more forcefully. She pulled away, leaving him to hold the ice in place himself. "I don't want it to be like this. I want—"

"Baby, I want the same thing."

She jumped to her feet and went around the coffee table, putting a barrier between them. "You're not listening. It's not supposed to happen like this. It's supposed to be special. Not like two animals on the floor of your sister's house with your nephew three feet away." She motioned at the playpen with an angry gesture. She took a deep breath. "I want to be married first," she said finally, a hint of tears in her voice. "I want to wear a white wedding gown and for it to mean what it's supposed to mean."

She smiled at his expression. "Relax. I don't mean tomorrow. I just don't want to be like everyone else. Nobody cares about propriety anymore, or decency. Chastity is a joke. You hear it all the time on TV. Marriage is a prison that only fools commit to. We're a couple of celibate freaks on that college campus. You know that, don't you? Free love, that's all I ever hear. 'How will you know what you're missing, Jamie, if you don't try it out first?' 'What fun is there in sleeping with one man your whole life?' Well, I don't want to try anything out first. I don't want to hop from bed to bed, and I don't want a husband who's done the same thing. I want to do it the way the Bible intended."

Eric stood up and took a step toward her.

She held up a hand to stop him. "I think it's better if you stay over there. My heart and my head are telling me I'm strong. I can resist because it's special and it's worth waiting for. But you—" she shook her head, "when you get near me, my body tells me something completely different. I shouldn't have come today. Not when you're sister's not home."

"Jamie, I'm not an animal waiting to attack." He smiled cryptically and lowered the hand holding the ice. "Well—not all the time. I want the same things you do. I shouldn't have let things go as far as they did. I'm the responsible one in this relationship. I'm supposed to honor you, not roll you around like an old bear."

"Eric, I don't need you to be responsible for me. I'm as guilty as you are. It's just very important to me that I wait until my wedding night. I know everybody doesn't feel that way, but I do. Unfortunately, I'm not as strong as I think I am. Being alone with you has made that painfully clear. So I'm going home now. Don't come around unless you're willing to sit in the living room with Grandma Cory, Cassie, and maybe the Ninth Infantry. I'm not trying to make demands on you; that's just the way it has to be, for my sake. I know what I want, and I know what it's going to take to protect me from myself."

He moved toward her. This time she didn't stop him. "This is important to me too, Jamie. I know we'd regret it if we did something before we were ready. I'll be good, I promise. I wouldn't do anything to make you lose respect for yourself or for me."

She stood on her tiptoes and gave him a quick kiss. "Thank you. I'll see you later. And I still want you to call your mother."

"I'll think about it."

"No, don't think, pray."

"Aye, aye, Captain," he gave her a mock salute. "Tell the Ninth Infantry I'll be over tonight around eight to watch television."

She grinned and headed for the door. "We'll all be expecting you."

# Chapter Twenty-six

After Jamie left Karen's house he knew he had to go home and find the engagement ring. He couldn't put it off one more day. He loved Jamie and he wanted to ask her to marry him. It wasn't the near fiasco on Karen's living room floor that demanded he act immediately. It wasn't Jamie's insistence that she couldn't have sex until her wedding night; he loved her, pure and simple. He wanted to be with her—tonight if she agreed—but he'd cheerfully wait a month, a year, or five years, whatever it took. He wouldn't even consider the possibility that she might decline.

The rest of the afternoon while waiting for Karen and the kids to get home, then during the inevitable argument over who behaved better—Christopher, who didn't bite anyone, or Rebecca, who though she'd cried, didn't throw up, and which of them had picked the better toy out of the doctor's treasure chest, Eric fretted over seeing his mother. Now Abby wasn't even home. Fantastic! No confrontations. No tears. No explanations about when, or if, he was coming home.

He didn't stop to wonder where she might be or what she might be doing, considering the fact she hadn't left the house after dark since April. Instead he hurried into the house and headed upstairs. He no longer cared about what he might find if he went through his dad's desk again. He'd worry about all that stuff some other time. He had no idea where Abby had gone or when she'd be back, and he didn't want an argument with her ruining his plans for tonight.

Abby put her keys in the dish on the end table and softly closed the front door behind her. She straightened her spine and took a deep breath to calm the hammering in her chest. For the millionth time she wished Jack was beside her. When she first turned onto Mulberry Street and saw Eric's car in the driveway, she had almost wept with relief. Then, almost immediately, she realized what she had to do. If only Jack were here. Even though he had much more reason to hate her than Eric, he would sit beside her to give her strength while she told Eric what he so desperately needed to know.

She heard movement in the bedroom above her head. He was here to find the lost engagement ring. He wouldn't stop this time until he found it, she knew it.

She shouldn't have attacked him the other day about getting married; another thing Jack was right about. He liked Jamie instantly and told Abby with some confidence after the first time Eric brought her home for dinner she was the one who'd steal their boy's heart. Abby refused to see it. Eric was too levelheaded to get involved with anyone before he earned his Bachelor's—or maybe even a Doctorate—she had insisted, and dismissed Jack's predictions. Now, here they were, two years later, Eric turning his room upside down looking for the engagement ring, and Jack nowhere around to gloat about being right.

In the three days Eric had been at Karen's, Abby had done more praying and meditating than she had in years. She felt like a brand new woman. The Scripture, "*old things have passed away, behold all things have become new,*" had been written specifically for her.

That morning she called Noel and told him they needed to talk. He told her to come by the house after he left the drugstore. She didn't sneak around the back of the house this time. Abby strode straight to the front door with no guilt or fear of what the neighbors would think.

"I don't know what to expect from him," she said to Noel after explaining what she planned to say to Eric. "He may never want to see either of us again, he might quit his job, or he may come over here tonight demanding that you explain how you let something like this happen."

Noel took the news much better than Abby anticipated. Apparently he had made peace with his sins years ago and was prepared for whatever repercussions Eric or their small town threw at them.

Finally Abby too, was ready to face the consequences for what she'd done. She no longer cared what anyone in Jenna's Creek said about her. She was confident in the Lord that she was forgiven; she was a new creature ready to admit her past sins. His was the only opinion with which she needed to concern herself.

She put her hand on the banister railing. *Give me the right words to say, Lord. Help me answer Eric's questions honestly, and touch his heart that he may accept it.*

She saw his bedroom door partially ajar when she reached the landing. "Eric?" She tapped lightly and pushed it open.

Eric stood in the middle of the room holding a broom the bristles pointed upward, sweeping along the ceiling for cobwebs. He spun around, startled. "Mom, I didn't hear you come in." He lowered the broom and studied her warily.

"I know. I just got home." She glanced around the room. He'd been cleaning. From the looks of things, he'd been here awhile. Did that mean he found the ring? "Um, can I come in?"

He shrugged and continued to hold onto the broom with both hands, gripping it like a weapon in case she got out of hand.

Abby took a few tentative steps into the room. "I'm sorry about the other night, I truly am. I was completely out of line. Did you find your ring?"

"Yes." His fingers moved protectively to his hip pocket where she noticed the square-shaped lump indicating the velvet box.

"Good," she said. "That must be a load off your mind."

"Yeah," his grip on the broom didn't relax.

She couldn't blame him. "Eric, could we both sit down?" She motioned toward the bed.

He shrugged again, relinquished his hold on the broom, and leaned it against the window frame. He perched on the edge of the bed, his carriage tense.

Abby felt like a bug under a microscope. She didn't want to say or do anything wrong. She prayed silently as she took the scuffed student chair from under the desk and positioned it next to the bed. She lowered herself onto it to face him.

She took a deep breath and reached out and patted his knee. "Eric, honey," she began tremulously, "you're my son, and I love you more than anything. I am sorry for those awful things I said the other night. I won't make excuses or say I didn't mean it because you know better. I always say what's on my mind no matter how inappropriate." Her voice grew stronger and more confident as she spoke. "All I'll say, is I've been a foolish woman thinking only of myself, and for that, I truly am sorry."

Eric continued to stare at her without saying a word. She recognized the resolute tilt of his chin, the narrowed, dark blue eyes, and the proud set of his shoulders. If he only knew how much he looked like his father at this moment.

"As you already know, I've known Jack Blackwood since I was a little girl," she began. "It was always assumed we would marry when we got old enough, but he went off to war and I fell in love with another man." There, she'd said it. She braced herself for his reaction. The muscle in his jaw twitched, his shoulders straightened a fraction of a degree, nothing more.

She took a deep breath and continued. "When Jack came home, we married right away. I cared for him and his family but my heart still belonged to someone else. Your dad and I built a life together and I tried to forget." Her voice caught, but she continued with barely a falter, determined not to get bogged down in a lifetime of emotions and wrong choices.

"We had your sisters, we bought this house, we suffered all the things young couples go through, but twenty-two years ago, I did something I never should have done. I turned to the man I loved in my youth. I know I was wrong. I knew it was wrong when it happened, and I know today it was wrong, but still it happened.

Before I could get the strength to end it I found out I was going to have a baby. The baby did not belong to your dad. I knew I had sinned against God and against my marriage vows. I prayed for forgiveness and ended the relationship.

"I always thought Jack didn't know. Looking back, I think I fooled myself into believing that, especially after seeing your face; I so much wanted you to be a Blackwood. No one noticed the differences. No one questioned me, so I began to think I'd gotten away with it. Not gotten away exactly, I mean, I still had to live with myself. I knew the truth even if no one else did."

Abby studied the gold band on her left hand and worked it around and around her finger. "Then, last spring your dad—he told me that night." She stopped talking and cleared her throat. She worked the ring around faster and faster. "He told me he knew. Jack knew and he forgave me. He said he always loved you even though you weren't—his…"

Her voice broke again, and she couldn't go on. She wanted to get up and get a drink of water, she needed a tissue, and she wished to be out from under Eric's impenetrable stare but she couldn't stop now.

"That's the worst part about the whole thing," she said after another gulp of air. "God forgave me for what I did, but I couldn't forgive myself for breaking your dad's heart. He never deserved it. He was a wonderful man who deserved so much more than I gave him."

Abby tore her eyes away from the ring and looked up at her son. He was no longer staring at her but at a spot on the wall above her head. The war of emotions battling inside him was evident on his face.

"Eric, I'm so sorry," she cried, unable to bear the silence any longer. "Jack did love you. He never said a word to me about what I'd done. He was too good of a man for that. I guess he figured it was between me and God. He was a wonderful man. We were both blessed to have him in our lives."

Eric stood up quickly and moved to the center of the room. He thrust his hands deep in his pockets, too overwhelmed for words.

"Eric?" Abby asked cautiously.

Eric spun around and put a hand in the air to silence her. "No, Mom, don't! I..." He turned away again though not so far that she could not see the expression on his face. He rubbed his hand over his jaw, alternately staring at the floor, the wall, and out the window onto the street below.

Finally he turned to face her. "That night in the hospital when Dad died I couldn't understand what he was trying to tell me. I thought it was the medication getting his words all tangled up but he kept saying it. Afterwards, I thought he meant I was adopted. I even went through his desk to see if I could find any papers. I never imagined..."

A sob wrenched itself from Abby's throat.

"I've had a lot of time since that night to think, to put the pieces together. The more I thought about it the more sense it made. And not just from what Dad said either, there's been more stuff I never paid attention to before."

He pushed his hands deep into his pockets again and returned his gaze to the floor. "It's Noel Wyatt, isn't it?" he blurted out, fixing her with his gaze. "He's my real father."

Abby felt the blood rush out of her face; she gasped and covered her mouth with a trembling hand. "Oh, Eric, how..." she choked out between her fingers.

Eric raked a hand through his thick dark hair and perched on the edge of the desk, pushing a pile of papers onto the floor in the process. "You went to see him the night I was diagnosed with epilepsy."

"What? I—"

Eric went on, cutting off any explanation. "And the way some of the people at the drugstore look at me, especially Paige Trotter. She talks about how I look like someone, and someday everybody will know the truth."

Abby was mortified. "She said that to you?"

Eric nodded and stared at his feet.

The remainder of Abby's resolve crumbled. She buried her face in her hands. "Oh, Eric, I didn't mean to hurt you," she cried. "I didn't mean to hurt your father. I'm so sorry."

Eric didn't move. He didn't even look up.

For a long time the only sound in the room was her sobs. She fumbled around for something to blow her nose on, and for lack of a better choice, she pulled the corner of the sheet loose from the mattress and blew her nose and wiped her eyes. Eric remained on the edge of the desk, his eyes fastened on his feet.

Abby dabbed the end of her nose with the sheet and dried her eyes again. She cleared her throat to speak.

Once again, Eric cut her off. "Why didn't you tell me before? I've been asking questions all summer." He didn't give her a chance to answer that question before firing off another one, his voice rising with indignation. He stood up straight and glared at her. "What about when I was seeing all those doctors a couple of years ago? They kept asking you and Dad about my medical history. You just sat there; why didn't you say something? My health was at stake."

She shrank away from his onslaught. "I was afraid," she finally mumbled, "not just for you, but for the girls too, and Jack. I didn't want to lose my family."

"You had to know we'd find out eventually."

"I was hoping you wouldn't. I know I was wrong, Eric. I should have told you the truth when you were old enough to understand. But I didn't think it would ever be necessary to tell you. I should've told you when you first started asking questions. I can see that now. If Jack hadn't told you he loved you like a son—"

Eric's mouth dropped open as realization dawned on him. "Then you never would've told me."

"Probably not," she answered in a small voice.

"Then why are you telling me now, because Dad opened this can of worms, because I've been bugging you to death all summer?"

"Yes, because you've been bugging me to death." Her voice rose to a pitch that matched his. "It was in the past. I didn't see any benefit in digging up ancient history. But I see now I was wrong." She took a deep shuddering breath. "Even if your dad hadn't opened this can of worms, as you put it, you have a right to know. You're getting married; you deserve to know where you came from and I didn't want you hearing it from someone else."

Eric shook his head from side to side. When he looked back at her, his eyes were filled with disgust. "What I want to know, Mom, is how could you—Noel Wyatt; why him of all people? Was it his money? Come on, Dad didn't deserve this." He walked over to where she sat on the chair and glared down at her. "He loved you. He worshipped the ground you walked on and look how good he treated me, your bastard son. He was better than this, Mom."

Abby jumped to her feet and laid a stinging slap across his face.

Eric didn't flinch even though a perfect handprint marked his cheek.

Abby withered at the sight of his face. "Oh, honey, I'm so sorry. You have every right to an explanation. I won't insult you by saying it just happened because it didn't. I knew what I was doing. I was an adult, totally capable of making my own decisions. You're right, your dad didn't deserve this, but it happened, Eric. All the 'I'm sorry's' and penance in the world won't change the fact that Jack Blackwood isn't your father."

Eric turned slowly and went to the closet. "I'm going to take a few more things to Karen's. I'll stay there until I figure out how to work things out about Jamie. In case you care, I'm going to ask her to marry me tonight."

"Oh, Eric, of course I care. Please don't leave, stay and talk. We need to get this straightened out."

"There's no straightening it out, Mom. You said it yourself; nothing will change the fact that I'm not Jack Blackwood's son." He turned around to face her. "You've stolen everything from me; my name, my sisters, even Grandma and Grandpa." His voice cracked for the first time. "Could I have a little privacy, please?" He stepped inside the closet and removed his green and white, South Auburn team ball cap from a peg and stuck it on his head. When he spoke again, his voice was muffled so that she had to strain to hear him.

"Don't worry, I won't say a word to Karen; there's no reason why you have to destroy her life tonight, too."

Abby left the room but she wasn't afraid. No matter what hurtful things Eric said in anger or even if he moved out and never came back she knew she would be all right. For the first time since realizing she had lost the man she loved, she was free. God was with her; she no longer had to carry her burden alone.

# Chapter Twenty-seven

J amie finished her chores early and hurried into the house to take a bath. She hadn't exactly been thinking clearly when she left Karen's house, so she wasn't sure if Eric planned on coming over tonight or not. He said he was but he could have been teasing because of her comment about watching TV with the Ninth Infantry. Either way, she didn't want to be caught unprepared.

As she towel dried her hair, she wondered if he was thinking anymore about what almost happened at the house. Her face blushed scarlet at the thought and she rubbed the towel roughly against her scalp. She couldn't keep getting herself into sticky situations with him nor could she allow him to accept responsibility for her chastity. Both times, she knew what she was doing. The other night at the pond was a close call, but lacking opportunity. But today—today provided opportunity; alone in the house, except for baby Alex, asleep by that time and unable to tattle anyway. Would they have been able to stop themselves if Eric hadn't hit his head on the bottom of the coffee table?

"You almost blew it, dummy," she scolded herself in the mirror.

She wondered if Eric thought she expected a proposal out of him with all her I-want-to-wait-till-I'm-married talk. She meant every word she said; it wasn't a ploy to get a proposal. More than anything, she desired to present herself to her husband on her wedding night just as she planned to present herself to her Savior someday, pure and unblemished; even if said husband didn't turn out to be Eric.

But if he kept hanging around, looking at her that way, whispering her name, with those lips, those eyes, and those broad shoulders and...

*Knock it off, Jamie,* she screamed inwardly. *Lusting in your heart is the same as lusting in body.*

As she finished her hair she tried not to think about anything. She went into her room and pulled on a pair of slacks and a dark green blouse that brought out the green flecks of color in her eyes. Just in case, she applied a touch of make-up. No sense getting all dolled up to sit in the living room and watch TV. She still wasn't sure if he was coming, but just in case.

It wasn't yet seven-thirty when she heard a car pull into the driveway. She dashed to the window and looked out, holding her breath in anticipation. *Please, don't let it be Uncle Justin,* she prayed. It wasn't.

Despite her desire to exercise a little decorum, she dashed down the stairs and out the front door. She got to the porch as Eric climbed out of his car. He was dressed in cocoa brown corduroys and a green and tan plaid madras shirt buttoned nearly to his throat. A green and white striped South Auburn team hat sat carelessly atop his tousled hair. She hadn't seen him wearing that hat since—since the night of his father's accident. He needed a haircut, she thought absently. She imagined smoothing the hair away from his neck with her fingers and stretching up to kiss him, his jaw smooth and fresh smelling from a recent shave.

He must have felt her eyes upon him. He looked up and spotted her on the porch. He grinned, exposing his perfectly shaped white teeth. His dark blue eyes sparkled. Jamie's heart dropped to her shoes.

She gasped and her hand flew to her throat.

*Noel Wyatt; he looked exactly like...*

She was instantly transported back to the day Lucinda Wyatt gave her the log cabin quilt. She remembered the picture she saw on her way out of the bedroom; a picture of a young Noel in his

South Auburn baseball uniform complete with green and white striped hat, standing on the pitcher's mound. How many times had she seen Eric in the exact position, his leg cocked in front of him, reared back to release a pitch?

By now Eric was nearly to the porch. "Jamie, are you all right? You look like you've seen a ghost."

She lowered her hand and gave him a tremulous smile. "N—no, I'm fine. I didn't know if—if you were coming tonight or not," she floundered.

"I'm here but I don't see any signs of the Seventh Cavalry."

"It was the Ninth Infantry," she corrected. "They called and said they're running late." She couldn't keep from staring stupidly at his face. Why hadn't she seen the resemblance between the two of them before? It was uncanny. Noel leaning over a ledger, his brow furrowed in concentration, a large, calloused hand pushing back dark hair, streaked with gray; Eric combing his fingers through that stubborn lock of hair that fell continuously across his left eye; Noel's apparent absent-mindedness when she first asked him about hiring Eric to work at the drugstore; Eric's confusion when she told him how Abby went to see Noel the night he was diagnosed with epilepsy—now it all made perfect sense.

"Do I have something stuck in my teeth?"

"No, I'm just glad to see you." She reached out to where he stood on the rock slab that served as a porch step and kissed him.

"Good. I thought you might still be upset over what happened at Karen's."

"I was never upset. I told you it wasn't your fault."

Eric wagged his head in the direction of the porch swing. "Could we sit out here for a little bit if I promise to behave myself?"

"Sure, as long as you don't get fresh." She forced her eyes off his face and led the way to the porch swing. She wouldn't stare. What would he say if she told him his father's identity was as plain as the nose on his face? Would he believe her? Would he see it too?

"I went by the house today," he said as soon as he sat down next to her. "I talked to Mom."

She exhaled with relief. "Good. How did it go?"

"I'm not sure." He removed the baseball cap and ran a hand through his thick dark hair. Jamie found herself staring again. She must have been blind to miss it for so long. "I'm going back to Karen's tonight if that tells you anything."

"Oh, Eric, I'm so sorry. I was hoping you two could work things out."

"We did talk," he began vaguely.

"And?"

He replaced his cap and leaned back against the swing. "She told me everything."

"Everything?" she asked cautiously. "What exactly is everything?"

"I was right about what I told you the other night. I'm not a Blackwood."

So he knew, or had Abby left out a few details to spare him? She put her hand on his arm. "Eric, I don't know what to say."

He shrugged like it didn't matter and stared out across the road, but he couldn't mask the pain on his face.

"Are you okay?" she asked gently, wishing she could think of something better to say.

She watched his profile as he worked his jaw back and forth. She tried not to notice the similarities between him and his real father.

"I don't know," he said finally. "I don't know how I feel."

Jamie nibbled at her bottom lip a moment before asking, "What all did she tell you?"

"She told me who my real father is."

Jamie clamped down on her lip and kept quiet. What if she was wrong? No, one look at Eric dispelled that possibility.

"She told me how it all happened, that she was never in love with Dad, I mean Jack. She loved this other man before she got married and—I guess she couldn't forget him. After the girls were born, well, things happened and she got hooked up with him again. That's where I came from."

Jamie's throat clenched at the pain on his face. She squeezed his arm compassionately but held her tongue. She would let him tell her in his own words and in his own time.

"It was such a shock hearing it come out of her mouth," Eric said, "even though I've been expecting as much. She said she repented and God forgave her, that it was a mistake. I don't know; I can't understand how she let it happen. She was a married woman, for crying out loud."

"Don't you think God can forgive a person of any sin?"

"Jamie, she wasn't a kid who let her hormones get the best of her. She was married," he repeated bitterly.

"A married woman who made a mistake," she said gently.

He snorted with disgust and set the swing in motion with a push of his long legs. "It's not that simple. She had three little girls at home. She was supposed to know better. She shouldn't have put herself in a position where she could fall into temptation in the first place."

Jamie was no stranger to the susceptibility of parents failing their calling. "She is a human being, Eric. Being a parent doesn't make her immune to falling into temptation."

"Are you saying you understand what she did?"

"No, I—"

"Do you mean you can see how easy it would be to do the same thing? That you could have an affair—"

Jamie planted her feet on the porch floor and halted the swing's motion. "Eric, stop! You need to back up and calm down. I'm not making excuses for anybody. I'm just telling you what the Bible says. If your mother says she's repented and received forgiveness you have to believe her. God is her only judge. Believe it or not, this isn't about you. I know it involves you more than anyone and it may seem like she's ruined your life, but this is about her. What really matters is that God forgives her and she forgives herself."

He snorted. "Forgives herself, that's a joke, how can she forgive herself after what she did to our family?"

Eric drew a ragged breath. When he spoke again the ire in his voice had been replaced by sadness. "I've been telling everybody my whole life what a great mother I've got. All this time, she's been lying to me and everyone who ever cared about her."

"Eric," Jamie said as gently as she could, "what she did has nothing to do with whether she's a great mother or not. She always loved you and your sisters but she's only human, like we all are. People fall. They make mistakes, even great mothers."

"Mothers aren't supposed to sin," Eric mumbled, "not my mother." A heavy sigh worked its way up through his chest. "I know; I'm being ridiculous. She was a woman long before she was my mother. But come on, Jamie, she lied to me for twenty-one years. She lied to everybody. Her whole life has been nothing but a lie."

"And she's had to live with that knowledge. Can you imagine how terrible that was for her?"

His eyes widened in disbelief, "Terrible for her? No one held a gun to her head. She deserved whatever torment she went through; and it's about to get a lot worse. Once everybody finds out..." He shook his head. "No, I don't feel sorry for her. She's getting what's coming to her. Dad knew the whole time, do you know that? That's the worst part. He went to his grave knowing I wasn't his flesh and blood." His voice cracked. He cleared his throat and resituated himself on the porch swing.

"Remember when I told you about all the cool father and son stuff we always did; the ball games, the camping trips? The whole time he knew I didn't belong to him." He shook his head in wonder. "What kind of woman could do that to a man; steal his only son from him? And now she's done it to me, she stole my dad."

Jamie worked at a callous on the pad of her hand and didn't answer.

"Everything's changed. I'm not who I thought I was. I don't even have the same family anymore. How are Karen, Elaine, and Christy going to react when they find out I'm not their brother; that I belong to the town's pharmacist?"

Jamie tried to look shocked for his sake.

Eric nodded. "Yeah, that's right. My mother was in love with Noel Wyatt. Who knows? Maybe she still is." He removed the baseball cap again and turned it around and around in his hands and then dropped it on the porch floor beside him.

"What matters, Eric, is that she loves you." She combed his hair away from his face. "She's afraid of losing you."

He stood up and stepped to the edge of the porch. "She should have thought of that before—before she did this." He turned to face her. "Jamie, I really didn't come here for you to try to make me feel sorry for her. I'm mad, okay? Don't I deserve to be mad? I'm not going to forgive her simply because she feels bad. I'm not going to pat her hand and say, 'It's okay, Mom, at least you told the truth. That's the important thing'. It's not the important thing, Jamie. She was wrong. She was wrong to cheat on my dad, and she was wrong to lie about it for twenty-two years."

"You have every right to be mad, Eric. I understand that, believe me. Parents aren't perfect but at least she told you the truth, the truth you've been hounding her about all summer. Now you need to be an adult and let her explain."

"Explain what?" he snapped, turning back to her, "That even though she was a married woman she couldn't keep her hands off another man. I don't need an explanation to understand that." He rubbed his hand across his jaw.

"I should hope not. Not after what almost happened at Karen's house this afternoon, or have you blocked that little indiscretion from your mind? I don't even want to think what may have happened if you hadn't cracked your head on the coffee table. I don't know about you, but it would've been very easy for me to let things go too far. I'm not proud of it and I'm glad it didn't happen, but it could have easily enough. But when you find out your mother made a similar mistake you can't forgive her? You're a hypocrite, Eric. How can you say you can't understand how she let it happen?"

"It isn't the same thing."

"How; how is it not the same thing?"

"She was married."

"I know she was married but sin is sin, regardless of the circumstances."

He sighed and shook his head. "You don't understand."

"You're right, I don't. All have sinned and come short of the glory of God."

He exhaled wearily and lowered himself back onto the porch swing. Several moments passed before he spoke again.

"Jamie, all I can think of is how badly she hurt Dad. I can't forgive her. Not tonight, maybe not ever."

"He forgave her."

"He was too soft hearted for his own good."

"Soft hearted has nothing to do with it. He loved her."

"Then why couldn't she love him?" he spat. "Would that have been so difficult? He was a good man. Everyone who knew him loved him, except her."

She squeezed his hand, feeling his pain and frustration.

"How am I ever going to go back into that drugstore? What am I going to say when I see Noel Wyatt after what he did to my family? I'm tempted to drive over to his house right now and just…oh, I don't know. Punching him in the mouth would sure feel good." He sighed and ran his hand through his hair.

Jamie didn't answer. She knew it would take some time before he worked through his anger.

"How am I going to look at my Grandma Blackwood again?" he continued. "She isn't a forgiving person, Jamie. She's always been critical of Mom. She'll eat her alive."

Jamie squeezed his arm and smiled encouragingly. "See? You do care about what happens to her. She'll always be your mother, Eric. You'll always love her."

He nodded and put his hand over hers. "I suppose. I'd do anything to keep her from getting hurt."

"She's already been hurt so much. She needs to know you still love her." Jamie pulled her hand out from under his and touched his cheek. "It's a lot to absorb all at once. No one expects you to get used to it today, but you will get used to it."

"I don't know if I want to. Noel Wyatt, of all people. Man, Jenna's Creek's going to jump all over this."

"Is that what's bothering you; that since everyone in town knows Noel they'll know your business, too?"

He shrugged. "Not really for myself, mostly for her."

"I'm sure all your mother cares about is what you think. She's lived her whole life trying to protect you. She could've been selfish a long time ago and done what she wanted, but she didn't. She did everything the way she thought would best benefit you and your sisters."

"That's what Dad said the night of the accident," Eric said, his voice cracking. "He told me not to be mad at her. For a long time I thought he meant about the way she would lean on me after—after he was gone. But I guess this is what he was talking about. He was trying to warn me of the pain that would come once I found out what he already knew."

Eric leaned forward and rested his elbows on his knees. Then he sat back again and rubbed his hands over his face. "Regardless of whatever pain and anger Dad must have felt at the time, he put his own thoughts aside and did what he was supposed to do; love his wife and forgive her, for the sake of all of us."

"He must have been a wonderful man. I wish I'd had the chance to know him better."

Eric looked at her in the waning light. "So do I, baby, he was great; just how great I'm only beginning to realize. You know, I almost wish I could go back a year to when I was blissfully ignorant. If Dad hadn't had that accident, I would probably never know where I came from. I might wonder from time to time why my hair wasn't red and I didn't have freckles on my face, but honestly, I wouldn't give it a second thought."

"You would have found out eventually. Something would happen and the truth would come out. It always does." *You might have looked in the mirror one day and figured it out for yourself,* she added silently.

"It's going to be tough on all of you for the next few months," Jamie said after a few moments of silence. "Noel is a well-known figure in the community and people love to see comfortable, well-liked people crash and burn."

He nodded. "Paige has been telling me ever since I went to work at the drugstore that the town was going to be set on its ear when it found out the truth. Now at least I know what truth she was talking about."

She put her hand on his arm again. "Try and remember the opinions of a few people in town don't matter."

He took her hand and raised it to his lips again. "Even though I've been a first-class jerk most of the time, Jamie, I don't know how I'd have made it through these last few months without you."

She smiled as he kissed her hand. "Don't worry, I'm not going anywhere."

THE END

Teresa always enjoys hearing from her readers.
You may contact her at: teresa@teresaslack.com

Coming soon:

# Evidence *of* Grace

The third book in the Jenna's Creek Series

Imprisoned for the murder of Sally Blake, a surprise witness casts doubt on Noreen Trimble's testimony. Was Noreen solely responsible for Sally's death? Is she covering up for someone else? Why would she be willing to sacrifice her own freedom in order to protect another?

Her old friend, Noel Wyatt, along with the attorney who first prosecuted the case, Judge David Davis, believe there is more to the case than even Noreen knows. In order to help her, they must uncover the identity of a reluctant witness and convince that person to come forward before it's too late.

Tim Shelton has problems of his own. He has spent his adult life distancing himself from the humble farm boy he once was. Married to a beautiful woman, he is the father of five and is well respected in his community. But suddenly the past is coming back to haunt him. What he knows can destroy everything he has worked his whole life to build. Can he risk it all to save someone from his past? If he doesn't, how will he face the man in the mirror who has already become a stranger to him?

# Books by Teresa Slack

*A Tender Reed*

The Jenna's Creek Novels:
*Streams of Mercy*
*Redemptions Song*